ALSO BY LINSEY MILLER

Mask of Shadows duology
Mask of Shadows
Ruin of Stars

BELLE
RÉVOLTE

"This is a memorable, sharply written character. While readers who identify on the GLBTQ spectrum may be easy fans as Miller handles Sal's identity with aplomb, that's certainly not the only point of note here; the impressive, intricate worldbuilding, tense action, and fierce competitors are equally strong."

—*Bulletin of the Center for Children's Books*

"Gory, well plotted, suspenseful on every page, and poised for the sequel."

—*Kirkus Reviews*

"This fantasy's genderfluid protagonist, Sal Leon, makes Miller's book worth picking up for diversity's sake alone. Her treatment of the gender issue is most notable in that it isn't really an issue... Violent and action-packed, this offering by first-time novelist Miller will circulate."

—*School Library Connection*

"Teen genre fiction featuring a strong genderfluid main character."

—*School Library Journal*

"Miller's setting is vividly drawn...a solid addition for libraries hoping to expand the gender diversity of their shelves."

—*Booklist*

"It is fabulous. Go forth and read the Hunger Games–like craftiness and intensity, Kaz Brekker-ish determination and moral question-ability, and utterly charming romance."

—*LGBTQ Reads*

BELLE RÉVOLTE

LINSEY MILLER

sourcebooks
fire

Published by Sourcebooks Fire, an imprint of Sourcebooks
P.O. Box 4410, Naperville, Illinois 60567-4410
(630) 961-3900
sourcebooks.com

Library of Congress Cataloging-in-Publication Data

Names: Miller, Linsey, author.
Title: Belle révolte / Linsey Miller.
Description: Naperville, Illinois : Sourcebooks Fire, [2020] | Audience: Ages 14-17. | Audience: Grades 10-12. | Summary: Told in two voices, sixteen-year-old Comtesse Emilie, whose yearning to be a physician is below her station, switches places with Annette, who needs training to develop her magic, as their homeland is threatened by war.
Identifiers: LCCN 2019032145 | (hardcover)
Subjects: CYAC: Impersonation--Fiction. | Social classes--Fiction. | Magic--Fiction. | Fantasy.
Classification: LCC PZ7.1.M582 Bel 2020 | DDC [Fic]--dc23
LC record available at https://lccn.loc.gov/2019032145

Printed and bound in the United States of America.
LSC 10 9 8 7 6 5 4 3 2 1

To everyone told they were not enough.

You are.

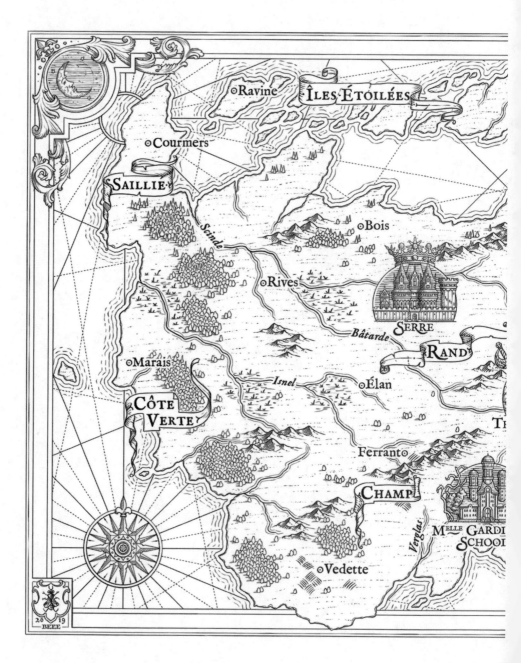

Ravine

Îles Étoilées

Courmers

Saillie

Scinde

Bois

Rives

Serre

Bâtarde

Rand

Marais

Isnel

Élan

Côte Verte

Ferranto

Champ

Verglas

Melle Gardi
Schoo

Vedette

20 19
BEEE

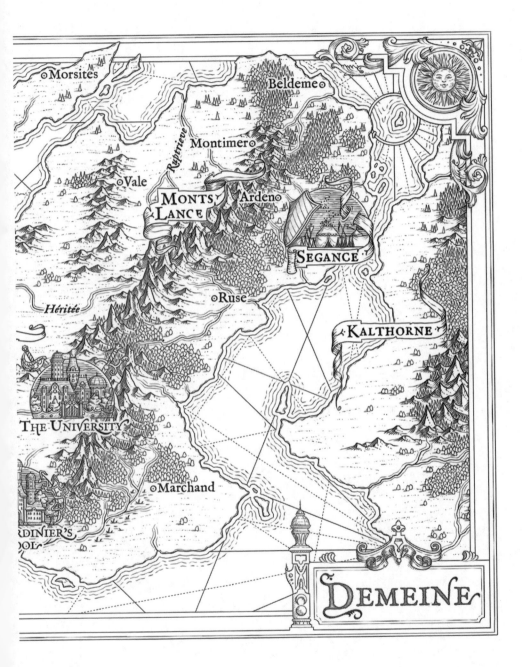

Morsites

Beldeme

Montimero

Réprieve

Vale

MONTS
LANCE

Ardeno

SEGANCE

Héritée

Ruse

KALTHORNE

THE UNIVERSITY

Marchand

RDINIER'S
OOL

DEMEINE

My mother did not shackle me despite my last escape attempt. It didn't matter—the corset, layers of satin and silk, and summer heat were chains enough. I was certain I would be the first young noble lady of Demeine to arrive at finishing school under the watchful eyes of two armed guards. My mother made it seem so innocuous, talking of nothing but her perfect days looking down upon the quaint town of Bosquet while learning the correct topics of conversation, the exact ways to divine tomorrow's weather, and wonderful illusions to cover up everything from blood stains to whole castles. The illusionary arts, the first and simplest branch of the midnight arts, were my mother's specialty, something the perfect daughter should have appreciated. I had neither aptitude nor interest in illusions.

Illusions were, as far as I could tell, nothing but lies. My mother was a wonderful liar.

"I love you," she said, her expression that emotionless calm all ladies of Demeine were expected to possess, "but I am growing weary of your rebellion."

I peeked out the window. We had been traveling for days, bundled up in the carriage and only stopping to swap horses. It was the carriage Mother usually took to court: wonderfully impressive on the outside, with gold and silver gilding running through the ocean colors of our family's crest on the door, and frustratingly practical on the inside. I had been staring at the same black velvet and single lamp since we left. No amount of fiddling with the lock while she slept had freed me yet.

"Let us rejoice, then, that your education means no one will notice I exhaust you." I tapped the thin skin beneath my eyes where she had hidden my dark circles as she hid hers every day. "You said you would let me study the noonday arts. Mademoiselle Gardinier's school does not teach the noonday arts."

The ability to channel magic was rare, and it was rarer still for it to run so steadily in a family. Traditionally, noble sons with the ability studied the noonday arts and either specialized in the fighting or healing arts. They became chevaliers or physicians. They changed the world by sword or by scalpel.

Noble girls didn't change the world.

"I said I would let you study them, not that I would allow you to partake in such powerful magic, especially after that abomination you used on poor Edouard. You could have killed him." She folded her hands in her lap, the tight sleeves of her silver overdress rustling together like moth wings. "You are a daughter of Demeine. You will learn the midnight arts, you will—somehow—impress someone well enough for them to marry you, you will have children, you will serve our people as the midnight artist and comtesse they need, and one day, you will understand why I made you do all of this."

Edouard, one of our guards, had caught me during my last escape attempt and laughed when I had explained my plan to join the university as a boy. Even common boys were allowed to be physicians if they were good enough and could pay the tuition.

"Being a boy's not that easy," he had said, angry for the first time since I could remember. "I would know. And you'd be doing it for selfish reasons. You don't understand. Listen to me, Emilie…"

When it was clear he wasn't going to let me go, I had knocked him out by altering his body alchemistry with my *abominable* noonday arts.

I tugged at the high collar of my dress, sweat pooling in every wrinkle, and scowled. "I could better serve our people as a physician."

"The noonday arts would wear your body out in pursuit of such a dream, to the point of death or infertility." She slapped my hand away from my collar. "Be reasonable, and perhaps you will learn you enjoy the midnight arts and the life you are supposed to lead."

My mother was always reasonable, as a good lady of Demeine should be, and unlike me, she never wore her emotions on her face.

"This will be good for you," she said. "Marais was too rural for you to make friends of the appropriate station. You will need allies at court."

"Yes, I cannot wait to meet them."

"I see sincerity was another of my lessons you neglected." She leaned across the carriage, fingers skimming my cheek, and recoiled when I flinched. "You are not a child any longer. You are sixteen, and soon you will be old enough to inherit your father's responsibilities along with the title you disregard. I remember when that was not even a possibility. You have so many more opportunities than girls in the past, than other girls now, and it is insult to refuse them."

I was an insult to our name, and my very dreams, to be a physician and study the noonday arts, to channel the magic of Lord Sun through my veins and save the dying, were the worst insult of all. I wanted the wrong things. I wanted too much.

"Noonday artists change the world, whether through the fighting or healing arts. That is a responsibility that comes with power you cannot comprehend. You are young. You will learn."

Demeine was blessed with two types of power: the noonday and the midnight arts. Each drew power from Lord Sun or his Mistress Moon, but Lord Sun was far stronger and even more fickle. The fighting and healing arts were used to change the physical world, and as such, required immense amounts of power. Such magic wore the mortal body down bit by bit until the ability to channel faded or the artist died.

Noble girls could not be allowed to handle such corruptive power.

There was nothing to learn. I comprehended the fact that I was a body, not a person, quite well.

"'I will learn,'" I said, the small nothing town of Bosquet rushing past our carriage window. "Is that a command or an attempt at reassurance?"

"Please, Emilie, we both know you are incapable of following even the simplest of orders." She twisted her first two fingers, broke the illusion hiding her fan in her lap, and flicked it open. "I prayed to Mistress Moon to console my grief at having to be apart from you, and she sent me a vision of you happy and content at court. You will be fine."

Mistress Moon's magic and the lesser power required for the midnight arts—illusions, scrying, and divination—wore the body down much more slowly but required excessive self-control. It was a safer, slower burn, but midnight artists couldn't change the world.

They only observed it, or, if they were good, changed how others observed it.

Perhaps Demeine was as it was, ruled by a court on the cusp of rightly losing control, because we let no one new change it.

I had to change the world. I had to prove to my mother that the whole of my being wasn't wrong, that I wasn't a disappointment.

"Maybe you saw a future where I became a physician," I said.

The gods could take the time to answer her prayers but not mine. How paradigmatic. Divination was guesswork, hardly quantifiable. A diviner could see a dozen different futures, and none might come to pass. If a midnight artist even could divine. Many never mastered the skill.

"Though, admittedly, you appeared to have taken none of my clothing advice in my divination; you were not wearing a physician's coat," she said. "You stand at the edge of a great future."

"Whose?" I lifted a silver chain, worth more than all of Bosquet, from my chest. The layers, the jewelry—I couldn't breathe much less move for fear of drowning in silver and sweat. No wonder we were expected to be silent and still. Even this left me light-headed.

Oxygen deprivation.

"All power has a cost," she said as the carriage slowed to a stop, "and you were born with power—your title, your wealth, your magic. This is your cost, Emilie des Marais, and it is your duty to pay it. Power demands sacrifice."

"This isn't fair."

She laughed, the apathetic mask she kept up at all times slipping. "Really? There will be girls at school who lack your name, your money, and your magic, and they will not treat you as kindly as I have. You are arrogant and stubborn. Mind your tongue, or you will have no friends, no happiness, and no future."

She had never called me a disappointment, but I could taste it in the silence between us. I was not the daughter she had always longed for. At least magic would never abandon me.

"You are my daughter, and I love you. I am pushing you to do this because I know Demeine will laugh you out of university. I do this because I love you." She ran her fingers through the strands of her silver necklaces, where she stored small lockets of power. Her illusion settled over me like snow, soft and cold and suffocating, and I knew no one would be able to tell how hot and miserable I looked. "Time to go."

We had stopped at a stable on the south side of town. The noises of Bosquet were louder now, and the shadows shorter, squat stains beneath our feet. The town had an open-air market and church at the center, and we had passed between storefronts and housing and orderly gravel paths shaded by linden trees with interlaced canopies. Our driver had already vanished inside the stable, and the guards lingered on the other side of the carriage. A crowd had gathered in the shade of the trees across from us. Behind them, a white poster with green ink had been stuck to the trunk of a tree.

At the edge of that crowd was a girl, who despite her flax dress dusted with dirt, despite her white skin spotted with sunburn and old bruises, and despite her brown hair in desperate need of styling, looked like me. I might have mistaken her for some unknown half-sister if either of my parents had ever been inclined to such affairs.

Perhaps Lord Sun had finally answered my prayers.

"Wait," I said quickly, grabbing my mother's wrist before she could leave the carriage. "Give me a moment to prepare myself, please."

I did not let go of her immediately as I usually did, and her gaze dropped to my fingers. She took my hand in hers and nodded.

"What do you think that crowd is?" I asked.

Her eyes didn't leave our hands. "Mademoiselle Charron is in town to inspect the artists in your class. I am sure she's providing free scrying and divinations to those who need them. All of her writings are in green for some ill-graced reason, but so goes the odd trends of youth, I suppose."

"That's nice of her." I moved my other hand, palm up and burning in a sliver of sunlight, out of her sight. "Can we wait until there are fewer people? You knotted me up in new clothes and shoes, and I have no desire for an audience."

She laughed, a sound I hadn't heard in ages, and nodded. "Very well."

"Thank you." I channeled the power I had gathered in my free hand to the one holding hers.

It slipped under her skin with the soft sizzle of heat against flesh. Her head jerked up, but I held tight, the magic slithering through the nerves of her arms to the dark little spaces of her mind, until the inner workings of her body shone with my power like a layer of gold silk. We were all nothing but lightning in a bloody bottle. I deleted the alchemical components in her mind that controlled wakefulness. These last moments would be like a dream.

My mother slumped in her seat, asleep, and I stepped out of the carriage. My own body would pay the price for this; I would not be able to sleep for a day or two at least. I had five minutes at most, and no idea if this would work. It was arrogant to think I would get away with it.

But arrogance and magic were all I had.

Even a chance was worth it.

I was far too overdressed for the crowd, but the people were more focused on the poster than me. My mother was right—it was advertising Estrel Charron's services—and the girl who looked like me was mouthing the words to herself as she read. I slipped into place next to her and tilted my head till my mouth was even with her ear. I was slightly taller and certainly heavier, but we had the same hazel eyes. The silver moon necklace at her throat glowed with power.

"Wouldn't you love to meet her?" I asked the girl.

She couldn't pull her eyes from the poster. "Love to, but it's tomorrow, and I've got to be home tonight."

"What if I could offer you the chance to not only meet her but learn from her?"

Her face whipped to me, and her eyes widened. She whispered with all the gentleness one said a prayer. "What?"

"I am Emilie des Marais, comtesse de Côte Verte, and I'm supposed to start my training at Mademoiselle Gardinier's today but would much rather study the noonday arts at university," I said, smile growing. She didn't stop me, so some part of her was listening. "How would you like to pretend to be me and study the midnight arts at Mademoiselle Gardinier's with your beloved Estrel while I take your last name and study the noonday arts?"

She stared. She did not say no.

"It will be dangerous, and I will do what I can to protect you if we are caught," I told her softly, "but some dangerous things are worth the risk."

"Yes," she whispered. "Yes."

I would prove myself, prove I wasn't a disappointment or insult, and I would change Demeine. If the world wouldn't give me the chance, I would take it myself.

I ate dirt as a child. Nothing grew the summer I turned six; Vaser's dry fields filled only with cicada husks. Lord Sun had not been merciful, giving us endless days of heat without rain, and Monsieur Waleran du Ferrant, comte de Champ, whose family watched over our lands, hadn't sent near enough help. Maman was pregnant with Jean, Papa was busy working, and Macé was seven and going through a growth spurt, crying till I gave him my supper. I'd cried too, but quiet, and pulled at my sides like I'd be able to pry open my ribs and scratch the hunger out of me. I'd been a good sister, then, and dirt was better than Macé crying. Tasted like the air after Alaine's funeral pyre.

"Your family must be proud." The shopkeeper smiled up at me and handed over the little satchel of everything Macé would need in Serre. "A varlet. There's a good career for a country boy."

I was not a good sister now.

"They're very proud of him," I said, tucking the packet into my bag. It wasn't a lie. They were. Of him. "He's leaving next week, and I'll be sad to see him go."

I'd be sad to see him go alone.

It was supposed to be us going—to university, not to Serre—to be hacks. We were supposed to study together, him the noonday and me the midnight arts, so we could both get jobs channeling magic for some rich artists who wanted all the results without getting worn down. I was supposed to go with him.

I'd always known I wasn't as good as him, but I didn't think Maman would make me stay in Vaser. Figured she'd be happy to see me go.

Probably why I'd been sent to pick up his supplies in Bosquet.

"Thank you," I said. "There a baker in town? I'm supposed to buy him something sweet to celebrate."

Our parents wanted to have a nice dinner before he left, and make sure he had some nice things to take with him so he wouldn't be too out of sorts from the others training to assist the chevaliers. So long as no one asked him to do something that required paying attention for longer than five minutes, Macé would make a good varlet. Macé would be a step above a hack, helping Chevalier Waleran du Ferrant stay alive and channeling the noonday arts for him during fights so his noble body didn't wear down too fast. They were honorable, varlets.

They were worth the money and time and sacrifice. I wasn't.

The shopkeeper told me how to find a baker—said Bosquet was too small for a proper pâtisserie, which I didn't believe for one second because there were more people and buildings here than I'd ever seen. As I'd left his store, he said, "Good luck to your brother, girl."

I froze.

"You're not as good as you think you are, girl," Maman had said yesterday morning. We'd been standing in the root cellar, she and I. The magic I'd been gathering to scry the day's weather had scattered when I heard her steps, and I itched to draw it all back to me and lose myself in the one thing I knew for sure. "Your brother's real good. The comte de Champ offered him this, and chances like these are once in a lifetime."

I'd run my finger along the rim of my bowl and refused to look at her. "He's not that good."

"Annette Boucher, keep that jealousy out of your mouth, or I'll wash it out." She'd bent over me, wobbling, and patted my cheek too hard. Like she'd forgotten how. "We're family, and family makes sacrifices. Now, you're going to Bosquet and picking up what he needs. You can get something small for yourself too."

She never asked. Just watched. She narrowed her eyes, the little crinkles of age bundled up in the corners like a handful of nettle cloth.

Bosquet was so much bigger than home. I slipped through one of the narrow alleys between two towering buildings, and wrapped and unwrapped my necklace around my fingers. The market was taking advantage of school starting up too, and nearly every available space was someone selling something. Country people brushed past rich merchant kids, and a rich girl glittering like gold in mud stopped at a stall serving food from our eastern neighbor Kalthorne. She bought dumplings topped with poppy seeds and dripping plum jam for her and her guards. She was nice at least.

She was still one of those destined for school, though. They'd use hacks, country kids like me who had magic but no money for training, to channel Mistress Moon's power for them. They'd get to do the magic with none of the consequences.

How noble.

I stopped, a rock in a river of people who couldn't care less about me. I couldn't see the end of the market, and the rows of trees leading past it were spotted with couples and families resting in the shade. A stall next to me sold sage water faster than the identical twins distributing it could pour, and the twin on the other side of the stall, clothed in a dusky purple and so focused on her work that her look of concentration made me feel like I should be working, lifted a jar of honey to the sunlight. A ribbon of power burned in it, the midnight arts trapped in a lemon slice. I leaned closer to get a better look.

"Drink it right before you need the illusion," the girl said. "It'll make it last a few minutes more than normal."

There were three types of midnight arts—illusions, scrying, and divining—and illusions were the easiest to master. Scrying was harder, but it let you observe what was happening anywhere in the present, so long as you had a looking glass to see through and knew what you were looking for. The hardest art, divining the future, showed artists all the different possible futures and let them puzzle out which one was true. Most artists never mastered it.

I'd never been trained in the midnight arts, but I could do them without wearing myself down too fast like most people. Even on dark, new-moon nights, magic called to me, thrummed in my heart and urged me to use it. Magic was the only thing that wanted me.

"Something small," I muttered to myself, walking away from the stall and onto the gravel-lined path beneath a line of trees. The interlaced branches were a blessing for my sunburned skin. There'd been no shade on the walk here. "Something small."

At the end of the wall was a crowd, and a kid holding a twig like a knife ran past me.

"Ask her where Laurel is!" someone shouted after the kid. "I want that five-hundred-lune reward on his head."

"Like His Majesty would ever pay up," someone else shouted. "Ask her how to join Laurel."

I took off for the crowd. Vaser got news two days late and two truths off, but everyone was waiting for news of Laurel. They'd started a petition for the king to release how much money the crown was spending, called the king a coward when he hadn't answered, and pamphlets had started peppering Demeine with copies of nobles' ledgers too specific to be fake. Papa had clucked and said they had a death wish. Macé had talked about nothing except the reward money His Majesty had offered up for Laurel's capture. Not even the royal diviner Mademoiselle Charron had been able to find them.

I nudged my way to the front of the crowd till I could read the evergreen words on the parchment.

MADEMOISELLE GARDINIER,
WITH GREAT THANKS TO THE GENEROUS DU FERRANTS,
IS PLEASED TO ANNOUNCE
MADEMOISELLE ESTREL CHARRON, ROYAL DIVINER
TO HIS MOST BRIGHT MAJESTY HENRY XII,
WILL BE PROVIDING HER SERVICES AS A MIDNIGHT ARTIST
FOR THREE DAYS TO THOSE IN NEED
OF SCRYINGS AND DIVINATIONS.
THE SESSIONS WILL BE HELD AT TOWN HALL
AND BEGIN AT DUSK.

Estrel Charron was here. The best midnight artist in the country, the only royal diviner of this century not born from a noble family, was in Bosquet. And I could see her.

I twisted my necklace till the silver crescent moon was pressed against my palm and drew out the magic I had hidden in it. Solane, who'd been a physician's hack before moving to Vaser for safety when the court and university started going after those "outside of Lord Sun's dawn and Mistress Moon's dusk and upsetting the traditional order," had taught me how to do it. Solane had said I had promise. They were nice to lie.

I read through the poster again, certain I'd missed something, and rubbed my eyes. The words itched at me, a little twitch on the back of my neck. Someone had written over the poster in red ink and hidden it with an illusion, ensuring that any artists, no matter how untrained, would be able to see the red message for at least three days. After that, the magic stored in the paper to fuel the illusion would wear down the poster. It'd rot before anyone without magic even noticed the secret note.

A KING CANNOT REST ON HIS LAURELS

NOT ALL ARTISTS DIE YOUNG

ONLY COMMON HACKS DO

WHY

A dripping red crown of laurel leaves had been painted above the words.

It was the symbol and call of Laurel, but they couldn't be in Bosquet. And why were they writing over Mademoiselle Charron's papers? She didn't use hacks.

Nearly all artists rich enough to afford them did. Magic corrupted, wearing down the bodies of artists who channeled it, so people paid country kids to channel for them. The artists directed the magic, but the hack bore the brunt of the power. After a few years of channeling, the hacks' bodies broke down till they couldn't channel or died. The artists were fine.

Most of Laurel's posters said using hacks was amoral. They were right, but being right wasn't much good when the folks we were up against had armies and weapons and decades of training in the arts. Without training, an artist channeling too much could wear their body to nothing but bone dust in a few days. I mouthed the words to myself.

A king cannot rest on his laurels. A king could rest on an army with weapons and magic, though.

"Wouldn't you love to meet her?" some girl next to me asked.

Didn't matter what I wanted. Maman and Papa would send people after me if I didn't get Macé's things home. "Love to, but it's tomorrow, and I've got to be home tonight."

"What if I could offer you the chance to not only meet her but learn from her?"

I turned to tell her to jog off, but the words stuck to my teeth. "What?"

She was all full moon, the sort of pretty only money could buy. Her silver dress was cinched tight, showing off the thick curves of her waist and hips, and a spill of pearls like snowfall was sewn into the silk. She'd long, brown hair twisted into an intricate crown of braids that were so slick, they looked fake. A signet ring, one of five, glittered on her left hand.

"I am Emilie des Marais, comtesse de Côte Verte, and I'm supposed to start my training at Mademoiselle Gardinier's today. I would much rather study the noonday arts at university," she said, as if comtesses said those sorts of things to me every day. She smiled, red paint smeared on her white, rich teeth, and all I could think about was how Maman would've chided me for such poor dress and manners. "How would you like to pretend to be me and study the midnight arts at Mademoiselle Gardinier's with your beloved Estrel while I take your last name and study the noonday arts?"

I'd no words for this.

Was I even allowed to say no? Did I want to?

"It will be dangerous, and I will do what I can to protect you if we are caught," she said, voice low, "but some dangerous things are worth the risk."

Nobles never risked anything. Only we did. We studied and learned, and none of it mattered because they used us as hacks and wore down our bodies before we hit thirty. Even midnight artists channeling Mistress Moon's mercifully gentle powers died sooner than later.

Midnight artists observe the world. You've already proven that's too much responsibility for you.

Maybe the world was as it was because we'd let folks do things without looking too closely at them for so long. Maybe Maman wasn't looking hard enough at me.

But I could make her see me.

"Yes." I nodded, glancing round. No soldiers. No chevaliers. "Yes."

"Brilliant." She looked back, gaze on a carriage bright as the sun, and touched my hand. "I only have a moment before my mother wakes up, but she will walk me to Mademoiselle Gardinier's estate and leave me there, assuming I will not be foolish enough to run off without money or a plan. However, if you meet me in the gardens, I can tell you everything you need to know."

Pulling away, she yanked a silver cuff prettier than anything I'd ever seen from her wrist. One of her hands was raw and red, the skin looked like it had been burned. Least she hadn't worn herself out too much. Her body could fix that.

"Understood?"

I nodded. "You'll have to send my family what I bought today. So long as they get everything back, they won't look too hard for me."

"Of course." Her nose twitched, and not even the red paint on her lips could pretty her scowl. "I can complete whatever tasks are necessary." Her expression shifted back to a wide smile. Mistress, this girl was fickle as fire. "Meet me near the cherry trees. If they don't let you in, tell them you saw a girl drop this and wish to give it to Mademoiselle Gardinier yourself because there's magic in it, and you don't want it to hurt anyone."

She pressed the silver cuff into my hand and darted away before I could speak. I tucked it into my purse.

Only a noble would throw away being a noble, but this was everything I'd ever wanted. Even if I were only there for a day, I'd come out knowing more than I did today.

And Estrel Charron was there.

She was as common as me and a genius. I could learn to be like her.

I could see the world and make it see me.

THREE

Emilie

Mother awoke a mere thirty seconds after I settled back into the carriage. I had leaned my head as if resting—it was so hot and our journey so long that the idea we had nodded off wasn't terribly unbelievable—and she jerked up. She would think it had only been a second or two if I had done it right.

"Emilie?" She blinked, the white cosmetics lining her eyelids sparkling, and touched her head. "Did I fall asleep?"

I yawned. "I think we both did. The crowd is clearer now, though."

"It has been a long few days," she said.

I stepped out of the carriage for the second time, and she took my arm immediately. She led me through the streets—bypassing water stalls tended to by pretty girls with bright smiles and sweet-smelling wares and slipping down an alley of vendors selling charms, all fake, to bolster the midnight arts and protect against the ravages of magical power—and we emerged on the other side of the market. The streets of Bosquet ended, and the path leading to the school began. Lord, this town was small.

The horizon cleared, and my mother pulled me close. She pointed to the mountains overlooking Bosquet.

The glass-domed spires of Mademoiselle Vivienne Gardinier's school glittered over the town. The towers were moon white and sharp against the southern sky, and my mother's relentless descriptions of her childhood home for years had not done the estate justice. The buildings were carved into the cliffs overlooking the Verglas River beneath, the rolling spokes of a waterwheel barely visible over the impeccably groomed garden blocking the ground floors and horizon from view, and a single observatory tower domed in silver marked the highest point for leagues and leagues. On the darkest of nights, it served as a light for the ships navigating the Verglas.

"It's pretty." I swallowed, the bitter tastes of sulfur and daisies heavy on the wind.

The half smile on her face was something I had never teased out of her. "I still miss it sometimes."

A dirt path laid with gray stones led to a silver gate twisted to resemble crawling ivy twined about saplings. The garden beyond, fruit trees and flowers so perfectly organized they resembled a rainbow of soldiers in marching lines more than a garden, blocked my view of the school. My mother approached the closed gate, and I followed.

At eye height, someone had knotted a cheap poster to one of the silver saplings. My mother ripped it down and handed it to me. Beneath the jagged sketch of a laurel crown read:

A KING CANNOT REST ON HIS LAURELS.

HENRY XII SAVED US ONCE AS A PRINCE BUT
HAS FAILED US REPEATEDLY AS A KING.
HE HAS FAILED TO SECURE PEACE AND HAS INSTEAD
SPENT OUR MONEY ON FIELDS OF GOLD & GILDED
PEACE TREATIES WITH NO GUARANTEES.
HE HAS FAILED TO FEED HIS CITIZENS IN TIMES OF NEED,
SAVING THE STORES FOR HIMSELF & THE COURT.
HE HAS FAILED TO PROTECT US FROM THE CORRUPT USAGE
OF HACKS BY NOBLE NOONDAY ARTISTS.
HE HAS BROKEN HIS PROMISES TO RAISE WAGES,
PROTECT OUR LABOR WHICH HE DEPENDS ON,
& ALLOW OUR TOWN LEADERS SEATS AT COURT,
BUT HE DOESN'T HAVE TO REMAIN OUR KING.
WE ARE OUR OWN.
LET NOT YOUR NOBILITY NOR WEALTH
STAND IN THE WAY OF DEMEINE.

JOIN US.

Next to that, someone had tied a flyer depicting the king's court as a handful of leeches sucking the blood from the arm of the Deme people.

"Unbelievable," my mother whispered. "I am appalled Vivienne has let those malcontents disseminate their nonsense here."

"I like this picture better than those old woodcuts, though." I ripped the leeches flyer down and peeked at the back. The signature of the protest's elusive leader was so splotchy, it looked as if a dozen different people had tried to write it at once. "Laurel is getting bold."

Laurel's revolt had been brewing for ages and finally had taken hold in the eastern province of Segance this summer, but the news of it had only just reached us. Côte Verte was a collection of salt-blown woods and port towns on the westernmost coast, and my father, Lord rest his soul, had been a terrible leader. He had spent money as if there were no end to it—there hadn't been, for there were always residents to tax—and he had died ten years ago, leaving me nothing but a title, a few debts, and copious amounts of shame. I had no doubt that many of my people would support Laurel. I wasn't sure I wouldn't.

I was already a terrible lady of Demeine. Why not live up to it?

"It's no laughing matter," said my mother. "We are lucky His Majesty has been so light-handed in dealing with them. They demand too much at once."

My mother was content to let justice trickle down through the ranks, but I suspected Laurel would not be so compliant. Small steps away from the ocean might have seemed like progress to those farther from the water, but when high tide came in, others would still drown.

"Come," said my mother, pushing open the gate and holding out her hand. "Claim your future, Emilie."

Within the hour, I would be on my way to Delest and the University of Star-Blessed Wisdom.

They would laugh me out if I attempted to become a physician, so I would be a physician's hack. I would prove to them how wrong they were. They would have to accept me after that.

I would not be denied my future as a physician.

I followed my mother for the final time. Golden honeysuckle brushed my shoulders. Ivy roses bloomed between the stakes of the fence, leaves a curtain of mottled green and butter yellow. My mother, shoulders relaxed and fingers skimming a row of knee-high lilies, led me down a stone path, and we wound our way closer and closer to the school buildings. The sweet scent of cherries hit my nose, and I turned my face into the breeze. My mother stopped.

Over her shoulder, beyond a thick wall of firs, were the doors to the school.

I shuddered. "Well, is this where you abandon me?"

With any luck, she wouldn't walk me to the door, which could complicate things. It was tradition for new students to explore the garden, but I was certainly not traditional.

"You're so dramatic for such a lucky girl." My mother pulled me into a tight hug, the warmth of her arms a mantle of comfort I hadn't received or wanted in a long, long time. I didn't know what to do. We fought too much, too viciously. Her nimble fingers tucked a rose behind my ear. "We are at a turning point in our history. Stay safe and study hard. Make me proud, Emilie."

I couldn't promise that.

"I have only ever wanted to help people." I hugged her back, but the gesture felt empty and awkward. "You understand that, don't you?"

She pulled away, nodded, and her face fell back into the expressionless mask I knew too well. "You will write to me regularly, and Vivienne will tell me if you attempt to run away."

"I will not attempt to run away," I said. I would succeed.

"Good," said my mother. "If you go straight, this path will lead you to the doors. You have an hour before you are officially late. Don't be, but do feel free to take a few moments to reflect. This garden is a work of art—Vivienne created it herself without the help of magic. There are, of course, guards at every entrance, whether you see them or not. Don't get in trouble before school even begins."

She studied me for a moment, tense, and said, "I love you."

She didn't, but I had known it for so long that the lie didn't sting. It was an old bruise, too yellowed and familiar to hurt.

"I love you too."

I did. What a terrible wound it was, loving her despite her lack of interest in me. I had cauterized it ages ago.

Proper ladies of Demeine did not cry.

They endured.

She didn't look back, and then, she was gone.

I wandered to the cherry trees. My eyes burned, tears pooling. It wasn't fair; she left me here so easily, without even a second thought. It wasn't fair how much it hurt, and worse, she would have chided me for my tears. I grasped a tree branch and ripped it free. Bark dusted my arm.

"What did that tree ever do to you?" a sharp voice asked.

The girl stepped over a thicket of blackberries, cheap dress snagging, and stopped before me. She didn't frown, but she paused before giving the worst curtsy I had ever seen.

"Sorry, Madame," she said.

I laughed. "I am a terrible noble, but at the very least, I must teach you how to curtsy."

Given my past, Mademoiselle Gardinier would be lenient with "my" manners. I hoped.

Mine were doomed; I hadn't even asked for this girl's name.

"Who are you, exactly?" I asked.

"Annette Boucher of Vaser," she said. "They let me in like you said." She tapped the wooden leaf pin on her shoulder. "The guard said Mademoiselle Charron can use this to scry whoever's wearing it, so be sure to give it back when you leave."

"Annette Boucher," I said slowly, the old Deme word a comfort. If I used her family name, I would be one of dozens and harder to find. "Thank you for doing this. Again, if you are caught, I will protect you and make sure you are not punished."

One of her eyebrows twitched. "Thank you, Madame."

She didn't believe me at all.

Well, I could only remedy that by proving it.

"Now," I said, clapping my hands. "We will change clothes, you will go up to school, I'll wait long enough to make sure you're not arrested immediately, and then I shall send your family what you bought today, yes?"

"Yes, or else they'll think I stole it. Shouldn't cost much to send, and you can take the money I have." She pulled out a small purse and handed it to me. "Can I send you money to Delest?"

"You can and you will." I weighed her coin purse—hardly enough to do anything with—in my hand. She had embroidered a crooked moon on either side. Or it was one very rotund cat. I couldn't tell. "If you do not, I will be caught swiftly, and I doubt I'll have time to send you a warning."

If she robbed me outright? Well, there was nothing gained without taking a risk.

"You don't mind me asking," she said, fiddling with the silver trinket around her neck. "Why do you want to do this? You've got everything."

"I don't want everything." I clawed at the lace scratching my neck. "I want one thing, and that is to be a physician."

"Here." She gestured for me to turn around, and her fingers skimmed the back of my neck, my necklaces bunching up as she lifted them free. She hung them from a tree branch. "You sure our clothes will fit?"

"There's only one way to find out, and you cannot walk into the school in what you have," I said.

She nodded. "Where do we start?"

"Help me remove this overdress, and then we may deal with this new contraption from Vertgana my mother insists is a corset."

She had imported it from the nation to our north as soon as she heard it was in fashion. It was wasted on me.

"You don't want to keep it?" she asked. The overdress she helped me pull over my head and hung from another branch. Her fingers lingered on the gauzy fabric. "How can you not want this?"

"I don't like the way it makes me look or the way it feels. It makes me feel as if I'm lying about who I am." Admittedly, the corset was much more supportive than the stays I normally wore under my clothes, but the pinch of it along my ribs made my skin crawl. "I have never been the lady my mother wishes me to be, tastes in clothes included."

Unlike her dress, mine was laced in the back—surely to keep me from getting out of it—and she took such care with undoing the ribbon that it took far longer to untie than it had to lace up.

"Like your parents assumed wrong at birth?" she asked.

A curious turn of phrase I hadn't heard before.

"I can't say my dislike for what my mother prefers has been since birth, but it's certainly been for a while." I mopped up the cooling sweat on my shoulders with my handkerchief.

"Never mind." She shook her head and went back to unlacing the corset.

"I know it's wasteful," I said softly, "but I hate it all—partly because I think I am supposed to love it and partly from my own dislike. I do not like the way I look in dresses; I do not like the chafing of them against my legs; and I do not like the way every part of this outfit constrains me. It is as if I am experiencing everything at once, my senses overloading, and it is unbearable. I don't feel right in them."

They were my mother's domain. She adored clothes, her own closet still limited since we had sold some old dresses to pay off my father's debts right after his death. I didn't love the midnight arts as she did, and all of the clothes and jewelry she wanted me to wear only reminded me of my failures. Dressing how she wanted was like wearing my wrongness for all to see. If they looked at me, they would know I wasn't meant for their world.

"I do not belong." I pulled the rings from my fingers and rubbed the pink welts they left behind. "Wearing things like this only increases that feeling of wrongness in me. They are a reminder of what is expected and what I am not." I laughed and forced myself to smile. It was no good wallowing. "And I do hate being wrong."

Annette hummed, taking great care not to brush my skin as she peeled the last of the corset free. "That makes sense. Not belonging. I don't either."

She adored everything I hated and was already practically the perfect lady of Demeine. My mother would have loved Annette.

"You enjoy the midnight arts, don't you?" I asked.

"It's the only thing I enjoy," she whispered. "Do you ever feel like magic is the only thing that understands you, even though it's not real?"

Magic couldn't think or feel, but it existed, and it wanted me.

"I know exactly what you mean, and yes, I do feel that." I stepped out of the gown and underdress, and Annette gathered them up as if they were the most precious things she had ever seen. "I feel broken. The world tells me I should want these things, but I don't."

Standing in a stranger's garden in nothing but a shift made it easier to say.

"If I go to this school, if I study the midnight arts, if I stay here and witness day in and day out the very things that make me feel broken for not wanting them, I fear it will kill me. I have felt out of place, unwanted, unimportant for so long with my mother, that I want something for me. Being forced to attend this school makes me feel like I'm not a person."

Annette's warm hand touched my shoulder. "As if when Lord Sun and Mistress Moon were weaving the world and all its people into creation, they dropped a stitch while making you?"

"Yes." I laughed and wiped the cosmetics from my face. "I think more than a few."

She pulled off her own dress and stays, and the simplicity of her clothes made me smile. The fabric was itchy and the dress slightly too tight, but I needed no help. Most importantly, my mother would have hated it. I kept my hose and gave her my shoes.

"I can't believe you're giving this away," she said, tracing the silver lines of my dress's bodice from pearl to crystal to pearl.

I undid the too-tight braids slicking back my hair. "I know I am lucky to have been born into my station, but you will appreciate that dress far more than me. You'll be wearing the jewelry too. They're heirlooms."

She picked up her own cheap necklace and compared the little moon charm to the sapphire collar that had been my great-grandmother's, and the silver glittered in her eyes. "I could buy a house or twenty with these."

"Please do not. My mother would murder us both," I said. "Speaking of, though, how are your mathematics?"

She hummed, gaze stuck on one of the mirrored necklaces my mother had hoped I would use for scrying.

"Annette," I said sharply. "This is important. Mademoiselle Gardinier is expecting me to be atrociously behaved, but she will catch on to our charade if you do not have the requisite knowledge, like mathematics, history, or reading. Your penmanship, as well, will—"

"I was reading a poster when we met," she said. "How do you folks always discount us, even when proof you're wrong is right there?"

I winced, flushing, and nodded. "You're right. I'm sorry. That was instinct, and a terrible instinct at that."

Her top lip twitched, as if she were about to sneer, but her face remained impassive. She was such a good stoic lady of Demeine already.

"Pedigree is more important than artistry or wealth anyway. You're the sole heir to one of the twelve families of the sword. If anyone ever questions you, simply remind them of your name."

She stared at me, shocked, and I took her by the shoulders.

"Enjoy your months of astronomy, embroidery, and whatever else they teach you." I plucked an orange from a nearby tree and dug my nails into its skin. "Madame des Marais, comtesse de Côte Verte."

She could be the perfect lady, the pristine calm of Demeine my mother had always wanted from me, and I could be the avalanche lurking underneath.

·CHAPTER·
FOUR
Annette

I was fixing to get hanged. Emilie might be able to pass for some merchant's runaway girl, but I didn't belong here. Even my hands looked out of place as I lifted the overdress from the branch.

"I have never really worn cosmetics, so I think you can get away without them." She tilted my head up and to the left, healing the little cuts and burns along my cheeks. Solane was a hack, but they did mostly surgery these days, not using their healing arts training unless they had to. Cost an arm and a leg too. I'd never been hurt bad enough to warrant the expense. "There. Try to stay out of the sun for a few days."

The last of her magic slithered out of my skin, and I shuddered.

"You've never been healed by a physician before, have you?" she asked and scrunched up her face. As if that were something I'd lie about. "But your arm? That was such a bad break."

"Vaser's got a hack, but they're retired and healing arts are expensive." I raised my arm, the little scar mostly gone thanks to Solane's salves. Beneath the sleeves of Emilie's dress, no one would notice it. "Wasn't worth it."

She narrowed her eyes at me. "You weren't worth a proper physician?"

When she put it like that, it sounded worse than it was.

"I'm not a genius or strong or pretty. I'm just Annette," I said. "I've got nothing but magic."

We sat on a little stone bench a few paces away, me pulling on the hose and testing out Emilie's slippers, and her finger-combing my hair so she could put it into place as hers had been. She did it more gently than I'd have thought she would, working out each knot instead of ripping through it. When I was little, Alaine had always brushed my hair.

"There was an accident when I was little," I said. "There aren't many artists in Vaser. My siblings and I all are, but we're it, and I'm the only midnight artist. It's easier for people to divine big things, like disasters, but I didn't foresee this."

"You were a child," Emilie said. "Children can barely understand what's right in front of them, much less divinations."

"We can't afford not to be perfect." I shrugged, and she hooked the last pin through my hair to hold it all in place. "I'm not good enough to get out of Vaser on my own. I'm a failure there."

Life in Vaser was like scrying—I was always outside of everyone else. Always watching. Never taking part.

Emilie stood first. She offered me her hand, the gesture odd. Even without all the clothes and silver, even in my elbow-patched dress, she still looked like a comtesse. I let her help me up, stepping carefully into the slippers, and she settled the overdress over me. It was like wearing winter air, and she laughed when I smiled. Her nimble fingers tucked the waist and shoulders in, so it wouldn't giveaway how big it was. She curtsied to me.

"You will belong here, Madame Emilie des Marais," she said. "And if Vaser does not miss you, it's the one missing out."

The word *madame* burned. Only noblewomen had the right to be called that, and folks hardly ever bothered to use *mademoiselle* with me. It was always *you* or *girl*. The title made our half-thought-out plan more real.

I tugged at the sleeves. "I don't look—"

"Half of looking like a comtesse is acting like a comtesse, so act like you know better than everyone else," she said.

"Like you?"

"Exactly." She laughed. "Order new dresses that fit you."

"That's too much—"

"Annette," she said, plucking an orange from a nearby tree. "This is from the Bèidexīng region of the Hé Dynasty. Do you know how much one of these costs import?"

I shook my head. "A lot?"

"This tree costs more than that dress, and my mother has a whole row of them at home," Emilie said, tucking the orange into my—hers now—bag. "Order new dresses that fit you. My mother won't even notice the expense, and if she does, she will be thrilled at the thought of me giving in to her tastes."

The idea of that much money made me itch.

"Now, we will have to communicate."

I shoved one of her silver cuffs into her hands. "You're keeping this, and you're scrying me with it. We have to talk somehow. I don't mind if you scry me from time to time to make sure I'm not caught, and it's certainly faster than letters."

"Not to imply that's a bad plan," she said slowly. "But I can't scry."

"Only because you don't know how." I gathered magic; it was day and the moonlight mostly gone, but using a tiny bit of Lord Sun's power wouldn't ruin scrying. *Same power, different source*, Solane always said. So long as I didn't gather as much as most noonday artists did, it would still work. "Focus on what you want to scry, imagine yourself next to what you're looking for, and want it."

She frowned but did what I asked.

It was fun bossing a comtesse about.

It took me a painful twenty minutes to get her scrying, but at least she was determined, even if she hated it. I clasped the cuff around her wrist.

"You scry me, I'll scry you, and we'll know what's going on with the other in a pinch," I said.

She spun the bracelet and couldn't hide her discomfort. "I have heard the best midnight artists are capable of communicating with scrying silver, though I have never read about how it's done."

I'd not either, but scrying was just looking at someone. Only the best could hear what their target was saying, but if you could do that, it couldn't be hard to communicate. Two people scrying at the same time would be enough.

"Well, let's hope I get real good."

Emilie laughed, and I laid my hands on her cheeks. She stilled.

"Let me make you a bit more Annette," I muttered, and channeled what little magic I could gather across her face and neck. It was easy enough to make her cheeks look sunburned and change the straight edge of her nose to a slightly crooked one. Her teeth, when she smiled, would be yellower. She opened her mouth a few times.

"I think you will get very good," she said, testing out the magic around her mouth. "How long will this last?"

"Half an hour." I withdrew my hands, the magic feeling more like a mask of ice frozen to her face than real skin to me. Hopefully, the guards weren't artists and wouldn't notice.

Then she was gone, tearing through the garden with a grin on her face and no care at all in her strides. She tore through a thicket, snagging a few branches, and didn't look back. I tugged at her dress, her life an odd fit, and scratched at the satin against my skin. Didn't rub but slipped, prettier and smoother than anything I'd ever worn.

"I can do this," I said, checking my hair. "Please don't get arrested before you even leave."

Emilie had felt like a friend when we were talking. I knew what it was like to feel broken and out of place because of what the world told you to want. Desires were complicated, living in a world full of contradicting ones doubly so.

"I belong. I can do this," I repeated.

I shoved my hands into the pockets of her dress, fingers crinkling over paper in one, and pulled it out, desperate to distract myself from this mess.

"A response to Mademoiselle Estrel Charron on *The Price of Clarity: The Effects of Divination on the Mortal Form* from a Healing Arts Perspective." I traced the spiky signature at the bottom. "Laurence du Montimer, premier prince du sang, duc des Monts Lance, Chevalier of the Noonday Arts, and Physician of the First Order."

What an ass. Estrel Charron was the only bearable artist from the higher ranks because she was common born and kinder for it. She'd tried studying at the university, and they'd made her a hack for the noble artists, content to waste her powers until she'd showed them she was too good to be ignored. She'd divined sieges and storms and spies. She'd written books foretelling the futures of Demeine—for noble perusing only, of course. A pearl amongst grit, they called her.

I could be too.

I tucked the paper away and pushed through the firs to a stone path. For all this fancy gardening, there wasn't a marker in sight. The path Emilie must've wandered off was stone, cut through with swatches of bright green moss, and I followed it eastward up a small incline. Around a bend of more orange trees, a pond of blue thyme, with yellow primrose spotted through like fish, rippled in the breeze. I skimmed my fingers along every flower and leaf as I walked, everything green and living, and pulled a poppy from a patch of red. We'd only enough land to grow what we needed in Vaser.

Winding closer to the academy, the observatory a great unblinking eye of glass glaring down at me through the holes in the treetops, I touched an orange. My stomach rumbled against my ribs. Most of the land around Vaser was too dry to produce such extravagance.

This was why Laurel was gaining so much ground—nobles wasting money on things like this.

"Pretend you're Estrel Charron," I whispered. "A winter, soft enough to be wanted and threatening enough to be feared."

If she could do it, maybe I could too.

"It would be best if you did not touch things you have not been told are safe to touch," a gentle voice behind me said. "It is not a good way to start your first day, Emilie des Marais."

I froze. The person behind me laughed.

"Turn, please. I prefer to see what I have to work with in its natural habitat, and your mother said you were quite the wild child."

"Yes, ma'am." I swallowed, turned, and straightened my back. Time to be a comtesse. "I'm sorry. It was real pretty."

"Don't worry, dear. I'm Vivienne Gardinier, and I'm here to help you." She was an older white woman, craggy lines like ice crevasses set deep into her skin, and clean brows shaped like snowcapped peaks brightened her forget-me-not eyes. Strands of curled white hair, escaping from the smooth knot at the back of her head just so, rustled against the shoulders of her pale-green dress. A scar split her pink lips from bow to chin. "Come—it is a normal day of instruction for the other girls, but your roommates have arrived, and I would prefer you acquaint yourselves with one another before attending classes. And don't worry, you're not in trouble."

I lifted my skirts and took her arm, the expensive beading of her dress rustling against mine. It made my stomach clench in a way that had nothing to do with hunger. "Yes, ma'am."

She swept up the path. "Mademoiselle when necessary. Here you may call me Vivienne. Only soldiers and sailors say *ma'am*, and you must remember to enunciate. Your accent will find nothing but scorn in Serre, I am sorry to say. You sound quite harsh, but it is a sad lesson we must all learn. People with power can be particular, can't they?"

As if she didn't have any power. Nobles were the ones who talked differently, snipping the ends off words with nasally sighs.

"Yes, Mademoiselle," I said. "They can be."

She patted my hand. She was warm, and this close, smelled of roses. "Your mother says you're very particular about your magic?"

"I won't use a hack." I swallowed. The building loomed above us, only a thin screen of trees separating us. "My magic's all me."

I was my own.

"An artist after mine and Estrel's hearts, I see." She smiled and pointed to one of the towers far above us. "Your mother said you took no joy from the midnight arts, but even so, I imagine someone so dedicated to their studies would appreciate a meeting with Mademoiselle Charron?"

Black smoke leaked from a half-closed window far above us, storm smeared against the sea of sky. I reached for it with my magic, and a teeth-chattering shudder ran through me.

Power—raw and ready.

"Yes," I whispered, feet moving on their own. "I would."

"Then I am very pleased to welcome you to my school, Emilie." We rounded a bend, and she paused before an open door taller than two of me and drenched in silver etchings of stars encircling the moon, white rabbits on onyx skies, and a brazenly gilded sun and moon. Most of the manors along the Verglas had been built to withstand sieges, and it showed. The doors were thick as my thigh, the locks an intricate web of metal gears and magic. Beyond, a hall of white marble and light wood stood empty. The muffled sounds of distant voices echoed through it.

Rivers of silver spilled through the marble and wood, slashes of metal so bright, they looked like they still flowed, and I couldn't bring myself to take a single step inside.

They'd know. They'd know I was all dirt and failure, a Vaser girl with ill-formed dreams. They'd know I didn't belong.

"Classes will begin for new students tomorrow, and one of the older girls will show you where to go in the morning." Mademoiselle Gardinier led me through the open doors. "Today is for settling in."

How could someone settle into this?

The entry was brilliant. The silver-seamed floor split into two hallways to the left and right, the floors shifting from marble to hardwood polished until it glowed in the light filtering through the tall, glass windows. A staircase of wood rose from the center and split into the two that spiraled away from each other, leading into the heavens of the school, and a rug of white with silver threads, impossibly clean, covered the steps. Silver gilded the edges of the furniture and sparkled in the portrait of the first King of Demeine hanging at the top of the first flight of stairs. Steel chains that ended in small candleholders hung above us, the blue candles unlit. Crystal drops dangled beneath them like rain.

There was no dirt anywhere but on me, and an army of servants must've been waiting in the wings. The very idea of keeping this place clean and running made my skin crawl.

"It is beautiful, isn't it?" Mademoiselle Gardinier asked.

I jerked. "It is."

"Come, let us introduce you to your new roommates, so you have time to speak before supper." She took me upstairs, past tapestries and wall hangings laced with gold and silver, past doors painted with alchemistry, so that only when I was right before them could I read the names of the three girls inside, and to a room at the end of a hall in the easternmost edge of the third floor. It was cracked open, the soft patter of tapping toes against plush carpet leaking through. She rapped on the doorjamb.

"Girls?" she asked, face impassive. She glanced away from me to rap again. "Emilie has arrived."

I checked my face to see if I was squinting. There was too much glitter and gilding, too much…everything.

The door opened wide. I couldn't help but peer in, the room full of gilded wallpaper and silk screens and fine silver. The rich girl I'd seen in town, the one with gold hair and a taste for sweets, leaned against the wall with one arm. She was distractingly pretty—full cheeks and lips, a slope of a nose dotted with too few freckles to be natural, moon-round eyes the same shade as clouds after a storm, and blond hair tumbling down her shoulders in tight curls. A single black beauty mark stood out against the tanned white skin beneath her right eye.

I'd never looked at someone and been attracted to them, but sometimes people would pass through Vaser who were so beautiful or interesting that looking at them was like staring at a painting, each glance revealing another exquisite detail. This girl was that sort of pretty.

"Coline, what have I said about your posture?" Mademoiselle Gardinier said evenly.

Coline let her arm slide down the wall, slowly, and straightened her back. "I try not to hold to negative comments made about me," she said. "It's bad for my esteem, and what if thinking about it makes me miss my beauty rest?"

"Then we will all suffer for your decline in beauty." Mademoiselle Gardinier removed her arm from mine. "Emilie, please allow me to introduce to you Coline Arden from Monts Lance. Coline, this is the daughter of the late Monsieur des Marais, Emilie."

"A pleasure," Coline said. She curtsied and kept her head bowed. The back of her neck was bared to me, and I couldn't help but feel she hated it. "My apologies, but I'm still a little uncertain—if she is the daughter of a late comte, doesn't that mean she inherits the title?"

Mademoiselle Gardinier did raise one eyebrow at that. "No politics unless you're in class. You are to be allies. You must learn to trust one another regardless of standing—a bond, when formed, creates power. This is the first rule of alchemistry, and it must be the first rule here."

"Of course, Vivienne," said Coline. "It is a pleasure to meet you, Madame Emilie des Marais."

Looking at Coline was like looking at a sword in a fancy sheath. Beautiful and vaguely threatening.

"You too," I said, curtsying instead of dropping to my knees and pressing my face to the dirt as I would've when I was Annette Boucher. "A pleasure, Coline."

Arden was a northern place of forests and hills in the Segance province, and it bordered the shores of the Pinch, where our island of Demeine came closest to touching our neighbor Kalthorne. My papaw still remembered when the last king made everyone pick family names and nearly everyone picked places. He hadn't wanted to be the fifth Jean Vaser, so the old Deme word for butcher had become our name instead.

"Propriety after breakfast." Mademoiselle Gardinier patted my arm and shooed Coline from the doorway, so we could enter.

All the money in the room—the walls, the portraits, the floors, the girls, their dresses, their damned skin even, so clear and clean—gave me a stomachache. The room was huge, and it was separated into three small sections with only paper screens between them. Each section had a bed, wardrobe, desk, and chair. A pile of clothes in bright reds and sunny golds covered the bed on the left. The middle bed was empty.

"It's a pleasure, Madame," said a girl with curly hair the same shade of ruddy brown as Papa's chopping board. Her slicked-back hair, so perfectly ordered, glittered in the light.

Mademoiselle Gardinier gestured to her. "And Emilie, let me introduce Isabelle Choquet from Courmers."

I nodded to her too, and she dropped into a perfect curtsy.

Courmers was one of those coastal cities out west. I'd always dreamed of seeing those oceans. Isabelle looked like she missed it, her fingers rubbing against the soft, blue-green dress that had been darned and reworked one too many times. Her brown eyes caught mine, and she blushed.

Coline was pretty, but Isabelle was interesting, from the purple paint stains beneath her nails to the single green and black earring in the shell of her left ear.

"It's nice to meet you," I said. "Thank you for introducing us, Mademoiselle."

I nodded my head to Mademoiselle Gardinier. That was polite no matter the standing, right?

"Vivienne," she said. "Call me Vivienne, dear."

"Yes." I swallowed. "Vivienne."

Behind her, Coline crinkled her nose and raised her top lip, mouth a crooked hourglass of amusement.

"Now," Vivienne said. "I do not wish to hover. Supper will be delivered to your room tonight. It won't be as of tomorrow. Meals are taken with the other girls, but I know so many new people can be overwhelming. If you are up to it, introduce yourselves to your neighbors and enjoy the evening learning about one another. Classes begin tomorrow."

She looked at each of us in turn, as if the phrase were threatening, but I couldn't imagine being rich enough to think an education a threat.

"I placed you together because each of you has distinct strengths and weaknesses that are in need of extra attention." She did frown at that, the first ungainly expression I had seen on her. "It is my hope that you find comfort in one another and learn to become outstanding ladies of Demeine."

We were problems.

Of course Emilie was.

Vivienne left. Coline shut the door, her steps a fencer's glide.

"If we are to be allies—a bold choice of words to be sure for a woman preparing us for life at court, but not wholly unwarranted given some of the people there—let us know what we are getting into." Coline's stormy gaze slipped from Isabelle's paste-and-glue hairpins to my rough hands. She threw herself onto the middle bed and patted the spot next to her. "We're the failures, aren't we?"

Isabelle huffed. "I'm not—"

"Sorry," Coline said. "But you're poor and female, so the nobles of court will consider you a failure. To them, it's simply another category like *scribe* or *servant* or *beneath notice*. Trust me, they will call you that whether you can hear them or not."

I sat on the middle bed, on the other side from Coline. "How do you know?"

"Because I have met nobles." Coline shrugged and stretched out, flinging her skirts back till her legs were bare all the way up to her knees. A knife was strapped in her left boot. A *knife*. "That's why I'm here—to be less of an embarrassment. Or it's a punishment. I wasn't listening when my father explained."

"Explains more than it doesn't," Isabelle mumbled. She sat back on her bed and pulled a leather-bound journal into her lap. The pages were thick with dog-ears and oil paint stains. "How do you know so much about court?"

"My family's fortune is from timber, and you know how it is, the only way to advance is to marry up or kill someone important." Coline picked at her nails. "There is a chance I was part of the group who attempted to free Segance from His Majesty's purview, and sending me here was a way to limit the rumors of my involvement with Madame Royale's attempted revolt with Laurel."

"She did what?" I asked. The little news Vaser got of His Majesty's only child was the priest asking us to pray for Madame Royale Nicole du Rand since she was *misguided* and *going against the current*. "Last I heard, she had promised to let Laurel and folks have seats at court."

"Their own ruling body. My aunt called it *atrocious*," Isabelle said. "She was trying to set it up with Laurel when her father caught her."

"A guard tipped off her father, who had most of those involved with the attempted revolt killed." Coline shrugged, teeth clenched. "She challenged her father to a duel, he refused, and she got locked away in Serre. It cost me an unimaginable amount to get the story from the guard who betrayed her, but it was worth it. Laurel found him soon after anyway and decided playing nicely was over."

Isabelle rolled her lips together. "Why would you pay for that story?"

"Because information is the only honest currency," said Coline. "I grew up in Segance. Many of those arrested and killed were my friends, and you cannot deny that something is very wrong in Demeine."

"I didn't know any of that," I muttered. "I'm like a baby."

Coline laughed. "People love babies, so I'm sure you'll be fine. What sort of trouble did you get into?"

"I wanted to be a physician and study the noonday arts." Emilie had left me with so little, it'd be a miracle if I weren't caught by breakfast. "At least here, I still get to study."

"A physician?" said Coline, but she smiled and it was kind...ish. "That's very untraditional."

I snorted. "I'm not a traditional student."

"None of us are, my pearl." Coline smiled and sat up. "We're about to meet dozens of traditional students from traditional families, noble and wealthy, and Vivienne and her staff are going to teach us how to run an estate, divine the weather, and hold political conversations without being too passionate. There's nothing wrong with any of that, but is it what any of us want?"

I swallowed. I wouldn't mind—the money that came with being a lady of standing could fix most things.

"I want to be a governess," Isabelle said quickly. "I like teaching, but I got removed from my last school."

Coline turned slowly to her, eyes wide. "What on earth could you have done to deserve that?"

"My aunt says I'm too petty." Isabelle blushed, sketching in her journal with a nub of charcoal. "One of the other students said something rude about hacks, and my brother's a hack, so I dyed her hair green. They said I would never be a governess with that sort of behavior, but Vivienne said I'm not hopeless, just rash and passionate." Her shoulders slumped. "I had to take out a loan to attend, though."

"And here we all thought I was the most interesting," Coline said to me. "Isabelle, I will pay you however much you want to help me out of this dress so long as you save me from drowning in wool."

Isabelle laughed again, and I stood to inspect the trunk at the foot of the middle bed. It had to be Emilie's. The wood was carved with delicate little sea stars and distant ships on ocean waves that must've been her home in Côte Verte. Coline let out a loud, unnecessary sigh.

"Thank the Lord." She gestured for Isabelle to help her. "I was trying to be nice, but we must get you into a dress and—" She eyed me, fingers picking at the seams of her dress. "That actually fits?"

"I don't really like wearing things like this, so most of the measurements were old." I flushed. "Is it that bad?"

"Yes," Coline said. "It is."

Isabelle grabbed the collar of Coline's dress. "I don't think you can tell a comtesse that."

"She doesn't care, do you?" Coline smiled. "The des Marais family hasn't been to court in ages. I quite like that about them, and now I'm curious. Emilie, what is it you want?"

Country girls from Vaser weren't supposed to want. Country girls from Vaser who were so bad at simply *being* that even their parents didn't like them anymore definitely weren't supposed to want. We were supposed to give.

"I want to study the midnight arts—divination and scrying and illusions. I want to be like Estrel Charron. I want to be the best."

"What's stopping you?" Coline asked.

She didn't understand. No one but people with money had time to be scholars and geniuses. They didn't have to do anything but what they wanted and pay people to do the rest.

"Nothing," I said. "Nothing is going to stop me."

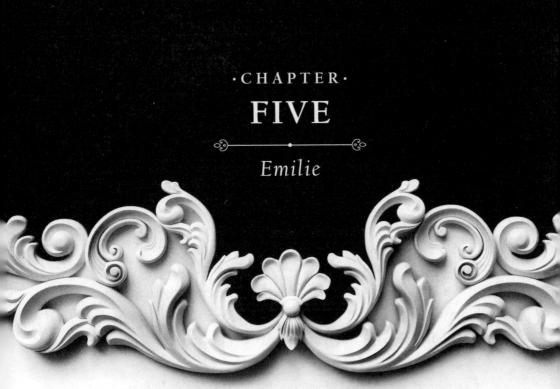

·CHAPTER·

FIVE

Emilie

The road to university was spotted with merchants. Robin-red packs wobbled atop shoulders and horses, the pungent taste of alchemistry ingredients burning every time a bit of sunlight slipped through the cloth and struck the brown jars. All schools started during the same two-week stretch, allowing those who weren't handpicked to prove their worth with exams and demonstrations. Fresh-faced priests returning to their churches and young apprentices returning to the chevaliers they trained under walked the road. The first king of Demeine had combined each noble family's soldiers into a singular military when he took over decades ago—it was how he had been strong enough to become king—and over time, the noble artists who led had adopted the title *chevalier*. They studied the noonday arts at university before training with the soldiers in Serre.

The university trained a number of people in a multitude

of subjects, but it was the medical school, the department that combined the physical knowledge—surgery—with the ethereal magic—physicianry—of the noonday arts, that employed the most applicants. Those without the appropriate family or connections could be assistants for surgeons or hacks for physicians. As artist Emilie Boucher, Annette's surname would do well enough and using her first would be confusing. I could only be a hack.

"Women can't do the noonday arts. It's too dangerous. Their bodies will wear out, and Demeine will die out," the old masters of magic in Demeine said, refusing to train women in the noonday arts and acting shocked when women died attempting to study them. "See? It killed her. It's not natural and can't be done."

I didn't need to be a diviner to solve that prophecy.

The head physician, Physician Pièrre du Guay, had to need a hack, and if I proved my worth to him, he would have to realize he was wrong. I would become a physician. They would have no choice but to accept me.

"Clear the road!"

The shout startled me out of my thoughts. Hoofbeats thundered behind me, bearing down, and I sidestepped left. Annette's skirts tangled around my legs, their thick presence an unfamiliar nuisance, and a chestnut-brown horse cantered past me. The rider was a long-legged slump of a white boy with a smear of inky hair tangled in a half braid. The road before him was crowded with carts and travelers, the people unable to move aside due to the bridge ahead. At least the noble had the decency to stop instead of demanding passage first.

"My apologies."

Something blew hot air down the back of my neck.

I spun, and a horse nipped at the shoulder of my pack. I clucked, no stranger to nosy rides, and nudged the horse away from my arm. It was a lovely seal-brown flecked with white, and the golden gear gracing its elegant head only made it prettier.

"Salt, stop it." The rider was clearly noble as well, and he patted Salt's neck till the horse let out a low-pitched nicker. "He's a terrible glutton who doesn't understand everything isn't for him."

I swept my skirts back and curtsied. The people of Marais never talked to me unless I spoke first, so I stayed quiet.

"I am sorry about him and my companion," he said, bowing his head slightly. "Salt didn't bite you, did he?"

"No, Monsieur. I shall make it to university intact." I stayed low, legs already bored of the position, and ran through all the noble families my mother had taught me. "Thank you for your concern."

I let the sound of the last letter hang in the air, so he knew I was waiting for his name and title and not being rude, and he raised the fingers of his right hand. A quick dismissal of propriety.

"University? My second year of medical school begins today." The boy nudged Salt into a walk and motioned for me to continue as well. He had a long nose and small mouth, and his red hair was loose, curling where the ends brushed the bottom of his shadowed jaw. Freckles peppered his pale skin. "If I may be bold, what are you studying?"

I glanced around. I was the only girl in this crowd, but with so many people around, little could happen to me or be done to me. The thought shuddered through me.

There were far more dangerous things a member of the court could ask a country girl.

"You may," I said, rising and stepping forward to keep time with the horse. "I would adore being a physician, but will settle for serving Demeine as a hack."

"How noble of you—settling." The wild grin he had possessed until now fell. "Good luck."

Country girls could be hacks, but still, it wasn't encouraged or favored. Most were shuffled off to study alchemistry or midwifery. Some were even made to study surgery, the bloody practice of healing without magic at all.

"Thank you," I said in the sweet, soft voice Mother had taught me to use when the answer was one the listener didn't want to hear. I was not good at talking, slow to catch on to the nuance of it, but my mother had spent years teaching me—watching me practice my smile in the mirror and correcting my inflection until it was perfect. "I appreciate it, Monsieur."

His lips twitched back up into a smile.

To think my mother believed I possessed no manners.

"Would you like some advice?" he asked.

"It would be much appreciated," I said, but I wasn't even sure I believed me.

The noble didn't look like he did either.

But still, he leaned down over Salt's back to point to the rider who had run through the crowd. We were only a little ways off from the bridge now, and the three wagons that had been blocking the pack were almost done crossing. "That is the comte de Saillie, and he very much demands people call him 'Monsieur des Courmers.' All physicians and apprentices demand their titles be used, except Laurence du Montimer. Call him Physician du Montimer. Never call him *monsieur*, use *grace* if he uses it first, and only use his titles if you have to introduce him before a stuffy crowd."

No wonder my father had hated him. Laurence was a genius, but his position as the king's nephew could only save him from so much splitting with tradition. *Grace* was a Vertganan honorific.

He sat back up. "He's the only one who doesn't make people babble during emergencies. It's so tedious."

"What about you?" I asked.

He sat back up and shrugged. "Apprentice—I earned that honor."

"Thank you for the advice," I said, bowing my head. "Nameless Apprentice."

He laughed. Then, he took off and caught up with the comte— Sébastien des Courmers if the memory of my lessons served me well—ahead of us. He was reading on horseback, waiting for the bridge to clear. The apprentice who had avoided giving me his name plucked the book, one of du Montimer's journals by the look of it, from the comte's hands. They laughed about something and threw back their heads.

If I did convince the university I would make a good physician, would I be free to be so open and fiery like them, or would I be forced to ascribe to the expectations of other ladies in Demeine— quiet, stoic, reserved?

I kept walking. The nobles made it easily over the bridge, the crowd splitting so they could pass, and vanished into the trees surrounding the school. The dense woods were the perfect training grounds, and the town of Delest had grown up around the school in twisting roads and dead-end alleys. The squat wooden buildings of town were crowned by stone spires, and the tallest, designed to channel and store the noonday arts so that the power could be used long after the sun had set, were glittering, gold-plated glass domes. The school commanded the skyline, every eave and tower gilded. I crossed Delest without stopping.

The raised stones over packed dirt of Delest's roads gave way to dark, damp earth sprouting a carpet of thick grass. I knew this path as well as I knew myself, the descriptions of the university front gates my bedtime stories. I let my fingers fall, feeling the scratch of the grass against my skin, the heat of noon on my face, and the quiver of power in my bones. I neared the fence, the wall of white willows rustling in the wind. The whole field was alight with sparks from their gold leaves.

The world was wild here.

The fence was impassable, the willows too close together and their golden leaves too sharp to reach through.

From beyond the trees, a clock struck noon, and the clamor of the bells rolled over the field. I moved from the side of the fence to the front of the gate.

"Lovely," I said, fingers skimming the golden bars.

The gate was taller than me, and the thick bars were styled like swords stuck into the earth at my feet, each golden blade bearing the name of the twelve nobles of the sword who had helped the first King Henry take Demeine generations ago: Estienne du Bois, Geoffroi du Montimer, Piers du Vedette, Jehan des Courmers, Simon des Marchand, Adrien du Vale, Léandre des Morsites, Hugh des Rives, Ignace du Ferrant, Henri du Ruse, Jean d'Élan, and there, the sword of Yvain des Marais with its waves emblazoned in vivid blue against the delicately woven guard. Above the swords rested a crown of gold irises inscribed with the name of the first king of the new nation of Demeine, the rubies and garnets making up the letters more fire than stone. A sun rose from the top of the gate.

My great-great-great-great-great-great-great-great-great-great-great grandfather Yvain from Marais, Chevalier of the Noonday Arts, had sworn an oath to Henry from Rand to serve him forever, and here I was, to serve Demeine.

"Such a gilded threat," a dry voice next to me said. "I could buy a house for everyone from my town and then some for the amount of gold in this."

A hand to my right touched the gate, fingers the nimble flick of someone familiar with the noonday arts.

"It was made ages ago," I said, turning to the speaker. "They had other things on their minds and plenty of money."

"Gold is gold, and metal can be melted down to make something new and better," the person beside me said. "I'm Madeline."

She was far better dressed than me and delicately put together in a way I had never mastered—umber cream lined her hooded eyes, her broad nose was pierced with a small pearl, and her pine-green dress hemmed with silver brought out the warmth of her dark-brown skin. The two-strand twists of her black hair brushed her slim shoulders as she nodded at me. Even that movement felt purposeful and controlled.

"Emilie." I nodded at her and smiled. She wasn't wrong; it was unfair of me to let off the university when they could be doing so much more. "I doubt they will ever tear this down, though."

"Of course they won't. They couldn't keep us out, then," said someone else.

Madeline sighed. "My older brother, Rainier."

"It was Physician du Guay yesterday," Rainier said as I turned. "There's no telling who it will be today. I hear they draw lots."

He bent at the waist and peered through the blades of the fence. Standing, he was Madeline's height—only slightly taller than me—but he lacked her easy style. His smile was wide and carefree, but the skin of his lips was dry and cracked, and his white skin was blistering from sunburn. The ends of his sleeves were worn from constant rubbing against a table. Dots of lampblack spotted his hands.

If I looked at Madeline, I felt she knew what she was doing.

If I looked at Rainier, I felt I should instead look to Madeline.

"You were here yesterday?" I asked. "What happened?"

"Showed up. Waited. Got rejected after I mentioned my interest in being a midwife since my mother died in childbirth." He rolled his eyes to the sky and clucked his tongue. "Stand back a bit. The gate opens on its own, and you don't want to get knocked out. Doesn't bode well."

We stepped back. Soon after, the gate opened slowly, no fanfare or hands, and a figure walked across the stone path to us.

"Two hacks were accepted to study the healing arts and work for physicians, five assistants to surgeons, and a handful to other schools." Madeline rolled her eyes, the action a perfect mirror to Rainier's. They shared a father, Madeline had explained while we waited, and Madeline's mother had adopted the two-year-old Rainier after marrying their father. "I didn't even bother once I saw it was Physician du Guay."

"Hacks are required to be tested," I said, doubt gnawing at my stomach. "It's a law. The university is fined if it bypasses—"

They both laughed, their identical bright brown eyes crinkling shut.

"Rules are only suggestions when you have enough money to pay the price," her brother said softly.

"Rainier!" Madeline elbowed him. "Hush. They'll hear."

This wasn't right. This wasn't right at all. There were rules, there had always been rules, and Demeine lived for them.

"You were laughing." He rubbed his sunburned cheeks. "You were certainly thinking it."

"Still." Madeline held out half of the pastry she had been eating to me. "For luck? Rainier already ate two."

"I need more luck than you," he said.

I took the pastry and knocked it against what was left of hers. "For luck."

I turned back to the gate, took a breath, and ate the pastry in one sticky bite. The ground beyond the gate was a mosaic of gold-flecked white stone, and tulips in every shade of red lined the path. The figure walking toward us wore the pale-orange coat of a physician apprentice. A shock of red hair crowned them.

Oh no.

It was the nameless apprentice.

"Welcome to the University of Star-Blessed Wisdom!" He raised his arms in welcome, the new coat a good fit for his sturdy frame and a terrible fit for his pale complexion. "I am Charles du Ravine, vicomte des Îles Étoilées and second apprentice to Laurence du Montimer, premier prince du sang, duc des Monts Lance, Chevalier of the Noonday Arts, and Physician of the First Order." Charles paused to take a breath. We were, it seemed, a stuffy crowd. "Physician du Montimer will select the new students to matriculate, and after that, you will begin the initial observation stage, so the masters may bid on which assistants and hacks they wish to employ in their departments."

Laurence du Montimer had started out as a chevalier's apprentice in Serre with a sword in hand instead of a scalpel, but it became clear he was far too skilled in the healing arts when he kept his chevalier and fellows alive during a skirmish with Kalthorne ten years ago. Now, he trained physicians in how to heal during natural and mortal-made disasters. He didn't even use hacks.

"Physician du Montimer is a very busy person," Charles said, fingers flexing at his side. "Do not argue with him if he rejects you. Come back tomorrow or next year."

That did send a whisper through the dozen of us here.

"You may, of course, still be accepted in Serre to serve our esteemed chevaliers, however." Even from a distance, Charles's scowl was clear. "Now, please form a line. It doesn't have to be straight, but it needs to ensure we can see you."

They wanted hacks for the fighting arts to serve chevaliers, not for physicians. Why would Demeine need more of those? We weren't at war. I tucked myself between Madeline and a lanky giant more long limbs than anything else, and Madeline shoved Rainier between us, muttering about quotas and appearances. A nervous energy twitched down my legs. The giant next to me tapped his toes. Mother would have killed me.

I tapped mine too.

Damn the expectations.

A figure crested the hill in the field behind Charles; he glanced back at it and clapped his hands together.

"We will start here." Charles gestured to the end of the line farthest from me. "If you have any questions, direct them to me and not Physician du Montimer."

Laurence du Montimer was reedier than I had envisioned the boy who had trained as a chevalier before becoming a physician, towering over Charles, and thin as the spikes of the gate. His spiral-tight black curls were unbound and tumbling over his shoulders as he walked.

"Once I get to you, hold out your hands." Laurence did not look up from the book he was reading until he was at the gate. He handed the book to Charles. "I will inspect your magical capabilities. If necessary, I will question you about your education in the arts."

That was it? Hands?

"You mean the noonday arts?" a person down the line asked.

"Did I ask if there were questions?" Laurence, weary, looked to them. "Yes, the arts. Noonday, midnight—the arts are the arts are the arts."

I wiped my hands against my skirt again. My nails were trimmed and cleaned, wholly unlike the hands of the giant next to me or Rainier's ink-stained, scalpel-scarred palms. Ladies of Demeine didn't have scars.

I had always had to hide my practicing on an arm or thigh. I could have paid one of the village kids to help, but the very thought of it left me nauseous. Some physicians did that, I knew; they hired people to serve as practice patients.

Physicians were supposed to save people, not ensure they died young by hiring them as a hack and watching magic wear them down.

Down the line, Laurence dismissed students one after another. I picked at the edges of my nails, peeling back the skin and healing it together again. Laurence directed Charles to inspect the giant's hands, and I turned away to avoid the flare of magic in my sight. He too was sent away after Laurence asked who he practiced on if not himself.

"Physician du Montimer." I bowed my head and held out my hands.

Laurence stooped to study them. Unlike Charles, he wore his coat, the dark scarlet of dried blood, open over a high-collared white shirt and wonderfully intricate doublet embroidered with silver. He had no insignia, no heirlooms, and no jewelry marking his rank as the male heir to the crown; only a golden artist's band on his right first finger and an opal drop hung from a piercing in his ear. He threw one arm back and beckoned for Charles.

"I spoke to her on the road." Charles didn't look at me. "It would be unfair."

We had barely spoken and hardly anything of import; was he trying to single me out?

Laurence hummed deep in the back of his throat and took my hands in his. The hook of his artist's band, designed to open skin and bleed the wearer for the trickiest, most costly of arts, dug into my palm. "Who are you?"

"Emilie Boucher." I bowed my head deeper than necessary. This was Laurence du Montimer, the man who had regrown a lung the moment it was needed—he had passed out for days, of course, but the patient had lived—when such speed of transformation was thought impossible. No one had been able to replicate it yet.

"You're from Côte Verte," he said, still staring at my hands. Behind him, Charles's gaze jerked to me. "Near the city of Marais, judging by the minerals in your bones."

I had seen him work no art.

"You have practiced quite a lot." He flattened my bare hand between his. His hands were a web of scars, most a shade darker than his brown skin but others burned in my sight, empty and yawning, as if the thin, sapped-of-color skin that had grown over wasn't really there at all. Scars from channeling too much power. "You want to be a hack, yes?"

"Physician, but hack for now." The words were out of my mouth before I could think. It was what I had said for ages when people asked what I wanted.

Laurence's eyes flicked up to mine, expression inscrutable. "Admitted. Join Charles."

A rushing filled my ears. My chest ached. I rocked on my toes until I was Rainier's height. "Thank you."

I joined Charles and the other hack admitted so far. My hands trembled, fingers clammy and sticking to my shirt. I stayed close to the line, and Madeline stared at me, brown eyes bright, until Rainier moved to join me, and Laurence turned to her. Charles glanced at me.

"You're not the first person to come here thinking that once you show them all how great you are, they'll see the error of their ways and let you be a physician," he whispered. "If that were anyone but Laurence you had said that to, being turned away would have been the kindest thing done to you."

I scoffed. "First person? Please. You can just say *girl*."

"I really can't. Girls aren't the only ones who have to prove they can be physicians." Before Charles could say more, Laurence called him over to speak to Madeline.

Laurence directed Madeline to the gate. Rainier whooped quietly, and she hid her face behind a hand.

"Please stop embarrassing me," she said when she got to us, "before we even begin studying."

I laughed. The other accepted students chuckled behind me. There were six hacks total and several assistants. Laurence dismissed the last two applicants and, head cocked to the right, narrowed his eyes at Charles.

"Did you lose my spot?" Laurence asked.

Charles held up the book—*The Anatomy of Self-Defense: A Physician's Guide to Mortal Immunity and the Arts* by Laurence du Montimer—and flicked the white ribbon hanging from the pages. Laurence sighed.

"Good. Thank you." He took the book back and flipped it open to the ribbon. "You all have an acceptable understanding of the arts to study and serve as hacks. Congratulations. Follow me.

"For the next two weeks, you will be taught the basics of human anatomy, common injuries, the noonday arts, and what every physician's hack needs to know. Your teachers will vary but the outcome will ideally be the same—you will be selected to work with one of us." Laurence glided down the stone path, long legs doubling his stride, and Charles motioned for us to follow. "Those of you not interested in being medical hacks, I'll hand over once we're inside. I don't know what they do with you these days. Any questions?"

If anyone had one, they didn't ask it.

We crested the hill in the middle of the field, the university towers becoming clearer and clearer as we neared, and my heart stopped as the full sprawl of the school came into view. A second gate loomed over us—great and gold and gaping, students fluttering behind them from building to building with arms full of vials and glass etchings. Magic bubbled around me, swimming through the air and gathering in the palms of students with the heirloom rings of lesser children from noble families of robe and bell, and my foot crossed through this second border with a shuffle. Power coursed over my skin, warm and wanting.

There was so much to learn, to do.

Let me prove myself. Let me prove them wrong. I am home.

And it hurt, burrowing deep in my bones till my teeth ached.

·CHAPTER·
SIX

Annette

Breakfast the first morning was a disaster. There were three long tables full of girls, each one prettier and more poised than the last. The walls were papered white with flakes of silver, tapestries depicting the cycles of the moon and stars decorating the walls, and silver mirrors were spaced so that every girl in the room could see herself in one from where she sat. The midnight arts burned in every corner of the room too, stores of Mistress Moon's power leaking from threads of silver running through the walls. Silver held the midnight arts well and could be used to save power for later. This was too much, though.

Too much money. Too much magic.

The excess made my head ache.

"Sit where you please, everyone." Vivienne stood behind her seat at the head of the center table. "Those of you who are joining us for the first time, please try to sit next to an older student. Our meals are, suffice it to say, unusual."

Isabelle picked a seat, and I grabbed the one next to her. Coline pinched me as she passed and took a seat across from me. It was easy to spot us, the new girls. We all shifted awkwardly and stared at the settings as if they were likely to bite us.

"I was new once. What fun times!" A tall girl with short black hair brushed back in flowing waves and a soft purple dress that looked divine against her dark brown skin touched my arm. She took the place setting to my left and nodded to another student wearing the same shade of periwinkle but their clothes were a fashionable pair of breeches beneath a long robe. "I'm Germaine and that's Gisèle. We arrived here the year Vivienne decided to sort everyone into rooms based on their first name, but it worked out all right in the end. She's not an artist either."

She winked at Gisèle and smiled, nose scrunching up in delight.

I opened my mouth and had to pause to get my name right. "I'm Emilie. It's nice to meet you."

We took our seats. I tried to sit as straight-backed and proper as the other girls. Germaine was gorgeous and smart, talking to Coline about politics I didn't know or understand, and Gisèle carried on a conversation with Isabelle about some sort of merchant route. Germaine sipped water from her glass without so much as making a sound. When I picked mine up, it clinked against the plate. I didn't belong here at all.

Couldn't even take a sip without being blinded by magic. It burned in the back of my eyes, so bright my vision was spotty long after I'd looked away from the water. A headache took hold.

Coline muttered something under her breath, fingers moving along the tabletop as if she were gathering wool, and Germaine made a motion as if snipping thread.

"This room is designed to bombard you with visions," Germaine said. "Vivienne wants you to learn to avoid revealing that you're using the midnight arts, and silver is so popular in most places, you can't avoid it. If you get used to the visions here, you'll be used to them elsewhere."

Magic wasn't physical like us. We didn't have to coax it out using soft words and gentle motions, but it helped.

"My new students, you have by now noticed that the contents of this room are designed to draw out your divining and scrying abilities." Vivienne rang a bell. "It has long been considered rude to react to the futures of those you are dining with for fear of revealing some horrible truth. Those of you with an aptitude in the midnight arts must learn not to react, to be as sturdy as the ice atop the rushing waters of the Verglas. Those of you without an aptitude must learn to help hide any reactions from prying eyes. Remember—"

She set down the bell and raised her hands, and from the corner of my eyes, I saw Germaine wink at Gisèle. Gisèle signed something with her hands that made Germaine snicker into her napkin. Down the table, another girl signed a response.

It must have been a common occurrence because several people laughed, and Vivienne's stoic expression nearly gave way to a smile. She made a motion for them to pay attention.

"Help those you can," the girls said in time with Vivienne. "Hold them not in debt but in heart."

"Though it does help if you need a favor later on," Gisèle whispered to us.

Germaine picked up my cup of water without looking and drank all of it as if it were her own. "Oh! How terrible of me. Let me get you another drink."

Even though it was in her hands and away from me, I could still see the ripples of power in the water dregs.

A black hack's coat, sleeves rolled up to the elbows. Sunburned skin. Worn-down hands grasping at a bloody neck. I blinked, and all that was here was a polished silver tea set, tall and thin and too reflective to be normal, set at the center of a mirror-topped tray. Another vision, *great clots of old blood*, dripped down the back of a silver spoon. The taste of ash clogged my throat.

"Here." Germaine poured me a cup of cloudy, steaming tea, too dark and unsettled to show me a vision in the surface. "Drink up."

I took a sip, hands shaking. "Thank you."

I'd been starving once, but now my appetite had fled as fast and far as Emilie. Didn't help when a line of servants entered with trays and started serving us. I didn't know what to do with my hands. Or eyes. None of the other girls looked at the servants, not even when they placed cloth napkins in their laps. I jumped.

There were too many knives and too many spoons, and the smell of oysters mixed with the faint taste of ash stuck in my throat. I drank tea and didn't eat. The gossipy puddle of leaves at the bottom were bad omens, and the silver rim was nothing but staring eyes. So this was what we were—visions in polished silver and sweet tea overflowing with portents of disaster.

I had to channel the midnight arts into silver, usually, and then focus on what I wanted to scry, but here the images were endless— flashing through the water and silver and mirror and broths so fast, it made me sick to my stomach. I focused on Vivienne instead.

"Mademoiselle Charron, unfortunately, foresaw a quite danger- ous accident occurring on the road during her charity work in Bosquet, and she will sadly not be able to join us for several days as she helps to prevent the event and subsequent issues from the change." Vivienne held up her hands at the disappointed whispers. "Don't fret, dears. She will be joining us for several days still, and those of you who excel in the midnight arts may attend those sessions instead of your other classes."

I slumped. I didn't excel. I couldn't even stand to be in this room, and I'd need weeks to get better.

When supper ended, Gisèle slipped me a soft, slightly squished roll, her spectacles hiding most of her worried expression. The light caught her glasses—*green lace lapping at a pale white neck and the shadow of a thick blade*—and I cringed. Coline and Isabelle helped me back to our room.

Most of me felt guilty for being so needful.

But part of me liked it, the anxious looks and oddly comforting pat Coline gave my shoulder when she didn't know what to do.

I had to get better. I had to meet Estrel.

But after that first night, I barely got better.

We spent the evenings after supper on *improvement* and *associating*. I'd followed Coline and Isabelle and prayed they'd known what it was. We'd just ended up back in our room.

Least the baths were as rich as the rest of the place—great stone pools dug into the earth and pumped full of hot water that filled the room with steam. I'd not known what most of Emilie's belongings were, but soap was soap was soap even when it had lavender petals in it, and I'd made do with only it. There weren't maids to look after us, thank Mistress for that, and I was more than happy to comb out Isabelle's hair after she combed out mine. She'd laughed and said she used to do it for her brother when he was little and they were alone. Maman had always done Macé's. I was too tender-headed and cried when she tugged, so she'd stopped combing mine.

I was too hungry to sleep, but fear kept me in bed. They'd know. They'd all know.

Couldn't divine. Couldn't sleep. Couldn't even make it through a meal.

They'd find me out, arrest me, and send me to the gallows, surely.

We woke to a bell at dawn. I woke up bleary, eyes stuck together with the crunchy leftovers of sleep. We ate in the silver room, quiet and focused, and my headache returned after two sips of tea and a piece of pastry slathered in butter. I survived three bites before giving up. Least no one noticed.

Gisèle had taken to slipping me rolls every morning, though, and whenever Vivienne questioned it, Gisèle only repeated her words back to her.

"Help those you can," she said, hand over her heart. "What sort of person would I be if I refused that call?"

We had to be allies, all of us as one, in order to survive.

Or, as Gisèle said one evening during associating, "We are our own."

Two days out of the week, I joined Vivienne and most of the other students in the small church on the Gardinier estate. We stood in the vast, empty hall, the altar of Mistress Moon and Lord Sun rising at the front of the church, and I let myself fade off as the priest spoke. Mistress Moon surely understood—the water spilling from her cupped hands still showed my scryings when I knelt at the feet of her statue. I kissed her talons, and she didn't strike me down.

Every day, we ate breakfast, and then the entire new group was herded to mathematics. There were twelve of us, the other students as skittish as we were. Numbers were the same no matter how much money someone had, and the teacher, an older white woman with black hair knotted up in a tight bun, let us work quietly for the start of class. The problems were easy, and my headache lifted. Returned in time for history where I knew nothing and couldn't keep up. Coline could recite every Deme king and what they were best known for two hundred years. I could name the current one.

Couldn't say what he was known for.

Would've given me away instantly.

After a light meal at noon, Vivienne rounded up Coline, Isabelle, and I for an etiquette lesson that melted into a class on hosting and conversation with the other nine of our earlier classes after two hours. We practiced sitting and smiling and saying the right thing. Apparently, I couldn't even sit right.

But the worst class was bookkeeping and home management. We spent the afternoon going over accounts and prices and the "delicate art of negotiation" with Madame Robine Bisset, who I couldn't take seriously. The numbers in the books, fake but still close enough to the real thing, were so high, so absurd, and so long that I couldn't comprehend them. This was how rich people ruined nations.

They saw 2.000 gold sols on a ledger, didn't realize how much money that truly was to most folks, and ran us all into the red.

The weekly cost of dress fabric for my fake household was three hundred silver lunes. I'd never even seen more than ten in one place. We didn't even pay that much to Waleran du Ferrant for our land in Vaser.

My fake household spent more on the horses and hunting hounds than the servants.

I crossed the hounds from the list and added the money to the wages.

"But how will you entertain guests?" Vivienne asked. "Do not sacrifice your own financial security for such foibles. You need not give in to such demands as higher wages like has become the fashion for certain peoples these days. There are many who would be more than happy to take the job. Hard work pays heartily. A good employee will understand that."

I added another zero. What did it matter? Once people were this rich, numbers weren't real anymore. Prices were just ideas.

Least the sums in my ledger were all right. Coline was terrible at mathematics.

There were other classes too—music and art, architecture and room decorating, flower arrangements and conversational Thornish, the business etiquette of Vertgana, and even the whole final year could be devoted to poetry, literature, and translation. I knew none of it.

And after four days of crawling from bed to breakfast, suffering through the silver room headaches and lessons with Isabelle and Coline by my side, nothing seemed even remotely better. If anything, I was getting worse in the silver room.

Only seven other students in the whole school could use magic. Isabelle's tuition, I learned, had been lowered because she could, making her a prize. Coline wasn't the best at it, but passable and rich.

Seven of us, drowning in divined futures and scryed presents, and only I had a ringing in my ears and white spots in my sight. Even my nose hurt.

"You glow with it," Isabelle muttered to me at breakfast one morning, her hands shaking as she ignored the silver tray before us. "You sure you can't divine? You gather magic without even trying, and I've never seen someone do that."

Scrying, observing present goings-on from afar, was easy, and really good artists like Estrel Charron could even scry the past. Divination—seeing the future—was like herding fainting goats.

There were dozens of futures, each one as fickle as the next, and not all of them came at once. Some showed up when an artist wanted them, but they weren't the right future. Other times the future an artist needed faded before they could so much as catch a glimpse of it. Finding the right future—and holding on to it until they could see what they needed—required more channeling and precision than any other midnight art. Every time I tried to divine, I ended up sick.

The future I wanted was always just out of my grasp.

"I can't divine." I squinted at her. "I was never trained in the midnight arts. I'm probably just not used to it, is all."

That evening before supper, Coline had passed a folded-up poster beneath the table as we waited to be served. I peeked at it, glad to look at something that didn't hurt, and almost laughed.

HIS MOST BRIGHT MAJESTY
HENRY XII KING OF DEMEINE
WEARS DOWN THIS NATION LIKE MAGIC
WEARS DOWN HACKS—
TO DEATH

Isabelle winced when she read it and passed it along. "You shouldn't have that. What if you get us in trouble?"

"I would rather get in trouble," Coline said. "At least then I know I tried."

"No point in being nosy about things that don't apply to us," some girl down the table said.

I did laugh at that. "Must be nice to be so rich, laws and death don't apply to you."

Coline shot me an odd look. I shrugged. Right, I was Emilie des Marais. Here, I was so rich that laws didn't apply to me.

"If you don't know why you should care about other people, especially the people who are dying for you," I said, not looking down the table, "then you shouldn't be in charge of anything, much less people."

After that morning, a stifling silence filled the silver room before breakfast. Mostly when I entered. Coline loved it.

It exhausted me.

I crawled back into my bed that fourth evening—a whole bed to myself!—and ran a hand along the soft pillows. The quilts were too heavy for summer, but I pulled them over my head anyway. The dark eased the ache in my head, and the thick cloth muffled Coline and Isabelle's whispers. It was evening, well past supper, and my stomach had finally settled. I'd managed a whole bowl of soup tonight. The fuzzy feeling of half sleep fell over me.

"Emilie?" a soft, musical drawl trickled through my quilt.

I turned my nose into the pillow cover, inhaling lavender and barberry. "One second, Alaine."

"You've slept in the same room as me for nearly a week, and I held back your hair as you dry heaved." A hand touched my back. "How could you have already forgotten my name?"

I jerked up, more awake than getting dumped in the Verglas would make me. Fool—my sister Alaine was long gone.

"Sorry, sorry." I leapt to my feet, chest cold and belly dropping, and wiped my face. My sleeves came away damp. "What's wrong, Coline?"

Coline was leaning against my headboard, one hand on the wall and one still outstretched to me. She was in a different dress than the one she had worn all day, this one a pale spring-green like fresh mint and spotted with little opalescent beetle wings. I hadn't bothered changing.

None of them fit anyway. Vivienne had brought a tailor to the school to have me fitted for new dresses, underthings, and even a new corset. At least Emilie seemed to have worn only stays like me before this.

"You're not getting better at ignoring the visions," Coline said, no trace of kindness in her voice. "You're only better at hiding your exhaustion from Vivienne, which may very well be part of the training given our expected comportment, but you need to eat real food, not only soup, a handful of crackers, and a sticky bun the size of your head."

I finger-combed my hair and smoothed out the wrinkles of my dress. "You gave me that bun."

"It was the bun or nothing, and so I picked the bun," she said. "Isabelle, please ally with me."

"Yes, Emilie," said Isabelle, not raising her face from her mathematics notes and probably unaware of what we'd been talking about. "Coline is correct. Listen to her."

Coline patted Isabelle's shoulder. I rolled my eyes and stretched, back creaking. If Coline's arrogance were rain, there'd never be a drought again.

"I'll go find the kitchens," I said. "Let me do it alone. I need quiet."

I tapped my head, and Coline nodded. "Fine. Go eat, or I'm asking Germaine what to do about you."

I wandered out of our room and down to the grand foyer. At night, the white marble was ghostly white, and walking across it was like gliding over ice, the cool breeze spilling in from the open windows the burst of air from pushing off. I checked the door for guards or servants, even though Vivienne said we were allowed onto the grounds so long as we didn't try to leave the estate. Outside, there was only the night and me. I raised my hand to the dark.

"Mistress," I whispered. "Please let tomorrow go better."

Light flickered overhead. A moth smacked into my hand. I lurched, palm stinging. The moth bumped into me again, feathery black feelers rapping at my knuckles, and the midnight blue fluff of its body pressed into the little crack between my thumb and first finger. I turned my hand over, and the moth settled there, spreading out its wings in a crown of pale moonlight. The wings were as deep blue as its body on the underside, but the tops were pure magic, smears of trapped power. A creature of clear night skies.

A Stareater.

"Aren't you a pretty thing?" I pushed on down a path I knew led to the kitchen buildings. "Hungry?"

Most moths were attracted to flames, but these went after magic. They fed on the power of midnight artists, churning the blood from their prey into pure power that glowed in them like stars. I'd only ever seen one before, and it had nibbled at Alaine's fingers till she flicked it away.

"I'm not much of a snack," I said to it. "You'll have to find someone else."

It folded up its wings, unfurled a single, long tongue from its head, and the light surrounding it faded. The tongue pricked the skin of my hand.

"Fine. Don't bleed me dry."

The dark had sunk beneath the leafy canopy and blanketed the whole of the grounds in the chilled smudge of night, rustling leaves and my soft breaths blurring the line between sound and silence. I glanced up at the starlight picking its way through the leaves in shaky slits. It was like Mistress Moon had reached out and run her thumb through the sky, smearing dark gray clouds across the purple night till only a dim moon remained behind. The yeasty scent of fresh bread hit me, and I followed it to a large, domed kitchen. The butter-yellow light of candles and fires leaked out the opened windows, steam dancing in the glare. I peeked through the cracked door.

Empty.

The kitchen was a small slice of chaos, bread proofing on one side and a whole course of things bubbling away above coals on the other side. There were five doors, three shut, and I crept inside enough to see. On one of the tables near my door was a basket full of vials that made my ears hum. My moth shuddered against the back of my hand.

Alchemistry.

There were a dozen different vials in the basket. The arts were complicated little alchemical things, not something I was familiar with. Objects full of magic broke down as quick as bodies.

It was the channeling that killed artists. We had to channel the magic through us to make it do our bidding, but the longer it was in us or the more that went through us, the more damage it did.

I picked up a small jar of honey infused with dandelions for protection, lavender for sleep, and a speck of magic to make all the ingredients last. I'd never met a real alchemist. They weren't as rare as artists but mostly worked in larger cities with physicians, surgeons, and apothecaries.

"You're not supposed to be here," a lilting voice said. "Mademoiselle Gardinier should've told you that."

I put the vial back. "Sorry. I didn't—well, the moth, and then these were interesting and…"

I trailed off, blushing, and shook my head.

Let the sky swallow me up, Mistress. Please.

"That's new," said a chef dusted in flour. She grinned, tongue between her crooked front teeth, and bowed her head to me. "I'm Yvonne."

I swallowed. It was the twin in purple, the one who'd been selling sage water the day Emilie and I had swapped places. She couldn't have been older than eighteen but walked like she owned the place. She might've for all I knew, and I stayed near the doorway, glancing round at the pot bubbling on the stove, and still-fresh greens scattered about the counters and cutting boards, and nets hanging from the rafters. Yvonne busied herself with the pot, brown sleeves of her blouse rolled up to her elbows, and brushed one broad smear of *something* from her skirts. The warm, black skin of her forearms was peppered with dark little oil-burn scars. Cooking wasn't the only thing happening here. The basket was hers.

"You're an alchemist," I said. "A proper one."

Alchemists could gather magic and store it in objects—using that power to extend the life of herbs, improve a coughing syrup, or bolster the powers of a poison—but not channel magic to use the arts. Most sold their creations in apothecaries or worked for physicians and surgeons. I'd never met one. Their wares cost too much.

"Yes, though that's the first time someone's called me a proper one." She cleared her throat, and I realized she'd been waiting for me to share my name.

I bowed back and smiled. "I'm sorry—Emilie."

"Well, you better come in and shut the door, Sorry-Emilie. I need the heat to stay the same." Yvonne beckoned me inside and froze. "You're Madame Emilie des Marais."

"No. Well, yes," I said. "But you don't have to call me 'Madame' or anything. You can just call me Emilie."

"Of course." She bowed her head again, shoulders stiff. "As you like."

I did not like this odd, new wall between me and maybe the only person who'd grown up like I had.

"May I ask what the magic you stored in these is for?" I gestured to the basket of vials, and the moth hopped from me to one of the vials, my blood staining its white wings spider-lily pink. "I can see the magic, but I've never been good at alchemistry."

There was nothing worse than being sick enough to take medicine but not sick enough to have lost your sense of smell.

"You can see the magic in this?" Yvonne reared back slightly, eyes widening and lips pulling into a grin. She pointed at the basket. "You can tell I've put magic in it?"

I nodded. "It's like looking at heated iron. Looks the same but the air around it's different. You can always tell."

"You know most people can't always tell, don't you? Not after the art's been worked?" she asked. "It took me an hour to convince the apothecary in Bosquet this was actually alchemical and I wasn't scamming him."

"Apothecary's a fool, then." I peeked at the other little vials. "They've all got a bit of the midnight power in them. Not a lot and not doing anything. Have you ever used a hack? If you did once, maybe they could prove it for you?"

She glanced at me over her shoulder, wide eyes a bright amber in the light. "I have not. I wouldn't even know how to go about hiring one. Mademoiselle Gardinier is very particular about hers, and they're not allowed to work with anyone but her students to limit the damage."

"I've never worked with one either," I said. "Was it one of the fancy apothecaries?"

"Very," said Yvonne, smiling now. "What can I do for you, Madame?"

I shook my head. "The silver room makes me sick to my stomach and then not eating makes it harder to sleep and being tired makes it harder not to get distracted over breakfast, and I was wondering if I could get something to eat. Nothing fancy." My stomach rolled at the idea of pigeon pie or heavy red wine–braised lamb, which had been the meals for the last few days. "Less fancy the better, probably."

"Of course. Allow me a moment." Yvonne vanished into another room or pantry and returned with a little bowl and small loaf of bread in her arms. "There's a clean stool to your left if you'd like to sit. Unfortunately, this isn't the main kitchen. Mademoiselle Gardinier is allowing me the use of this building in exchange for some recipes and alchemical work. It's not as well stocked as the main kitchen, though."

"That's fine." I folded myself onto the stool. "Do you need help?"

"No, but the offer is appreciated." Yvonne focused on her pan, the violet tucked into her left hair bun bobbing. The familiar sound of sizzling egg hit my ears, and she flipped it with all the grace of a juggler before the king. In no time, she presented me with a small plate of bread with a fried egg in the middle. "Madame."

"Thank you!" I shooed the moth away from my hands. "You sure there's nothing I can help with?"

Yvonne's pleasant facade shifted.

"Actually, Madame," she said with a wide, tense smile. "I would like to ask a favor of you, since you are apparently very gifted in the arts."

No one had ever called me gifted. "What's the favor?"

She ducked her head in a half bow. "If you are willing, I would very much appreciate it if you could be witness to the fact that my alchemistry is real and sign a short note attesting to it, so I can have proof for the apothecary."

"What's the point in being noble if I can't do something like that?" I looked around. "Do you want me to do it now?"

Emilie wouldn't mind. Probably. And Vivienne was always going on about our responsibilities to the Deme people.

I wrote out a quick note with some paper and a quill Yvonne had nearby and signed it with a neat little signature far smoother and straighter than anything I'd ever written.

Looked like the words of a proper lady of Demeine.

I'd been practicing Emilie's signature in case I needed it for Vivienne or Emilie's mother.

"Good enough?" I asked.

She nodded, distractedly tucking it into her pocket. "Thank you very much. It is harder than I thought to start an apothecary."

"Can I ask why you're working as a chef, then?" I finished off the last of the toast, and she took the plate from me. "And in Bosquet? I saw you selling tea with your sister."

"Oh. Yes, that's Octavie's thing. She's saving up to travel with some cartographer to map the world before someone else does. Our parents were merchants, and our mother's from a small city-state north of Kalthorne. They have a shop in Lily-in-the-Valley." She waved off my question politely, and part of me relaxed now that she had. It was nice just talking to a person. No rules. No Vivienne judging. No lies. She talked with her hands too, great passionate gestures as if she were painting a picture. "I have some of her family recipes. We moved here before the Empire got huffy about worshipping the Lord and his Mistress. Mademoiselle Gardinier asked my mother to help with some Kalthorne recipes, but my mother wanted to stay at her shop. She's enjoying having Octavie and me out of the house. So I took the job instead. It's not a full job and doesn't pay much, but it's a job."

She didn't say *they're a bit hard to come by*, but I heard it in the way she paused and her jaw tightened.

"I'm glad you did." Listening to her be happy made me happy, and the alchemistry looked fascinating. "Thank you."

"And you, Madame," she said. The tone was light enough to be a joke to test the line.

"Really, I know folks say it all the time and don't mean it, but I would like it if you used my name. If you want," I said quickly. "I've never really used the title before."

"Emilie." Yvonne lifted her head. "Thank you."

I woke up the next day to the moth, scarlet and fat, fluttering near my head, and at breakfast there was an extra place set beside Vivienne. The other girls whispered to one another, and to me, even though I heard none of it. Coline shook her head to some question Isabelle asked. The mirrored comb in her hair sparked and caught my gaze. I froze in the doorway.

Shaking, bloody hands knotted in gold hair. The slack-jawed stare of death in storm-gray eyes.

The vision snapped. A shock, white hot, shot through me like someone had lit a match right before my eyes. I squeezed them shut.

Couldn't even get in the door, and I was crumbling. The magic wasn't wearing me down yet, but even the midnight arts could break down a body over time, and I was failing so spectacularly at controlling my divining that surely I'd be nothing come winter.

I sunk as low in my chair as my clothes and manners would allow, and Isabelle, frantically blinking away a vision too, touched my arm. I shook her off.

Estrel Charron would *know*. Oh, Mistress, what if she'd scryed it? Divined it?

No, I wasn't that important. She never would've looked for me.

But she didn't need magic to see how much of a failure I was.

A server set down a squat bowl of fruit, and a vision swirled in the reflective silver—*blood splattering across a white gown*. Why were none of my scryings normal things like a lightning storm or caravan arriving home three days early?

The vision lingered. Silver specks drifted through my sight like snow, a hook of blue splitting the room in two.

"Students!" Vivienne's voice forced me to look toward the front of the room. She was a smear of white. White hair. White skin. White dress. White snow powdering around her.

Mistress, this was worse than ever before. Artists didn't have to be able to see to do magic, but seeing nothing but this white forever would be annoying.

"I am aware that some of you have had the pleasure of meeting Mademoiselle Estrel Charron at court, but please bear with me as I introduce her to your peers," Vivienne said, and even through the snow, I could see she was smiling widely. Her hand reached out and found an arm. "Students, this is Mademoiselle Estrel Charron, the royal diviner. Estrel, these are my current geniuses."

The others tittered and nodded, already sitting. Estrel was too country to demand standing, even if she was the royal diviner. She was only a blur of green and red to me.

And across the table, across the fourteen girls between us and a dozen trays and pitchers, across the onslaught of silver that still burned my eyes, my vision cleared and Estrel Charron stared straight at me. I couldn't see anything but her eyes.

"Please, call me Estrel. We'll start after breakfast," she said, gaze sliding from me to the next girl. "Every midnight artist in this room needs quite a bit of work."

·CHAPTER·
SEVEN

Emilie

We had spent a week studying human anatomy, whispering bones in our sleep and muttering common ailments over our meals. At dawn we rose, Madeline and I earlier than all the rest, so we might bathe without interruption or scandal in the dreary bathhouse set aside for hacks and assistants that seemed to hold more mold than steam, and then we did our laundry while the other students got ready for the day. Madeline had taught me how, graciously not mentioning the atrocious way I treated my clothes. I had never had to think about it before.

We were the only two girls in training, and all the older female hacks we might have asked for advice were working elsewhere in Demeine. Our requests for their names so that we could write for advice had been dismissed. The university didn't want us "gossiping." It was unseemly.

The habit of apprentices to send hacks and assistants, our

counterparts for the rest of academia who did not possess the ability to use magic, to run errands felt more unseemly, especially since we were given instructions that led us to breaking rules we hadn't been told about. Madeline said we were lucky that was the worst that had happened.

Rainier had been asked to channel a bit of healing arts that had worn his body down so quickly, his blood hadn't been able to clot for a day.

I had been asked to deliver papers to the anatomy laboratory, and they had neglected to inform me of the letter box right outside the door or the six-day-old corpse dredged from the river currently resting in the room. One of the lecturer's assistants, running their own errands, had been nice enough to put down their flyers and offer me mint oil to offset the scent.

At least I had finally been able to see the building where real medical students attended classes—the light wood polished till it shone like copper, the golden sconces shaped like hearts, the doors carved with the school's symbolic skeleton clutching a book and knife, and the displays of preserved journals and discoveries. They even had a whole case of entries from ancient Physician Guy de Calciare who had documented the night plague's effects hundreds of years ago. Still we reeled from those dark days of rotting limbs and failing lungs.

Most believed it was a physical manifestation of spiritual uncleanness—a reminder from Lord Sun that we were not all-powerful. Physicians had worked themselves to death trying to cure it and died before they could unravel its mysteries. So began the use of hacks.

Cleanliness was next to godliness, and so hacks were here to do nobles' dirty work.

All of our classes took place in one long room that looked dimmer and bleaker now that I had seen the halls of the rest of the school. Our class was the same pale wood, but we were in charge of cleaning it when we left every day, and the shine had long left the floors. There were no skylights—we were below ground—but three narrow windows were at the top of the back of the room. The floor was sloped so the room was five different levels, the instructor on the lowest level at the front. Four long tables with chairs filled the other levels.

Every morning, a physician's apprentice stumbled through the systems of the body, a new one graced us with their presence every day, and neither Charles nor Sébastien had yet made an appearance. Our afternoons were owned by the physicians who hoped to hire us one day. They watched us, beady eyes on other, more important things, while we cleaned their instruments and work spaces. I adored those hours, peeking through journals and observing their work while cleaning up after them. Each physician had different rules for different things. Already one student who had complained had left in the night.

I had never been more bored in my entire life.

The only thing I had learned—truly for the first time—was how much of a pain it was to get ink out of wool.

At least Madeline shared my boredom if not my apathy, though I was certain it would lead to atrophy by the end of the week.

"It looks better if you take notes," she whispered to me, as yet again we sat in the lecture hall, her with her notes and me with nothing.

I leaned my chair back until it rested against the wall behind us, and the breeze snuck through the shutters of the windows above us. "Who cares what I look like if I know it?"

I was lucky—I had a noble's education, but no one else in the room could say the same.

"How have you not been arrested for insulting some duc yet?" she asked, never raising her face from her notebook.

She took meticulous, lovely notes in midnight-blue ink with handwriting that would have given the royal printer a run for its money. The ink, an alchemical substance of her own making, was delightfully, terribly permanent. Most of her dresses were the same shade of blue to keep the stains hidden.

"There's only the one, and I doubt he cares so long as we show up to the exam," I said. At the end of this week, we were to sit for an exam on anatomy and alchemistry to determine if we were trained enough to be hacks and allowed near real people. The physicians and their apprentices would pick which of us they wanted. "Regardless, only Physician du Guay's opinion matters."

He was the head of the medical school, the oldest physician living, and I would prove him wrong. I would be his hack, prove I was good enough, and make him regret his policy that girls couldn't study physicianry.

"Suit yourself," Madeline muttered as the door to the hall opened.

"I always do."

Most hacks only survived ten years after beginning. Most physicians, even with their hacks, survived thirty. Even with only ten years, I could actually change something for the better. That was more than my father had ever done. I owed my people that.

Charles du Ravine, clothes a mix of colors beneath his orange coat and his tangle of red hair pulled up into a messy knot, stepped inside the room. He wasn't carrying much, only a book and a glass tablet with a smear of notes inked across it. The room quieted.

"I hope you remember who I am from your first day here. You can call me Charles; it saves time in emergencies." He set his glass tablet against the desk at the front of the room and picked up the ink brush at the base of the glass writing board that covered the whole front wall. "I will be going over some of the most common injuries seen in soldiers and chevaliers today—wounds and blows to the head."

I leaned forward. This might finally be useful.

"He's so starry," Madeline said and sighed. She rarely dropped her serious mask, but now she was all smiles. "Smart too. It's very unfair."

I twisted to glare at her. "I'm certain the gorgeous, genius vicomte needs little more to feed his vanity."

"Just remember, you said 'genius.' I didn't."

"I'm already trying to forget," I said.

"Mademoiselle Boucher!" Charles's call cut through the room, and my cheeks burned before I could even turn to look at him. "How many bones are in a human skull?"

Of course. Finally I could prove one of the people with my fate in their hands wrong, and I hadn't been paying attention. Everyone in the room turned around—Madeline and I had claimed the chairs in the very back of the room, so no one could talk behind our backs—and I pressed my hands together, forefingers against my lips. It was an incomplete question.

"What age of human?" I asked.

My model skeleton—I had named it Basil and decorated it for winter solstice until Mother had disapproved and given it away—had always stood, labeled, next to my desk at home.

"Do not play with me or waste my time. There's no room for that in an emergency." Charles scowled. If we had been at court, I would have called his glare cutting and expected no one to speak with me again. "Who do I work for? How many children do you see on battlefields?"

"Several," I said. "Some pirates will not kill children, but that does not mean children are not in the line of fire. I thought specificity in triage was important?"

His face softened. "Boucher, how many bones are in an adult human skull?"

Someone in the room snickered, and I said, "Twenty-two."

"Thank you," he said. "Now, unfortunately, our brains are quite often in the line of fire…"

He did not call on me again.

I didn't mind, though it felt like punishment. He was a good teacher, and by the end of the class, I somehow felt more ass than student.

It *had* been a vague question.

"It was not a vague question." Madeline didn't raise her eyebrows as we left the room, the model of restraint.

Rainier, wiping the blue ink from his white hands, snorted. "That could not have gone worse."

"Yes, it could have," I said. "I could have gotten the question wrong."

"What happened is making sense now." Madeline led us to the courtyard for lunch. "You think every question asked, no matter what, is for you."

"If a question is asked of me, I answer it." I threw up my arms in surrender. "It has worked until now."

We sat on a bench in one of the many courtyards and ate lunch. The proper students, the nobles and children of the wealthy who could afford to attend university for longer than a season, banded together on picnic blankets and tables set out by their assistants, varlets, and hacks. Our trio sat in the shadows of the medical school, away from prying eyes.

"If it were only you, this wouldn't matter, but this isn't about only you." She sat next to me, shoulder brushing mine. "They'll take whatever they think about you and apply it to me."

I picked at a savory pastry stuffed with cheese and onions. "The other students don't matter. Only physicians."

"Why are you even here? Girls like you have other options," said Madeline. She nibbled on half of an apple.

The money I had taken from my purse had been enough to cover tuition, an appropriate small wardrobe, and supplies. The amount I had left was questionable at best. The price of food was far higher than I had anticipated.

No wonder Laurel was gaining ground.

At least Annette was sending me money to arrive in the next day or so. Her last note had been short—she was ill—and to the point, which was a small blessing given her handwriting.

"I want to be a physician, but it's not appropriate or allowed," I said. Madeline and Rainier could certainly hear the bitterness because it was so strong, I could taste it. "And I'm not rich right now."

It was not a lie.

"I'm sorry." I offered her half of my pastry—what else did I have when my word was questionable at best—and she laughed, refusing. "I will do better."

If Demeine were a fire, I was simply inhaling the smoke and calling myself a victim when I could've been helping others escape.

We returned to the building only to find pockets of people crowding the doors. I pushed my way to the front and froze.

Propaganda from Laurel. On highly guarded, mostly noble and wealthy university ground.

WHY MUST WE BREAK OUR BODIES FOR THEM
AS WORKERS AND HACKS

WHEN THEY WILL NOT SO MUCH AS BREAK BREAD WITH US?
ALL ARTISTS DIE YOUNG, BUT HACKS DIE YOUNGER.
IF WE WERE ALL TRAINED,
IF WE ALL SHARED THE BURDEN OF POWER,
THE MASTER ARTISTS WOULD ONLY DIE FIVE YEARS EARLIER.
HACKS WOULD LIVE TWENTY YEARS LONGER.
WHY DO THEY PREFER US UNTRAINED?
WHY DOES THE KING PREFER US DEAD?

"Are they on any of the other buildings?" a boy next to me asked.

I shrugged and shook my head. "I don't know."

"Can you scry it?" He glanced around, eyes wide with fear, and ripped the poster down. "Midnight arts it or whatever?"

"What do you think we're studying here?" I snapped. "*You* 'midnight arts it or whatever.'"

The flyer was passed from hand to hand until I lost sight of it, and I slipped through the crowd to rejoin Madeline and Rainier. The silver cuff Annette had made me keep was in my room under the bed.

"Your attention, all of you," a voice called.

We all fell quiet and turned. It was Physician Pièrre du Guay, the First Physician of Demeine and responsible for keeping Henry XII, King of Demeine alive. He could reattach limbs and reconstruct half a heart, and here he stood before me. He was a stout white man in his fifties, square jaw clean-shaven, and scraggly eyebrows the same gray as snow slush in dirt grew wild above his sharp, blue eyes. The red coat he wore was not one of the newer ones that was made with red wool but had once, when he had been first named a physician, been white. His work had stained it over the years, and his magic had kept the color but not the mess.

"Where is it?" he said

From our small group of a few dozen, the three flyers nailed to our buildings made their ways to Physician Pièrre du Guay. He crumpled them in his hand and gestured for us to follow him. We did.

The courtyard where we had eaten was empty, and in the center was a body. It was a hack, black uniform speckled with blood, lying face up on the grass. Pièrre circled behind him.

"I know I have not had the pleasure of making your acquaintances before now, so forgive my bluntness. I am sure many of you are entirely dedicated to your future work," said Pièrre. "However, please allow me to introduce to you Florice, who was formerly my most-trusted hack. In fact, I spent all morning working with him to save three lives."

Florice's chest heaved. A thin line of red seeped across his stomach, the stain more like veins than blood loss. He was steeped in power, magic from overuse of the noonday arts burning in his skin, and I could see it all the way down to the marrow of his bones. He was a skeleton still dressed, dead save for the soul still in him. There was no coming back from this without a physician to intervene. But Pièrre wouldn't let him die.

"It has come, most unfortunately, to my attention that Florice had a hand in this garbage appearing here, but I know for a fact he had an accomplice place them. I need to know who."

The magic that had been building in Florice's bones for years was devouring him, gnawing at the threads of his life, changing the smallest ethereal aspects of him, and working its way out. The red stain grew.

Bisection was a mortal wound.

Pièrre was a physician. He had a responsibility.

"Please," Pièrre said, his hands spread wide as if to embrace whoever gave him what he wanted, "tell me if you saw anyone."

Next to me, Rainier and Madeline shook their heads. My hands shook against my thighs, the bright burn of Florice's life all I could focus on. The tissues of his intestines gave way beneath the magic that had finally become more than his body could handle. His ribs were webbed with cracks. His very blood was a poison.

He could still be saved maybe. It would take work. It would take action—now.

"Now," Pièrre asked, "I will ask once more—did anyone see Florice's accomplice?"

Pièrre was letting Florice die. His hack! The assistant he had worked with for years, the assistant who had worn down his body channeling magic so Pièrre could heal.

It might have been magic wearing Florice down enough to end his life, but it was Pièrre who had killed him by not helping.

"This is a trying time that requires loyalty and solidarity," he said, "and as we have only recently welcomed you into our school, it would be beneficial to demonstrate your loyalty."

No one spoke.

Pièrre nodded, clasping his hands together behind his back. "Then I am hopeful that none of you are involved in this nonsense and that we may care for Demeine together. All infections must be burned out, of course." He glanced at Florice. "And if any of you need a reminder of what I mean by that, let Florice be your demonstration. Anyone found with such propaganda from the coward Laurel or aiding him will be dealt with swiftly."

He left.

Then we went on with our day as if nothing had gone wrong, none of us able to save Florice, and the eyes of the people around, from the varlets to the guards to the physicians to the other hacks, too threatening to let us near him. We all, I hoped, disagreed with Pièrre.

But disagreeing wasn't enough. Thoughts weren't enough. Words weren't enough. Inaction—Pièrre's calculated inaction—was a killer. What sort of comtesse was I if I didn't act? What sort of person?

That night I told Madeline I was going to take a bath, but instead, I snuck back to the courtyard.

Pièrre was going to let Florice die the slow, painful death of sepsis, and there was no part of me that could swallow that truth.

But when I reached the courtyard, a dark figure was already bowed over Florice, magic flowing from him to Florice's injuries. Stareaters fluttered about them, white and threatening, and their light flickered across the grass in quick cuts. No one else was around as far as I could see. The fool tending Florice pushed more magic into him.

That would only wear Florice down faster. All we could do for him was take away the pain or kill him quickly.

"Stop." I sprinted to them and paused. "Rainier?"

He spun, breath leaving in a terrified, stilted sigh. "Lord, you know how to not sneak up on someone?"

"What are you doing?" I took his hands and used my own magic to stop Rainier. It was night and it was harder, but there was enough left in me to do it. "It'll kill him faster."

Rainier, white skin ghostly in the moonlight, nodded. "I know. He knows too."

"Hacks never do have survival instincts," Florice said. Up close, he was younger than I had thought, and that hurt more. His coat and vest were undone, and his shirt had been pulled up, revealing the hole that had once been his stomach. Two brave Stareaters crawled along the yawning wound, their wings a sickening shade of pink. "You all shouldn't have come."

He smelled of damp earth and singed hair, magic leeching the life from his body even now. A mushroom stalk grew from the jagged edge of a rib, the same way a spine grew—slowly folding in on itself over and over until more cells bloomed. The cap was the pink-streaked gray of brain matter.

Power corrupted, taking what we were and making us into someone else. Something new, terrible, and incompatible with mortal life.

"But we did," I said, and before I could speak, I felt the tug of magic behind me. I spun and raised my hands.

Madeline appeared from the shadows. "What are you two doing?"

"Apparently," I said and dropped my hands, the magic I had gathered dwindling, "we all had the same idea."

She sighed and her shoulders slumped. I nodded her over to my side.

"One of us want to keep watch while the rest of us work?" I asked.

"I can." Rainier pulled his blue coat back on. "Someone sees you, they investigate. I can at least distract them."

"You new hacks?" Florice asked, coughing.

Madeline nodded. "I can stop you from feeling pain, though. May I?"

He nodded, and she began to work on his more painful wounds. His fluttering gaze drifted from her to me.

"You're good at this." He wiped his nose on his shoulder. Blood speckled his teeth. "And you're breaking a lot of rules for someone none of you have met."

"We're hacks. It's what we're supposed to do." Madeline laughed softly, her magic a balm against his body's betrayal. "You are a very good patient."

Pièrre was going to let him die. His own hack.

"It's what physicians are supposed to do," I said. "Risk their own lives to save others."

"Noon. Bloodletters." Florice coughed and shook his head. "You want to save others, you go there and do something about Demeine."

Laurel.

"I will," I said softly. "You're going to live a while. The arts will wear off by then, as soon as the power eats through the nerves she's blocking."

Madeline glanced at me. "You can see the ones I—"

"Yes." I licked my lips. "I can make you think you're something else, somewhere better."

Florice laughed, and the Stareaters leapt from his chest, the wound wider now. "Changing thoughts is physicianry and even then, most don't bother with alchemistry."

It had been easier, as a child, to change my thoughts rather than change the world around me.

"I had to run away to come here and used body alchemistry to do it," I said, and it was only a half lie. I had tried to run away and failed. "I can, but you have to let me in."

Back home, I had a guard named Edouard who was wonderful and kind, whose mind I had crept into. It was harder to filter through to what I wanted since he had fought me, but eventually I had sent him to sleep, a little twist of alchemistry here and a little nudge of his body there. I had made sure his dreams were nice. He deserved that much.

"Do it," Florice said.

I pulled the power I kept in me free and gathered it in my hands, letting the pieces sink into the smallest, most ethereal pieces of Florice's mind.

"Think of your favorite memory," I said. "Then keep thinking of it."

I had not done this before, not on this level, and I had known Edouard for ages. He had been my personal guard since I was three, but an oddness swam in Florice's veins with me. His body was in a panic, every part of him shutting down slowly as the magic of the noonday arts ate away at him. I tucked my power into his body and calmed myself. His body mimicked me.

One breath, one thought.

The memory he had selected played out, sparks of life, between the gaps of his brain. I latched onto it, dug my magic into his mind, and forced the sparks to replay over and over again.

Like lightning.

A hand closed over my wrist. "He's dreaming."

Madeline.

"We have to go," Rainier said, hand on Madeline's arm. "Now."

For a brief moment, my magic still alive, we were all connected, and I could see the power in all of us.

I shook my head and my vision cleared. "Let's go."

The connection faded as quickly as it had come.

Estrel started with the older students. I went to classes like normal, new clothes fitted to me and worlds better than the old ones. Breakfast got worse, but I wasn't so bad Estrel took notice, and Isabelle was getting better. Watching her go from endlessly blinking and tense with clenched hands, to a steady smile and a chin held as high as Coline's was the only good part of my mornings. And Coline was getting better at mathematics.

I wasn't getting better at faking interest in bookkeeping with Madame Bisset. Isabelle and I had taken to sitting together, mostly so we wouldn't have to keep correcting Coline's miscalculations. Isabelle paid attention in each class as if her life depended on it, something I did in all our other classes, but Bisset's was still a struggle. We were going over the sections of the ledgers Laurel had stolen from Chevalier des Courmers, and Bisset had a whole list of advice for the folks who were as outraged about the expenses as

Laurel. More and more posters were showing up in Bosquet, driving a wedge between most of us. A lot of the students were sad about the state of things and wished they could do something. Bisset had taken to providing us advice we could tell folks who needed it.

"Frugality," she said one morning. "It is not a word but a way of life, and it is very important to save money when you can."

I groaned, and Isabelle kicked my foot.

"Buying leaner cuts of meat may save only a small amount, but it adds up," said Bisset. "Frivolity leads to failure, and it will be your job to look after the household expenses."

"That's terrible advice," I whispered to Isabelle.

A person could only buy cheaper things if they had the money to buy things. Buy less wasn't good advice for the folks who liked Laurel. We didn't have money to be frugal with. We paid our dues to whomever owned our land and survived. Least we had land too. Folks in cities depended on whatever they got paid.

She glanced at me.

"It is!" I hissed.

Isabelle rolled her lips together and muttered, "It's good advice and common. You just don't like her."

"I can dislike her and think her advice is bad."

All of Bisset's advice was for people with money who made bad decisions. Or at least ones she considered bad.

"Girls?" Bisset asked. "Is there something you would like to share with the rest of us?"

I looked up and found the whole room looking at us. Isabelle withered.

"No, Madame," she said. "I'm sorry. Please continue."

That afternoon, Vivienne sat next to me as I was reading with Germaine between classes.

"Emilie," Vivienne said. "I find it curious that given your mind for mathematics, you would have such trouble with bookkeeping. Your mother, when first broaching the topic of you coming here, said much the same—you had the mind for most things but no desire to apply that knowledge as required."

Germaine stared studiously at her own book on Deme fencing history. I had been reading Emilie's most recent letter—*Perhaps foolishly I believed that my time here would be easy, but the world is not as I anticipated, and I must admit, on this side of it, I wish I had learned how to scry.*

"Madame Bisset says I get distracted." That much was true. It was easier being Emilie des Marais than I thought it would be. She'd spat in the face of most of this knowledge, but it meant my being bad at most things was expected. "Sentimentality, she called it."

"Ah." Vivienne patted my hand. "Sometimes, we must present the appearance of acceptance while working toward change. Practice doing what Madame Bisset says, dear. If nothing else, you'll learn how to better control your expressions. And do try not to embarrass Isabelle during class. Unlike you, she does not have a legacy to fall back on."

When Vivienne was gone, Germaine lowered her book, face unreadable, and said, "Vivienne had to hire Madame Bisset last year at His Majesty's insistence."

"Why?" This was a school for people he hadn't even let into the lawmakers' court until a group of nobles pushed for laws so their daughters could inherit. "And bookkeeping's normal, it's just—"

"They think Vivienne has grown soft in her ways and needs a noble hand to guide her," said Germaine. "You've never been to court, but I have with my father. It is believed the Laurel issue is because we have weakened and given ground to needless sympathy. Kalthorne has taken advantage of us, and now our people follow their example."

Germaine's father was the baron de Beldeme in the north-east corner of Demeine, far too close to Kalthorne for comfort, and too small now that there were a dozen different taxes imposed on Thornish trade. The court said it was because Kalthorne was too stingy.

"But you're in charge of nearly all the bookkeeping for your lands and the crown's lands," I said. "You know that's not true."

Politics, so far as I could tell, was lying until the truth got too worn down to care.

"So I do." Germaine marked her place in her book and closed it. "Did you know that in 1268 Before Midnight, a Deme duchesse challenged the marquis who was set to inherit her estate to a duel for it, pretended he had mortally injured her, and then as he approached to check, disarmed him? It's a fascinating tale, but it was ripped from most books. His Majesty hates it."

So what? I should let Bisset think she'd won? That wasn't enough. I wanted more. I wanted to do something.

"I'm deaf in my left ear," Germaine said suddenly, fingers crushing the book. "It's hard to notice—I was taught to deal with the world, the world wasn't designed for me—and I love Vivienne, but sometimes she is misguided. She doesn't understand the small aggressions some of us deal with every day. Instead of asking me to leave or taking you outside, she pretends I'm not here." She sniffed. "Demeine makes the people it doesn't want invisible. Does that make sense?"

"I know what you mean." I shook my head when she raised an eyebrow. "Not the same thing, not at all, but I know what you mean about Demeine making us invisible."

She studied me for a moment and nodded. "Help those you can, but especially help one another."

As Emilie des Marais, I had enough power to help without getting hanged, and I wanted to help Demeine.

"Thank you," I said, gathering up my things. "For everything."

After supper, I lay in bed, Coline's sleeping mask across my eyes, and asked if she knew the story of the Deme duchesse.

"It's my favorite," Coline said, and I could hear her sneer. "They called her the Dishonorable Duchesse, and she said her people were worth far more than her honor. Her direct line ended when Henry du Rand overthrew the last queen and tore the names of every family who stood against him from the history books. I wish I knew her name. I think Laurence du Montimer's family is distantly related to her, though."

She broke no rules, only a noble's pride, and kept her estate.

"Are you visiting the kitchens tonight?" Coline laughed and smiled in that breathy way that meant nothing funny was happening. "For sustenance."

"I usually eat toast," I said, confused. "Why? You want some?"

Coline closed her eyes and shook her head.

The door creaked open. I lifted the mask, spying Isabelle peeking around the door. She blushed when she saw me.

"I embarrassed you, did I?" I asked.

"Yes, but I didn't, you see, I—" She sighed and shut the door behind her. "She asked me what was wrong, and I couldn't lie, so I told her I was still a little upset about class. You didn't get in trouble, did you?"

I shook my head. She collapsed onto my bed next to me.

"I feel stuck," she said. "I want to do something. I know you're still having trouble with the silver room—"

"That's putting it kindly," Coline muttered.

"—you don't know the meaning of the word," Isabelle said

quickly, eyes rolling to glare at Coline before she turned back to me. "But even though you're having trouble, I know you can see things. I mean, I know you can scry."

"That's sort of the point." I pulled one hand free and tucked a blanket over Isabelle's hands. "I can't stop seeing things."

"But they're clearer than what I'm seeing," she said. "I need to scry my brother."

"That's against the rules." Coline lunged across my lap and bed, ripping the blankets off with her—she only ever managed to mess up my bed—and grabbed Isabelle by the shoulders. "I'm so proud of you."

Isabelle swallowed. Even when faced with Coline, she managed to keep her emotions hidden. "I don't care."

Mostly hidden.

"I love a good nighttime sneak about," Coline said and rolled off the bed. She started riffling through my wardrobe. "We'll wear socks—they're quieter—and I'll keep watch. If this were illusions or some foray into the noonday arts, I would join you, but this will keep me out of the way."

"Least we found a way to do that," I told Isabelle. "Why do you want to scry him?"

"He's a hack for a chevalier, and he hasn't written me in a while." She shifted. "And if you could divine him, I would appreciate that too."

When Isabelle was thinking, she chewed on the dry skin around her nails, and Vivienne, no matter how many creams and oils she provided, had not been able to break Isabelle of the habit. I pulled her hands out from under the blanket. Red lined the cracks around each nail.

"I can't divine," I told her, hands still clasping hers. "But I'll try to scry him. Just promise me if I ever say something embarrassing again, you'll come to me instead of talking to Vivienne."

Isabelle threw her arms around my shoulders. "Thank you."

"Excellent," Coline said, throwing open the door. "Let's go."

We crept downstairs and stole a bowl from the silver room, sneaking into one of the private study rooms with a skylight. I sat on the floor, back to the wall and moonlight streaming in from the windows behind and above me, and Isabelle sat next to me. It was a crescent night. Vivienne wasn't holding lessons in the midnight arts tonight because Estrel was here, and Estrel insisted on teaching during the day when we were at our weakest. There was so much power in the night, ribbons of moonlight that pooled in my palms and seeped into me, and I channeled it into the bowl. Isabelle's thigh pressed against mine as she leaned in closer. A ring fell into my open hands.

"His name is Gabriel," she whispered. "He gave that to me."

And there he was, my magic plucking the leftover pieces of him from the ring. Everyone, especially artists, changed the world wherever they went. Imprints of power left behind. I dropped the ring into the bowl.

"As I said, I can't divine, but I can try to scry him."

My lungs were too tight, my breaths too fast, the flutter in my heart too heavy, and all of it felt wonderful. Divining was all about the details, the magic a touch less controllable and its power several touches less than Lord Sun's. There were as many possible futures as there were stars. I hadn't divined since I was a child, the wrong stars were all that I found. Scrying was safer.

A chevalier in armor light as ash. A one-handed sword in a hack's worn-down, bandaged hands. He ran a palm down the sword, magic bubbling and burrowing into the steel, and handed the chevalier the hilt. The blade thinned and lengthened, deadly sharp point bright in the sunlight of a battlefield strewn with bloodied wheat.

"You have a month before Kalthorne," a rough voice said. "You must be prepared."

"He's alive," I said, voice raspy. "He will be for a while. I saw him with his chevalier in a wheat field."

Were we going to war, or was that training? If we went to war, what would happen to my brother Macé? Varlets weren't fighters, but they were always with their chevaliers.

I shook the image from my mind. We couldn't go to war. The army was all country kids, and to fight Kalthorne, we'd need more soldiers. They'd have to offer up money for joining, and then most of them would still die and not get the payout, and everyone who was a hack would get called up to work. Emilie would be on the edge of the battles looking after the wounded. My brother Macé would be a varlet. They'd need them to replace the ones who died.

He'd die. I couldn't let that happen again.

Laurel, I thought, eyes fluttering shut. I breathed in magic and channeled it into the bowl with an exhale. *I have to help Laurel and all of us who'd die.*

The nobles wouldn't. They rarely did, even though it was only a king who could declare war.

I want to help Laurel stop Henry XII. I want to save us. I opened my eyes, face awash in moonlight, and an image, not in the bowl but in the glass of the skylight above me, ghostly and larger than life, shone. *How do I find Laurel?*

An older man in a soldier's uniform. Wrinkled hands pinning a laurel leaf to a shirt collar. Worn boots walking the perimeter of the school at night, no one else nearby.

Thank you, Mistress Moon.

I let the vision die and turned to Isabelle. "I can't see anything else. Just that."

"Let's get you to bed." She pulled a cloth from her pocket, pressed it to my nose, and cupped my cheek. "You're worn out."

Late that night, it was easy to find the guard who'd given me the wooden laurel leaf pin and let me inside the day I'd swapped places with Emilie. I'd used the midnight arts to disguise my face. Still looked like me but more like Emilie than me, and it wasn't like I was important. He'd not remember.

He was pacing before the servants' gate, whistling a tune I didn't know, and he stopped when I stepped from the garden path. He spun, fists up fast for his age. A proper soldier.

"I'm sorry for startling you." I laughed like I was embarrassed. Vivienne said when girls did that, it took men so off guard, they were more likely to be quiet and listen. "I have a slightly odd question for you, if you would oblige me?"

He bowed at the waist, the low dip deep enough for a comtesse and too deep for me. As if it weren't midnight and this weren't odd. "Of course, Madame. I would be happy to be of assistance, but perhaps I should escort you back inside?"

"No," I said, enjoying the taste of a word I had so rarely gotten to say. "We should have this conversation out here when no one's around."

He straightened, face in shadows. "Why is that, Madame?"

"Your laurel leaf pin," I said. "It's a lovely idea. I was wondering where you got it?"

Vivienne had taught me many things, but above all else, she

had taught me how to speak to other people in compliments and half-truths.

"It's one of a kind, I'm afraid." His arms crossed behind his back. "How did you see it? I can't recall having made your acquaintance, Madame."

"I was scrying, and I saw something bad." I clenched my hands in the folds of my skirt and dropped my voice. "In the midnight arts, it's safer to share power than to hoard it. That's probably true for other things too. Like information."

"This is too risky," he said.

I cut off whatever other complaints he had. "Some things are worth the risk, and I think things are about to get real risky."

"Wait here." He crossed the distance between us and stuck the laurel pin to my shoulder. There was a pause between him reaching out and him pinning it to me, as if he thought I'd run, but I was winter. I endured. "You scryed something bad?"

"Yes," I said. "And I want to help stop it."

"Don't move," he said. "You might have company soon."

The guard slipped through the gate. The key clicked twice, locking behind him. I slunk back a bit, into the boughs of an apple tree, and the soft crack of underbrush behind me made me lean into the trunk. A tall shadow, backlit by the light from the estate, stepped into the clearing before the fence, and the familiar scents of yeast and sulfur drifted to me. Yvonne, hair covered in a dark hood, lifted her face to the gate and looked around. What good company to have.

Her shoulders tensed, lifting up to her ears. The soldier had told me I'd have company, and she was getting anxious. Talking to her couldn't hurt.

"Yvonne?" I stepped into the clearing.

She spun, skirts a swirl of silver and dusk. "What?"

"Hi," I said with a laugh. A real one. "I might've interrupted your meeting."

"What are you doing here?" She crossed to me and fell short of touching my arm. "You can't be here."

"I have to help," I said. She hadn't touched me because I was Emilie des Marais to her. "I want to help, and I scryed something that led me here."

She didn't know me. Her head tilted to the side, the starlight flickering fires in her brown eyes. "Emilie…"

She didn't even know my real name.

The gate creaked, and we both spun around. The guard had returned, and with him was a stout person, hood drawn so low I could see nothing of their face. The guard let them through the gate and nodded to Yvonne. She swallowed.

"They are who you want to talk to," the guard told me. To the newcomer, he muttered, "This is Emilie des Marais."

"So," they said, lifting their head and not pushing back their hood. They'd a wide nose and hooded eyes, blue a softer shade than spring skies, and their clothes were the slightly worn of someone who worked every day in a shop. Dust and wrinkles, a few good tears, but mostly just ink stains at the wrists. "You're a comtesse who wants to help?"

Their tone was not promising.

"Laurel," Yvonne said quickly. "She's noble, but she's all right."

"That's the best compliment anyone's ever given me," I said. "You're Laurel?"

"We are all the laurels because our king and his nobles rest on us," said Laurel. They brought their hands up, their leather gloves the sort embroiderers and tailors wore with thimbles in the tips. "What did you see?"

"War," I said, and Yvonne stiffened. "A chevalier with a hack, but they were in all their armor and in a field fighting. Didn't look like normal training."

"That's fair specific for divination," they said. "Sounds like a lie."

"Scrying; I can't divine. The chevalier told their hacks they had to be prepared by the end of the month. I'm not the best midnight artist, but I'm not sitting by while people die." Emilie hadn't written back after I'd asked what to do if Estrel found me out. If I was getting hanged, might as well make it for something bigger than impersonation or thievery. "I can't divine or leave school, but I can scry. I can be useful."

"You could hear them speaking?" Laurel asked.

I nodded.

Yvonne cleared her throat. "She can see arts after they're done. She's the one who wrote that note to the apothecary. We've only got you and me in Bosquet. We could use someone who can scry."

"We could." Laurel gestured between us, their mouth twisted up. "Yvonne, this is very dangerous."

"The world is dangerous," said Yvonne. "And I'm done of waiting for it to get less so."

"Then you listen to me." They grabbed my chin with one hand, fingers digging into my cheeks. "You don't put either of these two in danger, or I'll send you to the pyre myself. Scry what you can about this war, Henry XII, his court, his chevaliers—anything that comes to you whether you think it's the future we're heading toward or not—and tell Yvonne anything you overhear while here. You're our spy now, Emilie des Marais, and you answer to Laurel. Understood?"

I nodded. Couldn't talk with their grip so tight.

"Good," they said and let go. "Anything you tell us that seems false, we'll make sure you take the fall with Henry XII for anything that happens, comtesse or not." They turned to Yvonne now, stance softening, and touched her cheek. "We need to get you better friends."

She glanced at me. "I like mine fine. Here—red vial bad, blue vial good. Don't mix it up, and don't take the blue one on an empty stomach."

Yvonne pulled two glass vials from her pockets, their tops sealed with a thick crust of wax, and handed them to Laurel. Laurel held them, gently testing their weight. The guard whistled.

"Time's up," he said, and the distant toll of a bell marking one in the morning echoed across the garden. "We're all good?"

Laurel nodded. The guard escorted them to the gate, glancing back at me once. I mouthed *thank you*, and Yvonne touched my forearm, her fingers cold despite the heat. We walked to the main building, mostly silent, and she held me back at the path that led to the kitchen. It took a moment for the words to come.

"What are you doing?" she asked.

"What I want for once," I said. "I'm tired of people telling me what to do."

Her brows came together, the little line between them new but deep. I shook my head.

"I'll tell you one day what I mean, but for now, I just want to change me or the world or something. Does that make sense?"

"It does." She pulled her hood down and took a step onto the path to the kitchens. "I'll see you tomorrow?"

I nodded.

She almost left, but I couldn't hold it in any longer. "Was that the real Laurel?"

"No." Yvonne turned back to me. "Every city has one now, and the first Laurel sends out letters to them. Divinations and advice, news from court, and the like. But that one you met tonight is my friend, and if you betray them, I will never forgive you."

She said it softly, surely, with so much care that the shake of her voice only made the threat more real. I nodded.

"If I ever betray you, please don't."

·CHAPTER·
NINE

Emilie

We did not see Florice again. He died in the night, at peace I hoped, and was moved by the time we woke. Rainier was quiet, Madeline was too, but in a determined way, and we met early in our lecture hall two days later for our exam to determine if we had learned enough. Nearly all the hacks staggered in with the tired eyes of people thinking too much. If I were home, Mother would have demanded I illusion them away. I was wearing mine today, though.

"Late night?" Pièrre du Guay, here to oversee our test, said to me as I entered.

He did not say it to anyone else.

I was tired—this place had made me tired—and that was the kindest thing it had done to anyone here. I wasn't hiding my truth to make him comfortable.

"A productive one," I said, head bowed. "How was yours, Physician?"

Sometimes, Mother had taught me, we had to bear the storm.

"Restful." He clapped his hands together and gestured to the rest of the room as I took my seat in the back near Madeline. "I do love a good exam!"

The board at the front of the room was covered with a cloth, gold and gilded as if it had been pulled from a table in the physicians' dining hall and not meant for us.

"Now, despite the unpleasantness of yesterday, I find myself hopeful that you are all on the road to becoming excellent hacks, one of the most necessary parts of our great institution." He cleared his throat and touched the table at the front, his fingers tapping along the glass tablets that were our exams. "Our physicians are the best minds of Demeine, and you are to be their hands. Several fully qualified physicians are in immediate need of hacks—me included, given the events of yesterday—and while this examination has been set by us to test for what we consider integral knowledge, it is by no means the deciding factor. Our apprentices observed and taught you. We do take their opinions into account, so I do hope you were nice."

He paused, and some of the others in the room laughed.

"There are fifty questions on the board behind me. Once you have been handed a tablet and pen and the board has been uncovered, you have two hours to impress us, and I am certain you will." He smiled, lips pursed, and clapped again. "And I encourage those of you more inclined to stoicism to let go of your coldness and embrace the necessary impromptu problem solving and creativity medicine requires."

I didn't gag, which as far as I was concerned was enough to warrant making me king, considering Mother had often declared me as indomitable as a puddle.

I pulled the glass tablet passed back to me into my lap, fingernails clicking against the words and a faint red stain shining from my hands through the glass. My brush shook, and my signature was crooked. These were easy questions with my education but would have been hard if all I knew was what they had taught me this week. The last question would have been easy, too, before I came here.

Is there a physician you wish to serve?

I glanced around the room—Pièrre du Guay had slipped outside a while ago, and none of the other students seemed to be having issues. I whispered "good luck" to Madeline and Rainier and stood. The water clock I passed on my way out said it had only been an hour.

Outside, Pièrre and Laurence were in the midst of an argument, du Montimer trapped in the corner of the hall across from me. Pièrre, back to me, readjusted his stance every time du Montimer attempted to leave.

"You had no authority over him," Pièrre whispered through clenched teeth. "He was an example."

"He was a corpse in the courtyard, and you neglected to mention what you wanted to do with him. Of course I had him moved." Laurence waved his hand as if to banish the conversation. "It is a child's game. It will be fine."

"It is treason, and you would be wise to pay attention to it, considering it is your uncle they wish to depose." Pièrre grabbed Laurence's arm. "You cannot stare down such a threat with passivity. You have let them fester in Monts Lance for too long, and now you allow them funeral rites? Take action. Be a man!"

"I'd rather not," said Laurence. "You know I loathe politics, but if you had denied his family funeral rites, it would have come out as another slight against us. Laurel's desperate. He'll cling to anything after that last debacle."

Laurel had tried to rob a storehouse last week in a city north of Serre—two guards and five traitors had died. No one had come forward to claim them, and the news of the deaths had started a whirlwind of rumors.

Laurence lifted his head and spotted me. I studied my tablet as if it were the only thing of interest. Laurence patted Pièrre's hand.

"So really, my absentminded mistake is a blessing in disguise," said Laurence. "Go. I will watch our intrepid hacks."

Pièrre stormed down the hallway, red coat a blood stain in my vision when I blinked, and through the haze of my glass tablet, I saw Laurence raise his hand to me.

"Oh." I feigned shock and bowed. So Laurence du Montimer had seen Florice dead and shipped his body back to his family. He was notoriously oblivious to anything not a patient or his research, but at least the results were good. "Physician du Montimer, I—"

"Didn't see me here?" he said with one huff of a laugh. "Do you have a question, Emilie?"

"The last question," I said. "What if there's a physician we don't want to work with?"

He held out his hand. "Leave it. No reason to offend his sensibilities."

I handed over the tablet.

"You're free until the morning, then." He tested the ink with a finger and tucked it under his arm. "Personally, I would go into Delest for the day. You won't have time soon. There's a lovely place with wine. Enjoy your time before the work begins."

He smiled, and I mimicked the expression, but I could feel my lips sticking to my teeth, mouth suddenly dry.

Madeline, Rainier, everyone behind me—we would be worked to near death and then left for dead eventually.

No, *they* would. I had options. It was unfair of me to forget what I had, even if I wanted desperately to forget it.

"Thank you for the advice." I bowed again, not as deep, and left.

Florice had told us to go to Bloodletters at noon, so I would. I pinned a note about where I was to Madeline's bed. They would join me or they wouldn't; it was their decision. I wouldn't blame them for avoiding Laurel and his plots. Madeline had told me one night when we were worried about the exam that I didn't know fear, and I had laughed.

I didn't know fear. Even now, I had a net woven from my family name and money to catch me if I fell. They didn't.

Leaving the university held none of the awe that entering it had. The gold fence and fluttering willow trees felt vulgar next to the squat wooden plots that made up Delest. The city *looked* nice, polished wood buildings and raised stone streets full of vendors and open-air stores selling all sorts of finds, but the prices were all wrong. They were too high. The fruit was too pretty. The people were too involved. It was a stage play of a city.

I found Bloodletters at the end of a crooked alley in the north-ernmost tip of the city. It was a bar, a single server inside with four guests working their way through glasses of pale wine. I ordered a glass, which was good, and a bowl of soup, which was not, and with an hour and a half until noon, waited for Madeline and Rainier. The other patrons glanced at me every now and then, and the server checked on me once. They asked if I wanted to leave or order more.

It was half an hour to noon.

I bought three glasses of wine and waited. Rainier peeked through the door. I raised my hand to him, and he pulled Madeline through with him. He flanked her when she sat, and one of the patrons lifted her head. Bloodshot red eyes glared at us through the dim room.

"I haven't seen anyone," I said, "but I got you these, and I don't think they're poisoned."

Madeline checked anyway, power slipping into her wine with a breath, and she shook her head. "You finished the exam early."

"And I overheard something interesting." The hair on the back of my neck rose. A low hum built in my ears. "Do you feel that?"

Madeline nodded, and Rainier shook his head.

I spun around. There was only a patron and the server, a cup of wine in their hands. The familiar tug of the midnight arts, soft magic and tight control, slipped over me, and Madeline reached her hand across the table. We hadn't worked since last night, and even though it had left us exhausted, she flung out her power in a whip. It broke through whatever vision the server was trying to scry. The water in the cup turned to steam, ruining their scrying surface. They jumped back.

"Rude of you to scry us," Rainier said loudly. "Could have just asked what we were talking about."

It was so little magic, but the server's hands were shaking.

The bloodshot patron rose, dragged a chair to our table, and sat. I downed the last of my wine.

"Who are you?" she asked. She couldn't have been more than a few years older than us, but her face was haggard, and the cut of her clothes was slightly too big, as if she had lost weight and muscle in recent weeks. A scar beneath her left eye was still shiny.

Madeline and Rainier at the same time said, "Hacks."

"How'd you hear about today?" she asked. "Don't lie. I'll know."

"Are you better with magic than that one?" I asked and pointed at the server. "Because if not, you will have trouble seeing as we can all control our bodily responses to stress as well as other people's."

She turned to Rainier and pointed at me. "This one always an ass?"

"Yes."

I scowled.

"Well, that was truthful, so I think I've still got it," she said, running a hand over her recently shaved black hair. "Now, who told you to come here at noon?"

Madeline set down her wine. "Florice."

"He's dead, but nice try." The girl dropped an elbow on the table and leaned in. A strip of leather knotted around her throat held a small curl of icy-blond hair in a locket cut like lacework. "How did you really hear about it? You're not our standard fare."

"We know he's dead," I said. "We were there for it. He told us to come here before he died. If it helps, it would've been around two in the morning when he told us."

"Shit." She dropped her forehead into her hand, massaging her temples. "Physician Pièrre du Guay left him as an example, didn't he?"

I nodded. "Laurence du Montimer didn't know and sent Florice back to his family at least."

She nodded and rocked in the chair. "Your names?"

We told her who we all were—perhaps a mistake, perhaps the start of something better—and she cleared her throat.

"Here's what you're going to do, then." She stood her first two fingers on the table and walked them about as if explaining battle positions. "We already have eyes inside of the medical school, but they can't get close to Physician du Guay. We need to know what he's up to and what he's thinking. Can you do that?"

"Who's this 'we' you're talking about?" I asked. "And what should we call you?"

"You lot don't call me anything. Last time I told folks my name was in Segance, and I'm not getting arrested again." She rolled her eyes at me. "But let us say that a physician, like a king, should not rest on his laurels."

She was one of the Laurels.

"But you asked for our names," said Rainier.

"I did," she said. "Problem?"

"No." Madeline shook her head. There was a thump, and I was sure she had stepped on her brother's foot. "He's picking a new hack from our class. We can talk to whoever it is and figure out what to do."

"Good," she said, standing. "Send word through one of you. Don't all come tromping back here at once. We can't survive another Segance. Now get out of here."

So we downed our wine and did.

"Madeline, if you'd had Charles's education, would you be as skilled as him?" I asked later that night in our room.

"If this is a veiled insult, your veil's not thick enough," she said, head leaning back on her folded robe.

"It's not. It's a question." I spun the silver cuff in my hands, gathering all my memories of Annette and channeling magic into the metal. "If you were a comtesse, things would have been different. Was he lucky that he had the education he had, or was it predestined?"

She rolled her eyes to stare at me but didn't say anything.

"And I don't mean in the way the Empire's new ministers go on about predestination. I mean it in the political way. Is it luck if the world is designed to ensure he got that education?"

"I feel like this is less a question for me and more you working through some sort of issue." She whistled a tune and threw a wadded-up blanket at me. "Stop spinning it."

I glanced up at her. "Can you scry?"

"Oh yes. I refuse to sacrifice what I love simply because it's too feminine for a physician, whatever that means," said Madeline. "Hold it still. Moving won't let the image take hold."

"Thank you," I said.

But the silver still showed me nothing.

The next morning, we were shuffled to a tailor bright and early. Madeline and I went in last, and while we waited, I held up bolts of fabric to her to see which looked best. We settled on physician-coat scarlet, but the tailor had strict orders on what to fit us for. Old, donated dresses in cheap cloth and pale colors were thrust into my arms, and the pitch-black coat of the hacks—so as not to show our mistakes—buttoned from our collar to our hips. I paid the tailor's assistant double for a pair of trousers like Rainier had been given earlier. The money I had brought with me from Bosquet was gone, the disgustingly expensive sets of supplies and texts from the university responsible for most of it. Annette had sent me more, of course.

Everything well. Haven't done anything dangerous. No one suspicious. Scrying notes on back. Also, everyone hates your handwriting. Sorry.

I had not asked her if she had done anything dangerous, and for such a short letter, it begged so many questions.

"I bet you a silver half that Physician du Guay picks first and makes a speech about it," Madeline whispered to me.

I grinned. "Deal. I bet he makes his hacks walk to meet him and doesn't bother coming here."

We were all dressed in our uniforms. The coat over our long-sleeved blouses and thick skirts was uncomfortably hot, dredging every drop of sweat from my skin. Madeline had buttoned her blouse and coat to her chin, a much more feminine fashion statement, and I had rolled up my sleeves like Rainier and most of the others. I pulled at my collar. Rainier leaned back to say something.

The door to the lecture hall slammed open. Laurence du Montimer, scarlet coat neatly buttoned from throat to knee over his white shirt and black hose and his hair plaited back so that only a few stray curls framed his face, swept into the room. Every part of him was put together, despite the early hour. He held up his right hand and pointed to the back of the room. Two gold rings with opal slivers glittered on his fingers.

"Rainier, Emilie," he said, turning to leave. "You're mine."

Arrhythmia.

Madeline grabbed my arm.

I stood and Rainier did the same, staring at me. "Good luck. You owe me some silver."

Madeline looked at me, eyes slightly too wide, lips slightly too tense, and Rainier and I walked after Laurence. I marched after him—my strides too wide to be polite and my arms crossed against my chest; an inappropriate lady of Demeine—and licked my lips, the sting of sulfur and seared skin thick in the air around him. He led us out of the building and to an area far on the other side of university. We stopped before a thick wooden door carved with the creation of the universe. Laurence laid his hand against the dual sun and moon etching.

"You've met my second apprentice, Charles, I believe." Laurence pushed open the door and beckoned for us to enter. "He's opted not to have a hack, but Emilie, you will, when needed, assist him with non-ethereal and surgical medical work. Rainier, you will be working with my first apprentice, Sébastien. I typically do not permit the use of hacks for my apprentices, but I let them decide this year."

Wait—was I not going to be working as a hack? Did he think I couldn't work with the noonday arts? That I shouldn't?

Laurence ushered us inside. A prickling of gooseflesh spread over my arms, sweat chilling on my skin. The familiar thrum of the noonday arts around me pounded in my head, powerful and demanding, hungry to be used, and I breathed it in, let it steep into me until Laurence spoke again.

"This is the laboratory," Laurence said, sweeping one reedy arm out to gesture at different tables. No wonder his hands were so worn down. He must channel so much for this amount to have lingered here. If this was what he hadn't used yet, I could only imagine what he had. "My research is mostly in long-term ethereal solutions to physical problems, adjusting body alchemistry and healing the small veins we haven't quite mastered closing with surgery yet."

A glass tablet no bigger than my thumb rested on a table nearby, and a red drop was crushed between two planes. I peeked at it, fingers on the table edge. Charles darted in front of me.

"Don't touch things." He said it softly, so Laurence wouldn't hear, and tapped the pair of thick, protective spectacles atop his head. They had left little crescent moon indents on each side of his nose. "He has a whole list of rules I'll give you two later. He always forgets."

"Sorry." I shrugged. "I'm very curious."

"Yes," Charles said. "That is the word we have used to describe you."

Behind me, Rainier snorted.

"Familiarize yourselves with this layout," Laurence said quickly. "In the event of an emergency, which does happen on occasion, you might need to traverse it without sight or sound."

It was a large, high-ceilinged room with windows of curved glass for privacy. Vents spotted the ceiling, to redirect bad air and fumes, and if I were to divide the room in even quadrants, I was sure the four tables of the room would fall in the exact center of each quadrant. Small lamps—flameless, alchemical things of glass and magic that cast an odd, yellow light across the room—hung from the ceiling, sparking in the various glass jars, vials, and distillation setups on the tables. At the back of the room sat Sébastien practicing stitchery on a pig flank. The table to the right of the door, Laurence's table, was meticulously cleaned and organized. At its center was a small steel box.

As Laurence turned to move it, Charles mouthed to Rainer and me, "Two explosions."

It took everything in me not to laugh.

"That," Laurence said, pointing to Sébastien, "is my first apprentice. Do you want to introduce yourself or should I?"

Sébastien didn't seem to hear. Laurence only nodded.

"That is Sébastien des Courmers, comte de Saillie," Laurence said, voice overly nonchalant. "He is too busy to select which one of you he wants to work with—"

Sébastien turned around. His dark hair was braided back but escaped strands dangled across the sides of his face, giving him the look of a person interrupted whilst in the middle of something of great importance. His spectacles were artfully drooping down his straight nose, and the bushy brows above bright green eyes were naturally full and arched. "We agreed. I get Mercer."

"Just making sure you're paying attention." Laurence pushed Rainier toward him and moved to sit at his desk. "Acquaint yourselves."

Charles held up his hand. "You forgot to introduce yourself."

"I hate small talk." Laurence dropped his pen.

"You're intimidating without it." Sébastien cleared his throat. "But it's only because you're so smart."

"Complimenting me to make me do something I hate?" Laurence asked. "Really?"

Charles and Sébastien glanced at each other and said, "Yes."

Laurence sighed, his shoulders rising and falling with the effort, and he held out his hands to us as if his next words were an offering. "Please call me Laurence or Physician du Montimer. Please do not break anything. No eating in the laboratory, and no excessive use of the arts without my permission." He glanced at Sébastien. "Better?"

He nodded.

"What's your favorite color?" Charles asked. "Everyone has one. It'll make you seem more personable."

"I have apprentices to be personable for me." Laurence rolled his eyes but smiled. "I like dark green and hate apples. Personable?"

"Very," Sébastien said.

I glanced at Charles. "Laurence said I would be working with you, but that you didn't want a hack?"

"No," Charles said, grin pure malice. "I see he also forgot the entire purpose of today. You're working with Laurence." He patted my shoulder. "My condolences—I don't think I slept for two months when Laurence first took me on."

I shuffled to Laurence's desk, unsure of what to do. He had already set to taking notes and staring at some sort of alchemical agent I had never seen. He glanced up at me after a moment.

"Right." He narrowed his eyes and pushed his glasses to his forehead. "I need an assistant who knows how to alter the alchemistry of the human body, and judging by your exam, that's you. I won't use you as a hack unless necessary, but you will do exactly what I say. Understood?"

I bowed. The new stays and shift scratched at my spine. "Yes. I am glad I can fill that need."

Laurence tilted his head to one side, plait bouncing against his shoulder. "You bow quite often, so I'm assuming you don't normally wear skirts. Wear what you're comfortable in." He slipped off his physician's coat and handed it to me, gesturing to the hook on the wall behind me. "And please stop bowing to me. If you do it every time we see each other, you'll end up face-first in a dissection cadaver."

Finally! We would get to learn something.

"Thank you."

"You'll go with me on my rounds, as will the others, but they are studying minor surgeries and bonesetting now. We'll start tomorrow. I spend most of my days between research and free infirmaries when not at university," Laurence said, tossing his journal on the table at the back of the laboratory. "It's tedious work, but it has to be done and be done right, no matter how much the patient can pay, and while we are here, we work in Delest every day."

The world needed reordering, me included, and maybe this was my first step in helping. I would hear all sorts of things about court and Pièrre from Laurence.

I sat on the stool across from Laurence. "Where would you like me to start?"

"Here." Laurence reached beneath his table and dropped a stack of books heavier than the earth before me. "Start reading."

·CHAPTER·
TEN

Annette

B reakfast was the same except Estrel didn't show, and I nearly vomited after eating a pastry oozing with cinnamon that had looked too good to pass up. I sat on a bench next to Coline in mathematics, head on her shoulder, whispering the answers, and the teacher didn't bother us about it. On my way back to my room, the pull of channeling magic took hold of the power around me. Someone was divining in the silver room.

It was an hour before supper. The sun was still up, burning through all the windows. Whoever it was gathered power like their life depended on it, channeling the midnight arts and noonday arts into their work, and it was too much. Even being near it made my teeth ache. I crept to the door.

Isabelle, awash in magic, sat bowed over the same silver bowl I'd used for her brother. She was ethereal, cloaked in ribbons of power that threaded through the air to her open hands. Thin strips of flesh peeled away from her hands where the magic poured from her body to her bowl. Instead of water, she'd used quicksilver to keep the artistry steady. Red smeared across the silver.

"Stop!" I rushed to her and yanked the bowl from her hands.

The skin touching it tore away. Isabelle didn't even shriek. The bowl, solid silver, shattered against the floor, and I pulled Isabelle's chair away from the table. She didn't move, didn't speak, didn't drop her hands from where they'd held the magic. Her teeth chattered.

"Isabelle?" I knelt in front of her. The pieces of her skin the magic had worn down were raw and open, not so deep they made me shudder, but unnatural enough they gave me pause. Like a paper cutout made with fire, except her flesh was the paper and the cutouts a perfect view of the inside of her forearm. They weren't even bleeding. Drops of quicksilver beaded up along her veins. "Isabelle, can you hear me?"

Sometimes, if an artist didn't have the money to pay a physician and enough power had channeled through their skin, the wounds killed them. Too many common artists died from healable injuries like this.

"I saw a future," she whispered. "I had to know if it came true."

"You were killing yourself." I pulled her handkerchief from her pocket and wrapped it around her hands. "Can you walk? We have to take you to Vivienne."

"No!" She ripped her hands from me and fell back. "No, no, no, no, no. Vivienne can't know. No one can know."

Someone behind me cleared their throat, and I glanced back. Coline, arms crossed, stood in the doorway. Germaine and Gisèle peeked into the room from behind her. They were always together, Germaine on the left.

"If you want to get away with this, you have to move," said Coline. "First rule of breaking the rules: Never stay in the same place too long."

"Then help me carry her, Mademoiselle Crime." I rose and wrapped the cloth back around Isabelle's hands.

Tall, sturdy Gisèle with her wide smile and strong arms came forward instead and swept Isabelle up in her arms. "It is times like these, I am glad I don't have the curse of magic."

Coline, Isabelle, and I were the only first-year students who did.

"Thanks." I gathered up the mess, Germaine helping me clean, and stared around the room. Most of the power had faded. "Well, that could've been worse."

Germaine, Vivienne's favorite student when it came to comportment, only hummed.

"What was she trying to do?" Coline asked.

I shook my head. "Divine her brother, but she wouldn't say what about."

"It must be bad, then, to wear herself down so much for one divination, yes?" Germaine asked. "I have never understood the appeal of knowing the future, but Isabelle talks of nothing except her brother."

She was a good sister.

"They're all each other have," I said. "Their parents are dead, and she's got something that's supposed to help but doesn't. It's infuriating."

"I'll find another bowl." Germaine dumped the shattered pieces into a decorative vase. "If she gets in trouble—"

I grinned. "I haven't seen you since class."

I left, saying goodbye and thanking Germaine again, and raced back to my room. She agreed to make our excuses at supper—Vivienne loved nothing more than us banding together to protect the others, so us keeping an *indisposed* Isabelle company would delight her. Upstanding ladies of Demeine didn't let a bit of uncomfortableness affect them, even if it meant they were in too much pain to stand. It was more seemly to excuse yourself.

Couldn't do it every day, and only for one hour. I'd already tried with household management.

"What were you thinking?" I said, shoving open the door to our room and looking round for Isabelle.

She'd been tucked into her bed, her hands wrapped in gauze, and Coline sat at the foot of her bed.

I paced between her bed and mine, and pulled the lockbox I'd stolen from one of Emilie's trunks out from under my bed. Inside, I'd been storing little things, mostly. A few tonics for pain or fever, some silver lunes, and most importantly a half-empty tin of balm to help with damage caused by magic that one of the girls had left in the silver room on accident. There was no telling when someone would find me out. I had to be ready.

"Here." I sat it on the high wooden back of Isabelle's bed frame. "What did you see?"

"Him dying," she whispered. She stared straight ahead, eyes red. "My aunt keeps telling me he's fine, but I *saw* it and know she's lying. Blood and steel or a noose and gasping or his body wearing out and crumbling or once a horse hoof to the head. So many possibilities and all of them death."

I pulled Alaine's necklace out from under my dress. It was always best to use things well-loved. "You and Gabriel aren't alone anymore," I said softly. "You don't have to be ever again."

I held the image of her brother—mousy hair like hers that he kept long and knotted at the nape of his neck, her nose beneath a startling set of blue eyes that were all his, and the black coat of a hack covering him from neck to knees—in my mind. I rubbed my hands together as if I were gathering wool, and power condensed around the silver crescent moon. My skin grew cold and clammy. I didn't need to open my eyes to see this future.

I had gathered so much power, too much of Mistress Moon, to ensure that what she sent me was the future that would come to pass. Most divinations didn't.

Gabriel, bloodied and worn down, on his back in a field. Black-hearted bruises speckling his white skin. Blood in his throat. No pain. Only stars above and memories.

My first divination in ages, and it was certain death.

I tried to pull my hands away, but they held fast, the divination arts not done with me. Part of the danger of working the midnight arts was not knowing when to stop and getting trapped—the illusion, present or future, playing out forever. A pair of small hands grasped my wrists and pulled them apart. I opened my eyes.

"What did you see?" Coline asked, her hands holding a cloth beneath my nose. "Emilie, that was the most power I have ever felt anyone pull together without preparation."

Isabelle's trembling arm pressed to mine. "Please don't lie. What did you see?"

I glanced at her. She should know. She'd done it downstairs and nearly worn her hands out. "You—"

Pain tore down my throat. I coughed, choked, and Coline pulled back the cloth. Blood drenched it. I dropped Alaine's necklace against my chest, the soft tap of it painful, and touched my nose and mouth. Blood dripped down my fingers, flecks of silver magic floating in the red. It clotted almost instantly.

"I—" Instead of words, blood and snot filled my throat. I sniffed. "This is why I don't divine. It never works."

Coline pressed the cloth back to my face. "Stop talking. I know it will be hard but try."

I scowled, but she couldn't see it through the cloth.

"Did you see him?" Isabelle asked softly.

I nodded. Even that hurt.

Gabriel would die, worn down far too much to be saved.

Not all artists die young. Only the common do. Why?

Because they were killed, by magic or by their artist's hands. I needed to talk to Yvonne. Something bad was coming. Rich folks always needed hacks because hacks kept them alive. They wouldn't kill them for nothing.

Demeine wore us down as surely as magic did.

"The last time I saw someone gather that much power, his heart stopped," Coline said. "And he had to resort to hacks."

I waved her worry off with a hand and picked up my necklace. Some of the power I'd gathered but not used still lingered in the room. It curled around my shoulders like a mantle of wool on the hottest day of summer, and I gently pushed a single strand of it into the necklace. I had enough in me for one more midnight art. Something quick and easy.

If I was going to help Isabel, Gabriel, and Laurel, I needed to be better, and for that, I needed Estrel. But she wasn't teaching us yet, focusing on the older, better students instead. How did she get better?

Hands, calloused and scarred, flipped through folded pages. A language I couldn't read that looked like ancient Deme. Neat, stylized handwriting in red ink. A flash of magic so powerful... My eyes outside of the vision burned.

I jerked back. The magic fell apart, slipping through shaking hands. That wasn't possible. The midnight arts weren't physical. They couldn't affect physical things, especially not through divination. It was just...watching.

"Are you incapable of taking care of yourself?" Coline crumpled up the cloth and threw it on my bed. "Stop. You're hurting yourself."

That one hadn't hurt at all, and I tapped the corner of one eye then nudged Isabelle. My vision blurred.

"You saw it?" she asked. "You saw something bad?"

I was terrible at divining, and maybe, if that were Gabriel's future, we could stop it now that we knew.

I shook my head.

Knowing your sibling was about to die and not knowing what to do was the worst feeling in the world, and I would suffer no one through it. I had to find a way to help Gabriel first.

Footsteps echoed down the hall. Coline turned to the door, and I covered my face with my hands. Blood pooled in my cupped palms.

Let it be Vivienne who probably wouldn't kill us too badly. Please, Mistress, anyone but Estrel.

I blinked, and it didn't get better. The footsteps grew closer, the clack changing to a shuffle on the hall's narrow rug. The headache I'd carried since coming here gnawed at my temples. The door opened. Isabelle stiffened.

"It's rude to scry on someone without their permission," a voice that was not, could not, but absolutely did belong to Estrel said.

"I tried to divine earlier and failed," Isabelle said quickly. "It's my fault."

"I know. I don't mean that. Unlike Vivienne, I find power and trouble go hand in hand and expect such experimentation from my students." Estrel laughed, breath rippling between her lips, and the red-crowned smear that was her crept closer. "Now, which one of you scryed me?"

I lifted my head and tried to deny it, but the words were a bloody mess.

"What for all the gods have you done?" Her voice was a rough, low thing with no humor, and the bed to my left dipped. Warm hands touched mine. "It was an accident, wasn't it?"

I nodded.

"I cannot believe you two let her do this," she said. "You should have helped."

"Is that even possible?" Coline asked. "We're not trained as hacks."

"Are you asking me is it possible for you three to do what the majority of artists do? You don't need training to share, I would hope." Estrel's fingers tilted my face back and forth, her gaze unreadable from all the snow in my vision. Then, after what felt like a century, she brushed my hair from behind my ears and slipped her spectacles onto my face. "I can't believe Vivienne didn't notice you."

Why would anyone ever notice me?

The whole bottom of my stomach dropped out. Maybe this was it. The worst fate in the world. My legs were numb and my brain was of fire and the little bundle of nerves I'd been keeping in my belly since she'd arrived was finally eating me in two. Maybe I'd get lucky and there'd be nothing left of me to be embarrassed. I was so bad, she wished Vivienne had told her about me.

"Open your eyes," she said. "Does that help?"

I blinked, the world tinted orange-yellow, and the snow in my vision cleared. The power I'd been seeing everywhere was gone. My head still ached and my stomach still rebelled, but this was better. The little itching pain in the back of my mind since first entering the silver room faded.

I nodded again.

"You two rest, and no more midnight arts. If you do any, I will know and I will not be happy. I know you are Vivienne's rebellious group for the year, but this is really beyond the scope of her capabilities," said Estrel. "Understood?"

They both agreed.

"And you." Estrel Charron, the best midnight artist who had ever lived and maybe the best artist of the decade, gently took me by the shoulders and smiled. "You are coming with me."

Estrel led me to her quarters on the upper floors. The halls looked different, stained gold by her spectacles, flickers of magic dancing across the lenses when I looked sideways. She'd a real laboratory with divining bowls in every shade of silver and glass, vials of quicksilver and water full of arts, and two gold-plated tables lined with tall gold stools, and she swept me through the room before I could get a good look at any of it. The bitter-clean scents of vinegar and lemon peel filled my mouth when she opened a door in the back of the laboratory, pushing me into a small, cushioned chair. Water flowed through a clock in the corner, trickling down the hour. Four trunks stood open and messy along one wall.

Maybe she'd kill me. Couldn't be embarrassed if I were dead.

"Now, don't speak," said Estrel, sweeping to the large desk taking up most of the room. "Vivienne told me you call yourself Emilie des Marais."

I pushed her spectacles up my nose and nodded. She must think me weak compared to her.

She was the country girl so good with magic she'd tried to join the university and they'd accepted her as some half-real student so they could keep an eye on her as she studied the midnight arts. Hope had whispered through the villages from kids' lips to kids' ears because if she could do that alone, what could we do together?

She'd teach me how I could help, how I would be worthy, surely.

"Drink this." She pressed a small cup into my hands. "It will help your throat."

The familiar scents of sage, barley, and honey hit my nose. It smelled like Yvonne's kitchens and the hum of her alchemistry trapped in the honey soothed me. She was so talented.

After I'd been sipping for a while, Estrel asked, "I'm curious—did it work?"

"What?" The word was a croak.

"Your scrying—you were looking at my past," she said. "Did you see it clearly?"

I shook my head. Scrying the past was possible, but no one ever did it. It was only slightly easier than divining but took too much power to make it worth it.

She laughed, the sound of two old book pages rubbing together. "Divining is the hardest midnight art and provides us with the most dangerous knowledge. Do you want that sort of power?"

She stood barely five foot and three thumbs, smiling, but still the words wouldn't come. What if she thought what I wanted was silly? What if she laughed again and the sound was ruined forever?

"Emilie?" she said softly but firmly. "There's no wrong answer."

She wasn't soft or still or stagnant like Maman always said I should be. She was sharp and moving—one finger tapping against the tip of her hooked nose, pointed jaw tensed so tight, her muscles twitched, red curls bouncing free and wild around her shoulders as she shifted. Two starry clips bright as her brown eyes flickered near her ears. She pulled a spare set of spectacles from her pocket and put them on. Opal slivers sparkled in the arms.

My vision for faraway things was still blurry, but at least it showed me her.

"Yes," I said. "I want to be the best. I want everyone who told me I couldn't be to know they were wrong. I want to save people and help people and be something to someone, so it doesn't all feel like nothing. I have to be the best."

If I wasn't, what was the point of me even learning magic?

"Good. I love ambition." She came to me from around her desk, shoulders squared as if her well-tailored plain clothes were armor instead of her origins, and sat on the footstool before me. "I'll talk to Vivienne in the morning, but you need to start training immediately. This"—she tapped my brow and then my throat—"is because you are much more capable of gathering magic than most other artists. Does it feel like magic is calling to you? Like it wants you to channel it?"

I nodded.

"You are innately talented, but because of that, you are more susceptible to wearing down."

I knew it. I wasn't trained enough for it. No wonder I'd been more wince than girl in that room.

"How much more training?" I asked. "Am I far behind the others?"

"Behind?" Estrel laughed, hands fluttering around her like excited Stareaters. "The amplification effects of the school are affecting you quite badly, as they did me. I mean that in the best possible way, of course."

"I don't know what you mean, though."

The embarrassment had died, and in the hollow place where my stomach had been, a warm, curling feeling like dry heat after a humid summer day had taken over. She was brilliant. Of course she'd say things I'd not get. And she was nice, bedside manner more sisterly than strict. Her thumb tapped my jaw.

"Oh, darling, you think you're terrible at magic, don't you?" Her fingers tilted my chin up, and she pulled the spectacles from my nose. Least her smile was as cutting as I expected from the smartest person in Demeine.

"I know I'm not the best, but all I want is to be better," I said. "Everyone always told me I was bad at it, and I can't divine."

"I'm going to put a drop of castor oil in your eyes. Blink and it should help." She touched my chin. "Not to be the bearer of bad news, but everyone lied to you or didn't want you to grow into your power. And I would bet that you can divine."

She held open my eyelids and let two drops fall into each eye. I blinked them away for a few minutes, the two of us sitting in the tense but comfortable silence of two people who didn't know what to say, and my vision slowly cleared. I was sitting in a chair with a tall, cushioned back near the door, and the rest of the room was a barely contained, cluttered mess of books and glass and bowls and kingfisher feathers spread out across the desk and table and shelves. A map of the sky with each constellation outlined and the meanings for reading portents decorated the stone wall behind a complete human skeleton on the side of the room across from the door. Tiny scrawls of black curled around each separate bone. Estrel's wooden desk was in the corner to the left of it, covered by a series of knives and telescopes.

She leaned away from me. "Better?"

It was nice being cared for.

"Much. Thank you," I said. "So, what has been happening to me? Feels like you're laughing at me."

"I'm sorry," she said. "You remind me of me a little bit in how shocked you are by all of this."

Well, that was a lie. We were nothing alike.

"Sometimes," Estrel said, "there are people like us who are so affected by the ethereal power of magic that it can have more detrimental effects on our physical bodies when we aren't trained. Power begs to beget power. It wears whatever it touches down over time. We tend to gather it innately, store it in things without realizing it."

"Us?"

"Us." She leaned toward me, hands on her knees, and stared into my eyes. "You are a wonderful midnight artist who needs training, but you taught yourself control and all the intricacies of scrying, didn't you? Power comes in many forms, some that we might not recognize at first, and some that others seek to disregard, and I want to help you recognize yours. You're not alone."

I couldn't even nod. The tears on my face had nothing to do with the pain from earlier, and she reached out with one steady hand to wipe them from my face.

"You need better training than I received, and it will be hard." She reared back and chewed on her thumbnail, eyes staring through me. "I am supposed to return to Serre in three days, but I can leave Vivienne instructions."

"Whatever you want," I said, the burn in my throat almost gone. I was no one, and she wanted to teach me.

I wasn't bad. I was useful. Maman was wrong. She'd lied to me.

Estrel looked up at me. "I want you to promise me that you won't gather that much power without supervision."

I swallowed, set my cup down, and nodded.

Wasn't a lie. Mostly.

"I mean it. And another rule." Estrel picked up the chain of Alaine's necklace with her finger. "You have to stop wearing this and stop using it for divinations. When you gather power, you gather a lot without meaning to, and when you use this necklace with it, some of that power stays in that necklace. It leaks out and wears down whatever is near it."

I grabbed the charm at the end, silver warm in my hands, and swallowed. "It's holding power and wearing me down faster?"

"It's wearing down the parts of you it touches." She tapped her own throat right where a short necklace might have once sat. "Why do you think I sound like this? Those with the money to pay physicians may wear such trinkets, but this silences us. Which is probably why they don't warn us of that."

The phrase stuck to my mind long after she escorted me back to my room. Isabelle was sleeping in the two-bed infirmary, and Coline was reading by moonlight in my bed. She didn't look up when I entered, but her eyes caught the light as they followed me, watching as I pulled out the lockbox and laid Alaine's necklace into it. Coline turned the page and sighed.

"You lied to Isabelle," she said. "Why?"

Her tone was even. Maman always got quiet when she got angry, and Coline seemed the same sort.

"Do you have any siblings?" I asked.

I knew she didn't, but I wanted to draw her through my thoughts like how Vivienne taught us mathematics.

"You know I don't," she said. "The only family members I don't hate are my aunt and cousin, but I'm no longer permitted to speak to them."

I tugged at the edges of my clothes and eased myself out of them. There was still a thrum in the air, like seeing someone scry made me feel, and I rubbed the back of my neck. "Is there anyone that you love? Any sort of love?"

"Yes," said Coline, but she said it so softly, I might have missed it.

"Have you watched them die?"

"No, and Isabelle shouldn't watch that either." Coline closed the book and set it aside. "We have to make sure it doesn't happen."

Coline came up to me and turned me around, and she undid the tight braids I'd knotted my hair up into that morning. We were meant to learn to help one another. I wondered, sometimes, why some rich and noble students needed the reminder. Coline dropped the pins from my hair on my bed.

"You don't have to say who you watched die," she said very gently, more gently than I thought she was capable of being, and squeezed my arm. She didn't let go. "But a lie of kindness is not always a good lie."

So she was Mademoiselle Crime *and* Ethics now?

"What are we going to do?" she asked.

"We're the troublesome girls. I imagine us doing something wouldn't be wholly surprising." I turned to face her. "He's worn down, but why would they wear him down that much and not have a physician heal him?"

Coline had lived in Serre for a time. She knew more than me.

"If he disobeyed or betrayed them." She shook her head. "I have a cousin who is a physician, but I haven't spoken to him in ages."

"Physician du Guay wore down one of his hacks on purpose after finding out he was a part of Laurel," I said. I had only been able to read that letter from Emilie once. "We need to find out if that's what's happening to Gabriel or if it's something else."

She nodded. "How? We're stuck here."

"What if I told you I had agreed to help some people scry," I said slowly. "And that maybe it's related to that?"

A hack kid serving a chevalier would make a great spy.

Her hands fisted at her sides. "Some people?"

"People trying to help Demeine."

"If you told me that," said Coline, "then I would like you much more than I did yesterday, and I would say we have a lot of work to do. Laurel had gained quite a lot of ground in Segance and was working with Madame Royale Nicole until the king arrested them all. I was lucky enough to escape. Others weren't. We can help them."

I froze. "Wait. How much did you like me yesterday?"

"Doesn't matter." She waved the question away. "Tomorrow, when Isabelle is back with us, and you're less whatever is happening with you, and we're on our own, we're figuring this out. We help. Even if we break the rules?"

What was breaking a few more rules compared to this? "We help."

We slept fitfully. Coline snored as she always did, her presence a comfort. I wasn't used to sleeping in silence, the root cellar always alive with sounds from upstairs, and Isabelle had become the sounds in the night for me. She slept rarely, sketching by the light of a hooded lantern most nights, the pages a soft rustle in the back of my mind, the sighs of her breathing like the wind through the cracks of the house I'd always known. There were no cracks here, at least none that I could hear. Money bought silence.

It unnerved me.

I woke up at dawn. Isabelle was only just returning from the infirmary, and I slipped from my bed onto hers. She sat, lacing our fingers together.

"Our father was sick before he died," Isabelle whispered. "I was seven, and our aunt and uncle told Gabriel and me he was getting better. That we shouldn't worry. Everything would be fine. So we didn't worry, and then one morning he was dead. I can't wake up and find out Gabriel's dead. I can't do that again."

"If he's about to die, then let's save him," I said. "We're artists. We're smart. We can do something, so let's do it."

She nodded. "Should we tell Coline?"

"No." I helped Isabelle out of bed and gathered up our bathing supplies. "She's too grumpy after waking up. We'll tell her later."

By the time we made it to breakfast, Isabelle was smiling. Estrel handed me the yellow-tinted spectacles when I walked past her, gesturing for me to put them on. I did, marveling at the room as some of the other girls must have seen it, and my stomach growled. Germaine and Gisèle took the seats on either side of Isabelle and me.

"What happened?" Germaine asked, voice soft.

Even Coline looked to me to answer.

I glanced at Vivienne and Estrel at the head of the table, laughing. "Nothing," I said. "I scryed after you left, and Estrel caught me."

"Caught you scrying?" Gisèle asked.

Germaine laughed. "That's not against the rules."

I shrugged and tapped the spectacles, but before I could answer, Estrel tapped her spoon against her water glass. She stood and dropped it with a clatter.

"Morning, all," she said, and magic flickered at her throat, pale and sunny through the tint of these lenses. An illusion. I hadn't noticed she hid her voice. To hold that all the time must have been exhausting. "I have so greatly enjoyed meeting most of you and must apologize that I haven't had time to meet all of you, but I hope to rectify that." She leaned against the table like we were never supposed to and stared at me. "I have decided to stay and help teach the midnight arts this term. Power and rebellion often go hand in hand, and it would be far too dangerous to leave you all on your own."

I leaned forward too, able to see the world plainly for the first time in days, and my mind blessedly clear.

I knew what I had to do.

ELEVEN

Emilie

W e woke at dawn every day. Laurence required that we attend morning rounds with him at one of the Delest clinics, teaching us the basics through example. Our school sessions were over, the education of hacks largely lacking in academia and built solely upon practical experience, and we would remain with Laurence's group until they returned to work in Monts Lance after the term was over. After an hour, Sébastien would lead Rainier away to work as his hack and deal with the patients Sébastien didn't want—inevitably, it was the children and pregnant patients, which suited Rainier fine. I was always stuck competing with Charles for Laurence's attention, gleaning as much as I could from over Charles's shoulder. We fell into an easy pattern.

"Mademoiselle Marie here has had trouble balancing and has experienced ringing in her ears over the past few weeks. Why do you think that is?" Laurence asked Charles and me. "But don't worry," he said softly to Marie. "I promise I do know what's happening, and you'll be fine."

"Growths on the nerves," Charles said, as I asked, "Both ears or only one?"

"Charles is correct; though, it wouldn't hurt to ask more questions." Laurence sat with Marie for a while, channeling magic from his hands to the nerves near her ears, and dealt with the first step of her recovery.

Charles glanced at me. I sniffed.

"Do you think your first guess will always be correct?" I asked.

He laughed. "I suppose high intelligence would appear to be guessing to some."

By the end of the first week, Charles was winning, and he was insufferable about it. Not that he said anything; no, he never stooped so low as to mention our little competition. But he looked at me with his face all calm and unconcerned. I knew he was thinking it.

Unbearable.

"Now, Henry is an alchemist and several days ago cut himself with a small knife," Laurence said one morning as Charles and I stood behind him.

"Overgrowth," Charles and I said at the same time. I cleared my throat and added, "Overproduction by the vascular tissues inside of vessels."

Laurence nodded. "Very good, Emilie."

Henry, an affable white fellow with alchemistry scars stippling his brown skin and a head of thick, white hair, laughed.

Charles didn't.

"Stop baiting him," Madeline said one evening as we recovered from our day. "And don't say you aren't. You like being smarter than other people, and you've finally met someone who won't let you boast."

Physician du Guay, the most contradictory man I had ever had the displeasure of meeting, had selected Madeline as one of his hacks since she scored the highest on the exam; however, he refused to let her use the noonday arts. Instead, he was using her as little more than a maid or surgical assistant.

It took all the fun out of being jealous of her score.

"You're smarter than me and I don't fight with you." I was sitting on the windowsill, and the last dregs of sunlight were still warm against my bare arms.

She wrapped her hair in a silk scarf, carefully checking the hairs around her face. "I might be smarter than you, but you're smart enough to know that I'll win any fight we have."

"True." I pulled Annette's latest letter from my pocket and unfolded it, the scraggly ink of her words already fading. For all our writing, her penmanship was still atrocious. "Laurel put another poster up in Bosquet, this time about Waleran du Ferrant's excessive spending. Did you know the church funds the upkeep for the town and Mademoiselle Gardinier's garden? People are not pleased."

"Shocking." Wrapped in a thin robe, Madeline sat next to me in the window. "Physician du Guay is plotting something."

"Doubly shocking," I said. "Did Physician du Guay say anything today?"

This week, many of the older hacks had resigned with no warning, and physicians around Demeine had been left doing their work alone. The Laurel from the bar had said the original plan had been to organize a mass retirement of all hacks, but there were many who served the countryside. All the Laurels had voted against it; they wanted His Majesty to hurt, not Demeine.

"He counted us like a dog herding sheep." Madeline groaned and let her head fall back against the wall. "But no, he said nothing."

An unspoken tension pulled at all of us—the physicians inserted themselves into conversations any time they heard the word *poster*; they made snide comments about responsibility and idleness; they plastered up placards about the natural order of the world and how the abolishment of hacks would put undue pressure on the overworked physicians; and one physician had given a talk about how to budget one's money, but he had, absurdly, not bothered to find out how his own income varied from a hack's. He had advised investing with one's extra money.

Rainier had leaned over to me and whispered, "What's extra money?"

Beneath that universal tension, a singular worry tugged at me: I didn't belong here.

While I knew how much hacks were paid, the full hilariousness of the presentation was lost on me. It was as if, because of my upbringing, I had been staring out at the dark world from a brightly lit room. I couldn't see what was right in front of me because of the privilege of affording candles.

Which were, I had learned, very expensive. Madeline, Rainier, and I were spending a fortune on them, but there was no other way to study after dark.

Laurel's passive presence at university had snuffed out a light and showed several of us the world.

Of course, I wasn't sure Laurence du Montimer knew Demeine was on the cusp of trouble.

"Your free time is your business," Laurence said the next morning when Rainier asked for permission to go into Delest that afternoon. "I don't care what you do so long as everything I tell you to do gets done."

Sébastien sighed. "Please stop saying things like that."

"Yes," Charles said, nudging Sébastien with his elbow. "Laurence, you should really pay attention to politics more."

It was hard to hate Charles when he was so terribly bearable outside of our competition.

"That is hardly what I meant," said Sébastien. "We need less politics these days. Everyone takes things so personally."

Charles turned to glare at him, and Sébastien flushed.

"They do," he muttered, as though saying it again made it true, "and I don't want to get arrested because Laurence is bad with words."

"I can hear you." Laurence snapped his book shut. "What am I not paying attention to?"

I covered my laugh with a cough, and Charles glanced at me. He rolled his eyes.

Lord, he made hating him so hard.

"Laurel," Charles said with a shrug. "Have you even noticed all the posters and suspicion?"

Laurence groaned and made a hacking sound in the back of his throat. "They've stolen my name. Do you know how long it took me to convince everyone it wasn't me? I am intimately familiar with Laurel, trust me."

Sébastien rounded on Rainier. "If I find out you are mixed up in that nonsense, I will not hesitate to get rid of you. I'm not sullying my family name because someone is softhearted."

"Of course, Monsieur," Rainier said and bowed. "I will not sully your name, though I cannot promise that my heart is as hardened as yours."

"Leave it." Charles gently smacked Sébastien's shoulder and shooed him away with Rainier. "You walked into that one."

Laurence let Charles and me wander the infirmary. It was a

comfortable routine, the two of us walking in silence. Unlike the stifling atmosphere of the university, Charles and I felt no need to fill the void with idle gossip or assertions of our innocence, and the most we spoke was to exchange notes on a patient. We checked over those who were still recovering and stayed out of the other's way. Until today.

"Not like that!" Charles smacked my hands away from the young girl I was working on. "Too much power. You'll wear yourself out and them before you even notice."

I froze. The magic gathered in my palms dissipated, leaving a slight red flush in my fingers. Charles spread his hands wide, magic so carefully collected that I could barely feel it, and urged the skin along the patient's sliced arm to heal much more slowly. I had never bothered to take my time, but I had only ever healed myself before this month. It had never worn me out before.

The patient recoiled and wouldn't let me near them for the rest of our time there.

Before we left, Laurence held Charles back. I lingered, cleaning up the table slowly.

"I know you haven't been taught how to teach yet, but let this be the first lesson—do not correct people in front of others unless the mistake is dangerous or rude," Laurence said. "They will eventually be glad for the correction. They will never be glad for the humiliation. And never strike them like that. Did I ever do that to you?"

Charles shook his head. "Was it humiliating?"

Laurence cocked his head to the side and raised one eyebrow with the graceful aloofness of someone who practiced the move in a mirror. Charles groaned.

"Emilie, stop eavesdropping." Laurence patted Charles's shoulder and walked to the door. "Talk it out before supper, you two."

We stood, silent, for far longer than necessary.

Finally, I said, "You don't have to apologize."

"No, I do." He dropped his face into his hand and pushed his hair from his eyes. "I should not have slapped your hands. I just—"

"I know." I knew exactly what he had been thinking and probably would have done the same thing. "Remarkably, we are quite alike."

"I had noticed."

"Actions mean more than words," I said. "Please don't do it again."

"I won't."

We stood, silent again, and he cleared his throat.

"There's a public autopsy tomorrow if you would like to watch it," Charles said. "I'm sure Laurence won't notice if we're late to laboratory."

"I would like that." I gestured to the door. "Hacks don't get much in the way of real anatomy training."

The next morning, Charles met me at the infirmary with a box full of financiers speckled with tea leaves and blueberries. I hated sweets.

"Thank you," I said, "but you didn't have to."

"I definitely shouldn't have smacked you, but none of it was called for." He pushed them into my hands. "Please take them."

"Thank you," I said again because I had no idea what to do. Of all the hours I had spent learning propriety, my mother hadn't taught me how to handle this situation. "Would you like to pretend it never happened and go back to work?"

"Lord, yes." Charles let out a long breath and held open the door to the infirmary for me. "I enjoy our competition."

"Yes, I imagine you do." I slipped past him and set the box on one of the tables Laurence had stolen to use for supplies. "It must be so freeing to finally be able to show off your knowledge to a hack a year behind you in education."

"You're right." He smiled. "I should stop letting you answer the easy ones."

I glanced at him, eyes narrowed, and his smile widened.

"Are you the cadaver for the autopsy?" I asked.

"No?"

"I'm not sure I'm interested anymore."

He laughed and escorted me through the halls I never got to see in the section of the medical school solely meant for physicians- and surgeons-to-be, and we passed the rest of our time together in more comfortable quiet. The anatomy theater was small, and we sat in the back, out of sight of the other students. It was a more than bearable way to spend a morning.

When I got back to my room after work, a note was resting on my pillow.

4morn

I went alone. There had been no note on Madeline's bed, and if she were caught, the trouble would be greater for her. I stopped by the infirmary to grab the box of financiers—and make sure the guards saw me heading into the infirmary but not out of it—before slipping deeper into the dark streets to Bloodletters. It was the only thing the note could have meant, and if not, I had pastries at least.

I rapped on the door once. The girl from before, one of the Laurels, appeared in the crack, her eyes narrowed. She yanked me inside, and on a table in the center of the bar rested a small person whose entire right arm was drenched in dried blood. Laurel shut the door behind me and gestured to the newcomer. I dropped my financiers on an empty table.

"What happened?" I asked, already gathering magic.

"Save your healing arts," Laurel said, nervously fiddling with the locket around her neck. "This is another Laurel. They took a knife to the arm. You can stitch, right?"

"Of course." I peeled back the newcomer's sleeve, and they hissed. "How long ago was this?"

The newcomer winced. "Half a day? I was traveling for most of it."

"The blood has stuck your shirt to the wound," I said. "I'll need water."

I set to peeling the shirt away. The cut wasn't too deep or damaging, but it took long enough that I was only halfway done when they started up their third conversation over my head. They spoke about soldiers and quartering, unease in Bosquet which made me nervous, and a few missing old hacks they couldn't find. I used my healing arts, channeling it slowly into the nerves, despite Laurel's warning; there was no need for this newcomer to deal with the pain. They didn't seem to mind and muttered their thanks after the first few passes of the needle.

"Am I allowed to know your chosen name?" I cleaned out the bottom edge of the cut.

"Would you like to know a secret, hack?" my patient asked. "We're all Laurel."

"That's very confusing." I opened the satchel the newcomer had set before me and shifted through the supplies. "Have you ever had a bad reaction to pain syrups?"

"Yes!" They beckoned my Laurel over and held out their coat.

"The normal ones make my heart race, but I have an alchemist who makes me some."

Laurel searched through their coat until she found a small blue vial and handed it to me. I uncorked it, inhaled—amazingly concentrated—and handed it to the newcomer.

"That is very strong. Don't take it until you're ready to fall asleep or won't need to walk in a straight line for a while." I pointed to the financiers. "And take one of those."

Laurel looked in the box and whistled. "You sure you want to give these away?"

"I don't like sweet things." I hadn't wanted to tell Charles; it was a kind gesture. "And you definitely shouldn't drink any of that without eating."

"Yeah, she warned me," said the newcomer.

I cleared my throat and paused cleaning up. "You said there was unease in Bosquet?"

"I did." The newcomer looked me up and down, all the exhaustion leaving their face. "Why? That accent, you're not from Bosquet."

"No, but I have friends there."

"People are uncomfortable with some of the comte's new statements about Laurel." Laurel grinned. "Something's coming. We've got two people scrying for us, and Demeine's army and its chevaliers are on the move to Segance."

"The scryers gave me the whole guard schedule for Serre's barracks," said the newcomer. "I only nearly got caught because there was some sort of meeting tonight, and I wanted to see what it was about."

"We mean to be ready when it happens, and Bosquet's probably getting there a touch sooner because Chevalier du Ferrant's being ornery." Laurel put the box of pastries back in my empty arms and led me to the door. "We're going to needs hacks to heal us. You all right doing that under Laurence du Montimer's nose?"

"Yes." Change was coming, something good, something worthwhile. It was the least I could do. "Of course."

After that, Laurel called Madeline, Rainier, or me to heal her and her visiting Laurels often. I went more often than not, Madeline and I afraid of her being even the least bit conspicuous given what Physician du Guay had done to Florice. A few times I had noticed my Laurel with healed wounds or new scars, and I knew there had to be others at the university supporting Laurel. From the healing arts used, it was someone good—a powerful hack or physician's apprentice. Rainier and I never discussed it during the day, too afraid of the others overhearing us. The rest of the university seemed as equally on edge as us; Laurel's latest flyers had appeared without warning one day at noon.

LABORERS WORK SO THAT THEY NEED NOT
HACKS CHANNEL SO THAT THEY NEED NOT
SOLDIERS DIE SO THAT THEY NEED NOT
WE DON'T WANT TO FIGHT
BUT WE WILL
UNITE! ORGANIZE! DEMAND!

"He has no idea who puts these up," Madeline whispered to me as we got ready one morning. "I already told our Laurel, but he's demanded one of his older hacks join Laurel to find out who's behind it. The hack's about as obvious as a cat in a rat's nest."

"Good." I was growing tired of Physician du Guay's public shaming when no hack could provide him information on Laurel. "Let him worry over that for a while."

"What about you?" Madeline asked.

"Nothing as interesting," I said, using the phrase we had started understanding to mean I *didn't help Laurel last night*. "Charles and I are trying to isolate the bodily alchemistry that causes fever responses. It's going nowhere, but Laurence says that impossible tasks build character and make us think creatively. I would rather build a wall between my table and Charles's."

"Play nicely," Madeline said as we rounded the corner where we would part. "It's not as if you have to drink the ocean. You only have to work with him."

I sighed and shrugged. "I suppose."

Drinking the ocean might have been an easier task.

"Late night?" Charles asked, mouth twitching at my poorly concealed yawn.

I hadn't even been in the laboratory for one minute.

I rubbed my face. "Rewarding night."

If boys were allowed to be disheveled and tired-eyed, I wasn't going to worry. I had, at least, washed the grit of too little sleep from my eyes. I had used the healing arts with Laurel the night before last—she had returned with an arrow in her stomach—and my arm was still a little worn down where I had pressed it to her while channeling. The larger the surface area, the more magic I could get into her at once. She was lucky the arrow had hit no organs.

"Actually," I said, pausing by his table instead of continuing to my own. "I have a question, but I am going to say a statement before the question that sounds harsher than I mean it."

Charles turned and leaned against the table, the glass of his distillation setup jingling. "I love it when people have to add caveats before they even start talking."

"I already regret speaking to you. However," I said, ignoring his laughter, "I do not normally enjoy sweet things. Those financiers seem to be the exception, and I am curious as to where you got them?"

"Really?" Charles asked. "I thought opposites attracted?"

I tried to raise one eyebrow like my mother always did when annoyed. "Couldn't think of a better insult?"

"Give it time. I'm sure you'll do something ridiculous soon enough."

"Fine. Don't reveal your secret pâtissier. I will find them on my own." I waved him back to his table and set to rolling up my sleeves.

Charles followed me. "So you're not a sweet person?"

"No, I hate the aftertaste," I said, "and much like plants, my bitterness is a warning to leave me be."

"Fair. I shan't eat you, then." He grinned, but it lacked his usual crook of sarcasm. "Chef Vin, thankfully, is completely susceptible to bribery. They're saving up for their wedding. They work in Delest."

"Do they?" I said, drawing out the words. Oh, that was dangerous these days. "Do you think I'll die if I only eat pastries from now on?"

"No, you should definitely do that." He gently touched my arm, pulling away before I could even react. "Wrap this. Worn-out skin is weak and numb, and this is why most hacks die of blood loss. They don't even notice they're bleeding."

I glanced at the raw skin on my arm from healing Laurel. A few syrupy beads of blood oozed from the wound. "Damn. Thank you."

He walked back to his table, tossed me a bandage from the kit beneath Laurence's workbench, and went back to his business. I had only just finished wrapping my arm when the door to the laboratory slammed open. Rainier and Sébastien shuffled inside, Laurence looming behind them.

"Good. You're both here." Laurence locked the door behind him. "All of you have a seat."

We did. Silently.

I glanced at Rainier, and he shrugged.

It had to be bad. Laurence's coat was unbuttoned and flaring around his knees, and he twisted and untwisted the loose strands of his long hair as he paced before us. He normally put thought into his clean-lined appearance, and it wasn't the flighty, finicky, flashy look that most men at university spent hours perfecting and fussing up. Sébastien behaved as if he were the ideal, though—intelligent, wanton, a creative genius too busy to pick out his clothes or wash his hair. To be fair, he was a remarkable artist, but I could tell the ink stains on his sleeves had been made for show.

Laurence never so much as had a wrinkled shirt sleeve until today, and I was certain the ink stains were unintentional.

"Demeine, as of several days ago, has decided to attack Kalthorne and declare war," Laurence said through clenched teeth. "Ostensibly, it is to remove Thornish forces from our border in Segance and retaliate for their role in the small uprising that occurred there this summer."

"Ostensibly?" Charles and I asked at the same time.

Demeine was separated from Kalthorne and the rest of the continent by the Pinch, a sliver of water too wide and deep to bridge but narrow enough to see across, and Segance was a crescent-shaped strip of land on our eastern shores. Its northern tip had connected us to the continent at one point, but over time had been worn away by water. Now it was a line of small islands and watery settlements. A nebulous border with a dozen or so Thornish towns technically living on Demeine land.

"My sentiments exactly," Laurence said. "This will force a good number of people away from home, and while war generally does good things for the economy, that is because it does bad things for mortal life."

It would distract people from the problems of Demeine and give them a common enemy that wasn't His Majesty. It would move people across the country, breaking up established communication systems. Once a soldier, always a soldier; it was a crime to desert, so anyone who had been in the army and part of Laurel would not only be in danger but unable to help Laurel anymore. It was one huge, murderous distraction.

His Majesty would get us all killed, simply to protect his rule and squash a possible revolt. If most of Laurel died in the war, His Majesty couldn't lose—war hero, brief economic boon, and his adversaries would be dead.

If Kalthorne didn't crush us.

"People are going to die," Rainier said, voice unsteady.

Charles shifted. "It's subtler than a massacre."

"Shush." Laurence shot him a quelling look. "I must apologize to all of you. I did not think it would come to this, but since I already officially employed you all, we must answer the call."

There would be people from Marais fighting, people I probably knew. If they had a chance of dying, it was only right I took the same chance.

"When do we leave?" Sébastien asked, his voice wavering. "They'll evacuate Kalthorne civilians, right?"

"I don't know, and we leave in the morning." Laurence folded his lean body onto a stool and slumped over the table. "Take tonight to write home, pack, and do whatever you feel the need to. While we travel, I will teach you how to survive and channel during a fight. It will be our jobs to not only heal the wounded after fights, but keep the chevaliers alive during them. And Emilie, I am sorry. There are not many other women in the first groups being sent to the border, so you will have to make do with us for company, but I will make sure you feel comfortable. We will discuss it tomorrow." He waved for us to leave. "Go. Get your lives in order."

Rainier and I ran to the room I shared with Madeline. She was already there, pacing between the beds. Rainier practically tackled her. I let them mutter to each other and began packing my scant belongings. Physician du Guay wasn't part of the initial group being sent, and Madeline would not be there with us. She wished me goodbye.

I told them I had to take care of something in the laboratory, so they could say their goodbyes alone.

Laurence was in his little office. I pattered about the laboratory, not doing much of anything. I could write to my mother, but what would I say?

Oh, remember that thing you hate? Well, I did it, and now I might die.

That would go beautifully.

Instead, I wrote a letter to Annette asking her to scry for me if she could. Segance was days away, and she might not be able to see that far. She would likely be commandeered by the court to scry anyway.

If you have the time and health to do so, I would feel much safer knowing you are scrying and divining me, given the fact that such advantages are usually only for chevaliers. I'm not quite sure what will happen if I fall, but please feel free to take as much money as you can and run for it if it comes to that. If nothing else, it would give me a good laugh from beyond the grave.

What else was there to say?

The door creaked open. I folded the note into a thin strip and turned to see who it was. Charles saw me and sighed. I set the note aside.

"I need to talk to you," Charles said softly. "It's about something important."

I nodded. He had a little, unusual furrow between his brows. "Are you sick?"

"What?" He shook his head. "This is nerve-racking."

"Do you want to talk over tea?" I gestured to the kettle in the corner of the laboratory where Rainier had taken to making tea whenever Laurence wasn't looking. "My mother says it makes talking easier."

It mostly gave me something to do with my hands. I never knew what to do with my hands.

He laughed, not happily, and shook his head. "Thank you, but no."

"Is it about our competition?" I pulled out the stool next to me. "I know we don't get along and all, but I do enjoy it and since we are about to wander into a war, I want to make that clear. I do trust you as a physician and person. Probably more as a physician, but what makes you such a good one is your remarkable dedication to others. If you think us working together in a serious situation will be an issue, I assure you, it won't."

"That's actually why I'm doing this now." He sat and set both elbows on the table, his fingers laced beneath his chin. "I do trust you, even if you are the most insufferable person I have ever met."

"It's mutual," I said. "And only insufferable? Please, that's what everyone says—insufferable and stubborn. You can do better than that."

He laughed softly, but his body tensed. "When I was born, the physician and my parents assumed I was female. I am not. I have always been more dawn than dusk."

Annette's words—so similar, so long ago—came back to me. She had been asking me if I was a lady, and I hadn't understood, had never heard the words or thought on them. How isolated I had been. How foolish.

Henry XII wasn't only attempting to corral girls, but anyone not like him. Even outside of magic, anyone who didn't fit neatly into the ideals of Lord Sun and Mistress Moon—and only ever those two options—wasn't really a part of Demeine.

"My parents are overjoyed they have a son, and I am lucky I found dear friends in Sébastien and Laurence. They, and now you, are the only ones who know outside of my family. You are all the only ones who can know right now. Though, I am hopeful that the future I am working toward won't always be like this." He took a slow, long breath and exhaled, hand held up between us so I wouldn't interrupt. "I want us to be friends. I think, given time, we could be good friends, but considering where we are going, I wanted to make that clear in case anything happened. I hope I am right in thinking I can trust you."

"I want us to be friends too." I didn't say anything else. I let the moment sit and tried to think of anything, the best thing, to say, but what was there I could offer that he hadn't already heard?

Being a boy's not that easy. I would know. You don't understand.

Edouard was right. I didn't.

"It would really help," Charles said, "if you said something."

"Sorry. I'm sorry." I shook my head and held out my hand for him to take if he wanted. "Something someone said to me just made sense. I was too much of an ass to listen to him before."

Even without gathering magic, I could hear the frantic panic of his heart.

"Oh. Good. I think a slight subtraction of ass would do us all good." Charles took my hand, threading our fingers together.

I squeezed his hand. "Thank you for trusting me and also still wanting to be my friend. Perhaps my initial temperament was spurred by some small jealousy-like feelings I harbored, given my own desire to be a physician."

"The terrible truth comes out." He unlaced our fingers and smiled, still nervous. "Perhaps I antagonized you due to some choice comments."

I winced. There must have been so many people Demeine had discounted and erased who had come before me. If only scrying allowed me to punch my past self, then perhaps I would be interested in learning it.

"We are our own," I said. "Do you think the Laurels mean that more broadly? That we get to decide who we are, not Demeine, our parents, or the king?"

"Probably," he said, "and I imagine that anyone Demeine has cast aside would find a home with them."

Another thing I had never thought to ask.

"I won't let anyone find out, and if anything happens, I'll help," I said slowly.

He sniffed. "Good."

We lapsed back into silence, and I shifted.

"I'm not good at reading moments emotionally—my mother always said I had the emotional depth of a puddle during a drought—so this might be off, but do you want to find a practice hog and work on our surgery skills?"

"Absolutely." He raised one ruddy eyebrow at me, and his starry cheeks dimpled as he smiled. "Have you ever worked on facial wounds?"

"No, not really," I said and leapt off my stool. "Why?"

"Because I'm going to be so much better at it than you," said Charles. "They bleed atrociously and are common to see in the field. We need the practice."

"You've had a whole year more than me to practice," I muttered. "You won't be better for long."

He hummed. "We'll see."

Charles was much, much better at it than me. We worked for a good while, Sébastien eventually joining us around supper. By dusk, we were lagging, and Sébastien slapped Charles on the shoulder to pull his attention away from his stitchery.

"You have to write your parents before you leave," Sébastien said, "or they will murder us both."

Charles blinked up at his friend. "Don't be ridiculous. Laurence would save us."

We said our goodbyes until the morning. I walked slowly, not wanting to interrupt Rainier and Madeline's time together. I had never had a sibling or even a friend closer than an acquaintance, but Madeline might have been that if we had more time. Rainier too.

"Thank you," Madeline said as I entered the room. She was sitting on her bed with Rainier next to her, several leaves of paper between them, and she patted the bed next to her. "We're writing letters home."

"And to each other, in case we die." Rainier handed me a blank scrap of paper as I sat on Madeline's other side. She leaned her head against my shoulder. "Join us."

I fiddled with the pen, hooked an arm through Madeline's, and nudged her head off me. "No peeking."

She laughed but turned away.

I wrote the only thing I could think of to both of them to read in the event of my death.

Please, do not follow me.

TWELVE

Annette

It was easy being Emilie des Marais. I hadn't been before. I'd only been using her name and wearing her clothes and drifting through her life like a fake ghost in an ill-fitting costume, but I *was* Emilie des Marais here. I was a comtesse. I was powerful.

Madame Bisset cleared her throat, a thick ledger in her hands. "Now, what would you do with the leftover funds?"

I could afford the fall.

"Stop charging rent on my estate and hire a full-time surgeon for each area in the province." I had spent the last ten minutes working out the numbers, and Emilie des Marais could do that and still be making money every year. Not as much money, sure, but what else was she going to do with it? "Maybe a physician for the ports."

"Emilie," Bisset said in that calm, smiling voice most folks used for toddlers. "Why?"

Least she didn't question my calculations.

"Because I can," I said. "The point of living in a society is taking part in society. We make sure roads and bridges are well cared for, but not the people who need them? Not the people building them? Not the people doing all that work for me?"

"You already pay them." Bisset sighed. "The order of the world is as it is, and I don't know why you are so hung up on this aspect of your education."

I didn't shrug or scowl or do any of the things she would've used against me. I simply turned my head slightly and tilted my chin up. "I don't know how to explain that I care about other people's well-being."

I got in trouble, of course, but it was nothing compared to back home. I was a comtesse! They made me polish silver.

Not that we'd silver for me to polish at home, but it wasn't much of a job. Vivienne had written Emilie's mother. I almost felt bad about that.

Emilie, please, darling, stop misbehaving. I know you are unhappy, but I promise this is for your own good.

Emilie seemed to be getting up to about as much trouble as me. She was incapable of brevity, though.

I don't have much to say. There have been some curious goings-on here, and I suspect something big is about to happen. I cannot fathom a guess as to what, however, and while I am pleased that you have started studying under Estrel Charron, please do not send me any more of her research. Laurence was quite cross when he saw what you sent last week.

That had been the first page.

Of five.

And I got a talking-to from Vivienne about respect and elders and using my position responsibly, and I'd not even nodded to let her know I was listening. Emilie wouldn't have.

"Mademoiselle Gardinier," I said softly. "I appreciate how much you care for us, but I'd rather be responsible than respectful."

Vaser had asked for things. We'd asked nicely. We'd begged on bended knees. We'd been respectful when refused. But we couldn't ask nicely in the face of death. Respect only served who was being asked, and if they expected it, they'd reject any request as disrespectful.

"Are you going to hold people accountable the way you wish to be held accountable?" she asked.

I froze. That was a saying from one of Laurel's new pamphlets.

"Go to class, Emilie," she said softly. "Please do not fight with Estrel. She's far more likely to kill you, and it's only your first lesson with her."

I met Isabelle and Coline outside of Estrel's quarters. Isabelle paced, her gloved hands fluttering at her sides. Coline, too, was nervous.

"You're late," she said with a snap.

I snapped back at her. "Does snapping make me get places sooner?"

"Hush." Isabelle stepped between us, hands raised. The gloves were delicate little things of silver lace and white leather, and Coline had given them to her this morning. The wounds were well, but the scars were there to stay. "What's Estrel like?"

"Smart," I said. "More amused by what I did than angry. She talks like she's smart, and I couldn't understand all of what she said. She's flighty too."

"She's not what the court expects of women." Coline crossed her arms. "Laurence du Montimer once called her the worst sort of hummingbird."

The door to Estrel's laboratory opened, and she leaned in the doorway. "It's because hummingbirds are gorgeous creatures." One auburn eyebrow arched. "If you're going to gossip, at least gossip about the fun stories."

"Fun stories?" Coline spun the locket—the only jewelry she ever wore—and ran her short nails around the edge. "Like when you showed up to a party you weren't invited to?"

"To be fair, that party was a funeral Laurence du Montimer threw because he thought I was dead, but no one ever talks about that part." She opened the door wide and beckoned us in. "Wonderful food, though."

The room was mostly as I remembered. Soft, warm light crept in through the high windows on the western wall, dusk settling over the countryside like dust after rain. Estrel gestured for us all to sit at a long table in the center of the room that hadn't been there before, and I took a seat facing the window so I could follow the slow sinking of the sun beneath the twining body of the Verglas. Coline and Isabelle crept in slowly, glancing around at the boards and skeleton and tapestries. The glass top of Estrel's desk was half-covered in a mostly marked-off list of things to do. Isabelle sat across from me. Coline took the seat next to me.

"Now, I know your names, but I want to know what each of you can do." Estrel stalked to her desk, none of Vivienne's easy gliding, and picked up a set of four small bowls. "Why are these wooden? Why is the tabletop stone?"

I lifted my hand and left behind a greasy print on the marble.

"It's less bouncy," I said. Divinations I'd done in wooden bowls were smooth and clear, but in metal, they rippled. The magic jumped about between the littlest pieces of metals.

Estrel nodded. "I see what you were going for, Emilie. Thank you. Would anyone else like to try?"

"Metal conducts magic, more so than stone or wood." Coline's low tone sounded more like a reading from some old tome she found unbearable and boring, than from her. "The ethereal makeup of wood, the way its smallest parts are organized, prevents conduction and stops the midnight arts from leeching out of the bowls and weakening our arts."

Isabelle and I stared at her.

"As good an explanation as any." Estrel poured water into each of our bowls. "Power breaks the bonds of the world—the ones holding iron and carbon together to form steel, and the boundaries of time—which is what allows noonday artists to transform a sword into a shield or midnight artists to divine a possible future."

Estrel showed us the old scars on her hands. "Power breaks bonds and corrupts what it flows through, including mortal bodies. That is why many artists use hacks, but there will be no hacks here. Scry for me now. Show me what you can do."

We did nothing but scry—what color ink Estrel was holding behind her back, how many fingers she was holding up, what the note on the very top of her desk read—and I saw none of it. My hands shook against the bowl, and a cold pit opened up in my stomach. I felt as if I were continually falling. Sweat pooled along my forehead and chin. Estrel laid her hand on my shoulder.

"Stop. It's all right," she said. "Let's discuss portents."

Estrel pulled out a chart on different divination forms from hares to doves to snowy owls. We each had an eye to a telescope and were staring at the stars by the time she sent us on our way. Isabelle was painfully studious, trying so hard and channeling so much power without thinking, I worried a cut in my lip. Coline stared at me until I changed out of the fancy dress I wore during the day and into the plainest dress Emilie had.

"What's wrong with you?" Coline asked.

I shrugged, and that only made her frown more. "I can't divine."

We went to the baths and studied in our room, and after Coline and Isabelle had turned in for the night, I went to see Yvonne. The door to the kitchen was open, and she had divided the small building in half. One side was covered in glass stemware and narrow burners, jars and vials full of bubbling, sticky substances littering the tabletops. Each was labeled, and the controlled chaos of what she was doing lived in the taut line of her mouth as she measured the rate at which a clear substance bubbled in a vial. I waited for her to finish her notes.

"What is it?" I asked.

We hadn't spoken since I met Laurel.

"Nothing," she said far too quickly. "Let me show you this!"

She pointed me to the other side of the room and lifted a domed glass cover from a beautifully decorated three-tiered cake covered in thin white icing and peppered with edible petals. Balanced precariously on the top tier was a sugar-work moth that glittered as if made of glass.

"You're a pâtissier," I said, dying to know what the cake tasted like but wanting to save that moth forever. "And an alchemist who makes poisons?"

I turned and pointed to the apricot kernels she had boiling in alcohol.

"I have many talents." She reached behind the cake and the moth's wings moved.

I whistled. "Is it weird if you're my friend and my hero?"

"No," she said, blushing. "Hero worship does lovely things for my complexion."

"I know I'm not supposed to be looking at that," I said and rolled my eyes to the alchemistry setup. "But can I scry while you work?"

"I don't really have time to talk," she said. "Or make you food."

"You don't have to do any of that, and you can tell me to leave." I reached for Alaine's necklace and found nothing. My fingers itched. "I just need normal company."

One of her eyebrows arched, and the flour stuck to it snowed across her cheek. "Then by all means, Madame, scry away."

I scryed at a little stool and table in the corner of the room, thyme and rosemary branching above me, and the thick scent of yeast heavy in the air. It was almost like I was home, tucked in the root cellar, but there'd never been the threat of alcohol fires in Vaser. I muttered guard rotations and news for Yvonne to pass onto Laurel.

I slept uneasily after that, but the days fell into a steady pattern. I woke in the morning and bathed with Gisèle, Isabelle, and several other girls—Coline didn't like waking up earlier than she had to. Estrel slipped the gold-tinted spectacles over my face each morning, wearing hers as well so I wasn't alone, and they kept me from being constantly assaulted—*Stareaters scattering against a blue sky, boots splashing though a thin stream, blood seeping through crooked teeth*—each time I looked at silver. In class, I started answering when the teachers asked questions, especially in mathematics and household management. Gabriel, still alive, was a blank image whenever I tried to scry him.

Estrel kept me after the evening classes were over. The spectacles tempered my power, she said, and I needed them because, like her, I was very good at seeing the magic in things. Divining had always come easily to me, but not in useful ways. Estrel set me in the comfortable chair in her laboratory and shook her head. She didn't push me to scry.

"What on earth have you been doing?" Estrel turned my hands over in hers. "Your nails are purple."

I told her I'd helped Yvonne make red ink out of beets. She'd laughed, clapped, and asked me how we'd done it. Yvonne seemed pleased about that when I told her. She baked and titrated and passed on my news to Laurel. Sometimes we worked in silence, the comfortable type, and I caught her watching me in the reflection of my scrying bowl. Sometimes we talked about life.

I told her about my mother and that she hadn't tried to talk to me.

And sometimes, I tried to scry Macé, but all I saw was the magic-gilded smear of Serre, all the power held there too bright to let me gaze at it. He must've been a varlet by now. I hoped he was happy.

I didn't try to scry Vaser. If I saw them in some future, happy without me, I didn't know what I'd do.

My fourth day training with Estrel, I got a note from Emilie.

A dear friend has taught me how to scry, and while I have not accomplished it well, I will attempt it on the next full moon night at twilight.

Which was tonight. Letters were worthless; we had to figure out something faster. I wrote out a little note to her—*If you can read this, you're scrying*—and left it on my desk. At twilight, I sat before it.

An hour later, I scryed her and caught the end of her laughing about it. She looked well, if not tired, and on her bed was a glass tablet that read: *I know you're scrying this. Thank you.*

And that was how we spoke from then on. It went like that, day after day, classes in the morning, the midnight arts with Estrel in the evening, and Yvonne's warm company at night. Every night at twilight, Emilie and I scryed each other and exchanged quick notes. I made her scry first, and I spoke during her time, hoping she'd figure out the right amount of power to be able to hear me. She only ever caught bits and pieces, though. She was channeling too much power into the silver. It made the scrying harder to control.

But she was getting better, even if she was sneaking out most nights. If I didn't know better, I'd have thought she was working for Laurel too. Maybe she did have some sense.

All of it would've been easier if I could divine.

Least I was useful in other ways. Estrel got a letter one day from Pièrre du Guay, and I loosened one of my rings and let it roll off under her chair. Estrel ducked to pick it up. I twisted so I could read the letter.

"—reply immediately with what your scrying uncovers or you will be—"

Of course. The only part I'd uncovered was the closing and his threats to strip her of her titles if she didn't comply. What an ass.

Estrel set the ring on top of the letter. "You're very lucky I don't care about keeping his secrets."

"Sorry," I said. She smiled, but I could feel the heat spreading through my cheeks. I was too tired to work an illusion to cover it now. "Do you like being the royal diviner?"

"It's certainly a better job than an orphan from the Pinch's shores could have gotten normally." She pulled a pen toward her and started making a list of things for us to do tomorrow. "But I am still serving a crown who cares little for me as a person. It has its own unique problems."

"You're the most powerful artist in Demeine," I said. "You could tell them what to do."

"Emilie." She laughed softly and ducked her head. "The king is an excellent noonday artist with endless hacks and chevaliers at his disposal, not including the army he commands. I could, maybe, kill two chevaliers, but more would take their places, and by then, I would have worn my body completely down. Your faith in me is refreshing, but I am still only one very human person. To 'tell them what to do,' the court and chevaliers would have to be split up and dealt with only a few at a time."

Ten minutes later, in my room with Coline and Isabelle, my moth fluttering from one to the other before finally landing on my hand, I shut the door.

"I have a problem," I said. "I need your help."

Coline shoved a letter into my hands. "We are all about to have a very big problem—Demeine is declaring war."

THIRTEEN

Emilie

I t took twelve days for us to reach the Pinch. I tried to scry Annette as she had taught me, but the farther we went, the harder it got. The camp in Segance was large, crowded, and constantly moving, despite the uncertainty of what exactly we were supposed to be doing when. The first day, we settled in, me setting up my sleeping roll a few paces away from the small tent Sébastien, Charles, and Rainier were sharing, and Rainier and I organized the supplies that Laurence would need to run the infirmary. That evening, Laurence told us the first attack on Kalthorne, a surprise, would be the next morning at dawn. Charles and Sébastien were to heal Chevalier Waleran du Ferrant, comte de Champ, the mounted fighting artist who would lead the charge. Rainier would be serving as hack to Sébastien. Laurence, with me to help, would be in charge of keeping everyone else alive.

He made us go to sleep right after dusk. I was half asleep when Sébastien crept from the tent and waved to me.

He tossed a woolen blanket to me. "This is for you."

"Thank you?" I unrolled it—a very lovely, very warm blanket clearly meant as a gift and not some soldier's supplies—and spread it out across my legs. "Why?"

"It gets colder here at night than you're probably used to," he said, looking anywhere but at me. "It would be embarrassing if a physician's hack froze to death."

"Of course." I smiled. "Thank you."

He nodded and started walking away. "You're all right. Don't die."

I didn't freeze to death; though, it was a close call. Laurence woke me well before dawn, and I spent my time scrying Annette as I waited for orders. Rainier stopped by once to kiss my cheek and wish me well, and I hugged him for a bit longer than was probably necessary. I had not ever wanted a brother, but I wouldn't have minded Rainier.

Charles grinned when he stopped by and saw my new blanket. "Sébastien's nervous habit strikes again."

"Did he make it?" I asked, standing with Charles's help. "It's very nice."

"He made a very tiny hat this morning. Couldn't sleep." Charles offered me his arm, and I took it. "Did he tell you not to—"

A sliver of a shadow crossed between us. I squeezed Charles's arm, and he gently let me go. Laurence beckoned us both.

"Now," he said. "Quickly."

We took up positions along a stretch of land outside one of the Kalthorne settlements. The area had soldiers stationed about it, common ones and maybe a few artists who were in charge of keeping the peace and acting as town guards. The chevaliers, alchemical armor blots of power on the eastern horizon, motioned for us to move, and

I followed after Laurence. The silver bangle on my wrist grew hot, an itch burrowing through my skin. I glanced at it.

Nothing.

I gathered the last dregs of the midnight arts, even though it wasn't much, and focused on Annette—the determined glare of her brown eyes and excitement over having the chance to study. Her voice rolled down the back of my neck as though she were standing behind me.

"Oh, thank the Mistress, you figured it out."

I startled and nearly yelped. "Annette?"

"It took me all night to find you, but I'm scrying you now."

Laurence paused, walked backward to me, and pointed to my silver cuff. "Are you scrying someone who's scrying you?"

"She's scrying me," I said. "But yes."

"Good." He hummed and tapped the silver cuff wrapped around the entirety of his left ear. It was always impossibly full of magic. I didn't understand how his ear hadn't worn away yet. "Two midnight artists are better than one." He winced. "No, not you. You're obviously the best of the two," he said, waving his hands at the air as if he could shoo his midnight artist away. "Follow me exactly, unless your scryer tells you something different."

"You are scrying me. Badly, but still. I'm scrying the soldiers around you," Annette said in a tone my mother would have been exceptionally proud of. *"I can't divine the exact seconds you would need to anticipate an attack, but I can at least tell you who's about to attack you."*

"I am happy with whatever you can offer," I said. "Is Estrel Charron divining for Laurence?"

"Must be. I don't know anyone else who can do this."

Laurence and I hung back as the chevaliers and soldiers attacked. They tore through the guards around the city in a flash, Chevalier du

Ferrant only suffering a single slash across his forehead from an arrow. Sébastien healed it with a quick channeling. Laurence stiffened.

"Run," he and Annette said at once.

He sprinted down the hill to our right, and I took off after him. In the distance, a screech echoed across the land, black alchemical smoke pouring from town, and I felt the gathering of immense power. Blades stored with the noonday arts sparked as they hit each other, shearing off iron and igniting it. Fire flared where the chevaliers had been.

Thornish artists.

Something tore past my left with a whistle. Flames licked at my back.

Laurence healed a soldier's burned leg as we raced by him, and I channeled enough magic into him to get him moving again. We wove between trees and sheds, Laurence healing the worst of the injuries and me healing the easiest. A Thorne, hiding, nursed a twisted ankle, and I fixed that too.

Ahead of me, Laurence sidestepped left. I did too, and a volley of arrows rained into the area we were running from. Another whistle, another tightening of the magic around me. I could feel the world unsettling, hearts speeding up, veins tearing open, and I dove into the wounds without seeing who they belonged to. Deme, Thorne— none of it mattered if we were all dead. Skin was simple. It was almost always the same. Scabs bloomed as quickly as I ran.

"*Duck.*"

Laurence and I ducked at the same time, and another whistle flew overhead. I had never been interested in stories of valiant chevaliers, honorable battles, and the destructive powers of the noonday arts, and had no idea what we were up against. Laurence was untroubled, though. Prescient, he dodged left.

"*Right.*"

I darted right. Another bead of lead whistled past me, burrowing into the tree we had used for cover. The air shivered, and stored magic burst into the world. The iron sheared from the bead and, still lingering in the air, combusted. The oxygen rushed out of my lungs and into the reaction. Breathing grew heavy.

No, no, no—the mortal body produced plenty of things that decomposed into oxygen. Magic wove through Laurence's skin, and I copied his arts without thinking, dragging up fresh blood. Blood beaded across the palm of my hand. I cupped it over my mouth.

"*Three steps, you're out. Five steps, stop him.*"

One. Two. Three. Air!

Stop who? The world was chaos, and I was not prepared for this. A crossbow bolt caught a Deme soldier in the shoulder. Laurence dove for him, air hardening next to Laurence's forearm like a shield, and knocked another bolt aside. A chevalier's apprentice in the cover of a nearby tree took aim with a longbow.

"*Stop him.*"

I was a physician's assistant. I was never supposed to hurt anyone.

"*Look.*"

I glanced down at the cuff and saw a Thornish soldier running away, raising the alarm as they ran, a crossbow in their hand. They were retreating.

The apprentice's arm tensed. Alchemistry was too slow; I couldn't put him to sleep, but I was already in his veins and my magic coursed through him. An old scar on the back of his hand ripped open. Blood splattered across his face.

He dropped the bow and shrieked. Laurence whipped his head to me, his hands on the soldier who had taken an arrow, and I channeled more magic into the apprentice. This time, I healed the wound for good. Laurence's magic overpowered mine, snaking beneath the apprentice's skin. I turned away from them.

"*Safe.*"

"Annette," I whispered. "Tell me where the hurt Thornish soldiers are too."

She was quiet for a moment. She might have been gone. She might have been worn out. Then, "*Broken leg a few paces to your right.*"

I found them easily, and they scrambled back. Thank the Lord my mother had insisted I learn Thornish. I healed their leg and turned away. They ran.

Laurence, channeling magic so the branches before him had transformed into a sturdy shield, nodded to me. "Come. We've more to do."

He didn't mention what I had done to the apprentice or the Thorne fleeing, healed, behind me.

"*Fight's over. Artist dead. Chevaliers capturing people.*"

"Is it over?" I asked Laurence softly. It had only begun a little while ago, and the sun was a low crown atop the trees.

Laurence nodded. "Chevalier du Ferrant killed the only artist here, and the soldiers surrendered. Some will try to flee."

His unspoken *let them* calmed me.

Until another chevalier's apprentice tried to stop a Thorne from dragging an injured comrade to safety. Surrendering was supposed to put an end to the fighting and give time for healing. Laurence shouted for the apprentice to hold. They didn't.

Laurence channeled his magic into the dirt. The power slipped through the threadlike roots of the grass and fungi and shot up into the bodies of the three dozen people around us. They all stilled.

"Check the injured, Emilie," Laurence said, blood pooling in the mud around his shoes. "Now."

He was controlling the alchemistry of three dozen people and hardly breaking a sweat. I swallowed and got to work. The paralyzed soldiers creaked like dead trees in cold wind.

The Thorne had a spearhead in his shoulder.

"Leave it in," I told him, my hand steadying what was left of the shaft. It shook as he shook, and each jitter was a threat. "It's holding the veins shut."

"I'm going to let everyone go now," Laurence shouted, "and you're all going to help us with the injured because as you may have noticed, I healed you all. There's no excuse for such behavior in a quick fight."

It didn't take long to get the most injured back to the infirmary. Charles, Sébastien, and Rainier met up with us inside the long tent, none of them injured, and Sébastien helped Laurence clean the dirt from his face. Apparently, so the chevaliers said, the town had surrendered the moment their artist died.

"A blessing," Laurence said, slipping gracefully from his coat despite his shaking hands. "The apprentices already broke our common understandings and kept fighting after. Keep an eye out for them if we're in another surrender."

There were only three injured Deme, two injured Thornish civilians, and seven injured Thornish soldiers who Laurence was to heal after the chevaliers were done talking with them.

I was the only hack that could speak Thorne, and the physicians' apprentices were doing more important work.

"Please don't move," I said as gently as I could in Thorne. "Does anything hurt?"

The civilians were understandably uneasy, and one of them, as tall as Laurence and as rough as he was elegant, gestured to the other despite their own blackened eye. I healed the cuts easily enough.

Clot. Inflame. Proliferate. Age.

I didn't look at the guard looming behind me, but I *saw* him—a heartbeat and a half step away, a river map of coursing blood, a lightning bug against the backdrop of all the world's power—and the little cut on his cheek that he had refused to let Charles heal. Scabs and bruises, he had said, were a sign of a winner's battle. I entered his veins through it.

Small things, imaginary things like itches where nothing was, were easy to cause and easier to explain away. I had learned to stop them in my own skin; starting them in someone else's was nothing. He scratched at his neck and turned, looking for the insect he thought had bothered him.

"Only seven people here speak Thorne," I whispered, wiping the blood from their wounds and healing the worst ones. "The chevalier, the tall physician, the redhead and blond in orange coats, and me."

I wasn't supposed to fix the soldier's fractured ankle, but I did.

"Pretend it's still broken." I stood, hands dirty and trembling. "Don't let them know you can run."

When I went to wash my hands in the infirmary, Sébastien had finished healing one of the Deme soldiers and was wiping his hands with a clean white cloth.

Physicians are noblemen, and a nobleman's hands are clean.

"Would you like me to refill the basin for you?" I asked.

"My family hasn't worked with their hands in hundreds of years." Sébastien shook his head and huffed. "What could possibly be on them?"

He tossed the red cloth to me, the damp blood seeping across my clean skin, and left.

That night, tucked beneath Sébastien's gift and the silver cuff pressed to my chin as I cried into my hands, Annette's soft voice rolled over me.

"They all lived. It'll be all right. So many more lived than would've."

"We shouldn't be here," I whispered.

"I know, but you are there and I'm here, and we're going to save so many more."

FOURTEEN

Annette

R un."
My fingers had long since gone wrinkly and numb, but I was too deep in my scrying to pull them from the bowl. A country kid from a farm only two days away from Vaser was racing through the forests of Segance, a Thornish artist at his heels, and neither of them were dying today.

Lying was easy when it saved a life.

"Stop. Crouch. Don't fight. You'll lose."

They didn't know I couldn't divine something like that. Laurel had passed along the news that anyone who could scry had me looking out for them. This war might've been a distraction to keep Laurel at bay and kill some unwanted Deme citizens, but no one was dying so long as I could stop it. Deme or Thorne.

"It's safe. Run back to camp and don't look back."

I pulled away from the magic finally and sighed. Every night was the same. Our days had become a somber affair, the teachers shifting from how many flowers to buy if the duchesse came calling to how much spark was needed to set off a flour bomb.

It was a distraction, and it was working.

Bisset talked about how to manage lands during wartime depending on location, and it was hard and different at first, but after a while, it was easier. Soldiers got two square meals a day, folks got to take up the job they left—if they left one—and war needed a lot of things to work. Metal workers, farmers, messengers. For now, we'd profit.

And with over a quarter of the people either running away from the fighting or running to it, there was no one left to revolt. They were either conscripted, convinced we needed to take back Segance, or dead. Even Yvonne and I were too busy. No telling where the Laurel who'd been running Bosquet was.

Coline said it was overkill and laughed bitterly as she said it. "They want the people moving against the king dead, the people who might've listened to them distracted, and the king to play the role of hero."

Every day was the same too, but not as rewarding.

It was our job to make sure the king and his chevaliers survived to be heroes. Everyone else was a necessary casualty.

On our third day of war divining together, I yanked myself away from my bowl and pressed my palms into my eyes. "Chevalier du Ferrant's walking into an ambush. Throat slit. Physician with him gets attacked when he goes to help." I groaned, sure I'd never get the taste of drowning in my own blood—the chevalier's blood?—out of my mouth. "I'm getting real tired of red."

The physicians' red coats. The soldiers' red blood. Alaine's red hair still haunting me when I tried to divine. Red hands under white ice.

"At least yours are specific." Perenelle, one of the older students who studied the midnight arts, gestured to the array of portents on the table before them—the fall of ash, the curls of smoke, and the fresh splatter of a hare's blood on its white coat. "This makes me feel poorly read."

I laughed into my hands. Reading portents was a gentle terror. We knew terrible things would come to pass. We knew we could only wait and see if we helped avert them.

We laughed at everything and anything now, and my mind clung desperately to the sound.

The portents beneath Perenelle's hands were good at least. Estrel looked over their work and wiped their hands clean.

I stayed with her after every session. From dusk to three in the morning, Estrel taught me *everything*. We read through books and journals, her explaining terms I'd never heard and me flipping through pages till I got what she was saying. I wore her spectacles constantly, the headaches worse now, as if every future were knocking at my mind to be let in, and she let me drink tea and sit at her desk while I made list after list of questions. Some were silly, I knew, but she never laughed.

"When you're divining for the king and the chevaliers, do you see their hacks?" I asked as I was leaving. Our schedules were backward now. We slept for most of the day and were up for most of the night, so that the midnight arts were at their full power. My flickers of the futures were narrow. I only ever saw a single person, even now. They were clearer, though. "Do you see the whole scene?"

Do you see a boy too young to be there with hair like mine and hazel eyes? He's scared of mice and never been away from home, I wanted to ask.

Macé's future was tied to Chevalier du Ferrant's, and my divining was always unsteady.

"Sometimes." She looked up at me from her spot behind her desk. Estrel slept less than all of us, working during the day too. I didn't know where she channeled her power from in the early afternoons when all of Mistress Moon was gone. Estrel's powers seemed endless. "Why?"

"Do you warn them?" I asked, and she laughed.

"Darling, of course I warn them. The crown may have first rights to my skills, but I haven't forgotten who I am, and I'm certainly not one of them." She pointed to the great tapestry of Lord Sun and Mistress Moon on the wall of her office. "Why is the sun a lord but the moon his mistress?"

I shook my head. "Because they are."

"But why did we separate magic by them?" she asked. "There's no need. It's all magic. All power, only different levels upon a spectrum of power. Why do they divide people?"

"Because we're easier to kill when we're alone."

"Yes, but we are not alone."

On the fifth day, Physician Allard was on the name of every Thornish soldier I scryed, and I wrote each one down in excruciating detail so he could avoid them all. Two days later, I learned he lived. A Thornish house had burned, and due to my warning, he hadn't entered it to save the soldiers. I didn't scry that day.

I sat in the kitchen and helped Yvonne make all sorts of inks and tonics and drinks for the people at the front. She said it wasn't my fault.

"Have you heard from Laurel?" I sliced vegetables and chopped herbs, kneaded bread for tomorrow, and did all sorts of things

Annette Boucher used to do. We had a system, Yvonne and I, and it worked.

She shook her head and rubbed her cheek, smearing charcoal across her face. "They had to leave. Henric can still get some news to them, but I think it's over for now. It had just caught on, and there wasn't enough wood to keep the fire burning."

"Do you think Henric could get letters to common soldiers?" I wiped the charcoal from her cheek, and she scooped the diced onions from my board. The soldier who guarded the gate and had introduced me to Laurel, Henric, had been on edge of late. "Not only the ones working with Laurel?"

We had orders—who to scry for, who to divine for, what sorts of illusions we needed to work on in case they were needed—and they didn't include all the kids from our homes who'd gotten called up to fight or the hacks at death's door next to the chevaliers.

"Maybe," she said. "Why?"

"They deserve to have someone look out for them too."

Time passed a blur of working nights and sleepless days. Vivienne tried to keep the rest of our lives as ordinary as possible, as if some of us weren't waiting for letters with news of the dead. There were two girls here with fathers and brothers who were chevaliers. They'd taken to staying up with the scryers and diviners while we worked. Like at breakfast, they helped us hide our use of the midnight arts.

I ripped myself from a scrying—*hands red and blue and trembling before me as the spear came down*—and gasped.

"You're done for tonight," Gisèle said. She shoved a wadded-up cloth into my left nostril and gagged. "I can't fix nose bleeds with paints."

Gisèle was an excellent painter, and her cosmetics covered my dark circles and worn-out skin better than any illusion I could've created. I'd an eye to see where they'd been used but no skill at the art of creation.

"Worth it." I cleared my throat, voice raw. My bones hurt from how much magic I'd been channeling. "Soldier with Chevalier du Ferrant. I need to add him to the list of warnings."

Knowing it might not happen eased the ache in my chest. I could suffer through any number of futures with disemboweled soldiers and dead physicians so long as I knew they weren't set. Those futures could be changed. The people could live.

The next night, I was a Thornish soldier, her heart beating fast as the hooves of her horse, her black shirt plastered to her skin with sweat. Green lands I'd never seen sped past. Her fingers tightened on the reins. Steam rose from the horse in clouds.

A spear, transformed by the noonday arts and dripping with Chevalier du Ferrant's magic, tore through her shoulder and knocked her off her horse. Chevalier du Ferrant stood over her corpse and pulled the tag decorated with cornflowers from her chest. He set her aflame. They wouldn't be able to identify her.

"I don't want to scry for Chevalier du Ferrant anymore," I told Estrel as she packaged up all our letters.

She stared at me over the edge of her spectacles, bright brown eyes gold in the candlelight. "All right."

I could not live my brother's death. I could not live another loved one's death.

So I didn't. I never scryed Macé, I never tried to scry him, and my self-loathing shook my hands until my letter to Emilie was nearly illegible. He deserved someone better looking out for him.

A hack, black coat torn, bleeding out in the grass of Segance.

I ripped myself from my scrying and dry heaved the water that wasn't in my throat. I could feel it, seeping, but there was nothing there.

"Take a break." Germaine rubbed stinging, green balm into my worn-out hands, the power I'd been channeling the last few days finally taking its toll in a visible way, and she pulled the divining bowl away from me. "Do something that's not magic."

I was tucked into a corner of her and Perenelle's room. They'd pulled the quilts off the beds and covered the floor so that everyone could sit together. Perenelle, exhausted from storing the midnight arts in case we needed them during the day, was snoring softly in their bed above me. Coline, too, was asleep but jerking awake every few seconds and pretending she was fine. I coughed and nodded.

"You got the letters?" I tried to stand, and Germaine had to help me to my feet. "Thank you."

"Don't pass out," she said, leaning until she was even with my face, and tweaked my nose. "Here."

Germaine was the best calligrapher in all the school, but even better, she knew all the ways to make ink disappear without magic. We didn't want soldiers to get in trouble for distracting us.

I made my stumbling way to the kitchens and dropped a small letter on the table near the door. "More letters if you can get them out."

Yvonne hummed an acknowledgment. She was bent over the

table, measuring the dip of liquid in a cylinder. The liquid was viscous, not like water, and she'd gone off a few days ago about how precision for such small things mattered, how whether the top of the liquid curved up or down mattered. She was too busy to talk now, but watching her work was soothing. She was so sure of herself.

"Why don't you divine the hack?" she asked after about thirty minutes of wonderfully comfortable silence.

"Bad things happen when I divine." My Stareater was dead, probably, but there were new ones. They fluttered around the windows like dawn gone wandering, red wings beating against the glass, and I had not seen the white wings of one in days. Two lapped at the softly bleeding skin of my fingers. "It doesn't matter anyway. Divining only helps if you're near enough to tell them in time."

I shuddered, suddenly cold, and organized the little bottles of wound salve and fever tea into their crates. "Why do you sell water instead of these?"

"People trust hawkers selling drinks. You can't go wrong with water, but things can go so wrong with a coughing tonic," she said. "These aren't perfect. They're for soldiers and civilians. People like me have to be perfect when you lot only have to be good enough."

She sucked in a breath through clenched teeth, and I laughed, trying to make her feel better. I liked when she forgot who I was.

"I really didn't mean that how it sounded." She turned slowly. A smear of powdered cherries lined one cheek like a soft blush, and the skirts of her dress, ruched so they cascaded round her knees and left her free to dart from counter to pantry, twirled up a foggy puff. She'd shoved a whole tin of fruit breads into the oven before switching back to alchemistry. "You're not just good enough. I meant the world."

"You don't have to make me feel better," I said. "If me being here makes you tense, I can drop the letters off and leave."

"Don't you dare. I need someone who can see the midnight arts to help me." She held out a new crate of unorganized vials.

I smiled and took it. "I can do that."

Dawns later, I clung to the last rays of moonlight and channeled them into a still pond. I had stayed outside after visiting Yvonne, the garden a quiet calm. Estrel's spectacles were inside on my desk, and a flicker of red had darted through the water as I passed. I forced the magic into the water, fingers shaking—*bloody hands picking apart a bloody arm.* Someone shrieked. My concentration shattered. The image vanished.

I stood, glanced round, and waited. A sob, high-pitched and crackling with snot, broke through the silence. I followed the sound toward the main building. The familiarity of the voice bothered me. Coline or Isabelle.

Another sob. They blew their nose.

Coline would never cry where someone could hear. But Isabelle never cried or panicked. She got nervous, twitchy sometimes, and she cared a lot, but she was an unchanging pine thriving through passing seasons. I'd have thought her a quiet crier.

I pushed through the dark gray of a blackthorn. Curled up in the gnarled roots of an old, rotting juniper with bees thrumming in its empty trunk, Isabelle muffled her cries in the skirts bunched at her knees. A silver bowl meant for scrying sat before her. Would she even want me to see this?

It had to be Gabriel, but every time I tried to divine him, all I saw was death, and I hadn't figured out how to stop it yet. Every future, every attempt to change his fate, was smeared in blood.

"Isabelle?"

She tensed and looked, snot shining on her upper lip. "Why are you here?"

"Heard you and got worried," I said. "Want me to go?"

She dropped her face into her hands.

I sat next to her, not close enough to touch, and pulled the bowl into my lap. He was already dying. I'd only scry him for a moment, and nothing bad would happen. It took familiarity to scry, though, and all I had was Isabelle. So I thought of Emilie. I could still picture her, wide-eyed, passionate, and trying not to panic when she approached me in Bosquet. She had smelled of rosewater and money. All good intentions bundled up in bad history.

An image boiled to the top of the bowl. *A jagged bone stained red and spotted with holes.*

I dumped the water into the grass and set the bowl next to Isabelle. Vivienne had taught me well.

"It'll be fine," I said, hands shaking, though my voice wasn't. She couldn't see. "We'll find a way to help him."

Every future ended the same—with death. There were no warnings I could give. At least with divining, people knew it may not come to pass, but the blood in my mouth was the last gasp of a dying man.

"I'm a midnight artist," Isabelle said into her hands. "I'm supposed to know when death comes."

"Sometimes, the worst times, things happen and there's no reason to it at all, and all our little plans and artistries leave us with nothing but a pyre full of ash and head full of memories blowing away in the wind."

Ice. Cracking.

"If your brother's dead, we can't undo it." I couldn't do it again. I couldn't die in someone's head. I couldn't swallow back the blood or water or ash of their death that scrying gifted me. "But he's not dead yet, so don't make ghosts where there are none."

"I would do anything to save him," she whispered. "I can't stand being able to do nothing."

Isabelle was a good sister.

She deserved a good friend.

I rapped on Estrel's door. She answered, red hair in a fuzzy braid and silk robe hanging off her crookedly. The lurking death in me, the knowledge of it, the weight of it in my skin, was an ache so deep that even her spectacles couldn't keep it at bay. I kept them on anyway, and she led me to the cushioned chair. I pressed my fingers to the bridge of the spectacles, scared she'd take them off. I had nothing. Not really.

Families were supposed to love one another no matter what. That's what everyone always said. Mine didn't, not anymore, so what did that say about me?

"I divined my sister dying," I said quickly. "I was five and she was fifteen, and Maman wouldn't let me go ice skating with her because I'd gotten in trouble for hiding a broken cup instead of coming clean, so I filled her favorite bowl with water. Alaine was real good at scrying, and I'd seen her do it plenty of times. I wanted to watch her skate, but I didn't know the difference between scrying and divining."

I'll be back soon. I promise.

She'd flown, quick and poised, inky hair streaming out behind her and breathing a trail of fog in the winter bite. She'd always been so free. Untouchable.

"She fell through the ice. She was so cold, the water I was using froze over too, and I could feel her in me, all that panic and water and hope, but the creek was deep and the current fast, and her nails scraped against the bottom of the ice where she'd been skating. She held her breath for a long time. Long enough to tear her nails clean off." I closed my eyes and ducked my head. Water pooled in the curve beneath my nose and bottom of my chin. I covered my mouth with my hands. "I felt everything, and then there was nothing."

Estrel's hands curled around my wrists. Soft. Warm.

"The bowl broke," I whispered. "My hands were bleeding, and I coughed up water. I got scared. I hid the bowl under the house, and I didn't tell anyone, but they found Alaine when she didn't come home, and Maman found the bowl, and I didn't tell anyone. I didn't think it was real. It felt real, but like how nightmares feel real when you wake up."

All that time. Trapped under the ice. Alone.

And I could've saved her.

"I didn't tell anyone she was going to die. I didn't save her."

I sobbed for a long, long time till my face was hot and sticky, and Estrel left and brought back a damp cloth. She gently pulled the spectacles from my face and held the cloth to my eyes. I curled up, knees to my chest. I wanted to live in the dark behind my eyes. Estrel sighed.

"Thank you for trusting me with that," she said softly.

The bells of the observatory chimed midnight, and I ran my hand along the chair Alaine would never see in the school she would never attend.

"She should've been here," I said. "She was so good."

"Don't punish yourself for surviving." Estrel's voice cracked. What necklace had she kept so close, it wore her voice away? "It's not your fault."

If it wasn't my fault, it wasn't anyone's fault, and I couldn't bear that world.

"You're good, you know." Estrel touched my shoulder then my cheek, like Papa sometimes did when I was little and too sick to know who was there. She brushed my hair from my face and wiped the tears from my cheeks. "I've said it before, but your mind's twisting it into an insult every time. You're allowed to excel. There is such power in you that you could make Demeine tremble, and you shouldn't feel ashamed of that. You are not the people who love you or the people you've lost. They're parts of you. You are so much more than you've been led to believe, and you could be better than me. Don't limit yourself. Please."

"I can't be better than you," I muttered, unsure of what to do with all her words. "You're the best."

Estrel laughed. "Fine, but let's make you second best, agreed?"

I nodded.

"People are going to underestimate you," she said. "When they do, teach them not to do so again. They will not give you respect. Take it. Make them regret disregarding you."

I would. For Alaine. For Gabriel. For Macé. For Emilie. For all the rest I'd see.

For me.

The Stareaters scattered first, a red stain against the blue sky. I looked up and paused, and Rainier stopped behind me. It was late afternoon, sunlight and shadows stretching across the field where we had newly camped at the western edge of Segance, and the noonday arts shifted around me, as if a great hole had opened and was draining them away. I followed the tug and turned east. Rainier touched my arm.

"What's wrong?" he asked.

"You don't feel that?" I gathered a bit of power, channeled it through my heart to get it used to the rhythm, and sent my awareness out with it through the air and over the hill of tall grass. "Someone is channeling a lot of power."

Rainier and I were the only two at this edge of camp, save for the soldiers guarding it a little ways out. We had been in need of quiet, Sébastien and Charles tired and touchy after their days spent healing Waleran du Ferrant during fights so he could continue, and Rainier and I had a few free moments before our next shift in the infirmary. The shift in the noonday arts hummed in my bones, low and deep like distant thunder, and I shoved Rainier behind me. The hum built to a whistle, the air around us tight with power.

"Someone's fighting," I said. "Someone's using the noonday arts near the camp line."

"Fuck," Rainier muttered and grabbed my hand. "Come on."

We sprinted down the hill and into the thick patch of woods stretching before us, gathering power as we ran, and we crashed through a thin stream run through with blood and dirt. I hadn't thought to bring my bangle for scrying. Rainier turned upstream, and I followed. Shouts echoed through the woods.

And died.

Ahead of us, power condensed. Rainier sidestepped and so did I. A volley of arrows gilded with the fighting arts cut through where we had been, and the trees they hit burned from the inside out, the fire contained to their outer bark. I could feel the world unsettling here, hearts speeding up, veins tearing open, and Rainer stumbled into a copse ahead of me. A group of twelve Thornish soldiers had attacked the squad of soldiers sent out to scout. They'd been chased into this clearing.

Rainier started healing the soldiers before taking cover. The magic hooked into the skin of the nearest soldier, transformed the arrow in his chest into clean water, and healed the wound. Rainier wiped the sweat from his forehead.

One of the Thornes whipped to us, their hands empty of weapons, and hurled a small bead. The magic Rainier had been gathering snapped.

We were used to it by now.

Rainier pulled himself to his feet and followed my lead. We both sucked in aching breaths. I threw out a web of power, found a cut on the Thorne's hand, and sent him to sleep. The other soldiers, Deme and Thorne, finally noticed we were there. Rainier grabbed the nearest Deme soldier and dragged him away. His broken ankle snapped back into place.

"Go!" I waved Rainier on. Saving one was better than nothing, and he was already wearing out, the effort of fixing such a bad break burning through his hands. "Warn someone."

He nodded and pulled a vial from his pocket, opening it with his teeth and dumping it all down the soldier's throat. I gathered enough power to get the next nearest soldier up and walking. Pain ripped through my cheek.

The green glass vial in Rainier's hand exploded. His mouth opened in a little gasp of shock, the breath bubbling in his throat. I stared at his eyes, unable to look down, and Rainier collapsed behind me. An arrow trembled in his throat, and another had pierced his hand. Another ripped under my arm and into his chest. I fell with him.

"No, no." The arrow that had cut my cheek was in his throat, and I clung to the ethereal pieces of me in him. He was losing too much blood, but I was already in. I clotted the holes in his veins and arteries. I couldn't keep it long. His brain needed blood flow. "Hang on."

Rainier gagged and choked. Behind me, someone screamed. Horses broke through the underbrush, and magic poured over the field in a thick wave of the fighting arts. Demeine's army had arrived, but how could they be so late?

Rainier needed new blood. I channeled more power into him. If I removed the arrow, he would bleed out, but his neck was so damaged that I was certain he would need a new trachea. His body replenished his blood, using the alchemistry of mine to do it, and I sunk into my channeling. What parts of me made up a trachea? What could I take to make him a new one?

He let out a wheezing gasp. Stopped breathing.

No, no, no. I was fine. I just needed a lung. I could live with one lung if I—

"No!" A pair of arms hooked under my armpits and hoisted me up. "He's dead. Stop."

The magic I had been channeling broke. My grip on Rainier loosened. Laurence dragged me away from the fight, and I dug my heels into the earth. He lifted me higher.

A man in gold armor atop a golden horse raised his hands and killed every Thornish soldier with a single sweep of the fighting arts, magic turning the air in their lungs to ash. My shriek tasted like funeral pyres.

"I can fix him," I said. "No, no, Laurence, you can fix him. You have to. His trachea and his lungs and his hand. You can fix them."

He yanked me back a final few paces and kept one arm firmly around my shoulders. "I can't fix death. It nicked his heart, Emilie."

"We'll get him a new one." I clawed at Laurence's arm, and still he didn't drop me. "We can make him a new one."

"No," Laurence said softly, "the price for that is something Rainier would not want us to pay."

I sobbed. Laurence swung me up and carried me back to camp. It was alive with shouting and cheers, and he tucked me into a bed at the end of the infirmary. My hand was red and bloodied, the skin worn away, and an odd wound like that from an arrow in my palm. Laurence healed it and made me promise not to channel for a day. I only nodded.

A sharp, breath-stealing ache burned in my throat. Sébastien and Charles sprinted into the tent and skidded to a stop near my bed. Sébastien, eyes narrowed at me, slowed and opened his mouth. Laurence shook his head.

Rainier was the first hack to die in this new war against Kalthorne.

Sébastien sucked in a breath and turned to Charles who wrapped him in a hug. Both of them were worse for wear, hands twitching and skin raw from channeling. Laurence made them leave to recover Rainier's body and make sure he was cared for. I stared at the Stareaters above.

"Emilie," Laurence said, "listen to me—you cannot break your body down like that to save others. It will only leave you dead."

"Rainier's dead. What's the difference?"

He sighed and rubbed his temples.

A shout went up from the beds near the opening of the infirmary tent. Henry XII was certainly as handsome as a king was meant to be, and he spoke like he expected us to watch his face and not listen to his words. His hair was a sunny gold held back loosely with a gold tie, and his expressive mouth was easy to get distracted by. Each emotion, each scowl and triumph smile, rippled across his face like river water. Ice-blue eyes flickered from face to face. He spoke to each patient in turn, largely ignoring the hacks. His gaze glided over them the same way it glanced over scalpels or potentially interesting salves. He would have ignored Rainier.

He had. It had been so easy for him to stop that attack. Why hadn't he done so sooner? We shouldn't even be here.

Laurence clamped a hand over my mouth. "Do not say what you are thinking to him."

"Rainer and a lot of others are dead because of him," I whispered into Laurence's palm. "More will die."

"And saying so now will help nothing but your pride." Laurence removed his hand. "Why do you think I never talk politics?"

"Because you don't care."

What a privilege we nobles had to simply not deal with politics when they so rarely affected us poorly.

"Because when I did, my uncle didn't like my politics, and I'm not fool enough to think he doesn't have scryers listening to me now." He set one hand on my shoulder. "If you move against the king, he will crush you, and he will crush anyone he thinks agrees with you. He will gain popularity. Do you understand?"

I nodded.

Laurence hated politics. He avoided it, driving his peers to postpone passing laws as he missed court dates and ignored summonses, and I couldn't understand him saying this to me.

His Majesty spoke to everyone injured but me. When he looked up and saw Laurence, he threw up his arms.

"You were supposed to be healing Waleran," said His Most Bright Majesty Henry XII, King of Demeine. "You deserted your orders."

"My apologies. Two of mine were injured in the fight, and I didn't think you would require my assistance given your returned prowess." Laurence bowed, graceful as ever, and smiled at his uncle. "Congratulations on your victory, Your Majesty."

Returned? I glanced up, but Laurence's eyes were focused on His Majesty's feet. Henry XII, King of Demeine, had been a great noonday artist in his youth, his battle arts renowned, but he had worn out his body past repair during the war with Vertgana twenty years ago. So how had he channeled all that power today without his body collapsing? There had been no hacks with him.

"Come here, boy." His Majesty Henry XII opened his arms and let Laurence embrace him. He did not hug him back. Laurence hugged him quickly and stepped back. Next to each other, with Laurence not bowed, he towered over Henry's wiry frame, and

Henry reached up to touch Laurence's cheek. "You've got so much of your father in you."

They were so different that I had forgotten Laurence was His Majesty's nephew.

"Thank you," said Laurence, but he stiffened and slouched so they were the same height. "How did you find this morning?"

"Refreshing." Henry gestured for Laurence to leave and started walking away. "I expected more of them, but they put up an enjoyable fight."

At that, Laurence did look at me.

Trust me, he had said.

But what had he done?

I stayed in the infirmary that night. One of Allard's hacks, Louis, tended to my injured hand and throat. He was nice, clever, and if Rainier had lived, he might have been like Louis someday. It made the ache in my chest hurt all the more.

But the worst was when Madeline arrived. She wailed, the pitch of it digging into my soul and burrowing into my bones, and a shuddering, aching wrongness filled the air. I could hear her all the way across camp. I heard her sobs in my sleep, long after she had stopped. His death would hurt so many people.

It should have been me.

Laurence made me take a day off, forcing me to stay in my tent and sleep. He got in trouble for not healing Waleran during the fight, and even Sébastien had scowled at that. Madeline could not be moved from Rainier's corpse, and it hurt worse that she was not the only one grieving. A dozen had died. Sébastien brought her food. I brought her nothing.

I had let Rainier die. What could I possibly offer?

I didn't sleep. The nobles of camp took on a haughty, anxious air, as if impalpable armor had been slipped over their shoulders in the night. I wandered about when others fled to the safety of dreams and listened to what the chevaliers talked about—the attack that had left Rainier dead was the start of a real war with Kalthorne. It was as if the last days had been nothing more than rehearsal for a play, and the rest of the army was being transported here. Laurence had no siblings or children, and if he died, his title would revert to His Majesty's family once his mother passed. His Majesty seemed to have no problem having him on the front line, though.

Charles, too, had no siblings, and his parents had somehow already written him. Sébastien was the youngest of three.

"I'm the spare," he said, sneering, as he watched Charles fold up his letter. "They're much more worried about my older brother, the *chevalier*."

He said it the way most people said *no, thank you*, and I had never related to him more.

We were gathered in Laurence's small tent awaiting our briefing now that the war had changed. I stood alone where Rainier and I might have leaned against each other for support once upon a time. Charles, the only one of us who had been working for a full day nonstop after one of his soldiers collapsed a lung, was in the only chair. His red hair was stuck to his face in serpentine strands. Half of it covered his eyes.

"My parents and I will be very sad if you die," Charles said, hair fluttering with each word. "Laurence certainly will be as well."

I clasped my hands together to keep from pushing his hair back. Usually, he kept it in a knot while working.

"If it helps, Sébastien," I said, and it was the first time I had called him by his name and not his title, "if my mother knew I was here, she would be furious, but because I'm an only child and not because she likes me."

Sébastien laughed through his nose. "I should have known—you have the same brand of self-preservation Charles does. No one ever taught you how not to get trounced."

We all laughed at everything now. Sébastien had paid to have Rainier returned home, offering Madeline a seat in the wagon if she wanted. She had refused, according to him, and gone back to work with Pièrre du Guay. I hadn't talked to her yet.

I couldn't.

"We'll save so many more," Annette had said, but what was the point when Rainier was dead?

Laurence threw open the tent flap and slouched inside, a touch too tall for his own space. "We're leading a full-out assault on Kalthorne as of now. Segance was the start, and since it wasn't heavily guarded, His Majesty has taken it as a good omen."

All of us fell silent.

"Does that mean their artists are here?" I asked. A war with Kalthorne would last for years. His Majesty had made his name and set himself apart from his father as a war hero, and now he would be one again.

"Let's be honest for once with each other, Emilie," Laurence said, tone far more sarcastic than I had ever heard, and yet I still felt as if I were missing something. "We're going to try and conquer Kalthorne because it's a convenient distraction, and no one can overthrow the king when everyone is fighting, dying, or barely surviving."

Sébastien frowned. "How can you say that?"

"Easily because I am the premier prince du sang and duc des Monts Lance," said Laurence, the old Deme words for his rank making Sébastien flinch. "I can't get in trouble for saying so like others would; however, considering we're at war, I imagine all punishments will be rather grim."

He had, as Charles had once put it, gone full duc since his last meeting with Pièrre du Guay. His curly black hair was plaited back from his face, little spirals feathering out around his cheeks in asymmetrical strands as was popular, and his clothes were so well made that my understanding of envy had changed. His scarlet coat was open over a gray vest and white shirt, and for the first time, I could see the black lining was embroidered with little silver stars and red planets. The family rings had been hung from a fine gold chain around his neck. Even his gloves, supple black leather, had been branded with the Demeine crest.

"I would, of course, prefer not dying," Laurence said quickly, "but the people of Demeine and Kalthorne are worth my death if it comes to that."

"You're talking about treason," Sébastien said quietly, suddenly. "Our names would mean nothing for us or our families."

"And a lot of people would live." Charles tilted his head to Sébastien. "Do you want your legacy as a physician to be one of death or life?"

"There's no reason for this," I said, "so we're clear. This is a way to distract Demeine from Laurel?"

Rainier and I had sent word to the girl in the bar about everything we had and hadn't discovered, but we had heard nothing back from Laurel.

"Yes." Laurence laced his fingers together and held his hands before his mouth. "Keep with your jobs for now. As we move into Kalthorne, are we all agreed that our goal is to preserve life?"

We all nodded, and Laurence dismissed us. Sébastien returned to his tent, muttering that he needed to sleep before tonight. Charles and I returned to the infirmary. He had been working for far too long, and I went over his patients with him, doing any work that needed to be done. He followed, flipping his hair out of his face every now and then. His instructions were delightfully detailed without being condescending. By the time we were done, the back corner of the infirmary was empty.

I held out the ribbon I had used in my hair earlier to Charles. He glanced at it, wild-eyed, and then looked at me. I sighed.

"For your hair," I said. "You keep pushing it back."

"Thank you," he said, laughing, "but I held my arms in the same position for three hours and cannot lift them that high."

"Do you want me to do it?"

"Do you want to?" He raised one eyebrow at me, arch perfect. The ass. "If you would be so kind. Sébastien is terrible at it."

I stepped behind him. We were the same height, and he slumped a bit to give me access. I gathered up his hair in my hands, dragged my nails along the back of his neck to get the sweat-sticky strands, and pulled his hair into a loose knot. I tucked one of the too-short bunches of hair behind his ear. Charles leaned his head back to stare up at me.

"You're being nice," he said. His cheeks were pink as if from a sunburn.

I shrugged. "Perhaps I'm a nice person."

"Even you don't sound like you believe that." He yawned. "I don't hate you, you know. Not anymore. I always trusted you, but you were so…"

"Bitter?" I offered up. "Most people call me stubborn, but only when they want to be polite. If they don't want to be, they use *insufferable*."

"You treated your training as if it were a joke, as if you were the only one these societal rules affect," Charles said softly. "You sat in class as if it were a waste of your time."

I swallowed. "To be completely honest, every class excepting yours was a waste of time. There was no unified curriculum. It's a miracle anyone knows the femur from the fibula. Most of what we learned was self-taught after class. At least you answered questions and talked about useful things."

I could see the thought rolling through his mind, crinkling up in his brows and thinning his lips into one pouting line. He wore his feelings as well as he wore his clothes.

"Are you going to try and convince me that your terrible attention span has noble reasons?" he asked.

Why would I do that; I knew I was terrible. It was plain as day.

I shook my head. "I was only being a little smart with you. I don't handle surprises well."

"Good place we're going for that." He let out a deep breath. "I was only being a little smart with you when I called on you. I like to be taken seriously, and you irk me."

"That's the least insulting thing anyone has said about me."

"See how free you are with words?" He glanced up at me. "If your family name is Boucher, I will eat this coat."

"I cannot believe you're going to make me change my family name."

He snorted. "Come again?"

"I'm changing my name to Boucher. Not to make it all about me, but I would like to see you eat that coat. It would be hilarious and wonderful for morale."

"Your funeral, since it would make me sick and you would have to deal with me," he said, standing. "I'll vomit on your favorite shoes."

"I don't have a favorite pair of shoes."

"I'm understanding the insufferable comment now," he said, but he smiled when he said it. "Would you like me to walk you back to your tent?"

"No," I said, glancing around the mostly empty infirmary. "I might sleep here. No one can call me dishonorable for that."

I was supposed to share a tent with Madeline, and I couldn't suffer through her seeing me alive. Maybe they would think me a corpse and let me rest. Maybe they would burn me with the rest, and when I died, Rainier would wake up.

"That's not going to work for your spine or for tomorrow." Charles came back. "Come on."

"Is that an order, Apprentice Physician du Ravine?" I asked.

"I'm trying to help you."

"Everyone's always trying to help me," I said. "For my own good, they always say, but rarely is that true."

"Emilie," Charles said, holding out his hand. "You're in charge of my patients in the morning. It's in my best interest that you're well rested." He swallowed. "And you saw Rainier die but haven't talked about it. I want to make sure you're all right."

"I'm not," I said, taking his hand, "but thank you."

He walked me back. Sleeping there didn't help—I stared at the top of the tent, sweating in the late summer heat. Eventually, once night had settled over the camp, I crawled out of my sleep roll and made my way to where they were keeping the Thornes captured. The guards wouldn't let me near, turning me away since everyone was living, and I wandered on the outskirts with my face to the breeze and my nose full of ash. I couldn't see the pyres that were certainly burning in Kalthorne. A week, and so many dead.

A fly, iridescent and annoying, landed on my arm, and I brushed it away. Then another and another, and my whole head itched before long, even though I knew there was nothing there. The guards didn't notice. They brushed them away and paced.

But I had seen enough maggots to know what flies meant.

One winter, in the deep of night when fog rolled thick as snow and rain froze long before it hit the ground, one of the scullions had spilled oil on her legs. She was twenty-five and I was eight, and I had borrowed the mouser's kittens to keep her company. She couldn't move, and the physician had set up a little screen to separate her legs from the rest of us, meant to keep away contamination from the air. I had peeked, once.

I hadn't looked again.

"Death has set in," he had said. "We need to get rid of the flesh too far gone."

They had laid maggots against her burned skin and let them feast till the rot was gone and they could replace the lack of flesh with magic and bandages. I had helped with the maggots after that.

The flies, gently touched with power, had glowed gold when I looked at them.

I followed them. We were supposed to turn over the dead to priests for funeral rites, not leave them to rot on the ground. The flies led me farther from camp, deeper into Segance, and smoke stung in the corners of my eyes. Here, a house had stood, but Demeine had burned it down. I stepped through the remnants of a kitchen, candles flickering in the dark before me.

It was the king's tent. We were still far back enough from the lines and camps of soldiers guarding the new border, but of course he would want to sleep on Segance—now Demeine—soil. Cloth of white and gold fluttered in the warm night breeze, holding on the tent poles glittering in the light, and the expanse of earth between the tent and me was clear of guards. The golden glow of flies flitted through the air, streaking from ground to guards to grass. Shadows danced across the tent walls.

There was a great tug at the edge of my awareness, the one I usually ignored because it was simply my mind telling me magic was here, but there was no ignoring this—the noonday arts and midnight arts, every source of power nearby, gathered in the hands of artists in the tent. A line of thin windows, shaded and covered in a golden mesh, lined the bottom of the tent. There were no guards near me.

My skin prickled, uneasy, and the hair on my arms rose. I pressed forward. It was easy to slow the beat of my heart and soften my breathing. No artists would sense me, not with this much power gathered here. My boots squished through the damp muck beneath me, air filling my nose with the sickly sweet scent of rot and long-damp earth. No wonder the guards avoided this place.

I knelt and peeked through the meshed slits. His Majesty lounged on a cot, his back propped up by pillows. Physician du Guay was bent over His Majesty's right arm, the king shirtless and sweating still, and scars, twisted and deep, webbed His Majesty's skin. Welts crisscrossed his right arm, the flesh bubbling as if he had been held far too close to a fire. His channeling this morning *had* worn him out.

Greatly. The flesh was the frightening white of a burn so deep the nerves had died. The apprentices around du Guay—only two, each of them struggling not to tremble and neither thankfully Madeline— must have been the ones gathering magic. One of them had a hand on a young chevalier's hack stretched out atop a cot. Power, so strong it burned when I looked at him, threaded through his veins.

There were no other hacks in the tent. There were no guards. There were only nobles.

"They were warned. That attack this morning was a distraction so the Felholm homestead would have time to raze the fields. That's lost land and a traitor," His Majesty said. "I'm here to rip out the Thornes and retake the fields, not be king of a salt flat."

Pièrre du Guay pulled one hand up—the work must have been delicate if he was bothering with physical gestures to control the magic—and His Majesty slammed his free hand onto the table.

Pièrre gestured for one of his hacks to block the pain. "Apologies. There is more damage to the surrounding tissue than I thought. The bone has worn away. It will need to be replaced."

His Majesty exhaled with a low whistle and spat out a glob of blood. "How's the replacement?"

"Good, good," Pièrre said. "He's quite the artist, and this shouldn't affect your arts as much as the last one did."

A chill settled so deep in me, I was sure that winter had come. I lowered myself to my knees, mud seeping through my clothes. The flies, gilded from feeding on noonday artists' flesh, crawled across my cheek. I did not want to watch this.

This is your cost, Emilie des Marais, and it is your duty to pay it. Power demands sacrifice.

I gathered a few small strands of the noonday arts not quite pulled into Pièrre's gathering yet.

The hack was breathing and aware, but he couldn't move. I could feel his panic rapping against his chest. He could feel—Pièrre's hands along his ribs, the knife beneath his skin, the pull of power hooking in his bones—and couldn't do a thing about it. Pièrre and his apprentices set the work above him.

They removed his bones, his muscles, the threads of his nerves, and the little strips of yellow fat. They broke him down piece by bloody piece and built up the healthy tissue inside of His Majesty the king.

And the hack *felt* it. I felt it, my right arm burning.

I snapped the nerves in his spine, let my power eat through them as he breathed out. The panic softened.

I yanked myself out of his consciousness with a heavy cough and slapped my hands over my mouth. Eventually, Pièrre's apprentices carried out the hack's body and threw it into the dark, steps from me. There was nothing left of his arm, and the skin of his chest and shoulder had been worn away by the noonday arts. The bones they hadn't removed were nothing but dust, his common body broken to support a noble one. A slow, unsteady thump echoed in my head.

His heart—it slowed and stuttered and stopped.

I tried to channel the noonday arts through me, tried to restart his heart and dive back into his mind to keep him awake. Blood could be regenerated so long as bones were intact. But his were hollow.

Channeling power allowed an artist to control it, to use it as they wanted. By running it through their veins, it became a part of them, and it wore them down. His Majesty shouldn't have been able to channel the power he had today. But he had.

We are not our own.

They had undone the damage done to His Majesty's body, the damage that was irreversible after so much had been worn down, by replacing parts of His Majesty's body with a hack's. This was what Pièrre du Guay had been researching, had been testing, and they must have thought Laurel knew some part of it, so they needed a distraction. They had gone to war rather than let people find this out.

Laurel hadn't gathered enough help yet, but if people knew this, no one would serve the king again. Everyone would have backed Laurel.

And now I knew.

·CHAPTER·

SIXTEEN

Annette

I got more sobbing than scrying done the next few days in Estrel's office. I slept there that first night, the dam of my heart open and me drowning. Estrel wrapped me in an old, worn quilt and brought Vivienne to see me. They spoke in hushed tones, Estrel telling her that I'd revealed the traumatic event I'd seen the first time I'd ever scryed and that was why I hated the midnight arts, and Vivienne had wrapped me in a gentle hug. She smelled like ice and mint, and she muttered that it was all right. I shook my head when she asked if I had ever told my mother.

Maman knew, but I had never told her exactly what I had seen. I couldn't live with it. How could she?

"Can I stay here?" I asked. I couldn't let the others see me like this. Isabelle was already too worried about her brother, and Coline was busy with the other girls, organizing letters and plotting how to sooner warn the soldiers we weren't given orders to divine for.

They'd bigger things than a decade-old death to deal with. "I don't think I can sleep."

After Vivienne had left, commanding Estrel to let me take it easy, I'd lifted my head and said, "Teach me to divine. Please."

Estrel had sat next to me. "You need to deal with your grief as well. You can't just work through it. Trust me—it catches up with you eventually."

I wasn't running away. This was my normal run, and Alaine was right beside me.

"I need to learn," I said. "I need to do something. I'm not made to be still like this. Does that make sense?"

Eventually, she agreed.

She sat across from me, ready to stop me or shake me if I started coughing up water, and walked me through the steps of divining one by one. We divined gentle things at first. When chicks would hatch, who would walk the hall later, and what they'd serve for breakfast tomorrow. I cried sometimes. A lot of times.

Half of it was off, though. That hollow sobbing of knowing I should be sad but couldn't feel it. Like a burn so bad, it didn't hurt anymore.

Alaine's death had seared my soul so deeply, I couldn't even feel the pang of her loss.

"What's happening with you?" Coline asked after three days. "You've barely been able to do anything, you spend all your time with Estrel, and you come back with red eyes. You're acting like something has happened, and we're supposed to be your friends. What's wrong?"

"Remember how I couldn't divine?" I swallowed. My eyes were still that tight puff of crying, and I knew I was being unfair. "I got tired of not being able to help and told her what happened last time. She's teaching me to work around it."

"You've been helping more than most of us can," Coline said. She stared at me as if I were out of focus. "What happened the last time you divined?"

"I watched my sister die."

Coline narrowed her eyes at me, her mouth open in a little circle, and shook her head. "I thought Marian des Marais only had one child?"

Oh.

Oh fuck.

"I have to go," I shouted over my shoulder.

I reached Estrel's office as she was leaving. She took one look at me, sighed, and opened it back up. "Realized it, have you?"

I swallowed all the words I'd prepared on my sprint up here and nodded. She ushered me inside and shut the door. I didn't sit.

"I don't know why you're so nervous," Estrel said, sitting on one of the stools. The laboratory was clean and gleaming, the mess of our midnight arts gone now that it was four in the morning and time for bed. "But I would like to eat before I go to bed, so—" She held up her hands. "Who are you exactly?"

"You don't know?" It left me in a stutter, and I inched along the wall to one of the stools. "Why haven't you turned me in?"

"The fact that you believe I would is remarkably insulting," she said. "No, I don't know your real name, but I know you are not Emilie des Marais."

I couldn't look at her, but I heard the soft shuffling of her clothes as she rose, the rub of her shoes against the floor, and the soft hiss of her laughing at me.

"Since the moment we first spoke, I knew you weren't Emilie," she said. "You're as common as I am."

"Oh." I wrung my hands together, rubbing off the leftover stains of Yvonne's kitchen. Maybe she'd give me a chance to run. "How?"

"Your teeth. They're crooked and a bit stained." She stopped a few steps short of me and did a half bow till she could glare into my eyes.

I lifted my head. She pulled her top lip up in a sneer, showing off her own crooked front teeth.

"Rich people have enough money and time to get their teeth cleaned, bleached, straightened, and replaced by physicians, and there's no world in which a comtesse has your teeth. I've met Madame Marian des Marais. She's a perfectionist." Estrel inhaled a deep breath and blew it out through her teeth with an unintentional whistle. "They get their wounds healed, so they don't scar. They take their smallpox through the nose instead of in the arm, so no one knows they have to get protected like the rest of us. They have money to keep themselves healthy and happy, and they pretend they don't. You don't even know what to do with an extra lune much less all the money you're wearing right now.

"But mostly, you're me," she said. "Your accent comes out when you're tired. You walk as if your silk dresses are made of nettles. You stare at the silver as if you've never seen it before because until you were here, you hadn't. You stare at the food as if it's a mystery because you've never eaten before. You stare at the books and lessons and supplies in this school as if you want to devour them and keep them in you forever because you know this is your one chance. Ten years ago, I walked and talked and stared like you. When I told you I see myself in you, I didn't mean the midnight arts. I meant you. Whoever you are. I know the important parts of you, and I didn't need to know your name to know you."

I looked at her. "No one else has noticed."

"No one else knows our hunger," she said. "No one else has ever seen us, not truly, so they can't see you now." She touched my arm, voice soft and rough and sad. "I had no one when I was your age. No teacher, no family, no friends. So no, I'm not turning you in. You are my student, and that is a responsibility to protect and teach you that I will gladly take."

I could feel myself crying. Slowly. Quietly. No one ever wanted me.

"My name is Annette Boucher," I said. "I'm from Vaser."

Estrel smiled. "It's nice to meet you, Annette."

And I knew she wasn't lying.

Two days later, wrapped in the same warm quilt and sitting on the floor of Estrel's laboratory, moonlight streaming across the floor in silver streaks, I filled a bowl with ice-cold water and divined my brother. I held my memories of Macé in my heart—the sound of him snoring, the way his hand felt in mine when I walked three-year-old him around Vaser, the way he slurped his water from the cup and how horrible it sounded but how it was him, horrible or not. The water shuddered—*a soot-streaked hand gathered magic over a steel chest plate.*

The image rippled and ended.

Estrel leaned over me. "You're nervous. It's upsetting your art. Breathe and try again."

I nodded, and I let the chill of the bowl seep into my hands.

Macé, gaunt and sunburned, the clothes he was wearing a touch too big, and the frown he carried far too deep for his young face, paced along the outside of a tent gilded with gold ribbon.

"He's alive," I said. "He's alive."

"You divining doesn't make bad things happen." Estrel sat next to me. "Now, do it again."

"I have an idea on how to divine Gabriel," I told Isabelle early one afternoon after we'd woken up.

"Anything," she said. "I get nothing when I try. I'll take anything."

"I'm not great at it still," I said, but Isabelle cut me off.

"Don't do that." She didn't roll her eyes, but I knew she wanted to. "You're better than us. We know. You don't have to pretend you're not."

"It's because you are spectacular." Coline threw her head back and gestured as she said it, a perfect mimicry of Estrel's excited style of talking. "She thinks you're the next her. New her? How old is she again?"

"Twenty-four and waxing," I said. Her birthday was three months away, and I'd no clue what I could give her. "I can't be her anything since she's doing it still."

Coline dismissed me with a wave of her hand and nasally hum. "She finally has an apprentice, and she's delighted that someone knows what she's talking about when she teaches. She and Laurence du Montimer were at university around the same time, and they were the only people who understood the other's research. I heard he threw a chair at her once during a debate on the validity of the division between the noonday and midnight arts."

And I was back to not liking him again, except she agreed with him now. There was no difference. Same power, different amounts.

"You're being nice." Isabelle drifted into the room, arms full of paints but no brushes, and sat on the stool before Coline's window. "I've never heard you be nice on purpose before."

Coline pulled a locket from beneath her dress. "It was accidental, I assure you."

"Don't worry," I said. "I'll let you live it down eventually."

She opened the locket and shook her head. On the inside of the necklace was one small mirror with the sheen of a scrying surface and a lock of black hair knotted with a ragged leather strip. A lover's token.

"I store power in this sometimes," said Coline. "We could start storing it up and that might lessen how worn out the scrying makes you?"

"No." I shook my head and helped Isabelle with the tie to her painter's apron. "It'll wear down whatever it's in eventually, and we don't have time to store enough power to matter."

"We could pretend to be hacks. Gabriel and I used to—we would hold hands and see how far we could send an illusion of us walking down the road. Drove our aunt to tears." Isabelle dipped her fingers into opalescent paint and began to drawn the fringe of an orchid. She channeled power into her paints, letting it shimmer in soft illusions so the petals rustled in an imaginary breeze. "We could each do part of the scrying, so Emilie doesn't bear all of it."

I stared into the strokes of her flowers—*flies flecked gold with power gathering on the shores of Segance*—and the divining came easily.

"Isabelle," I said. "Is there quicksilver in your paints?"

She hummed. "Lovely color and keeps fungus at bay. So many of these colors tend to rot."

"It smells terrible," said Coline. "Open a window."

"You have any plain quicksilver?" I wrenched open the large window right behind Coline, who was doing nothing, and shooed the small gathering of still-silver Stareaters away. One, hoary with age despite its red, red wings, clung to my hand.

"No," Isabelle said. "Not here. Why?"

"Would an alchemist have it?"

"Probably." Isabelle nodded. "Almost certainly."

I nudged open the door to the kitchens. Bottles brimming with power—the power to lower a fever or fight back rot or scab a shallow slice from a sword—covered every surface. A pot of bubbling wax with the Chevalier du Ferrant's rosy colors sat on the stove, and Yvonne dribbled streams of it around bottles and vials to hold tight the cork tops. I rapped on the inside of the door to let her know I was there.

"I have not slept in forty-eight hours," Yvonne said slowly. "I'm afraid I will be terrible company, Madame."

I should tell her I was Annette.

It would be nice to hear my name from her.

"Let me, then." I touched her back, wished for a seat where we could rest side by side and work together instead of this awkward handoff, and carefully took the spoon and bottle from her. "Unless there's a secret alchemist way to do this, you should rest. I'm about to ask you a favor anyway."

She laughed, standing right next to me, and her shoulder brushed mine with each breath. "Ah, need to get on my good side?"

"You don't have a bad side," I said. "If you think you do, you need a new mirror."

"What do you want?" she said, smiling.

"Quicksilver, if you have any."

"Is that all?" She laughed again and moved to the little room off the main kitchen. "There's a minuscule amount in each of these. Not enough to poison anyone. It's excellent for keeping things clean, though, and I tweak it to make it harmless.

"Here." In one hand, Yvonne carried a small metal box that rattled as it moved and in the other, a large alchemistry apparatus that she poured like a pitcher. "Drink this and tell me if anything is off, and we'll call it even."

A crinkling layer of frost spread out from her hand on the handle, the light glow of the midnight arts a comfort. Ice bobbed at the surface, midnight purple and melting, of the copper cup. She shook the cold from her hand.

"What is it?" I asked. Floral and earthy, like blooming carnations crushed in mud, and the soft bite of something acidic and bitter at the back—black currants. I took a sip.

"Well?" Yvonne asked.

Wine? I swallowed what was in my mouth and stuck my tongue out, the bitterness clinging to the back of my throat. I sniffed it again—black currant juice—and ran my tongue over my teeth—dark wine undercut by something sweet. "It's an illusion?"

"Most of taste is based on what we smell, and I want to make medicine more palatable." She took the cup from me. "Also, I know you like illusions. Fun?"

"Very," I said quickly. I'd never even thought about making illusions with my other senses. "Can we talk about it one day when we're not falling asleep on our feet?"

She handed me the quicksilver box, and her frustration fell into the practiced, emotionless half smile I knew so well.

"I'll leave you alone." I laughed and turned to leave, rubbing my face. My eyes burned. "I should sleep anyway."

She always had to be on guard when the comtesse de Côte Verte was near.

"Wait." Yvonne caught my wrist in her hand. "You always do this. You leave when you know I'm working and need to focus, and I appreciate it, I do, but you don't have to always leave."

An odd, fluttery emptiness opened up in the pit of my stomach. Her hand still held my wrist, and I didn't mind.

"I want to stay," I said, and I grabbed her hand as she let go. "I like watching you work. It makes me feel like something's gone right in the world. But I have to do something now. I made a promise, and I can't put it off any longer."

Her narrow-eyed focus, the taut lines of her jaw as she gathered magic in her alchemistry, and how she scowled then smiled when something tricky went well. All the good in the world was here.

"Of course." Her head tilted to the side, and she tugged at one of the tight coils of her black hair, letting it bounce and then pulling it back down again. "Come back soon."

"I will." I clutched the metal box of quicksilver to my stomach.

Gabriel would too.

When the clock chimed four in the morning, when we knew most of the others would be falling asleep so the dawn light didn't keep them awake, the three of us—Coline, Isabelle, and I—sat in the bright light of our open window and filled a scrying bowl with quicksilver. Stareaters swarmed along the glass, wings thunking against each other as they scrambled into our room. A gibbous moon stared down at us.

"Think about him," I told Isabelle. "And when you have, channel all that magic and all those memories into me. I'll divine him. I just need to know him as you do."

Isabelle laid her hands on my shoulders. She didn't speak, but suddenly, laughter pealed in my head. Gabriel's laughter. Power rushed through me.

A gold sky. Flickering. My skin itched, but I couldn't move. It was too tight for me. To contain me. Magic pulsed through me, tugged at my bones, and settled deep. I rolled my eyes to the side. To see where the voices were. Muffled. Like sitting at the bottom of a river. Not a gold sky. A tent.

"It's not clear enough," I said. "I'm too close. I'm in his head. I need—"

I gathered up the moonlight arts spilling over me and thrust all of the power I could into the bowl. It shuddered. The image shifted. I wasn't watching it in the water. I was in the image with it.

I walked across the grass, looking down and seeing nothing where my body should've been. A girl knelt in the mud at the base of a tent, and my fingers passed through her shoulder. Emilie, the real Emilie, stared wide-eyed and horrified through a mesh window in the tent wall. I bent beside her and watched as well.

A physician laid his hands, glowing gold as the noonday arts, as the sun, as the flies humming in my ears, on Gabriel's arm. A knife slipped through his skin.

I gagged. Blood curdled in my throat, clotted and thick. All the magic, all the power, channeling through me dragged. It wore me down, ripping through my skin. Red tinged the quicksilver pink, and I reeled at the pain. A hand grasped mine, holding them to the bowl, and Coline gasped. She channeled some of the power through her, lightening my load. The pain eased. Welts rose on her hands.

But the image steadied.

I stood at the physician's back and saw Gabriel as he saw him—a catalog of parts, a collection of bone and blood and flesh ripe for the taking. He broke down the marrow of Gabriel's bones and pulled them out piece by piece. He felt the prick of Gabriel's pain in the back of his mind, and he pushed it away. He took.

And he gave.

I stumbled back, hands flying to my throat, and coughed up a glob of spit tinged red. The Stareaters fluttered to my feet and fed. A small, white mushroom cap crumbled to dust under the moth's prodding. The quicksilver seeped through new holes in the bowl. It was silver no longer, now a pale, pale red burnt at the edges, powdery and off-putting. It coated every crack in the floor. In my hands.

"We are not our own," I said, voice broken. "They broke him down and used the pieces to repair the king's injuries from channeling too much."

Coline leaned back against the wall, blanched by moonlight, and covered her face with her hands.

"No one will believe us." I turned to Isabelle. "I'm so sorry. I'm so sorry. I didn't know he would—"

Isabel, hands bloodied and face streaked with tears, shook her head.

"That is the future that will come to pass," I said. "And I don't think we can change it."

I crawled into my sleeping roll, didn't sleep, and rose to the scents of salt and smoke. For a moment, eyes closed, I was home.

"Emilie," a hoarse voice said. "Wake up. We need to talk."

I opened my eyes. Madeline, eyes red, sat cross-legged before me, her hands folded in her lap. The coat she wore had been Rainier's.

It hurt to look at her. I had no notion of what she was going through, and I could offer nothing. Anticipation leaked out of me in a clammy sweat, and I sat up, head bowed. She wrapped both of her arms around me. I stiffened.

"I need you to be my friend right now," she said. "I know you're sad, but he was my brother. I need you now."

"I'm so sorry." I threaded my arms around her, and she tucked her face into my shoulder. "What do you need?"

She pulled back a little bit. "I need some part of the world to stay the same. Do rounds with me?"

"Sure."

I tried to be the same as always but slightly less biting. Her torpor lasted a single day before anger burned it out of her.

"We shouldn't even be here!" She slammed her fists into her thighs. The tent we slept in was empty. "This is all his fault."

She meant the king, but she never said his name.

"He did something," I said quickly. I had tried and failed to find the courage to speak about it until now. "Something bad."

It was an understatement, but there were no words terrible enough to capture what His Majesty Henry XII and Pièrre du Guay were doing.

She settled back, legs crossed and skirts flared around her, and took my hands in hers. "With Rainier?"

"No, not during the fight. A few nights after." I swallowed and made sure there was no one else around us. "I know what the crown has been hiding."

I told her everything, whispering about Pièrre du Guay and His Majesty and the young hack they used to build our king back up, the hair on my neck prickling still, though I knew no one was around to hear, and Madeline's fingers tightened around my arm till I was afraid she would never be able to unclench them.

"I feel like I shouldn't be as shocked as I am," she said finally. "We have to contact Laurel."

"How?" I asked. "Everyone got scattered when this mess happened. It was exactly as planned—someone also found out, they created a distraction, and Laurel's whole system collapsed because people have to keep on living."

"Yes," she said, pulling me close. "They went through all this trouble because they knew that if people found out, Laurel would be the least of their worries. So how do we tell people?"

I shook my head. "I don't know. Let's start with what we know and go from there."

The next day, we were no closer to a plan. The war was still happening, the world still turned, and Madeline was stuck working with Pièrre every day. The only saving grace was that Pièrre's apprentices were too caught up in their work to notice that the hack channeling their art hated them. The three of us almost never left the infirmary for all the small works that needed doing.

I held a soldier's heart rate steady as she rebuilt a chunk of missing skin from his shoulder. Charles lingered at the foot of the bed, watching us work. He held up a thick fold of paper.

"Emilie, you have a letter from Bosquet." Charles held out a thin letter sealed with wax. A chromatic crescent moon shimmered with stored power above the seal. "Is that an illusion?"

I tore open the seal, and the crescent moon shifted into a single sprig of laurel. "Yes."

Staring at Charles from the corner of my eyes, I waited to see what he would say.

He only hummed and muttered, "You should probably burn that when you're done."

Charles followed us to an empty bed in the back of the infirmary where Madeline was cleaning. I glanced back at her and unfolded the letter close to my chest. She stayed on the opposite side of the bed.

Emilie,

If you do not see a crescent moon on the front, the wax seal holding our illusion was broken and this letter has been read.

I divined it. I saw it, and I saw you there. You've taken off the silver cuff, but I know what we can do. I'm doing something about it. I have been scrying this letter since it was sent. If you are amenable to helping, please touch your right hand to your nose. If you aren't, thank you very much for the money and education. You're dead to me.

"A bit much," I whispered and touched my nose. "Point taken, however."

"Here." Charles held out another letter with the same seal. "Messenger had specific instructions, but I am curious to a fault, so I tipped well to leave it to me."

"Thank you," I said, not meaning it at all. He laughed.

Well, at least someone was putting the family money to good use.

Good. That boy you saw was my friend's brother. His name was Gabriel. There will be no forgiveness for this.

I've been working with Laurel to scry for common soldiers and give them information about the court, and if we tell Laurel about Gabriel, they can tell the rest of the Demeine. Flyers, posters, placards—we tell everyone what they did to him. What they want to do to the rest of us. People may decide to believe it or not, but I think they will. We just have to tell enough people. We hope. That's what we need your help with—getting the word out. We can't leave the school.

Also, I've enclosed a letter for my brother, Macé. He's Chevalier du Ferrant's new hack.

I'm glad you're not dead to me.

"Me too," I muttered.

I tucked Macé's letter into my pocket. I gathered a few small strands of power, channeled them through my hands, and burned the letters to me in my hands. The ash, with a bit of material from my blood, I wiped away as nothing more than water. Madeline had come to stand behind me, and she took a deep breath. I nodded.

"We have a plan," I said. "Except…"

I looked across the empty infirmary bed to Charles.

He crossed his arms and smiled. "You really should be more careful about working for Laurel."

I felt the soft prickle of Madeline gathering the noonday arts behind me.

Charles must have felt it too because he held up his hands. "I have been informing Laurel of the physicians' and apprentices' movements for months. Brigitte, the Laurel from Bloodletters, told me you visited her."

Madeline's magic dissipated.

"But you adore Laurence and being a physician," I said. "Why?"

"Because Demeine is deeply flawed, and though it hates me, my family name provides me a safety others do not have. Demeine's society is a double-edged sword that I and many others do not fit into for one reason or another, and Laurel's goal is to make Demeine safe for everyone. A nation should be a shield, not a weapon," he said. "I won't lie. I was shocked you joined Laurel, Emilie."

That was when he had started trusting me.

"We have things we need to tell you," I said, glancing at Madeline. "But not here. Laurence's?"

Charles nodded.

I led us to the tent, Charles walking behind Madeline and me. She was about the only person I trusted there, but it wasn't odd now that I considered it, that Charles was part of Laurel. If he was lying, I was fairly certain the two of us could take him in a fight.

Probably.

Laurence's tent was blessedly empty. We made Charles enter first, and I nearly groaned as he grinned.

"This isn't a happy occasion," Madeline said in her flat tone. "Monsieur."

Charles sat down hard on Laurence's cot. "What's happened?"

"Pièrre du Guay used a hack's body as fodder to repair the king's wounds from using battle magic," I said. "He could feel everything, and when they were done, they left him to rot. With the amount of magic they channeled, I imagine degradation is accelerated. There were other bodies, and they were not fully human in how they were breaking down."

His jaw tightened, and a trio of wrinkles creased his forehead. His white skin paled till his freckles were nothing but flecks of rust on snow.

"We want to tell people," I said softly, "and we especially want to tell Laurel, if they can still get the word out. You know Brigitte?"

"Yes, I do. I knew the contact in Bosquet first, Aaliz. They were a friend of the family. They helped me..." Charles let out a deep breath slowly and rubbed his eyes. "I'll help. If people know, there will be no distraction big enough to make them forget."

"So, Laurel can help?"

Charles wobbled his hand back and forth. "The real Laurel—the ones who started it and said they would take the fall for any arrests— haven't been in contact with the others for several weeks. Brigitte was afraid they had been caught. Then, with Segance, she figured they were part of the group sent in. Laurel could be dead or in the infirmary for all we know."

"That's less comforting. What about Laurence?"

I couldn't imagine Laurence supporting this.

"He'll be fine," said Charles. "Leave him to me." A whistle came from outside the tent, high-pitched and cheery, and Charles cursed. "Act normal, and if anything happens, I'll take the fall."

He said it so easily, and I hated it.

I couldn't let him do that.

Laurence, whistling, threw open the tent flap and had his coat half-off before he noticed us. "How is it somehow always you three together when one of you isn't even working for me?"

Sébastien followed in after him.

"We needed someplace quiet to talk about things." Charles smiled at Laurence and got off his cot.

"Am I not allowed peace?" Laurence tossed his coat where Charles had been. "First His Majesty and now you lot."

Hypocrite.

"What did he want?" Charles asked Laurence and looked at me.

Laurence pulled a clean coat from the bag at the foot of his cot and shooed us out of his way. "Everything. Not to be surrounded by two hacks and one very nosy apprentice?"

"I am your favorite nosy apprentice," said Charles.

"Third at least." Laurence untied and retied his hair with shaking hands. He had been out all morning with another unit and opted to leave us behind.

Sébastien let out a low cheer and winked at Charles.

"I hope a tree falls on you," murmured Charles to Laurence.

Laurence laughed. "After years of teaching, it would be a mercy."

"You've only been teaching for three years," I said. "It can't be that bad."

"You have no idea." He showed us a strand of white hair. "This is all your fault."

"You look very distinguished, Laurence." Charles smiled, and it was clear how much he adored Laurence. "Like a sturdy, dependable mountain with fresh snow."

"Please never attempt to compliment me again." Laurence finished buttoning his coat and looked around at all of us. "We need to talk about how my meeting went." He pointed at Madeline. "You may stay if you wish, but it won't concern you."

"I'll stay." She curtsied. "Thank you."

"Well, firstly, everyone called me Monsieur le Prince, and secondly, His Majesty used my favorite phrase—*the opposite of the noonday arts*," Laurence said with all of the affection one usually reserved for dog shit on the sole of a shoe. "He wants me to find a way to store more magic in his sword and shield so he may use the noonday arts at night in the event of an attack, and I made the fatal flaw of suggesting he use the midnight arts instead."

The midnight arts couldn't be used for battle magic. They were too weak. Battle magic was strictly noonday, destructive and fickle. "Could he even do that?"

"Logistically, yes," Laurence said, "but personally, no. He's far too proud."

"No, I mean, can the midnight arts be used for battle magic?"

"Oh, yes, of course." Laurence shrugged and gathered power in his hands. "Most things don't have a natural opposite, magic included. The divisions are purely synthetic—for some reason, our world creates magic with lower energy at night. It's a bit like our alchemistry with sleep cycles if you think about it. As if the world is a grand beast waking and slumbering beneath us." He let out a great sigh, eyes glazed with the faraway look of thinking, and curled a strand of hair around his finger. "Transforming things at an ethereal level requires immense amounts of energy, so people use high-energy magic for it. Illusions and divining require more control and less energy, so there's no reason to use high-energy magic. All magic can be used for anything. You simply have to adjust to account for how much energy there is. And, of course, it's not all high and low. It's really more of a spectrum, like many things."

Laurence drew his hand through the air in a wave pattern.

"Eventually, the artists in charge categorized the arts into noonday and midnight," he said. "It's very misleading."

Charles glanced at me. "Would you like place a bet as to what sort of artists they were?"

"I don't take bets I know I'll lose," I said.

"Even Estrel with all of her little lists realized magic was high-energy and low-energy and capable of doing anything," said Laurence.

"I thought you kicked a chair out from under her when you discussed that in class?" Sébastien finally looked up from his journal. "My brother said it was hilarious."

"It was very much not hilarious, and that's not what happened." A slight flush reddened Laurence's cheeks. "Regardless, I got off track—His Majesty is hosting a small party next week once more of the chevaliers have arrived."

Madeline sighed beside me.

"Agreed." Laurence looked at Charles. "It's to celebrate our retaking of Segance and begin discussing our plans on taking the rest of Kalthorne. There will be a representative from nearly every major family in attendance."

My mother—where would she stand on this?

"There will be a simultaneous event in Serre to accommodate those families with members not serving currently or working as diviners with Mademoiselle Charron." Laurence's eyes flicked to me. "Emilie, you aren't invited. My apologies, but I imagine you will enjoy having a night off. You will have to cover all of Charles's and Sébastien's work. Understood?"

Oh, well, my gig was up. My mother would definitely be in Serre and so, almost certainly, would Annette.

I nodded.

"Excellent," Laurence said.

When he had left, I turned to the others and said, "In one week, we're going to use that party as a distraction. My friend in Bosquet is helping Laurel spread the truth to show people what happened, and it's going to be our job to get the posters out."

Before we died or I was caught, one way or another, the king was going down, and Demeine was not going to war.

Isabelle painted. She drew Gabriel's face in her journal, charcoal lines smeared and fading. She inked him onto the glass tablets we were supposed to use for work, leaving behind ghosts of him that materialized when the tablet caught the light, and sketches of him appeared in books and on tables. Gabriel, writhing. Gabriel, staring and unable to scream. Gabriel, the flesh of his arm pulled back to reveal the muscles and bones making him up. Gabriel, empty.

We found him on windows and bedsheets, in books and foggy mirrors on cold mornings, in blues and blacks and vivid, violent yellows the exact shade of the fat that had been under his skin. She drew him everywhere, each stroke of her fingers or brush or quill another line bringing him back to life. Dying a little bit every time.

Isabelle was an undercurrent of air, her presence like green-sky days when birds fell silent and lightning bounced on the horizon. Funnel weather, all power and constraint.

"Here," I said, setting a plate of savory and sweet pastries between us. "I can't possibly eat all of these, so you're going to have to help."

"No, thank you," Isabelle said, running her inky hands across a fresh canvas. Her fingers were a flag of dripping black, gray, purple, and green, and she painted Gabriel, his profile the mottled purple-green of a healing bruise, with so much care, it hurt to watch her. "I'm busy."

She had spent all day trying to perfect her shade of green for the grass outside instead of sleeping.

"Isabelle, I love you and I don't want to make you do something, but I remember how bad I got after my sister died and—"

"Really?" she asked, and her eyes rolled to stare at me. "Did you watch her die?"

"Yes. I did."

Grief was an old, familiar friend who came calling at all the worst times.

"Oh. Did it get better?"

I had lied to her so much that I couldn't do it again. "No. It got different, and eventually I got used to the different."

She hummed and went back to painting. Coline, still wearing her nightgown and a robe, looked up from her text on the fighting arts and made a motion for me to try again. I had told her my sister's death was a closely guarded family secret, and she hadn't brought it up again. I sighed.

"Isabelle, I'm going to hold this pastry in front of your mouth till you eat it, so either I'm haunting you with breakfast foods forever, or you're eating. Just one," I said. "You can't paint Gabriel if you're passed out from starvation."

"I'm not starving," she muttered, but when I held the food to her lips, she ate it.

Yvonne had made them. She'd the run of the one small kitchen and still prepared all the breads for the school, but it was slow work with long pauses. I spent the hours before sleeping with her, kneading bread and making sure it didn't burn, so that she could continue her alchemistry work. We'd finally found Laurel—their name was Aaliz, and they were five days away, stuck with their old unit training new soldiers. Yvonne's reaction to Gabriel's death had been quiet.

It did make sense, in a horrible way, once I'd thought about it. Coline was shocked it had happened at all, and I wondered sometimes if she would believe it if she hadn't been there. I didn't tell either of them we were working with Laurel. The revolt disbanded, still committed but distracted. It would be hard to rally people when the crown was playing war hero.

"Write exactly what you saw and send it to me. We can do this together," Aaliz had said in their letter.

"We can manage to make a few without anyone noticing, and you should send those to your friend in Segance," Coline said, not looking up from her book. She had been practicing illusions nonstop. "Aaliz will have to make copies for the rest of Laurel and send them out. Vivienne will definitely notice if we try to do that."

Serre—the crown was hosting a get-together for the important families of Demeine to celebrate taking back Segance and the plans for going forward. Isabelle and Coline were not invited. Emilie des Marais was.

Her mother, Vivienne had said, was too busy to attend, and so I was to represent the family alone. Estrel thought it hilarious.

I hadn't told her about Laurel or Gabriel or the king's hacks yet.

"I can help with some before I leave," I said. I poured a cup of cold tea from the kettle we'd all forgotten about and picked out the leaves. We would not be portents today. "Isabelle?"

At least she took the tea, even if she didn't drink right away.

"Good. You'll have Estrel with you, which is good. She likes you, and Bisset probably won't hang around you given your disagreements," Coline said. Vivienne was staying here. She wasn't noble, only useful. "I already picked out what you should wear, for which you may thank me later, but you'll either need to practice your illusions or take my cosmetics."

Seeing illusions was easier than creating them, and I much preferred portents and divining.

"Cosmetics," I said. "I think I'll have to wear Estrel's spectacles anyway if everyone's illusioned up."

Coline made a disgusted noise, and I glanced at Isabelle who would've laughed before.

She didn't now.

Yvonne was boiling down honey when I got to the kitchen. The sleeves of her blouse were rolled up, her skin ruddy from the heat. She laughed when I offered to help, but I didn't take offense. Emilie des Marais didn't know how to make syrups, so Yvonne must've thought my words an empty offer. I sat in the corner of the kitchen packaging up vials for Aaliz.

"Remember that apothecary I was selling to? The one you wrote to saying my work was legitimate?" she asked, voice biting as vinegar. "He's selling his business, and Mademoiselle Gardinier hired me mostly to help the head chef, but she knew I was looking for alchemistry work, and one of the people who came in to bid on the shop is an alchemist trying to make a line of alchemical agents to help counter and prevent dangerous reactions to foods and medicine."

She couldn't help her grin, even though she'd been scowling a minute ago.

I nodded. "You got a job?"

Her smile could've replaced the sun. "I'll need more training since I didn't go to university, but she was impressed by my theoretical knowledge and practical know-how. I'll be part of a team of other alchemists, university and self-taught. She was going to pay for us to travel to Amleth and study there since alchemistry's their specialty, but with the war, that's on hold."

Yvonne drew her hand through the air as if writing, and her eyes shone. Passion. Purpose.

Even in the middle of the mess, that was Demeine.

"I've wanted a job like this forever," she said softly. "No nobles, no hacks. Finally getting recognized for work. It could all go under, but it's something." She glanced at me, eyes half-lidded. "And she's one of Laurel's. I asked about her, and she was the contact in the north."

"Good." I pulled a violet from one of the dried bundles in the rafters near the door and sat at the table behind her. "I'll miss you, though, if you leave here."

"I won't be leaving quite yet," she said, sitting across from me. "Do you like violets?"

"I've never really thought about it." I rolled the stem between my fingers, feeling the gentle crush of it. "They're lovely, but seeing something pretty's never really spoken to me in the same way as everyone else, I think."

I swallowed, a fluttery worry in the pit of my stomach. Without precise words, talking was like drawing a map for a world you knew, but no one else did. You never knew if they'd understand your key.

"Oh." Yvonne reached out across the table, slowly, shakily,

and took my hand in hers. "We won't be able to talk for a while, though, and I want to talk to you. I like talking to you, even if it's only occasionally while we both work, or we don't say anything at all. I like spending time with you. Also, we might get arrested and executed next week, so this is it." She brought my hand to her lips and kissed my knuckles. "I want you to stay."

So I did.

Only Coline saw me get back to my room later that night. It didn't matter where we went so long as we did our work and didn't break any rules or leave the estate, so no one really cared. Isabelle was gone, probably painting out in the garden. We needed pictures of Gabriel in every pose and position so the illusion looked as if he were moving, and she refused to sleep until it was done. Coline and I had given up trying to stop her. Perenelle mostly sat with her now, helping with the paints. I'd written out everyone I'd seen, and Coline had even made an illusion depicting it to send to Aaliz before I left for Serre. The timing would be tight, but it was necessary. Everything had to be perfect. We couldn't afford failure.

I sat on Isabelle's bed. It was as far away from Coline as I could get.

"So," she said, drawing it out. "You're romancing the cook."

Coline was the sort of person who had the cunning to betray me behind my back and the arrogance to reap the rewards right in front of me, which was to say, she was as noble as any noble I'd ever met, eating my secret stash of biscuits on my bed without even laying down a cloth to catch the crumbs.

Which she'd done. And was doing right now. Metaphorically, as Vivienne had taught me in our literature class.

"I'm not romancing anyone." I knew what she meant—sex. People always meant sex when they said romance even though the two weren't the same. "Don't call her *cook*. She's a chef and an alchemist." I spun around. "Have you been spying on me?"

She let out a huge sigh and flopped back onto the bed. "I do love watching disasters unfold."

I knew her well enough by now to not take it personally. She was prickly with everyone. She was only funny-prickly with people she liked.

"But really," Coline said. "You're her superior. That creates complications. And you pick now? When we're on the cusp of war and revolt?"

"Like I could do it if I die tomorrow?" I scrunched up my face, hating the sensation but too furious to fix it. "You think you're superior to everyone, so how'd you romance whoever's hair that is in your locket?"

Coline didn't move or speak for a whole minute, and then very softly said, "I romanced her like one picks a rose—carefully and with permission."

"Is she the poet in the relationship because I don't think that metaphor works." She didn't laugh like she normally would've, so I sat next to her and softened my words. "Thank you for trusting me with that."

"I haven't seen her in months. She was arrested in Segance during Madame Royale's revolt. I'm living through you," Coline muttered. "And Mistress bless, are you boring." She rolled over to look up at me, her face as flat and emotionless as I'd ever seen it, and laced our fingers together. "We're not the same, but we must be allies. We shouldn't let the crown divide us. We're stronger together."

"We'll survive together," I said. "We will survive."

I lay down next to her. "Did your parents understand?"

"Not even remotely." She laughed and flipped over onto her stomach. "Yours?"

"I'm being merciful by letting her know now," Maman had said, hands on her hips while Papa paced the room. I'd listened at the door. "She'll have to learn to like it one way or another. She won't always have a family who will put up with her, and she can't make enough to survive living alone."

I shuddered.

I wasn't ever going back.

"No," I said softly. "You know that feeling when you miss a day of lessons and come back to all the other students knowing something you don't? Like you missed out on something everyone else learned and now you don't understand it like they do? That's how I feel about sex and attraction. Not that part of *me* is missing, but that my understanding isn't the same as everyone else's. I liked people in the past, wanted to romance them, but we had different meanings of romance."

Sometimes I felt like I was giving Demeine what it wanted. Men were lustful and women were controlled, the frozen calm of Mistress Moon that tempered Lord Sun's heat. But this wasn't control. I still *wanted.* Just not as some folks thought of want.

"There's nothing wrong with that." Coline laid her cheek against my shoulder. "You should talk to Alchemist Yvonne about it."

"Do you think if this works and Laurel does overthrow the king, things will change?"

"Yes. It's not only about money or the war or magic. All of those things are pieces of Demeine, and if we change them, we can change Demeine. Even the parts of it that feel set in stone." She glanced at me. "No matter what happens, we're family now."

"We'll survive," I said.

And Coline whispered, "We'll thrive."

·CHAPTER·
NINETEEN

Emilie

"D id Laurence teach you how to close sutures?" Charles asked, one hand still on a soldier's leg from where he had been cleaning a wound. The soldier had been an apothecary once, and it was safer, when possible, to close small wounds with physical rather than ethereal means.

I nodded. "Yes, he taught me physical suturing in Delest with Rainier."

His name pinched my heart.

"Good." Charles stepped back, his hand brushing my shoulder. "You can finish this, and I will clean up because"—he grinned, kissed his fingers, and flicked them up to the sun—"we are done for today. And we managed to save the best patient for last."

The soldier laughed and raised his flask to Charles.

"Of course, Apprentice du Ravine." I dipped my head down, not far enough to miss the roll of his eyes, and sat where he had.

Charles had already numbed the leg, and I could still feel the threads of his art in the nerves. I smiled at the soldier. "Please let me know if you can feel any of this. Otherwise, once it's bandaged, you'll have to keep it clean, dry, and watch out for rot like with anything else. The stitches I'll transform with some quick noonday arts once the wound has healed a bit. It will be like they weren't even there at all."

On any other day, I would have been thrilled to stitch up a cut or dive into the complicated alchemical tapestry that was the human body, but in the abyss of this wound, all I saw was the breaking of Gabriel Choquet. It had been as if some invisible force had picked apart his muscles and bones piece by piece. A gnawing fear had opened in me.

This soldier's skin did not peel back and vanish; the fat, muscle, and bone did not wear away; and he didn't die, heart pumping blood that was no longer there.

I hadn't been able to look at the posters of Gabriel's death when they arrived this morning after dawn, and I had shoved the disguised posters into the lining of my sleeping roll.

"It's very well done magically," Madeline said softly. Her usually bright brown skin was ashen. "It's like a nightmare trapped in paper and ink."

Madeline had watched the illusion play out three times and tucked one of the posters into the bodice of her dress.

I joined Charles at the back of the infirmary when I was done. He had gotten dressed for the party—such an abominable term for it—early and wandered the infirmary tent with me, pointing out things I might need to know. Everything in this tent was Laurence's responsibility, and we had made sure it was perfect. We could give no one reason to suspect us, which had necessitated telling Sébastien. He hadn't taken it well.

He had taken our plan better after seeing the placard this morning.

Charles ran a hand through his hair for a fifth time in the last minute as we pretended to work in the back of the infirmary.

"Stop messing with it," I said softly. "You look very nice."

"Thank you. For you to compliment me, I must look much more than nice." He dropped his hands and grinned. "That was even a *very* in there."

"Don't flatter yourself." I ducked and fiddled with my unbuttoned sleeve. "Words are cheap."

He snorted. "This suit was not, though."

He had foregone his orange apprentice coat for an evergreen suit with white shirt that brought out the freckles along his collarbone and didn't clash spectacularly with his red hair. Sébastien had told me it was the first thing Charles bought when he had been paid for his work as an apprentice. He had also demanded I not mock Charles for it. As if I would be so ill-mannered as to resort to insulting appearances.

"Yes," I said. "I don't think anyone could feel less than nice in it, though; even in the nicest dresses, I always feel more like a turnip pretending to be a person."

"And here I always thought carrot." Charles tucked a small journal into his coat pocket. He scowled when I laughed. "I have to have something to do during this, and you will not be able to convince me you wouldn't do the same thing."

I had done the same thing many times, much to my mother's chagrin.

I smoothed out the lines of his coat. "Translating ancient Deme anatomy texts during a party?"

"Sébastien and I make a game of it," he said and swallowed.

I leaned away from him and nodded. It was much better than that orange coat. "May I read it when you're done?"

"Why? Going to correct my translation?"

"Only if yours is very bad." I smiled and handed him a small vial of orange water I carried to clear my head after work. "Here—no one wants to talk to someone who smells like an infirmary."

He laughed, openmouthed, and tipped a few drops onto his fingers.

"You're late!" Laurence burst into the infirmary, words a hissing whisper, and beckoned for Charles to join him. "You are not getting out of this if I'm not."

Laurence du Montimer wore red velvet so dark, I might have mistaken it for black had I thought him inconsiderate enough to wear mourning colors to a celebration. The opal earring was not alone tonight—a collection of heirlooms glittered on his fingers in golds and reds, and a pair of dark brown leather gloves hid his hands.

Charles hummed. "If there are not at least two books hidden somewhere on his person…"

"Only two?" I laughed. It was nice, pretending I wasn't about to commit treason and maybe die. I whispered, "Be careful."

"You too," he whispered back and touched two fingers to his heart.

Madeline, grave-faced, found me in the infirmary several minutes later. We were not leaving a poster in the infirmary. We had only three—one for His Majesty's tent, one for the tent where the chevaliers held their meetings, and one for the post that nearly everyone passed every morning when walking about the camp. Our additions to this rebellion were mostly fear tactics since so many here were noble. It was the other camps that were crucial.

However, His Majesty had designed this war to tear us apart and stop us from working together. To stop him and this war, the soldiers would have to all agree not to fight. Only then could we hope to beat the chevaliers.

Luckily, though, Laurence's tent was near the edge, and we stopped in there and lit a few lanterns. Neither of us had any experience with the illusionary arts, and so we set up two coats to make it look as if we were studying. The setup cast two us-shaped shadows against the tent side.

We slunk out the back of the tent when no one was around.

The posters were heavy in my coat pocket. I had clipped the seam and slid them between the two panels of fabric for the coat, so they were hidden and easy to pull out. It was well after dusk, the darkness seeping across the horizon bleak and complete in this new moon night, and I walked with Madeline to the edge of camp toward where Gabriel had died. We stopped every now and then when people passed, pausing to look busy. There weren't many people on this side of camp. It was closer to Kalthorne.

A fly, young and golden, landed on my arm. I slapped it away, shuddering.

"We're close," I whispered.

It was almost comical—two hacks in black coats creeping through the bushes on bent knees, gilded flies flickering through the trees like hungry lightning bugs—the two of us crawling through the dark bushes toward a cloth tent of gold and silver. There were five guards now, and we stopped on the outskirts. They paced around the tent.

"This complicates matters," I whispered. I had expected three.

Part of our job here was to scare the king, but the other part was proof. Gabriel's body was rotting in the earth, the process accelerated and contained to prevent anyone from noticing. Somewhere, the metallic sun that bore his name was resting amongst his rotting uniform and degraded body. We had to find it.

Partly for Laurel. Partly for his sister. Annette had said her name was Isabelle, and I couldn't comprehend that grief. I couldn't comprehend how she could paint the posters.

"Here," I said, pointing. Two guards were circling the perimeter of the tent, avoiding the stretch of grass and ill-looking white growths between us. "I'll take care of them, but we won't have long."

"I'll get the name tag." Madeline sniffed. "Let's go."

I settled against the tree, back to the rough bark, and focused on the two walking soldiers. No magic flowed through them or any of the other three guarding the tent. It was easier to alter a person's alchemistry when touching them, but Laurence's lessons had been about necessity and not ease. I would not always be able to spare a hand.

The first guard was easy enough; his body was already upset with him. I channeled my power through me and flicked it to him like a whip. The lifeline between us burst to life, and I tightened my fingers into a fist against my stomach and twisted. His stomach gurgled.

"Well," Madeline said, "he's running. I don't know what you did, but he's running real fast."

"Good." I licked my lips, mouth dry, and focused on the second one. His laughter echoed in my head as if I were actually standing close enough to hear it. I had never met these guards, didn't know anything about them, and figuring out the right amount of nudging for his bodily alchemistry was difficult. He wasn't already ill. My own stomach ached. My ribs burned.

"Here." Madeline took my hands in hers and channeled more magic, so I could focus on the alchemistry while she controlled the power. "Let me help."

Madeline's channeling was a blessing. It was perfectly controlled and calculated, letting me slip back into the guard's body. My own nausea lessened. The guard heaved.

Madeline tugged me toward the tent, tearing through the grass in a rustle of skirts and fly wings, and I followed. I felt the tug of her magic lead her away, and I looked into the tent through the mesh vent. There was no one. I ripped up the spikes keeping the tent wall in the ground. She searched the field for Gabriel.

On the inside, the tent was even nicer. A thick flooring of reed mats had been laid down. The cot was wider and had a proper mattress, even if it was straw, and the sleep area was separated from the rest of the tent by a thick curtain of sunrise-red velvet. I pulled the poster from my pocket, folding and unfolding without looking at it, and walked around the tent. There was the table where Gabriel had been paralyzed. Here was the cot where His Majesty had sat while having a hack killed to save his arts.

It was like hiring a hack normally, except death had been faster and the exchange clear.

I felt sick for ever thinking it was fair.

"I want to scare you," I said softly, trailing my fingers along the wooden top of a desk. "You deserve to know Gabriel's fear."

He couldn't know it, not really. He would only be scared for a moment whereas Gabriel had had a whole life of living in the shadow of noble whims.

I unfolded the poster, crawled onto the king's bed, and broke down the roof of the tent above. It was easy; canvas was simpler than flesh and bone. They wouldn't be able to remove the poster bearing Gabriel's death. It was part of the fabric now.

An appropriate gilding.

The words were in the scarlet red of a physician's coat, and I could not bear to read the description of what had been done to him. Whoever had written this account had left nothing out. Every cut, every hurt, every horror was written out in exquisite detail. There was even a drawing of Gabriel with Physician du Guay leaning over him. Then at the bottom with Laurel's crown around the words:

The war is a DISTRACTION
Kalthorne wanted PEACE
HIS MAJESTY wanted POWER and
to KILL the people opposing him
This is what they do to hacks
This is what will they do to us
UNITE—ORGANIZE—FIGHT
We are not our own
But we are NOT theirs for the taking

I swayed and stepped from the bed. I raced back outside and redid the tent spikes. Madeline held up Gabriel's name tag.

"Did we actually get away with this?" she asked.

I grabbed her arm. "We'll find out in the morning."

We snuck back to Laurence's tent, broke the illusion on the walls, and settled down with texts on the noonday arts and anatomy. By midnight, the others had not returned. Madeline slept with her head on Rainier's bundled-up coat. She took it everywhere now. I nodded off with my back to Laurence's cot.

I woke up to Charles kneeling before me and tapping my foot. I blinked, sitting up.

"I'm assuming you weren't caught," he said, "and you need to go back to your tent, but you'll want to see this."

He pulled me to the door of the tent where Laurence and Pièrre were arguing several paces away. I narrowed my eyes. There was nothing unusual.

Charles leaned down and whispered in my ear, "Look for magic, not a poster. It's too dark to see here and probably until tomorrow."

There, stuck to Physician Pièrre du Guay's back, was one of Laurel's posters.

I had never thought Charles so bold.

I had never thought Charles so reckless.

"Lord, you didn't." Except here I was staring at it, and he had plainly done it. "He'll find out the moment he takes it off."

"Doubtful. His varlet may panic, but Physician du Guay is far too proud to let anyone know he was targeted," Charles said, dropping the tent flap and offering me his arm. "I hope the embarrassment doesn't kill him, though. Someone else deserves that honor."

TWENTY

Annette

Vivienne had given the maids sent with us strict instructions on how each girl was to dress and appear for the party—I still wanted to vomit every time I thought about some comte somewhere tossing Gabriel aside and then getting dressed for a party.

Even Estrel wasn't exempt from Vivienne's instructions.

"I'm sorry, Mademoiselle," the maid said, slicking back Estrel's hair into a tight twist at the back of her neck. "Mademoiselle Gardinier left me very specific instructions."

Estrel scowled. "Yes, I got her note."

Vivienne had left a lovely silver pendant on top of Estrel's clothes with a note that Estrel had read to me.

"Monsieur le Prince will be scrying from Segance, and you do not want to give him any more ammunition."

"Laurence du Montimer, despite his many flaws, has enough respect to leave my appearance out of our disagreements," Estrel had said to me as she set her spectacles atop my nose. "Some people aren't even worth your time. Don't bother arguing with the ones who don't see you as a person."

I smiled and nodded. "Do I look like a noble?"

"You look far too scared to be noble," she said, laughing. "Copy my expression and try not to gasp at the food."

"Plagued with shortages, and they got a whole roast out there I can smell and probably a dozen other things I've never even eaten."

I settled Alaine's crescent necklace against my throat. The gown Coline had chosen for me was a monstrously lovely thing of pale sea greens and blues, the silk softer than any of Emilie's other dresses, with pearls decorating the lining and hem, glittering across the turned-up cuffs. The half-moon neckline showed off far more than I was used to, but I wasn't some sunburned kid anymore. Weeks of Emilie's soaps and creams and indoor schooling without any of the work I normally did had left me pretty and smooth. Everything fit perfectly to me.

I could see how nobles forgot about important things. This felt like a dream.

I was not announced, my presence too symbolic for that and my importance nothing compared to the rest of the folks here. We'd arrived in Serre after dark, and the city had been nothing but looming shadows and yellow-toned alchemical lamps that made me think of Yvonne. Our rooms were huge, all stone and fur rugs. Estrel had promised to show me Serre properly once this was all over.

The hall, though, was all I'd hoped.

A great dome roof of woven glass and gold cast speckled evening light around us as we entered. Pillars of white stone split the hall in three, and tables spotted the floor. There were people. A lot of people. More people than lived round Vaser, and this wasn't even the entirety of the court. This was just one or two nobles from the families His Majesty liked.

They swished about, silk rustling over pale skin, and muttered in clipped whispers about how this was such a pity but such a blessing. We had gained Segance but lost some good soldiers, but oh, it was well worth it. No one had heard so much as a peep from Laurel. I followed behind Estrel, using her as a shield.

And then, the gentle pull of the midnight arts. A flicker of power awoke in the back of my mind, and I knew someone nearby was scrying me, trying to figure out who I was and where I'd come from. I spun and saw her.

Marian des Marais clutched a hand mirror in her white-knuckled grasp and headed to me. She was furious, but I only knew from the feel of her magic. She was painfully pretty and appropriately decorated, dark hair bundled up in a neat twist and white dress nearly glowing when the light hit it. She didn't stomp, she glided. It was somehow scarier.

I reached behind me and grabbed Estrel's arm.

"I hope you're hungry," I said, my mouth dry.

She spun back to me. "Why?"

"'Cause you're about to eat your words about Marian des Marais not being here."

"Oh no," Estrel whispered. "Of all the times to be sociable. Grin and bear it. If she tries to say anything, I'll stop her." Estrel wrapped one arm around my shoulders. "I promise."

I trusted her but couldn't help the way my legs tensed. The door was only a sprint away. The dress wasn't too bulky.

"Don't even think about it," she said. She moved to speak, but Marian held up one hand.

"You are certainly not the wild child I left with Vivienne," she said, smile sharper than any knife. "You look like a completely different person."

Estrel's hands tightened on my shoulders. "She's completely different and exceptionally wonderful, Madame, and I would love to discuss her progress with you."

I might've been about to die, but hearing Estrel say that made my eyes burn.

"How delightful." Marian held out her arm and gestured to an empty table near the back of the hall. "Let's."

She led us to the table. Estrel curtsied, form perfect. I'd never seen her do it before, and it drove the fear to my core. Estrel pulled out a chair for Marian and then for me, and she made sure there was a clear line from me to the doorway.

"Whoever you are," Marian said. "Let us get one thing straight—"

"No, I don't think we will." Estrel didn't even flinch when she interrupted the comtesse. "I'm going to talk first because I want to make it clear that if you threaten her, you will never have peace. The funny thing about noble power is that you only have it so long as people are willing to work for you. Do you understand?"

I glanced back at Estrel. Did she want to die?

"You cannot think I'm letting this go. Where is my daughter?" Marian's hands twisted in her lap, tearing at the spread of her paper fan. The illusion on it kept it all hidden, but the art she had stored in the fan showed it plain as day to anyone who could see magic. "Emilie has not been out in the world. She's not equipped to—" Marian brought one hand up and braced herself. "Where is she?"

"Segance," I said softly. Hearing she was in the middle of a war probably wasn't comforting. "She's one of Physician du Montimer's hacks."

Estrel inhaled at that. Marian looked as if she might be sick.

"She's fine." I held up my necklace, hoping the magic I'd stored in it would be evident. Estrel said one night wouldn't hurt me, and I needed Alaine with me tonight. "We write, and I scry for her so she's not hurt."

Marian bowed her head, covered her mouth with one hand, and closed her eyes. "No one thought to tell me my daughter was at war?"

"Emilie thought you would make her leave and have me arrested," I said. "She's a really good hack."

"Who are you?" Marian asked.

"Annette." My hands went to my throat, and I spun the moon between my fingers. "I'm from Vaser, and I was in Bosquet the day Emilie arrived. She saw me reading a flyer advertising that Estrel was in town, asked me to swap places with her, and it was too good to pass up. I wouldn't have been able to study otherwise. There wasn't money for it."

"You're the one who's been writing the letters to me, aren't you?" Shook her head, eyes rolling back. "I should've known. They were far too polite."

"Emilie told me what to write at first when she was still at university," I said. "She's getting all that money you sent too. That was for her. She and another girl were the only female hacks and had to pay for the whole dormitory."

Marian was quiet for a while and looked over me. "She's very skilled at the midnight arts, then?"

"More so than you can imagine." Estrel laid a hand on my arm.

I flushed a hot, splotchy pink, and Marian chuckled.

"Well," she said. "At least there's that redeeming fact. Someone is learning something."

"Annette is as gifted at magic as I am, and she has the mind for further education. If Laurence du Montimer hired Emilie, she is certainly as gifted in magic and medicine. Would you really deprive them both of learning how to control their abilities and risk them wearing down?"

"There is always that risk," Marian said. "And with Emilie using the noonday arts, that risk is far greater for her."

Estrel let out a little, awkward laugh. "No, you don't understand. Laurence and I, for all our differences, only teach people who are as powerful as us or could be, because given the types of magic we practice and the amount of power we regularly channel, it's dangerous if they aren't. If Emilie is with Laurence, she is far enough above other teachers, including the ones she would've had at Vivienne's. She would have worn out young, regardless, because of her innate abilities."

Marian tensed and eventually said, "You should not have threatened me."

"I'm sorry, Madame." Estrel bowed her head. "But we both know that in the current air, if you turn Annette in for thievery or impersonation, she will be killed."

"I'm not in the habit of having children killed, Estrel." Marian let out a large breath, shoulders slumping but only slightly. "I need to speak with Laurence."

"I can't do that right now," Estrel said.

"Don't play coy," Marian said. "I know you talk by scrying because letters are too slow. His mother says he complains about you constantly breaking his mirrors."

"That's his fault," Estrel said, sneering. "He's not channeling with the ethereal make-up of the mirror in mind and—"

Marian held up one hand. Estrel swallowed.

"Right. Sorry," she said. "I know he's scrying this meeting tonight to make sure the announcement is read for His Majesty. Give me a moment. I doubt he's noticed that his hack is lying about her name, so I won't give it away."

Estrel turned and pulled out a small mirror.

Marian sighed. "Do you like school, Annette?"

"Very much." I nodded and ducked my head. "I never thought I'd get to study everything. I thought I'd be a hack, but then even that was expensive. And the girls I'm with are nice. It was hard making friends in Vaser. There weren't many people my age."

"Do you like this dress?" Marian picked up the sleeve of my—no, Emilie's—gown and rubbed it between her fingers. "Emilie hated it."

"I like it," I said softly.

Marian laughed. "Good. Does your family know where you are?"

"No, they assumed I ran away." I didn't shrug. Vivienne would've killed me.

Her hand dropped, and she stared at me, face inscrutable, until Estrel turned back to us.

"Emilie is fine." Estrel turned the mirror facedown against her dress. "I'm not quite sure Laurence and I scryed at the right moments for him to catch all of my question, but he did say that 'Emilie Boucher is training to be my assistant, and that should be enough,' so I think she's doing well."

"Good." Marian's hands came together beneath her chin in silent prayer. "You are both sitting with me until this is over, and afterward, you are telling me exactly where Emilie is so I may write to her."

I nodded. Estrel bowed her head.

"Of course, Madame," Estrel said. "Let me get rid of Laurence."

She turned back around to her mirror. I peeked over Estrel's shoulder. The image in the mirror was blurry since it wasn't something I had scryed, but in it was a reedy man in red velvet. He held a silver mirror in his left hand.

"Why was I invited to this?" Estrel said, watching him in the mirror. The amount of magic channeling through her and into the glass made my teeth ache. "I hate things like this, and nearly everyone here hates me."

"I know." He was haughty, chin up and grin more sneer than joy, and he sipped a glass of red wine.

"I cannot believe you stooped to this level solely to annoy me," she said, tugging at the low collar of her pine-green dress.

He gasped and clutched his heart. "Annoy you? Perish the thought. I don't think of you at all most days."

"Who will you be scrying during the announcement?" Estrel looked out over the crowd. "Monsieur René du Ruse?"

"René." Laurence nodded, suddenly serious. "His Majesty is about to start. I have to go."

He pressed his hand to his mirror and the magic faded. Estrel turned hers over, so the reflective side was pressed to her skirt.

"Yours is a lot clearer than mine," I said.

Estrel laughed. "Laurence and I have been practicing this for years. You'll get better."

"And I could talk to you no matter where you were," I said. "Right?"

"Yes." Estrel smiled. "But I think you will be stuck with me for some time."

As if that were a bad thing.

Behind me, Marian cleared her throat. Estrel and I turned to face the rest of the room. A chime rang out.

Chevalier Waleran du Ferrant was certainly handsome like most nobles tried to be, and he spoke like he was the king. He was white-headed and gravelly voiced. I let my eyes unfocus so I could listen.

"My court, my friends, I come to you as the voice of the Premier

Noonday Artist of the Realm, His Most Bright Majesty, Henry XII, by the grace of our Lord Sun and his Mistress Moon, King of Demeine. This week, in the ninth month of our three hundred and forty-second year Past Midnight, we have finally taken back the land stolen from us by Kalthorne. Segance, once a home for our countrymen, was brutalized and wasted under Kalthorne's rule, but our people have been returned to us. I come to you tonight, though, with even more heartening news—the portents of Lord Sun and Mistress Moon have instructed us that now is the time to rid this world of this great Thorne in our side once and for all."

Estrel let out a growling exhale and stiffened.

There were no such portents.

"Our Demeine shall never suffer siege again but rise with the sun every morning and with the moon every night. Demeine will prevail. This treachery will never threaten us again." Chevalier du Ferrant threw his hands up as if in celebration or passionate prayer, and there was a soft cheer from the crowd gathered. "His Majesty, who served us so diligently and strongly in the war against Vertgana that his powerful grasp of the noonday arts wore him down completely, led the charge against Kalthorne in Segance, his vitality restored by the grace of our Lord Sun."

It was good that Isabelle wasn't here. If someone said that after killing Macé or Jean, I'd have killed them. I was certain she would've too.

"There is no progress without sacrifice, just as there is no power without sacrifice," he said, hands fisted at his sides. "We will bring Demeine to a level of power the world has never seen. Are you with me?"

People cheered and clapped, and I brought my hands together once. Estrel didn't even do that.

Power had a cost, but our folks were the ones who always had to pay it.

He held up the glass of black wine to us and those near a server held up their own glasses.

"Demeine!" he said. "Grace, honor, legacy!"

The room repeated the phrases, glasses high, and drank.

It went quickly after that, the evening devolving into a party. Marian hugged me when Estrel said we should leave. A real hug.

"I'll keep an eye on Emilie," I whispered, not sure what to do.

She patted my cheek but couldn't form the words.

Estrel escorted me out of the room, and her hands curled around my shoulders. "In the morning, we need to talk about what to do when you are found out and go back to being Annette Boucher. If we get things right, I think you may get away with this."

"I'll do everything right," I said. "I promise."

"I believe you." Estrel led me back to my room and stopped at the door. "But if you make a mistake, you're still my apprentice and it will be all right."

I nodded. We'd find out if it would be all right in a few hours.

The next morning at dawn, Estrel shook me awake. "We have to leave. They're scouring the city for Laurel."

"What?" I sat up and turned an ear to the window. Shouts and screams echoed down the streets. "What happened?"

I knew what had happened. The posters were up, Laurel had spread the news of what His Majesty had done, and people were angry.

We would be our own.

TWENTY-ONE

Emilie

I t was far too quiet for a military encampment the morning after the party. I lay on my back in my sleep roll, breath a fog above me. Madeline's soft snores were loud in the silence, a comforting reminder that she was alive and hadn't been swept off for treason in the night, and the others in the tent shifted and slowly snored themselves out of slumber. I crawled out of bed and got dressed as quietly as I could. Outside the tent, Louis, Allard's hack, paced back and forth.

"There was a poster on the opening to my tent this morning." He glanced around. There was no one about. There should have been people working, talking, preparing to switch shifts. "His Majesty's personal guards came through and ripped it down."

"A poster of what?" I closed my eyes and tried to feel out the magic being used in the camp. Nothing—as if Lord Sun had taken a hand and swept it all away. Someone was making it harder for noonday artists to channel magic. "Pièrre and Waleran are doing something to prevent us from channeling."

I had heard of battle magic's various uses but never studied them. Only nobles studying to become chevaliers had access to those texts.

"They're going to blame hacks. That's why I'm here. Make sure you've got your things in order if they question you." Louis exhaled. "What if they try to scry the past to see who did it? Whoever did it will be in danger."

His black eyes caught mine. I ducked.

"Scrying the past is exceptionally hard," I said, "and so far as I know, Estrel Charron is the only one who can do it accurately right now."

They would probably ask her, but surely someone with her background wouldn't turn Laurel in.

"Small blessings for traitors, ay?" Louis nodded for me to follow him. "I need your help with rounds—you can adjust alchemistry, right?"

"Sure."

The low hum of whispering filled the infirmary. This early, it was all common soldiers and hacks. Louis led me to a soldier in one of the middle beds. I sat next to him.

I had only spoken to Louis a few times before this morning. At university when Physician Allard had returned to pick his new hack, Louis had spent the day answering students' questions about the physician's work. Laurence had taken us into Delest that day. Louis's constant channeling for Allard had worn down his hands so much that he almost always wore a pair of dark brown leather gloves the same tone as his skin. He had said he was going to retire soon.

He was only twenty-five.

"Have you heard about Laurel?" Louis asked quietly.

"Incompletely," I whispered back. "Our tent isn't near anyone else's."

"The camp down in Adamesnil is refusing to work. Soldiers included," he said. "We've got too many chevaliers here compared to the others—they'd crush us—but none of the other hacks at any of the camps are working."

One of Allard's other hacks leaned over Louis's shoulder and muttered, "His Majesty found one in his tent and one left behind during the gathering last night. That was only nobles."

I whistled. "Good."

"No hacks, no soldiers, no war," Louis said. He hummed and pulled away from his patient. "I like Laurel more every day."

The infirmary flap opened. Charles, a beacon of orange, looked around. Louis stiffened and the other hacks fell silent.

"Everyone's fine without the noonday arts here, right?" Charles asked, coming over to Louis who nodded and bowed his head. "Good. Thank you." He beckoned to me. "Laurence is about to kill Pièrre and Waleran for doing this, so we have to go distract him."

Our moods had been tense for weeks, but Charles had his lips rolled together to keep from smiling as he led us to Laurence's tent.

"Some exceptionally brave person had the nerve to put one of those lies on the back of His Majesty's chair last night while no one was paying attention," Charles said. "Laurence is furious because Henry thinks he must know something and is covering for Laurel, and then Waleran decided to stop anyone from using the noonday arts near His Majesty, and now Laurence and Pièrre are furious at him. It's been a long morning."

"The other camps are refusing to work, though," I said. "It's working."

When we walked into Laurence's tent, only Sébastien was there. He was disastrously put together and wringing his hands.

"They're questioning Laurence right now," he said. "And once they are sufficiently sure he has no involvement in this plot, they're having him contact Mademoiselle Charron to scry who was responsible for it."

I glanced between Charles and Sébastien. "Well, good for them."

"Good?" Sébastien pointed one shaking hand at me. "Laurel has doomed us. Without a working army or hacks, Kalthorne could crush us in a war."

"Then we should broker for peace." I shrugged. "No war seems like a winning situation for everyone, and it's not like we had a reason for doing this in the first place. Especially considering how His Majesty is fueling his noonday arts."

"Your actions have put Demeine in danger." Sébastien planted his hands on his hips and shook his head. "I can't stand for it. What happened was terrible, but we can deal with it after we deal with Kalthorne."

I rolled my eyes. By the time we "dealt" with Kalthorne, His Majesty could have killed dozens of hacks. I walked to Laurence's rickety folding desk and picked up the stool.

"We shouldn't be dealing with Kalthorne at all," Charles said. "It's a distraction."

I set the stool before Sébastien. Charles stared, and Sébastien spluttered.

"Is this better, Monsieur?" I asked.

From the corner of my sight, I watched Charles open his mouth, shut it, and bury his face in his hands.

"What am I supposed to do with this?" Sébastien crossed his arms, chin shaking it was so clenched, and did not look at me.

Charles gave an overexaggerated shrug. "Sit on it, I would assume."

"Sébastien," I said, using his name for the first time that morning.

He jerked his head to look at me. I was only a few thumbs shorter than him, but my mother had prodded good posture into me. I pushed him onto the stool, keeping both hands on his shoulders. "Your brother is a chevalier, and you, one day, will be a very good physician, but if we go to war with Kalthorne, His Majesty will continue using the noonday arts, yes?"

Sébastien glanced at my hands and nodded.

"Which means he will have to continue using hacks." I let my arms fall. "And when he runs out of hacks, who do you think will serve him, then?"

Sébastien turned to Charles. "He wouldn't."

"Sébastien," Charles said. "We've talked about this. When one enemy is dead, one resource used, he will move to the next, and who do you think that will be?"

I let Sébastien stew and sat next to Charles.

"They'll try to find who did it, make them confess it was a lie, and use them as an example." He ran a hand over his face. "They might not even bother finding out who really did it and skip to the example part."

"They know someone in Laurel is a noble," Sébastien said, eyes closed and head leaned back. "He'll start there. We'll need a distraction of our own to keep us out of his sights."

Charles leaned into me and murmured, "Probably don't antagonize Sébastien."

"His existence antagonizes me."

"He's nervous." Charles flipped open his leather journal and ran a hand, fingers heavy with gold and ruby rings, down the page till he found whatever it was he needed. He had always styled himself impeccably, but there was an edge to how he carried himself now. He was fashionably disheveled but unbelievably precise. "Leave him be, please."

I sighed. "Fine."

Charles hummed and grinned.

Eventually, our silent meeting was interrupted by Laurence. He pulled back the opening to the tent and shook his head, the dark circles under his eyes impressively defined. Laurence flicked two fingers at Charles and me, and we leapt up. He collapsed onto his cot.

Charles leaned over at him. "Laurence, would you like us to leave?"

Then Laurence du Montimer, the consummate voice of reason and tranquility, closed his eyes and said, "What the fuck did you all do?"

"Nothing," I said.

"Nothing?" Laurence cracked open one eye and glared at me. "That is rich coming from you."

"Did you see who it was that—?"

"No," Laurence cut off Charles and waved the question away. "Do not worry about that."

"See!" Sébastien cried. "This whole thing was too presumptuous. Laurel should have waited and discussed it, not abandoned us to this."

Laurence winced and rubbed the bridge of his nose. "You cannot fix a decrepit house while standing inside of it. You must tear the house down and start again, though it is useful to get help and resources from inside the house first."

"That," Charles said, voice flat, "sounds like Laurel."

"Another poster appeared in Serre at noon signed by Madame Royale Nicole of Demeine," said Laurence. "We cannot simply wash our hands of this. Laurel is attempting to overthrow the king, and clearly they have selected Nicole as his successor. Using her means that our neighbors, Kalthorne and Vertgana, will recognize her as a valid successor and not attempt to seat their own. Laurel is planning a coup with Nicole."

Of course—all of our nations had distant ties to each other, and if they thought they had a stronger claim to Demeine than whoever ruled if Laurel won, they would try to takeover.

"I thought her father had her arrested," Charles said. "She tried this before with Laurel in Segance."

Demeine nobles could not have clean hands, but we had to help fix the mess we had made.

I couldn't keep this secret any longer, not if they were scrying for truths and liars in this camp. Eventually, they would find me out.

"Which is why her signature is curious." Laurence rolled into a sitting position. "Do any of you know why the first King Henry renamed our nation, our people, and our language?"

I knew he had, but all the historians made it seem triumphant. After the wars with Vertgana and the Empire, we had left our old name, the one that had seen us conquered again and again, behind.

"Because he thought this land was his and his alone." Laurence looked up at us. "Is a land its crown's or its people's?"

"It's people's," I said.

Charles nodded. "There is no nation without its people."

"Great!" Laurence clapped and stood. "That confirms my worst fears. When they question you, Charles and Sébastien, don't say that. Get out. I need to think."

Charles and Sébastien darted out of the tent. Laurence groaned.

"Emilie," he said, "there are very few conversations I am mentally capable of handling right now."

"I'm sorry. I need to tell you something." I was certain my bones were ice and all about to crack, leaving me a collapsed and worthless mess. "My name isn't Emilie Boucher. It's Emilie des Marais."

"Yes?" He glanced at me, not turning his body. "And?"

The little thread of control I thought I still held over my life snapped.

"You knew this whole time?" I asked. "You didn't send me away?"

"Did I not mention it before we came here?" He tilted his head up, black brows a confused, furrowed line.

I shook my head. "Not even a little bit."

"My apologies. I meant to," he said. "It's really irrelevant to most of my opinions on you, and you weren't doing anything untoward, so I might have—"

"You forgot," I said, "didn't you?"

He tried too hard to not be flighty and fickle like his contemporaries pretended to be, their well-controlled acts that ticked every box—half-done appearance, overly expressed emotions, and fiery temperament—and yet here we were. All of them wanted to look like the carefree genius who was too far above mortal concerns, but Laurence was.

"The intricacies of your life are not as interesting as you think they are." He stretched, face falling into his normal expressionless calm. "Why are you confessing this now?"

"I didn't want you to be caught unawares if Charron's scrying found me out," I said.

Laurence waved for me to leave. "She already knows. Your decoy is her apprentice, everything is fine, and I appreciate your honesty, but I dearly need to think. In peace."

"Of course. Sorry." I bowed out of habit and went to find Madeline.

The day went on as most days had, but more subdued. We stayed in the infirmary, checking injuries and taking stock of supplies. The three chevaliers in the camp walked through the little gatherings of people during supper, chatting with hacks as if they were old friends and not sniffing out traitors, and I ended up in Laurence's tent once again the next morning with Charles. Charles and Sébastien had been questioned and cleared. Sébastien was still twitchy, though.

"Stop thinking about it. Here." Laurence pushed a small leaf of papers into his hands. "Read this. You'll like it."

Sébastien clutched the papers to his chest, nodded, and left.

Charles picked up one of Charron's journals Laurence was flipping through, trying to find notes on scrying. He thumbed through the pages. "Exquisite."

"An exquisite pain," Laurence muttered. "If I leave you two here, will I return to find you both in one piece and none of my work worse for wear?"

"Yes." Charles sat on the cot next to me, book open on his lap. "I'll refrain from asking questions. That should keep us all safe."

Laurence laughed his way out of the tent.

"I was going to offer you the cheese pastry I had in my bag," I said, "but I'm rethinking that now."

"You should eat it." He smelled of vinegar and soap and something sharp like orange water. "You hate me. Why would you even want to share?"

"I don't hate you. I think you're"—I paused, the precise words not coming and shrugged—"insufferable and stubborn; however, you're intelligent and hardworking, and I know you put the well-being of patients over your current health no matter how foolish that is. You gave half of them your lunch. Please eat the pastry."

"You called yourself those things weeks ago. The insults only, though." He laughed and took the pastry from the bag at my feet. "How peculiar."

"Not really." I tore a piece of the pastry off and ate the plain corner. "I'm much meaner to me than I am to you. You should be astronomically insulted to share an insult with me."

"I'm astronomically concerned about how you think that's a normal sentiment." Charles took me by the shirt collar, gently, carefully, and tapped my lips with the pastry. "Eat."

I did, and Charles ate the other half. We sat in silence for some time, wiping our hands on Laurence's blanket—not that he slept or would use it—and talking about nothing. He leaned back, his left side flush with my right. My mother would have died if she saw us.

"I actually quite like you," I said finally.

He tapped his foot against mine. "I quite like you as well, Emilie Last-Name-Definitely-Not-Boucher."

"Let me keep one secret successfully," I said. "My mother shipped me off to Gardinier's finishing school before I could get away, and I had to improvise."

He let out a barking laugh, nudged my shoulder with his, and said, "I am very glad you ended up here, though."

"Me too."

Someone at the tent door cleared their throat. Sébastien shuffled his feet. "Charles, I need your help in the infirmary."

Charles glanced at me. "Later, then."

I nodded. He set the book back on the cot, and I stood as well.

The pair left. I fiddled around Laurence's stacks of journals, mostly things he had carried so we could continue studying. The odd haze that had interrupted my magic lifted, and I peeked outside. Waleran strolled toward the tent.

I gathered the magic in my hands faster than I ever had before and channeled it through me, the sting of so much power in my veins a pain I hadn't felt. I thrust my hands at Waleran. The alchemistry of his body lit before me.

Another soldier darted between us. A dozen more soldiers rising from the sides of the path. I let my magic fade and turned to run. A soldier yanked me up by my coat.

I stumbled.

"Please do not try to run," Waleran called out. "Any further attempts of escape will be met with retribution, either on you or Madeline Mercer." Waleran unsheathed his sword, a long, thin thing of artist-forged steel and magic. "Understood?"

"She had nothing to do with this," I said. "Don't touch her."

I lunged for him, and he flipped his sword up, ramming the hilt into my temple. I blacked out, knees hitting the ground. The world shifted beneath me.

"We're aware she's not involved, but I assumed she would make an excellent motivator." Waleran clucked his tongue against his teeth and wiped his hands clean. "Madame, please do not do that again. We require you alive for questioning."

We returned to Bosquet without stopping. I was in a coach with Madame Bisset and Estrel, watching her scry and divine and do a number of things with the midnight arts I didn't know how to describe. At one point, she started talking to the mirror, doing what she'd done last night with du Montimer, and she had to ask me to hold her steady as she scryed. The magic channeling through her was so powerful, I could feel how she was using it in the silver, peeling apart the ethereal threads of time to peek into the past. I stiffened when she stopped.

"Laurel has reemerged," she said, voice raspy. She wiped the sweat from her face. "Apparently His Majesty has been using hacks' bodies to repair his when it wears down, and Laurel revealed this truth last night."

Bisset tensed, her mouth falling open. "What? No, he—what?"

"So did we attack Segance just to distract from that?" I asked and hoped she would catch on.

"Oh, there are certainly people saying that." Estrel glared at me over the top of her mirror, and she sunk lower in her seat. Her eyes fluttered shut. "And it's very hard to go to war when all your hacks and soldiers are refusing to work until the truth is told and crimes are answered for."

"Are we in danger?" Bisset asked.

I turned to her so slowly, she flinched. "Why would you be in danger?"

"Those fire starters." She twisted her hands in her lap. "If Laurel takes power, they'll kill us all."

I shook my head and leaned against her shoulder. "Laurel's literally been saying the opposite of that all summer. Madame Royale Nicole of Demeine even tried to have a talk with them, and it was His Majesty who ruined that."

Estrel didn't stop staring at me the whole way back to Bosquet.

"How was your first court event?" Coline asked, sitting cross-legged on my bed and eating blackberries.

"It worked." I walked past Coline and sat next to Isabelle. "How are you feeling?"

"I feel sad," she said softly. "I didn't feel anything before."

"How are you not angry?" Coline asked. She spun a butter knife from the silver room between her fingers, blade skimming the skin of her hand. "Yes, people are resisting now, but His Majesty has been doing this for years."

Fresh anger was a delicacy of the powerful; otherwise, I'd have died from being angry and on edge all the time.

"What's the point in being angry here?" Isabelle picked up her brush and dragged it across the tablet, trying to read portents in the strokes of the ink and crooked hairs left behind by the brush. She held the tablet up to the midafternoon light. "Being angry won't bring Gabriel back, but being angry at the right people might get His Majesty dethroned."

"People in power don't listen to angry country kids, especially girls," I said. "Then, they don't listen to you ever again because you're emotional and you're not supposed to be."

Coline set her bowl of blackberries aside. "What?"

"I need to tell you two something, but it's a secret." I touched Isabelle's hand, tugged her to my bed and sat her next to Coline. She stared up at me wide-eyed, and how long I'd been lying hit me. Hard. "Please don't be angry—I'm not Emilie des Marais. My name's Annette, and I'm from Vaser."

Coline laughed, loud and barking, and I thought for sure Vivienne would come storming in to see what was wrong. Isabelle stared at me.

"You lied?" she asked. "Were you... Did Laurel send you?"

I shook my head. "The real Emilie wanted to study at university, so she had me take her place. All I wanted was to learn the midnight arts."

Coline kept laughing.

"You're joking." Isabelle dropped her tablet to the bed and rose up to her knees. "You have to be."

"I'm not." There was something ominous in the disbelief making it far scarier than Coline's endless laughter. "Estrel knows, but Vivienne doesn't. Emilie's mother knows now too."

"This is..." Coline said, gasping for air. "This is the most beautiful nonsense I have ever seen."

I stepped back to the door. "I can't tell if you're going to turn me in or congratulate me, so please get to your point."

"Congratulate you!" Coline leapt from the bed and enveloped me in a tight, painful hug. "How for all the stars did you pull this off?"

Isabelle kept staring at me over Coline's shoulder.

"Poorly," I said. "And full of fear."

I sat back down on my bed, Coline coming with me, and whispered, "Isabelle, if you're upset with me, that's okay. I can't lie to you anymore, and I was afraid if anyone knew, I'd get arrested."

"Estrel knew, though." She stared up at me, eyes watering. "You told Estrel before you told us, and we've known you longer."

"I didn't tell her." I took Isabelle's hands in mine. "She figured it out."

"Unsurprising," said Coline. "You did keep mentioning a sister despite Emilie des Marais being an only child." Coline flopped next to Isabelle and hooked their arms together. "You cannot stay angry at her. It was a matter of life and death."

Isabelle made a face. "She lied to us! Our classes. Our talks. All of it was lies."

"It wasn't. The only lie was my name and history. I meant everything I ever said to you." I leaned against her, her soft shoulder warm against my bony one, and sighed. "I promise. I meant every word."

"Oh." She sighed, her cheek resting against my scalp.

"I'll go get breakfast," Coline said, sliding off the bed. We were still on midnight artists' time—sleeping all day and working all night. "I think we could do with some food and only our company."

We didn't do anything the rest of the night. Vivienne didn't seem to mind, the whole of Bosquet being in such an uproar. Most of the other girls had gathered in their rooms, friends sleeping with friends and talking about the posters, and Isabelle painted and waited for news from her aunt and family. Surely they would recognize Gabriel. We were too isolated, too well-watched for it to have been Isabelle.

That's what Coline said. No one would think she'd pulled it off on her own, and how'd she get it to Laurel? Vivienne hadn't shown any of us the posters, but everyone knew what it was by now. We stayed alone in our room, the three of us, to keep the gossip out of Isabelle's ears.

The next day, Estrel was called back to Serre. She was, first and foremost, the royal diviner, and His Majesty needed her to find Laurel and keep an eye on Kalthorne to make sure we weren't attacked. She handed me a pile of books and mirrors and even a tiny silver knife no bigger than my little finger, instructing me to practice, and I found out later that her other students had been left similar instructions. Whole lists of things to do while she was gone. Perenelle took one look at their list and sighed.

"Try to find Laurel," they read from their list. "Don't tell Vivienne and don't report findings to anyone but me." They glanced at me, eyes narrowed. "We're on the same page in this book, yes?"

I nodded. "It's a real good page."

"Excellent." They gathered up the books and bloodletting knives. "If you want to work together, come find me. Germaine likes to hold salon while I work, so there's always tea and lovely poetry in the background. It's very bolstering."

I smiled. "Thank you. I will."

We'd stopped all working together after classes since the fighting was mostly paused, and we were mostly exhausted, bodies starting to show signs of wearing down whether it was bloody noses, sore throats, or burned hands.

I made my way to the gardens instead. The crash of the Verglas's current rumbled over the quiet grounds. I found a pond full of water hyacinth and cattails and tucked myself into a pile of rocks at the edge. The water rippled, and I gathered magic, letting the thrum settle over me. *Macé's familiar, calloused hands cleaned a set of steel armor.* So he was alive. Good.

I let myself slide free of the magic, the soft joy the image had inspired sinking in me. The leftover power I'd gathered scattered. I leaned my head back against the tree trunk.

"You burn when you do that," Yvonne's soft voice said from behind me. "It's a little alarming."

I turned. "What?"

Yvonne leaned against a short blackthorn tree, moonlight filtering through her hair. The sting of brimstone and nasty pinch of alchemistry still in the making hung in the air, and the last dregs of ash and blood cleared from my throat. She gestured to the bowl in my lap.

"I can't channel, and seeing magic is always a toss-up. Most of the students aren't anything. Vivienne is like a flickering star, but you and Mademoiselle Charron are like the whole night when you work, stars and moon and all. The steady beacon of a new world. You use so much power without even realizing it that it changes the way the world looks." She smiled, fiddling with the protective spectacles atop her head as if they were a crown. "And it's very distracting when you channel within sight of the kitchens."

"Sorry," I said, standing and stumbling on pins-and-needles legs.

Yvonne darted forward. She slipped one hand around my waist and one around my shoulders. "You're worn out. I think you've done enough for now."

"Hardly." I snorted and sobered. "You're too nice to me."

"I'm nice to people whose company I enjoy," she said quickly, dragging me into the kitchens. "Otherwise, how do I convince them to stay around?"

"Who doesn't want to?" I brushed a fallen leaf from her hair, dull green on shiny black, and settled my hand on her back. "Is there anything I can help you with?"

"Oh yes." Her fingers tightened at my waist. Warm. Firm. "I saved the washing up for you. Delightfully mindless. You can plot whatever it is you're plotting while cleaning."

"Thank you." My hand traced the stitching along her spine. I'd always tried to avoid touching. So many expectations. "It all worked."

"It all worked," she said softly, leaning me against a counter in the kitchen. "I'm dreading what happens now. They're still the ones with the weapons and money to buy a new army, but people are angry, and it's hard not to be pleased. What are you going to do after?"

"I like looking at other people's futures." My back bumped the counter. "Not mine."

She laughed and paused, arms on either side of my hips, trapping me between the counter and her, lips so close, I could feel them brush mine when she whispered, "May I kiss you?"

"Yes, please," I said without thinking, and then the burn of her hand on my hip shocked me out of it. "Wait. Wait. No."

She reared back and removed her hand.

"Don't apologize," I said quickly. "It's not you. I just want to, I mean, I like you, and I want to be clear about something so we're both happy—I don't want to have sex."

Yvonne's head tilted to the side. "We don't have to."

"Ever. I don't want to ever. I don't think about it. I'm not attracted to people in that way, but I like touching and romance and flirting, and I really like you but sometimes people think you can't have one without the other."

There'd been a boy, once. I'd liked him and he'd liked me, and Maman had even talked about marriage, but when he kissed me and called me pretty, he said I owed him. I'd stopped talking to him. Maman had told me he was wrong, but that one day I'd change my mind. That all girls learned to like it.

"Oh." Yvonne stepped back, and I loved her for it even though I missed her closeness. "That's fine. We can talk about it." She winced. "I mean our relationship, not sex. If you don't want to have sex, we won't. Ever."

"I got it." I smiled. "Last person I liked didn't think you could have romance without sex."

That I was obligated.

"We can," Yvonne said. "We are our own, and we will define what our love is, Emilie."

And the lack of my name, my real name, with those words killed me. *Mistress, let me die.*

"I'm sorry," I said quickly. "While I'm being honest, I have to tell you who I really am."

Yvonne froze, her mouth slightly open. "What?"

"My name's Annette. The real Emilie didn't want to attend, so she had me come instead of her, and she's off being a physician's hack. I'm not noble or anything. I'm just Annette." I stepped toward her. "I didn't mean to hide it from you. No one knew. No one could know. I'm not really anything, and you were—"

She stepped back and held up her hand. "You signed papers for me as Emilie des Marais."

The words and hurt within them were an avalanche, and I was drowning in cold.

"That won't hurt anything, will it?" I asked. "If I'm found out."

"I don't know." Yvonne pressed her hands together, palms flush. "I don't know anything, and apparently I know you the least."

"You know me better than anyone here." I ran the back of my hand beneath my nose, tears catching on the bow of my lips, and sniffed. "Talking to you is like breathing. Everything I told you is true, and you are the only one who understands half of what I feel. I don't have to pretend to be anyone with you."

"But I did." She covered her mouth with one hand. "All that time I worried about you being a comtesse, all that time I spent on edge, and you never told me?"

"No," I whispered. "I'm sorry."

"Then why didn't you?" She lurched forward, halfway to me. Her eyes glittered wet in the light. "Why?"

"No one ever wanted to talk to Annette. I was scared you wouldn't either."

"I can't right now." She held up her hands in defeat. "I can't talk to you and do my job, and frankly, it's more important than whatever this is. So tomorrow, we will talk, and you will explain. Then, you'll listen because I don't think you understand how much this hurts."

I left.

I didn't need to divine the future possibilities to know what would happen.

So I wrote a note instead, a cowardly thing, but Coline was in the room and I'd no words left in my chest. Isabelle hadn't come back.

Coline walked past me once and asked softly, "Your alchemist?"

"Everyone's cross with me."

Lies were easier when you were face-to-face. Nerves rattled them out of you. The truth and all its terrible details took time to set out straight.

"Sometimes lying is the only thing that keeps us alive." Coline set her half-eaten bowl of blackberries that she'd been working on all day next to me. "Let them cool off."

I rubbed my nose. "Whole world's falling apart, and I'm crying over this."

"You're part of the world," Coline said. "Cry as much as you want."

Yvonne,

I have seen so many futures full of possibility, and I cannot help but believe that the good fortune I foresaw in mine meant you. I meant to lie to you. It was intentional, and I can't excuse that. I'll understand if you don't want to speak again.

I didn't tell Estrel. She said she knew because of my teeth and because I study like I eat— desperately, like I'll never get to again. I won't. I'm not anything special.

My name is Annette Boucher. I'm from Vaser, and most of what I told you wasn't a lie...

"What should I do about Isabelle?" I asked Coline. "I thought we would be able to save Gabriel. I didn't realize I was lying to her."

"Give her time," said Coline.

I finished my letter to Yvonne, the handwriting shakier the longer the letter went, and folded it up. The little wax seal with Emilie's family sigil was too much of a slap. I pressed my thumb into the hot wax. The door creaked open.

"I'm sorry," Isabelle said quickly, sweeping in and out of the room. "We'll talk later."

The door slammed shut behind her.

"See?" Coline said from her bed. "It'll be fine."

It was something, more than I could say, and I went to sleep with it next to me. Things would be better in the morning.

"Out!" Vivienne threw back the bedcovers and yanked me out. "Shoes, coat, do you have food? Estrel always stashed food."

"What?" I stumbled, sleep wobbly, and swallowed. "Vivienne—"

"They know." Vivienne took my face in her hands and let out a stuttering breath. "Annette, they know, and you must get out of here."

She let go of me and woke up Coline. I grabbed my shoes and the little lockbox of lunes and biscuits beneath my bed. Vivienne grabbed one of Coline's cloaks and dragged us out of the room.

"There's a coach at the gate. I cannot believe you did something so atrociously blatant, Coline." Vivienne spoke in a harsh whisper, face a map of worries, and led us down the stairs and to the servants' gate at the back of the estate. "You put yourself and so many others in danger."

"I would rather be in danger than see my people dead," Coline whispered. She glanced at me. "They don't think Annette helped?"

"That is exactly what they are going to say, regardless of whether they think it or not," Vivienne said. "You created your own scapegoat."

The guard who had introduced me to Laurel was standing at the gate, a lantern in his hand. When we broke through the trees, he lowered it. Vivienne stopped.

"Oh no," she muttered, shoving us back. "Run to the church. There's another gate."

Coline grabbed my hand and yanked me back into the trees.

"She's here!"

The shout rang out from the garden. Coline's hand tightened around mine, pulling me closer. I gathered power on instinct, the midnight arts a comforting burn in Alaine's necklace, and Coline pulled a knife from beneath her nightgown. From the trees stepped Isabelle.

Coline hissed. "You snitch!"

"Me?" Isabelle's eyes were red even in the pale light, and she reared back at the word. "You knew he was going to die! You lied to me for weeks. I trusted both of you, and you made a fool of me, letting me think we could save Gabriel. You always knew he was going to die, and you did nothing to stop it. You don't get to just walk away."

So this was dying.

I had no answer to her, and knew none would matter.

Behind us, footsteps tore through the garden.

"Did you tell them what we did?" Coline asked quickly, eyes wild, hand clutching the knife so tightly, I could hear her knuckles cracking. "With the posters? Did you tell them?"

"No," she sneered. "I don't care about whatever rebellion you're leading. She's the liar and—"

Coline straightened. "Isabelle, I'm Madame Royale Nicole. They'll think Annette was here to work for Laurel. They'll connect the posters to you, then to me, and then to her."

"What?" Isabelle's smile twisted. "No, no—I only told them you weren't Emilie des Marais. I only told them you were a thief. You—" Her breaths came in quick, tight gasps, and she couldn't exhale without choking. "You stole my time with Gabriel. If I had known, I could've—" She glanced over my shoulder. "Oh, Lord, they'll kill you."

"I'm aware," and it came out of me in bubbling laughter because this was perfect. Least I was getting blamed for something purely my fault.

Coline grabbed my arm. "Why are you laughing?"

"Because this is hilarious," I said and buried my face in my hands. "You're Nicole, the king's daughter, and you've been supporting Laurel, so when they heard some impostor was parading about here, they took Isabelle seriously." I threw my head back. "I'm laughing because you were fool enough to think they wouldn't kill me for taking Emilie's place here. I'm not from a family like yours. No one's going miss me. I would've hanged for thievery, but now I get to be beheaded like some fucking folk hero when they blame me for Laurel."

The laughter wouldn't stop.

"Madame Royale," a deep voice called out from behind us. "I cannot say this is how I expected to find you, but I'm also not surprised."

Isabelle paled, gaze stuck behind us. Coline took a deep breath, raised her chin, turned. I turned too, laughing still, and the small crowd of soldiers, His Majesty's sigil branded into the leather of their chest armor, tightened around us. One held a bleeding Vivienne by the arm. The laughter died.

"Let her go," I said. "Now."

"Annette Boucher, you are wanted for treason," one of the soldiers said. He unsheathed his sword. "Please. It's much too late for a hunt, don't you think?"

"Let Vivienne go." I grasped Alaine's necklace, the silver warm against my palm.

"Gardinier is under arrest, as are you two." The soldier made a cutting gesture with his hand, and the one to his left stepped forward.

The moonlight caught in the soldier's short sword—*an arrow notched, a bloody arm*—and I ducked. An arrow ripped over my head. The soldier behind me screamed and stumbled, the arrow lodged in his arm. I licked my lips.

"Madame Royale, Boucher." The captain stabbed his sword into Vivienne's side. "I won't ask again—surrender."

I froze. Coline growled, throwing the guard who had tried to grab her aside. Vivienne's head fell back, her eyes steel in the moonlight, and magic flickered in her hands.

"Fine." He twisted the blade.

Blood bloomed across the front of her dress, and the magic in her hands died. Vivienne slumped forward. I screamed, sure my throat would tear, and Coline threw herself at the closest soldier. Her fist slammed into his jaw. He fell.

I flung myself at the one nearest to me, magic forgotten. My knees hit his chest, my nails raked his eyes, and we went tumbling down till his back was in the dirt and his blood was on my hands. Flashes—*arms closing around me from behind*—rippled in the steel of his fallen sword. I dove, dodging the arms. I grabbed the sword.

Another pair of hands ripped me up. The sword fell from my grip. I dug my heels into the dirt, dragging us to a stop. The hands tightened.

"Move again," the soldier holding me said, "and they'll put a bolt through your friend. You are the only two we need, and she is no one of consequence."

A history lesson in four words.

"Fuck off." Coline's voice cracked. A soldier wrapped an arm around her throat. Three soldiers were sprawled out at her feet. One had a knife in his neck and wasn't breathing. "If you touch her, I'll kill all of you."

"With what?" the soldier who had me asked. "A silver spoon?"

"If I must." Her breath escaped in foggy huffs. Frost crackled along her captor's lips. "Isabelle?"

Isabelle didn't—couldn't—hear. She'd eyes only for Vivienne, her body still, the grass beneath her red. An empty, aching wail whistled through her lips, and she collapsed to her knees, taking the soldier holding her down too. Tears gathered in the dip of her chin. Her mouth moved.

"We'll go with you," I said softly. The soldier loosened his grip. I didn't move. "Leave her here, and we won't fight you."

The guard holding the crossbow looked to the soldier behind me, paused—face wrinkling, eyes wide—and lowered his crossbow. The three soldiers loaded us into the wagon, dragged their friend with his clawed face inside, and shackled us to a bar in the back. Coline pressed her side to mine, blessedly cold, and whispered through her tears. I couldn't hear the words. It didn't matter. I wasn't letting go.

Not today.

Isabelle turned and watched us go, the smear of her hair in the blur of my gaze so familiar, I laughed as we crested the hill and left her out of sight.

"Run," I whispered, and the word vibrated from my throat to the silver of Alaine's moon, to the silver cuff around Isabelle's ear. "Run."

And she did.

I collapsed, and the guard I'd tackled laughed.

"Well," he said, slurring. "Between you two, the lot in Segance, and Charron, gallows are going to be full."

Estrel?

"Good," I heard myself say, braver than I felt. "I always wanted to be like her."

And she'd have surely given them every fight she could manage.

·CHAPTER·

TWENTY-THREE

Emilie

They'd threatened Madeline. I stopped fighting after that, afraid they would arrest her too. Waleran locked a pair of spectacles around my head and dropped me in the back of a wagon, his varlets and apprentices telling me all about the trial Annette and I would have in Serre. The spectacles stopped me from seeing magic, a hood stopped me from seeing anything, and after an hour with only my captors for company, he clamped a pair of shackles around my wrists that burned so badly, I wasn't sure I would ever be able to channel magic again. I wasn't sure if it even mattered.

Rainier was dead. Annette was arrested. I was bound and gagged and on my way to Serre.

"You will confess, of course," Waleran said to me as we prepared to leave Segance. "This terrible business with Gabriel Choquet. He died fighting for your country, and your use of him as some martyr for your cause is blatantly disgusting. You and your compatriots are surprisingly creative liars."

"Physician Pièrre du Guay and his apprentices killed Gabriel in order to restore the king." I swallowed. I couldn't see. I couldn't move. "It wasn't a lie, and I will confess to nothing."

"Most people say that at first." Waleran's footsteps paced before me on the dirt floor. The door to the small building I was in clanged shut. "We'll see how long you hold to that."

I slumped against the stone wall at my back. We had traveled for half a day perhaps, and we were still in Segance because we had not crossed the Pinch yet.

I was in the dark for days. Every few hours, Waleran or one of his apprentices would return to question me. They didn't hurt me, and they always called me *Madame*. My sight, my hands—tangible forms weren't necessary for channeling magic, but they made the actions easier and I was so used to them. My hands were shackled behind me, only tight enough to keep me from moving, and I rubbed my cheek against my shoulders until the hood slipped off. Blood from the rough fabric rolled down my cheek, leaving an itching trail all the way down my neck. One of the apprentices wiped it from my face with his sleeve, even though I refused to answer any questions about Laurel.

Annette was certainly not receiving the same treatment, and I had made a promise to her. I could not break it.

After three days—I counted the hours by the alchemistry of my body—of little water, no food, and barely any sleep, I was no closer to escaping than I had been previously. They came to question me too often and undid all the work I had done. Either way, I had no idea where we were. We had traveled intermittently and stopped this morning. The room I was in was as nondescript as the last.

"I need to speak with her." It was Sébastien, his voice muffled by the door. "It is of the utmost importance."

What an appendix of a person.

The lock clicked. The door opened. My head was still bound in spectacles that made seeing magic impossible and wrapped in a hood, but sunlight burned through the weave. I turned my face to it.

"Monsieur," I said, voice cracking, "how kind of you to join me. How can I be of assistance?"

The door shut. Even without channeling magic, I could hear the thump of his heart in his chest.

"You put everyone in danger." His feet shuffled in the dirt, closer, farther, closer, closer. Dust settled on my outstretched legs. "You have to say you're Laurel."

"I feel like you're not understanding what's happening." The hood choked me with each word. "I have already been arrested for it, and the girl who took my place—her name is Annette Boucher, and you must know that because you put her in danger—has been arrested, and we are certainly going to be blamed for it. I'm all right with dying in Laurel's place and letting them tear you down once I'm gone, but I have to figure out how to get Annette out of this. I don't have time for you."

His knees cracked. His breath puffed around my side—he must have been kneeling next to me—and he ripped the hood off. I blinked and flinched. My eyes took time to get used to the light.

"You—" He closed his eyes and covered his mouth with a hand. His skin was sallow, stretched across his round cheeks as if he hadn't slept in days, and the whites of his eyes were as red as the chewed skin around his fingernails. "I turned you in because you were putting people I care about in danger. It wasn't personal."

Endure.

I didn't even scowl. No anger leaked into my tone. I was flat and cold, and he was beneath me and my fury. "My father used to say it was never personal, which seemed odd since his politics only affected people who weren't like him. Of course it wasn't personal. He didn't consider them people."

It was good that he was dead. My mother wouldn't have been able to fix Marais if he were alive.

"I'm not here to argue politics. Demeine needs to change. It does," Sébastien said, "but you put Charles and Laurence in danger by involving them in this."

"Charles involved himself," I said. "He's capable of making his own decisions."

Sébastien shook his head and laughed. "He makes terrible decisions. He needs looking after, and you must tell them it was all you. Officially. Clear Laurence and Charles."

"What did they offer you, Sébastien?" I asked softly. "Or is this your moment to be better than your brothers and make your parents love you?"

He pulled away as if I had hit him, and I knew it was true.

Sébastien left and didn't return, but neither did Waleran or his people. They moved me from the room to the back of a wagon, my pale skin burning in the hot sun. After another day, we crossed the Pinch, and I was left hooded and shackled in the hay-filled stall of a barn somewhere in Monts Lance. The next morning, one of the guards made me drink beef broth and water till I thought I might be sick. Another loosened my shackles.

"Madame," someone said, too far away for me to really answer, but another voice did.

"Who are you again?" my mother asked, voice so steady and even, I could picture the exact expression on her face. "If you are so worried about her escaping in my care, perhaps your true concern should be how poor a chevalier that would make you. She's not even a half-trained hack, my artistry lies in minor illusions, and you are an apprentice to Chevalier du Ferrant. What could we possibly do?"

The guard muttered something, the blush evident in his voice, and hurried footsteps tore toward me. The hood flew off my head.

"Emilie?" My mother touched my face, my neck, ran her hands down my bruised arms and rattled the shackles, and wrapped me in a hug. The spectacles bit into her neck, I knew, but she didn't seem to mind. Her tears soaked my collar. "Are you all right? Are you hurt?"

"No," I said. "I'm fine."

She didn't smell of flowers. She always smelled of flowers, always dabbed perfume along the pulse of her throat and wrists. She always wore freshly cleaned clothes and her mother's silver, but her dress was wrinkled and dusty from the road. Her hands were bare.

"It'll be all right." My mother swallowed. Nothing in me knew the tense, empty expression on her face. "I can't get you out of here yet, but they have very strict instructions about your care."

She touched my scratched cheeks. My bruised hands.

"It's fine," I said again, and instead of looking at her face, I closed my eyes and urged my body to heal. It was easy, even without my hands to guide the magic. "See?"

She kissed my scalp again. "You can do all of that, even with these on?"

"It takes longer. I'm not used to it. What are you doing here?"

My mother shrunk, shoulders rolling down and hands retreating to her lap. They curled into fists. "You are my daughter. Of course I'm here."

"No, really, why?" I shrugged and nodded to our surroundings. "I have done everything you wanted me to avoid, so why are you here?"

It made no sense. I had dishonored the family legacy. Finally.

As we both knew I would.

"Of course I'm here. I love you," she said, crying and softly laughing all at once. "What are you talking about?"

"I'm not as oblivious as you think I am." I sniffed. "I am nothing like you wanted, and you can finally be rid of me."

"What?" She pressed her hand to my forehead, expression tight. "I don't want to be rid of you, Emilie. I'm here to—"

"You always tried to get rid of me. Piece by piece. All those little parts you hated—the things I liked, the friends I made, the way I looked, how I spoke, the arts I did. You rid me of them every day growing up. You wore them down till sometimes I hated them. How can you love me and say that, if every part of me is something you hate?" I sobbed and dropped my chin to my chest, her hands slowly sliding from my shoulders. There it was—debridement and Lord did it hurt. "Do you know how often I tried to show you what I could do and was met by punishment or horror? You looked at me like I was a monster! I was never good enough for you. I know it. I have known it for years. So stop lying to me and tell me why you're here."

She stared, mouth open, eyes so wet and wild, she looked nothing like herself, and whispered, "I'm so sorry."

"I have finally done something I'm proud of," I said through clenched teeth. If I moved any more, I would break. "Responsibility demands sacrifice, and if you want to be a good mother and comtesse, you will do whatever you can to stop Waleran because so many people are going to die who don't have to. If you help them, if you help His Majesty, disown me in death because I don't want your name on my grave. And if Annette is hurt for this, I will rip myself from death to make you pay."

"Emilie." Her fingers curled around my shoulder, loose and trembling. "Annette is fine. Vivienne Gardinier is dead, and Annette's arrest is more complicated than you think, but she is fine. I made sure of that."

"Well," I said, rubbing my wet face against my shoulder, "at least there is that."

"And you're not being executed. Laurel made a deal."

"What? No, no, no, they can't do that." I jerked forward, shackles weighing me down. "Mother, you have to stop them."

"Darling, they made the deal yesterday." She swallowed. "Laurence du Montimer and Estrel Charron confessed to starting Laurel and forming the group, and they provided quite a lot of evidence to prove it. They agreed to turn themselves in peacefully so long as certain conditions—like ensuring you, Annette, and anyone else arrested were allowed to live—were met."

"Laurence is Laurel?" I laughed, breath a whistle between my cracked lips. "No, he's not. He hates politics, and it's his name. He's not foolish enough to use his name for that. He bad-mouthed those flyers from Delest to Segance."

"It's his name and Estrel's," she said softly. "They started it when they were younger, right after the fights with Vertgana when Laurence abandoned his training as a chevalier and returned to university."

Laurence du Montimer and Estrel Charron—each one a half of the original Laurel.

"Laurence stayed out of politics in order to avoid suspicion while he funded the rebellion, and he exaggerated his feud with Estrel so when he was asked to find Laurel, he could clear her name. Then, when she began scrying and divining for the crown against Laurel, all she had to do was lie. The revolt has been years in the making, but Estrel gave it a name and—"

"She and Laurence agreed to take the blame if the revolt was ever in danger, didn't they? That's why they named it Laurel."

Laurel would die, the crown would be sated, and the revolt could live on and rise up, unsuspected. The crown could be taken by surprise, thinking Laurel was dead, and overthrown.

She nodded.

"They couldn't broker peace with Kalthorne, but no one else is to be executed for their roles in Laurel and, within the week, war or no, the crown must address Laurel's complaints and appoint a council elected by countrymen, not nobles. There are very strict stipulations that Demeine must follow." She took a deep breath and shuddered. "They designed a failsafe, you see. If their demands are not met, even after death, the artistry they did for His Majesty, the chevaliers, the university, and members of the noble houses will be undone. All of Laurence's healing will fail and Estrel's texts on disasters and futures and how to avoid them will burn. Her illusions at the borders keeping us safe will fall. Given how dependent we are on them, the court pressed His Majesty to agree."

Endure, she told me once, but how could I live like this when my lungs didn't work, my throat grew tight, and my heart was a hole in my chest.

"Is Laurence dead?" I asked.

"Not yet." She glanced behind her to the door of the barn. "He was transported to Serre for execution at noon today."

"Can you scry it?"

"Emilie, no." Her hand fluttered to my cheek, my hair, to the metal band of the spectacles around my face. She leaned her cheek against my crown. "You don't want to watch that."

"I need to." I didn't know what to do. I didn't know what I wanted now. "I have to."

My mother pulled her silver hand mirror from her pocket. The power in the air shifted, gathering in her and channeling through her hands. The silver flickered, reflection wavering, and she held it up between us, so we could both see the image rising to the surface of the silver. Serre, gold in the noonday light, burned into my mind.

There was Laurence, reedy figure towering over the others. His coat was gone, and he wore only a plain white shirt and brown breeches. His image blurred.

My mother's hands shook, the effort of channeling so much power rumbling through her, and I leaned against her shoulder. The magic spilled into me, my body sharing the burden of the channeling with hers. There were no sounds.

Laurence looked up once, face to the sun, and closed his eyes. His long hair had been gathered in a braid and wrapped around his head. An attendant rolled the high collar of his shirt down. There weren't many people near the scaffold at the top of one of Serre's towers. Most were members of the court. His Majesty stood, golden and scowling, next to the kneeling block where his nephew would die.

There, in the crowd, was Annette. She was shackled, hands bloodied, and gagged. A guard held her with one arm around her throat to keep her still and staring at the execution. His other hand held a hood like mine. The spectacles around her eyes were so tight, the skin along her brows had broken.

Another girl, blond and bruised, her hands bound, her mouth covered, and the guard at her back wearing two blackened eyes, struggled against her shackles. Annette didn't struggle.

Her gaze never left the face of the small, redheaded woman at her side.

Estrel Charron, shorter than I had always pictured, had the same haughty beauty as Charles but worlds more confidence. Her red hair was tucked beneath a coif, her neck bared by the low collar of her green dress. Her mouth moved. Laurence smiled.

He knelt, upright, and said his last words. I couldn't hear.

Monsieur du Ruse unsheathed the killing sword. He hefted the blade high, both hands tight about the grip. Laurence didn't even flinch.

It was a quick death.

It was still death.

The mirror went dark, and my mother gasped.

"Are you all right?"

"Yes," I said, and found that I was. I wasn't sad. I wasn't angry. I just was. "You should leave."

"Emilie..." Her lips brushed my forehead. "You make me very proud but also very, terribly scared for you, and I don't know what to do because I don't understand you as I thought I would. The idea of you wearing down or at war fills me with dread. The weight of it makes my tongue clumsy. I love you. I am proud of you. I am scared for you."

The little threads stitching what was left of my control together snapped. I tucked my face into her neck and cried, soft and still, no gasps or heaving shoulders, no snot or choking. I was a constant storm, a drizzle in the autumn months that never poured but never quite let up, and all the sad, sorry feelings seeped from me.

She was not lying.

She did not understand me.

She did not need to.

"Please," she whispered. "I cannot stay with you long. I must go back to court and make sure His Majesty holds true to the terms of Laurel's deal, but do not put yourself in more danger. Once that is done, they will release you into my custody."

"What about my work?" I asked.

They hadn't been able to stop the war, and Laurence was dead. How many would die because of that?

She shook her head.

"I'll be fine," I said, and it was not a lie either.

I would be fine because I had work to do.

On the fifth day, we were in Serre. They questioned me the whole way there, promising food and water if I talked. They'd locked spectacles like Estrel's over my eyes, tied a hood around my head, and shackled my hands behind my back, metal nipping into the divot between wrist and hand. I couldn't move, I couldn't see, I could barely hear through the thick fabric of the hood. There was no silver left on me, not after they had stripped me of anything shiny or sharp in the wagon on the way here. They'd taken my shoes off so I couldn't run. Coline had had another knife.

No, not Coline. Nicole, the Madame Royale of Demeine, had fought the whole way, and it made so much more sense. She wasn't only noble. She was royalty. No wonder she was so angry.

Life had never taught her that sometimes we just lose. That the world wasn't fair.

We did everything right and we died. The happenstance of death was that not even wealth made us immune to it.

And I thought I was the biggest liar among us.

They left me in a cell for days. I talked to myself. I screamed at Coline, so angry that she had so much power the whole time and used none of it. She had called that school a prison, but it was a blessing, and now it was dead. Vivienne was gone, and Isabelle had—

"Who helped you?" a guard I hadn't known was there asked.

I sobbed and laughed and threw myself back against the wall. "I helped myself because no one who was supposed to would."

The questions blurred together like ink smeared by a left-handed writer.

"How did you first get in contact with Laurel?"

"I prayed and Mistress Moon sent them," I said. "Do you think she would help you?"

I couldn't save Alaine, but I would protect everyone else come death or a different Demeine. Whichever freed me from this first.

"Did Estrel Charron assist you?"

I hadn't answered that for a long, long time. Long enough for their boots to grow heavy above my hands and my bones to crack. Long enough for them to call a physician. Long enough for them to forget the question.

And me.

They didn't come back for days. Then they did. A guard dragged me down a hall of stone, his arm locked around my throat. He carried me through the cool halls of a vast building and out into the bright heat of the sun. The stone floor burned against my bare feet, and I shrieked. The guard shoved a cloth in my mouth.

"This is a state function," he said, still dragging me. "Behave."

We were at the top of a tower, a crowd of nobles, gilded and dour, hung around the edges, and in the center was a raised scaffold. On it stood a stout man I didn't know in the golden armors of a chevalier, and behind him stood Henry XII, King of Demeine. Coline was at his side.

She screamed when she saw me. Her gag muffled the sound, and her bonds made her stumble, the shackles on her wrists padded but tight. She looked worse for wear, and her gray eyes were wide with wild fear. His Majesty didn't even look at her. Her guard yanked her back by her hair.

"The deal was she's not harmed, and that includes her feet." Estrel's rough voice sunk into me, and I turned. "Annette?"

She was wearing her favorite dress. Her skin was soft pink from being recently hurt and healed, the dark circles under her eyes deep as night. She sucked in a deep breath when she saw me.

"It'll be all right," she whispered and kissed my cheek. She slipped off her shoes and made me step into them. "Don't watch. You don't have to, and I don't want you to."

I tried to speak, but the gag held my tongue.

Estrel was on my left. She kept her chin up, the shackles around her hands clanking as she fidgeted. Laurence stood next her, looming, the bored expression on his face angering His Majesty until the end of his speech was pitchy and fast. Estrel leaned down once while His Majesty was distracted and kissed my crown.

"They're not killing you today. They're not allowed to," she whispered. "But this is very, very important—never feel guilty for this. It was my choice, and if it were not you, it would still be my choice. I made it years ago. Don't feel guilty. Promise me that."

I stared up at her, crying, and nodded.

Laurence went first, and his last words were in a language I didn't know, the rhythm of Estrel's name between unfamiliar words all I recognized.

I stared at Estrel. There was a sound like ice cracking. Estrel flinched.

I did what she asked.

I didn't watch.

"See what happens when you move against Demeine?" the guard asked.

He turned my head to see, and I closed my eyes. Safe in the dark.

They put the hood back on me, and they carted me back down the stairs, into the depths of Serre until I didn't know where I had come from or where I was going, and only knew that I was in the dark and the dark was in me. They sent no one else to me. Days slipped away.

Alone, in the dark of the hood and cell, I stayed. Estrel's shoes were too big, but I kept them on my feet. They were soft and simple, thin leather that knotted around the ankles, and I didn't tie them. I couldn't with my hands shackled behind me. Whatever deal she had made had saved me.

"I have to get out of here." Yvonne might have been in danger. There was no telling what His Majesty would do to Coline. What if they had caught Isabelle? The war with Kalthorne wasn't over. We, the country kids who became soldiers and hacks and varlets because we had no other way to survive, would die in a war we'd no business being in. The crown wore us down like magic—surely, slowly, till death. "I have to get out of here."

The hood scratched my lips, fabric catching on the tears, and I walked the walls of the cell. Three of stones, one of bars, none of them more than three paces. What would Estrel do?

Die.

I shuddered. I couldn't be sad. I couldn't give in.

She was dead. She was dead. She was dead.

"They're underestimating you." Estrel's voice was a distant whisper, broken, stuttering, but hers nonetheless, and the midnight arts trembled as she spoke. "What do we do to the people who underestimate us?"

"You're dead," I whispered.

She laughed. "You're not. So do something."

The hood was easy. I dragged my face down the wall, ripping it off. The shackles were sharp in my skin, the edges tight, and I stared at Estrel's shoes, the magic in me gathering. It was night, the magic in the air too weak for what I wanted to do, so I channeled it until my nose bled and clotted, till my skin stung, till it hurt even to turn my head. Everything, I pushed into the shackles.

They shattered.

Power, unchecked, corrupted.

I yanked Estrel's shoes from my feet and clutched them to my chest.

See what happens when you move against Demeine?

I set her shoes in front of me. In the left, in blood, was one word, and in the right was a time.

SCRY. 4 MORN.

I laughed. Of course she wouldn't leave me alone, not like this. All I needed was a surface, a reflection, and I could see her again. I reached up and tore the spectacles from my eyes, yanking out hair and bits of pinched skin with them, and the thick, dark yellow lenses glinted in the dim light from my one narrow window.

I held the spectacles up to the light, metal arms gold, and carefully channeled as much power as I could bear into the metal.

"Well, this is fitting." It was Estrel's voice, but the vision was blurred, slanted like light in rippling water. I pulled more power and refocused. Her familiar hands curled around the bars of a cell like mine. Her knuckles were bloody and bruised. Two fingers were broken. "If he still thinks we're the biggest threats and the Laurels are weak without us, he has another think coming."

"What else was there for us to do?" a deep voice raspy with exhaustion asked. "Let them die so we could carry on? What is a country and its leader if they let children die?"

"Let us not have our last conversation be about philosophy." Estrel pulled herself up until she was on her knees and leaning against the bars. Her red hair hung in knots stuck to her freckled face with sweat and blood, and one eye was completely swollen shut. She licked her lips. "Laurence, can you move?"

A hand, equally as broken and shackled as Estrel's, covered hers. "I can. The real question is will my broken ribs pierce anything important when I do?"

"I know we left out the don't-torture-us part on purpose to sweeten the deal," Estrel said and groaned. "I'm regretting it."

"He was so excited, he didn't question that wage clause, though." Laurence grunted. "No, can't sit up. Ribs are all over the place."

Estrel knelt down, so her cheek was to the floor and her face was near his. Her hand slipped between the bars and brushed his hair from his face. She twirled a strand around her fingers. He kissed her palm.

"I'm sorry you won't get to talk to Annette." Laurence's eyes fluttered shut. "I had to say goodbye to Charles. He said I was 'a very annoying older sibling he didn't ask for with a lot of advice he definitely never asked for but cherished.'" He chuckled and turned his face to her. "I named him my heir in my will, for my books and research if the title and holdings are disbanded."

I swallowed. The vision wavered, the power I was channeling rising up in my skin as welts.

"That has given me a lovely idea." Estrel sat up, kicked off her shoes, and gnawed open the wound on her hand until it bled.

"What are you doing?" he asked. "Take pity—it hurts too much for me to look."

"Annette is going to scry me, and I'm going to have my last words with her." Estrel scribbled in the bottoms of her shoes and let them dry. She tucked herself back up against the gate. Her forehead pressed to the bars. "I agreed not to speak with her. Me talking to nothing and her scrying me doesn't count."

Laurence laughed and turned his head so his nose was against hers. "You could've written a normal letter in your will. I did. It was very cathartic."

"There wasn't time," she said. "I didn't realize… It doesn't matter."

"You are such an exquisite pain," he muttered. "Have your conversation. It's not as if I can leave, though."

Estrel rolled up into a sitting position. She looked horrible and wonderful, everything I wanted but not here. She narrowed her eyes and glanced around. Then, as if I had really been there, her eyes stared straight at mine.

"Right, there you are, Annette," she whispered, tears in her eyes. "I'm sorry, darling, but I'm going to die tomorrow. Luckily, that's part of the plan. Unluckily, it happened sooner than I thought it would. I hope you didn't watch."

"I didn't," I said to the ghost of her that couldn't hear me. Couldn't know I'd ever see this.

"I don't have a title or land to offer you." She wiped her cheeks clean and closed her eyes. "I don't remember my family. I don't know if I had siblings, but I know that, if you wanted, I would have been very happy to think of you as one. And if nothing else, you were my apprentice, Annette Boucher. You are brilliant, and you are enough. You always were. They're probably going to attempt to go back on the deal we made with them, and that's fine. We expected that. They're going to underestimate you and the rest of the people, though. They think removing the instigators will remove the problem because they're shortsighted. Make them regret it. Make them acknowledge you. I love you."

The metal cracked. My magic broke, channeling slowing to a creep. I sobbed and bowed my head into my lap, face wet, throat tight. I couldn't say the words.

What did it matter? There was no one left to hear them.

"Mistress," I whispered. "We deserve better than this."

I sunk into my power like I always did. No water. No bowls. No quicksilver. Down and down and down to the little bits of me too small to be tangible, to where power flickered between my pieces, and I searched for other bodies, other people. A soldier guarded the door outside this block of cells, and his body was nothing but flickering parts. Illusions work by tricking the brain, laying down a blanket of magic and covering it over with what the artist want to show them. We believe so easily what the world shows us.

I dredged up the guard's memories of home. I made the world seem dark to him, like evening at shift change. The hallway to this cell block became the twisting roads and alleys of Serre, and he stumbled down them as if drunk. The keys in his pocket were to the room he rented. He opened my cell.

"Thank you," I said, standing to meet him.

He whistled and didn't hear me because I was in his mind and didn't want him to. He dropped the keys into my hands, thinking they were the table by his door. I pulled the cell shut behind him. He froze.

"What?" He spun, frantic, and shook the bars. "What did you do to me?"

I leaned against the wall across from them. Behind my back, my hands trembled. Everything hurt. Every part of me was alive.

"Nothing," I said. "Less than you did to me."

I didn't know I could be so cold.

The soldier laughed, deep and dragging out of his throat with a rasp. Alaine's silver necklace glittered at his wrist. "Do you know what they're going to do to you? You go out that door, you're dead."

It had taught me many things, this nation called Demeine.

"Yes, I know very well what they'll try to do." I ripped her necklace from him and tied Estrel's shoes. "They're going to under-estimate me, and I'm going to teach them not to do it again."

To any of us.

My mother left, and the soldiers—Chevalier Waleran du Ferrant's apprentice and two hacks—checked me over to make sure she hadn't slipped me anything.

"That's very insulting," I said to the apprentice. "Have you no respect for my mother or our name?"

This apprentice was my age, some younger son from one of the newer families, and he followed the orders Chevalier du Ferrant had left to the letter.

"It's not an insult, Madame," he said, head ducked. Even with me in shackles, he clung to the rules of polite society. "It's standard."

After an hour, he was still guarding me, and my mother was most likely far enough away.

"Are we still going to war with Kalthorne?" I asked him, sighing as if I were bored.

He glanced back, eyes narrowed. "Of course. And your needless outrage at His Majesty means we will be fighting ourselves as well as Kalthorne. Chevalier du Ferrant is having to focus on rousing up soldiers instead of preparing for those Thornes."

"Needless?" I stretched out my legs. "But not false?"

"His Majesty is more necessary than some hack," he said, but he shifted and looked toward the door. Neither of the hacks he worked with was here. "Without him, we are nothing."

My mother had left me with a deep, unsettling certainty that Demeine was going to crumble if this continued. A lot of people were going to die, and there was no need for it. Without the chevaliers, the nobles leading the charge, would the army fight? They hadn't wanted to, certainly. Kalthorne hadn't either.

There would be no safety while His Majesty and his court ruled, and this apprentice wasn't assuaging those fears.

"I was du Montimer's hack, you know." I focused on the parts of me in charge of panic and fear. Stopping my body from recognizing pain would be too much, given how tired I was now, and this would hurt. If I was in shock, my reaction would be dulled. That would be enough. "I would bet you were one of the soldiers I healed with him."

My heart sped up, my palms began to sweat, and a little tug of fear took hold of my stomach. A light-headed flutter filled me.

The apprentice shifted again, rocking from foot to foot. "I was very appreciative of our physicians while I was there."

I bit down hard on the collar of my shirt and dislocated my thumbs. Pain shot through me. The shackles clattered together as my hands, sweat-slicked, slipped from them. The apprentice glanced back at me.

"What are you doing?" he asked, stalking toward me.

I raised my hands, free and crooked, and channeled enough magic to slam my thumbs back into place and leave welts down my skin. He stopped.

I didn't need to do magic to know what had been done to him. The way his scar had healed, the way his bones felt strong and repaired beneath my prodding, was all Rainier. I pulled the spectacles from my face and threw them aside. He drew his sword.

I channeled magic without a care, drawing it through my fingers and twisting them, sending it out to the muscles in the apprentice's mouth where Rainier had healed a fractured jaw. I didn't need a way into this boy's body. Rainier was familiar enough. The muscles seized. The apprentice clawed at his mouth.

No wonder physicians and chevaliers used hacks. I could do anything—for a price. Already, my hands shook and thin strips of skin peeled away from my nails where the magic had channeled. My thumbs were black and old-blood brown with bruises.

"You got stabbed." I peeled away the old healing of Rainier's artistry from beneath this soldier's shirt. Bone fractured, vessels tore, flesh ripped open as if it had never been healed at all. "My friend Rainier healed it, but he's dead, and you don't get to reap the rewards of letting your people die for you."

A dark, dark strain seeped across his shirt, the linen gathering blood like I gathered magic, and he groaned. His sword hit the ground. Then his knees did.

"My mother didn't have to gift me anything," I said, staring down at him. "I have all I have ever had, and it will always be enough."

Me, alone.

I left him bleeding on the ground in Monts Lance. He wouldn't die; I didn't undo enough of the wound for that. There had been others guarding me, but they weren't artists, and it was easy to put them to sleep. There was no need to hold back now. I rode one of their horses east for three days.

No one questioned someone riding *toward* a war, and if the soldiers I left behind gave chase, they never caught up.

Laurence and Estrel had made a deal, but I doubted they were the true originators of Laurel. They were simply the ones who had agreed to take the fall when trouble came. There was little to do but think while traveling, and my time with Laurence repeated over and over in my mind. Of course he was one of the Laurels, and now His Majesty thought he had taken out the biggest threat. If we attacked Kalthorne, there would be no going back.

Chevalier Waleran du Ferrant and Physician Pièrre du Guay would have no mercy for the soldiers and hacks who refused to fight, and how many would die in the fights with Kalthorne that came after? They had to be stopped.

Smoke rose over the large military camp at Segance. I rode my stolen horse until I was close enough to see the line of soldiers walking the western border. Everyone would surely know what had happened by now, my name and what had happened all over, and there was no way I would be allowed to simply walk back into camp. I stayed on the edge and watched, timing the soldiers as they paced and kept watch. I couldn't handle all of them.

They came in twos. I crept closer, low to the ground and channeling as much magic as I could so I was ready. Two soldiers approached, laughing and chatting. I altered the alchemistry of the one nearest to me. They slumped and snored.

I slipped into the flesh of the other one, my mind melting away as theirs filled my head, and tried to prod their body to sleep. Their head jerked up to me, and I reared back. They tackled me.

Their knees hit my chest, their hands grabbed my throat. I gagged and flailed. They shoved me hard into the dirt. Their nails cut into my skin.

"Stay down," the soldier said, blinking back the sleep I tried to settle over them.

Insomnia.

I gathered magic and channeled through my neck, into their hands. They shrieked and smacked me. My vision went black.

Then they were gone. I coughed and rolled out of the way, sight coming back slowly. A blurry figure approached.

"Are you trying to die?"

I coughed again and rubbed my eyes.

Charles—lip busted and a purple bruise blossoming across the corner of his mouth, shirtsleeve torn and smoldering where fire had lapped at his skin, and hair a crown of bloodred tangles—kneeled before me. His arm curled around my waist and the other touched my throat, healing the worn-out flesh and crushed cartilage there. I leaned against his side and sobbed. His magic felt like spring.

"Emilie?" He tapped my cheek. "You're worn out."

"I'm fine," I said, voice rough. "We have to go before they get up. Chevalier du Ferrant and the phys—"

"One step ahead of you." Charles hooked his other arm beneath my knees and hoisted me up. "A lot's happened. Madeline is well. Laurence is dead."

"I know." My head lolled against his chest, the steady thump of his heart heavy in my ears, and I licked my lips. "I saw."

A few steps from the fight and after adjusting my alchemistry enough to keep me walking, Charles set my feet on the ground. "The other camps are refusing to attack Kalthorne, but Chevalier du Ferrant has Physician du Guay backing him up with a few apprentices and soldiers. They could kill us all, but then they would have no one and no power left to attack Kalthorne. We're in a standstill now."

I hummed. "How can I help?"

"I don't know," he said, sighing and failing to blow his sweat-heavy hair from his eyes. "It's a mess."

"Well," I said, brushing his hair from his eyes, "this might be the concussion speaking, but saving lives looks good on you. Thank you for saving me."

"Those were some of our dear chevalier's people." He laughed. "You're lucky I was over here."

"We need to get rid of him and Pièrre." I leaned against Charles as we walked. Each step, each breath, filled me with a renewed sense of purpose. "If we kill them, we remove their threat to the camp and prevent the attack on Kalthorne."

They were two of His Majesty's staunchest supports, and without control of his army, how much power did a king really have?

"I don't know how we didn't assume you were Madame des Marais. Such arrogance," muttered Charles. "Madeline nearly laughed herself to death when she heard."

"I know you're teasing me." I tilted my chin up and grinned. "However, I much prefer *confidence*. Nicer connotations."

We broke through the thin line of trees. The camp was oddly quiet, soldiers clumped in groups and whispering to each other. No one paid us much mind, most turned the moment they saw us, and Charles murmured that there had been several fights earlier. He led me to the infirmary tent, and inside, the hacks were busy. Soldiers with bloody noses sat to be healed. Madeline and Physician Allard's hack Louis ordered everyone around.

"Physician Allard's dead," Charles whispered. "He had an argument with Physician Pièrre du Guay. The soldiers broke up the fight."

Physician Allard wasn't noble. He had been one of the few common boys to rise from hack to physician.

"Sit here," Charles said, one hand on my shoulder holding me down and the other cupping my cheek. "Do not move. Do not channel anything. Rest for once in your life."

He joined Louis near the opening of the tent. They chatted and flipped through a journal that might have been Laurence's, and Charles started directing other hacks and a handful of apprentices on what to do. Power fit him well, his panicked expression calming as he and Louis counted up how many were here. Charles frowned, and I sighed. He had so much left he wanted to do, none of it killing.

He shouldn't have been burdened with stopping this war and getting blood on his hands.

"You know," a familiar, drawling voice said, "I was going to say all sorts of mean things to you for leaving with no hint of a note and then getting arrested, Madame."

Madeline sat next to me. A green silk scarf was wrapped around her hair, and smoke stained the collar of her dress. A new scar split her chin.

"Did you hear me, Madame?" she asked, my title on her tongue very much an insult. At least she was smiling as she said it. "But watching you pine might be better."

"I'm not pining." I scowled.

I wasn't—Charles and I were friends and colleagues, and half of our relationship was a lie, the other half stained with death.

I couldn't ruin my friendship with Charles. He was important to me. Our jobs were important to both of us. To have neither him nor medicine in my life would be a tragedy I couldn't accept.

"We have more important things to worry about anyway," I said.

Though, even if we had the time, Charles had no reason to like me. I was selfish. It wasn't a secret and I wasn't unaware, but it had never been an issue. It had been a blessing.

Cauterization.

It didn't hurt to be disliked if I didn't care about anyone else.

"Yes, but you look sad, and I'll be damned if I let that physician and his chevalier make me feel sad," said Madeline. "And looking at the mess you are right now makes me feel sad. So for my sake, please stop."

I glanced at her. "I'm sorry I lied, but I'm glad that lying led me to you. I wish I had told you the truth."

Her head tilted, as if the world were crooked, and she laced her fingers through mine. "Don't leave without saying goodbye ever again."

I dropped my head to her shoulder. "I got arrested. I didn't leave."

"I don't care," she said. "Figure it out."

I laughed and shook my head, and Charles approached again.

"What's the plan?" I asked.

He took a deep breath. "Subdue the soldiers and hacks coerced by Chevalier Waleran du Ferrant and Physician Pièrre du Guay. Then, kill them before they can attack Kalthorne."

So, we only had to kill the best fighters in Demeine.

"Lovely," I said. "Where do we start?"

Annette

M*ake them regret it.*

The words burned in me, cold and hot and all the pain between, like a portent I couldn't quite read. There was another guard outside the door to the cell block, and the spectacles seared my hand. Divination without limits was a whole new kind of knowing. I didn't even need to look.

"You're going to survive this," I said. "And you're going to change your name."

The guard spun, hands empty, and I ducked a full second before he swung. I got in close. Grabbed his arm.

His mind was a map of his fears, and the illusion seeped from my skin like sweat.

"You used to have nightmares about disappearing." Beneath my fingers, his arm began to disappear. His shoulder, his chest. "That was me."

He screamed and screamed and screamed, a flare of power in my sight that only someone with magic could see. Blood trickled down my arm.

The hallway I turned down was pitted with cells. Most were empty, the doors ajar and dust a thick carpet on the floor. These halls were underground, the thin windows running along the top of each cell half-covered in earth, and at the end of the hall was a soldier in the sunrise-red stitched with fiery-blue uniform of the Serre royal guards. A bend in the hall kept the final cell out of sight and muffled the voices beyond. I crept forward.

"Don't breathe it in. Don't touch it either."

The voice nearly froze me.

I rounded the bend. Yvonne, spectacles shattered and dangling from one ear, smoking vial clasped in her hands, scarf pulled across the lower half of her face like a mask, dripped something dark and burning onto the lock of a cell. Aaliz and someone else were backed up against the opposite wall. Aaliz's gaze jerked to me.

"Yvonne," they said, pointing.

Yvonne glanced back. Her hands stilled, whatever alchemical mixture she was pouring eating all the way through the metal beneath them. She corked the vial and slipped it into her pocket.

"What have you done?" Yvonne lunged and stopped. Her gloved hands fluttered near my face. "You're hurt."

I wiped my face with the back of my hand. "I'm fine. You're hurt. What are you doing here?"

"I got your note." Yvonne touched her pocket. "Bosquet's tearing itself apart over Vivienne's death, and we weren't sure what they were going to do with you. I have might have gone through your room looking for anything that could help."

I reached out and straightened her spectacles. "So you threatened to kill me if I ever betrayed you and Laurel, something about me being noble and playing at generosity."

From the cell, Aaliz and their companion laughed.

"About that," Yvonne said, and I shook my head. "Fine, then about this."

Yvonne kissed my cheek, softly, quickly, closer to my lips than to my ear, and I returned the gesture. I pressed my forehead to her shoulder.

"So, you're not killing me," I said. "How do you feel about killing the king?"

She blinked down at me, lips quirked up on one side. "That's the first time someone's suggested assassination in response to me kissing them."

Aaliz cleared their throat. "I'm really happy for you two and all, but I would like to leave now."

Yvonne and I knocked the lock from the cell door and pulled it open. Aaliz was worse for wear, a bit thinner, a bit older. Their companion I'd never seen before.

"Brigitte," she said, clapping me on the back. "The Laurel in Delest."

She was pretty, the same way forest fires were—hooded brown eyes beneath thick black brows, a square jaw with a bruise the size of a fist blossoming across the bottom half, old scars and new wounds running through her white skin. Her short nose had been broken once. She pulled two sickles from the guard and hooked them on to a leather harness beneath her coat. Aaliz took the guard's coat and short sword. They looked good in red.

"What are you all doing here?" I asked. "How'd you get caught?"

"Easily and on purpose," said Brigitte. "We needed to get in, so we could find our dear Madame Royale."

I scowled. "Right, Coline. How come you put up posters with her signature? Told everyone where she was."

"People like knowing someone powerful is on their side." Aaliz pointed to Brigitte. "And we'd been looking for her since she got caught working with us."

"They were plotting to overthrow His Majesty with the Madame Royale," Yvonne said to me. "Apparently we're all out of the loop."

Aaliz nodded. "It's a very small loop."

"You want to do it now?" I asked. Aaliz and Yvonne glimmered, the magic they could store as alchemists collected in their hands. Brigitte was blank. "We get Coline and kill them? We'd be breaking Estrel's deal, but—"

"If Estrel Charron and Laurence du Montimer made that deal thinking it would stick, they weren't half as smart as anyone thought." Aaliz sucked on their teeth and shook their head. "They made sure His Majesty couldn't touch us for now. The court probably knows it too. They were just buying time."

"Great," I said, clapping my hands together once. "Let's kill them."

Aaliz and Brigitte glanced at each other.

"We were going to wait for reinforcements," Brigitte said. "What's your plan?"

"Them sickles decoration?" I pointed to the weapons she'd hidden under her coat. "I can tell you when to dodge and when to swing, and none of them will touch you."

The future was mine, and they could not take it away from me.

Yvonne sucked in a breath, and Aaliz shook their head again.

"No one could keep up with that much channeling." Their brow furrowed. "Even if you could, it could kill you. You'd wear down faster than we could fight."

"There's only one chevalier here, and that's the executioner," I said. "Henry XII was one, but I'll bet I can survive longer divining than he can fighting."

Brigitte laughed. "You're—"

"She is that good," a soft voice said. "She is very good."

I turned to the little nook my back had been facing this whole time. Isabelle ducked when I looked at her, shoulders rolled in. She was smaller and paler and sadder than I'd ever seen her, and the distance she'd put between us hurt. I sniffed.

Yvonne pulled me back. "She's the one who told Aaliz and I what happened, and she helped me get in here."

"I'm still angry," I said. "But you'll help, right?"

"Yes." Isabelle came to us. A mottling of bruises speckled her arms and neck, and paint stained her hands. "Anything. I'm so sorry."

"Right," Brigitte said quickly. "Reunions when we survive. Let's go get our queen."

Aaliz stopped us at the stairs out of the cell block.

"I need to find the others and make sure there isn't a massacre in Serre. People are still angry, and they're not backing down. The court holds power because they have power, martial and magical, and they'll kill every Laurel supporter in Serre if things go badly." Aaliz sighed, the light catching in all the wrinkles of their face, and I realized they weren't that much older than me. Only tired. "Can you kill the king alone?"

I nodded. "We can do this."

And even if we couldn't, someone had to save everyone else.

"Good." Aaliz touched Brigitte's shoulder. "Until next time."

"There will be one," Brigitte said as Aaliz left. She turned to the rest of us. "Let's go."

I divined the guard positions. When they moved, where they

walked—I saw it all, and we wove through the building like shadows. It was easy, scrying, when I had nothing to lose, and Yvonne curled one arm around my waist, leading me down the halls as I was lost in visions of the present and pointing where to go. Coline was a star, a beacon behind the walls of this wing. She'd fought.

She'd bled, the magic her channeling had left in her smeared along the floor and walls.

I stopped us outside a door where a guard had been standing moments before. Isabelle had brought her paints, and she'd drawn an illusion so real, it made me wince when I looked at it. Gabriel, alive, sprinting down the hall. The guard had taken off after him.

I opened the door. A teacup shattered on the wall next to my head.

"You're welcome." I ducked, waiting for the next blow. "Madame Royale Nicole du Rand, duchesse de Segance."

I picked up the nearest thing to me and hurled it at Coline. She shrieked, arms up and blue ink splattering across her shoulders. A small pot of ink bounced off her arm. "Annette! What was that for?"

I swallowed. Permanent ink by the looks of the magic stored in the bottle. "You liar!"

"Like you aren't?" Coline, blond hair tangled behind her, threw up her ink arms, and flung more ink across the floor. "You had so many lies going, you couldn't even keep yours straight. Least mine was because my father would've killed me and everyone I loved."

That was a good reason.

I slunk more into the room and turned my nose up at her like she always did to food she didn't like. "I guess, but I'm still angry at you."

Coline flinched. "How angry?"

"Not angry enough to not be happy you're alive," I said. "Angry enough I might yell at you, though."

"Such syntax," Coline muttered. She dropped her knees at my feet. "I am very, very sorry I lied to you. Please help me kill my father."

I shifted. Pretty sure queens weren't supposed to bow like this. Ever.

"We were sort of coming here for your help with that," I said. "Get up. It's weird."

Coline stared up at me through her lashes, grinning. "Thank you, Madame."

"Get up." I leaned down and kissed her cheek. It was hard to be cold when she was alive, Isabelle was here, and we were all together again.

Coline kissed mine in return. "I'm glad you're here, though I was looking forward to saving the day."

I stepped aside to help her up, and she caught sight of the others behind me.

"Brigitte?" she said, the word a choked whisper.

"Hello again, Madame." Brigitte reached down and helped Coline to her feet. "Still dramatic, I see."

"You're not dead." Coline's chest heaved, and she let out a half sob. Her fingers skimmed the planes of Brigitte's face and taut muscles in her arms. "You're not dead at all. I knew it. I knew it. I also feared it, but you're alive and—"

Brigitte very gently kissed Coline's mouth and stopped her rambling. I glanced at Isabelle. She blushed and stared at the ceiling. I cleared my throat.

Coline pulled away only slightly, eyes half-closed. Brigitte smiled.

"Right," Coline said, breathless. "Let's kill my father."

No soldiers are supporting them, only their apprentices and a few hacks, but Chevalier du Ferrant was trained to take down a dozen soldiers without so much as sweating," Charles said to the small collection of soldiers and hacks crowded into the infirmary. "And he'll have Pièrre to heal him even if he does get injured."

The older hack Louis laughed, the bitter sound rustling from his tired body. "We probably can't win, and that's the hard truth of it, but it's better than dying in a war we didn't want with people we have no quarrel with."

We all agreed, and one of the soldiers muttered about already sending away those who didn't want to fight Kalthorne but had no desire to fight Chevalier du Ferrant. We had fifty confident soldiers, a handful of new ones, one half-trained physician's apprentice, and three hacks. Our odds were not particularly good.

"How many apprentices and hacks does Pièrre have?" I asked. "And Waleran?"

Charles's jaw tensed. "Five hacks total and two apprentices— including Sébastien."

"I'm sorry," I mouthed to him when the others in our group were talking a moment later, and he only nodded. That was unfortunate.

But Sébastien had always seemed, above all else, afraid of disappointing his family and not living up to his brothers. Relatable.

Much more unfortunate, but it couldn't be helped.

"Can we get close enough to undo their past healings?" I asked. It was not simple but it was quick; it would disorient the ones not used to such tactics. Perhaps we could subdue the hacks and apprentices without killing them.

Louis shook his head. "Chevaliers are trained to resist that, and Pièrre would recognize the attempt."

"But what if we focus on the hacks and apprentices?" I leaned up from the bed I had been sitting on, and Madeline grabbed the back of my shirt. "They're used to being the most important and always assume they're being attacked, so what if we don't? Without hacks or help, they'll still be good but not as good. They'll wear down as quickly as we do."

Louis shrugged. "True. I'd rather not kill the hacks, though, so we'd have to pull back and keep the wounds nonlethal."

"We could divide and conquer." Charles ran a hand through his hair and tugged at the ends. "Half of us keep the soldiers up, and the other half go after the apprentices and hacks once we're close enough and they're distracted."

"I'll take the lead healing the soldiers." Louis rubbed his forehead. His normally warm black skin was dull, little cuts and cracks marbling his face. "No offense, Charles, but I've got years of experience on you."

"I can't take any when it's true," Charles said. "If I make a mistake, I would rather it not be on them."

Madeline cleared her throat and crossed her arms, nails picking at the dry skin where her channeling had worn away the top layer. "I'll go with Louis, then. I have training and frankly fear what Physician du Guay will do if he sees me."

"Well, we're divided." Louis took a deep breath. "Let's only hope the rest of Demeine doesn't abandon us."

All in all, after Louis and Charles had spoken to everyone who had agreed to help, we were sixty-two strong, and yet I wasn't sure even that would be enough. It had to be. We had to be.

And whatever came next, we would be enough for too.

Charles had discarded his orange coat and pulled on the leather armor of a soldier who had left for home. Louis offered us each a vial of something mint-scented and blue that shot through us like lightning and jerked my body awake. Charles walked with him, talking about ingredients and methods. Madeline fell into step beside me as we searched the camp for supplies.

There was no armor that fit me. Madeline pursed her lips, rubbing the thin fabric of my worn shirt between her fingers. I held a helmet over her, waited for her to nod, and settled it on her head. The leather crushed her wrapped hair, but the flaps at least covered her ears and main artery. We even stole a pair of boots far sturdier than hers, the calves reinforced to keep the soldier wearing them safe, and I fiddled with the laces till Madeline could fit into them. It took both of us working to lace them up, me kneeling before her to make sure they fit right. I laid my cheek against her knee.

"Madeline," I said softly, "are we friends?"

I wanted to hear her say it, needed to hear her say it. I had heard my mother mutter *I love you* between caustic comments about my clothes or interests or ever-growing list of failures, and most of my life had been the same—mild disinterest and confusion were the only things I elicited from anyone. Never friendship. Never love.

Lord, even if it were a lie, I still wanted to hear it.

Her fingers fell to my forehead as if she thought I had a fever. "Of course."

I didn't know what to say to that because it wasn't a lie—Madeline was terrible at lying—so I squeezed my eyes shut and pressed my lips to the back of her hand.

"Please don't die." I rose and straightened her helmet. "I want to see what glorious thing you do next with your life."

Madeline dug her nails into my arm, not painfully; it was only enough for me to know she was there and not letting go.

"Hold on to that thought." She wrapped her arms around me, far too tight for comfort, and didn't let go till her hands started to shake. "I'm going to boss you around so much when we're physicians."

"You may try." I hugged her back. "Let's go."

Charles fell back in step with us. "Physicians and hacks always stay out of the fight near the back, so we'll have to circle around and hope they don't notice."

We stilled and let the others walk past us.

"I was supposed to be your hack anyway, wasn't I? Anyone else would have forced you to use one." I nudged his shoulder with mine and lingered. "At least now it's for a good cause."

He let out a short laugh through closed lips and nudged me back. "I'm not a good cause?"

"No, you're a good person, but even the best people need help sometimes." I couldn't save everyone—it was noble arrogance to think I could or should even try when I had done so much damage already—but I could be a shield. I touched his hand. "Don't panic about me wearing down. Don't get distracted. You're sweet to worry about everyone, but you can't now. It's fine."

"It is not," he said softly, taking my hand and holding me back even as the last group of soldiers walked ahead. "They don't know you're here and might think I left. If we don't have numbers, we should at least have the element of surprise." He blinked at me, autumn eyes wide, and leaned his forehead against mine. "I thought you hated sweet things."

"I'll make an exception."

"Please don't die." He kissed the tip of my nose and squeezed my hand. "We haven't finished our clinic competition yet."

Shouts echoed over the hill before us. Charles pulled me toward our right, toward the river separating Segance from Kalthorne. From the tree line, we could see the vast field of knee-high grass and trampled paths. We had a clear view of the fight, and there were more on Chevalier Waleran du Ferrant and Physician Pièrre du Guay's side than we had thought. A handful of soldiers protected them and blocked ours from getting near. Waleran sat atop a broad horse, his spear a golden needle against the bright blue sky. Already two of our soldiers lay unconscious in the dirt. The bitter tug of channeled noonday arts hung in the air.

Waleran wore alchemical armor, magic stored in the polished metal, so he could use it without wearing down. Behind him a good few paces stood Physician Pièrre du Guay, his red coat a stain on the horizon and the apprentices. Sébastien—orange coat replaced by the scarlet of a fully-fledged physician—looked as if he might be sick. Charles and I slunk as near as we dared.

"Sébastien might know I'm here," Charles said as we crouched in the tall grass. "He knows my magic quite well."

Thank the Lord for his narrow-mindedness.

"He doesn't know mine." My ears were full of heartbeats—rabbit-fast panicked ones and the slow, steady thump of unadulterated confidence that had to be Pièrre—and it took me longer than normal to find the hacks in the cacophony. "Which one first?"

"The one channeling for Sébastien," Charles said. He didn't question if I could do it, didn't explain what we would need to do. "We make it appear as if he fainted, use the time as they check that to get the others out of the way, and it removes Sébastien from play for a little while."

We were in the midst of a mess and yet his simple trust sustained me.

"Understood."

I gathered magic and held it in my chest, waiting for Charles to channel his magic through me, and his shoulder leaned against mine. The magic slipped between us like a breath, low and soft, and for a moment, I feared Charles was holding back until a jolt shook through my arm, my chest, and into the magic I had gathered. I channeled all into the ground and got lost in the feet of the grass, more power than a person would channel alone coursing through me. I jumped from minuscule cell to minuscule cell, riding the lightning of the living things between us and the hacks. None of the power was lost like it would have been if I channeled through the air.

"Oh," Charles breathed next to me. "That's why you always channeled down."

"I probably should have explained this," I said.

"Explain after." He shifted the magic, directing it up into the hack working for Sébastien. His body lit up in my magical sight, nerves constellations in a bloody sky, and Charles threw the hack's response system off balance.

The hack's heartbeat raced, the pressure of the blood in his veins dropped, and he plummeted to the ground. The art he had been channeling with Sébastien faded away.

I withdrew the magic we had channeled into the roots of the grass, so Sébastien wouldn't sense it. Charles's magic tested the other hacks.

"Wait," he whispered, watching them kneel to pick up the one who had fainted. "Until they're holding him up."

If they were all touching, we could channel the magic through them and remove three from the field at once.

We needed all of the advantages we could get.

The soldiers fighting with us were no match for Waleran. Madeline burned with power, healing our soldiers as Waleran's magic tore them down. She bled herself to replenish the blood a soldier had lost, channeling magic so it broke down her vein and built the veins up in them; the healing arts that Henry XII had twisted for his own means. She saved his life and urged her own body to replace the blood it had lost. The five soldiers who had sided with Waleran were dead. Pièrre and Sébastien hadn't healed them at all.

"Now," Charles said. "Do it now."

I looked away from Madeline and channeled for Charles. The magic slipped between the hacks, settling in the little gaps between their nerves, and between the two of us, it took nearly nothing to nudge the hacks' bodies toward sleep. They collapsed, tangled together and snoring. Sébastien whipped his head to us.

Charles shuddered, and I took the lead, channeling my own magic into Sébastien. From so far away, he should have been able to resist it, to alter his body alchemistry so that it countered what I did, but all he did was stare, wide-eyed, at Charles and me. He didn't try to fight the tug of sleep at all. He stumbled, not down but certainly out.

"Thank you," Charles whispered. He stood slightly, balanced on his toes, and took my arm. "We need to get closer if we want to get the rest."

A crossbow bolt tore through the grass next to us. Charles fell back, taking me with him. A burn, gathering noonday arts, so much magic the air around it shifted, stole my breath, and Charles lurched to his feet. Across the field, Waleran's apprentice, who was protecting Pièrre, readied another bolt and gathered more magic to attack Charles. He pushed past Sébastien.

All at once, the magic I had left in Sébastien vanished. He knocked the apprentice's hand aside and twisted his fingers as if making a surgical cut with the noonday arts. A bruise bloomed along the apprentice's neck. He clutched his throat and gagged.

A shout echoed across the field, and Waleran lashed out, transforming the tip of his spear into the thin point of a needle. The noonday arts swimming in the metal burned, and he whipped the spear upward. The sliver sheared from the spear and flew toward Sébastien.

He touched his chest, impaled, and opened his mouth once. His heart stopped. Twice. The alchemistry of his body stilled. He looked at us, mouthed *run*, and fell.

Charles howled. He gathered more magic than his body could handle, skin blistering as the power channeled out of him, and tried to heal Sébastien's corpse. When it didn't work, he threw himself forward.

"Charles!" I grabbed his arm and pulled him back. "Charles, no. He will kill you."

Magic gathered behind me. I twisted, hands tight around Charles. Waleran was staring at us, his horse still in the middle of the soldiers around him, and he shifted his gaze to Madeline. She was kneeling far from the fighting and healing a soldier whose head had been dented in by a blow.

"Stop him," I told Charles and pointed at Pièrre. "We haven't so much as nicked Waleran. I'm sorry about Sébastien, but we have to stop them now. The two of them alone could level a Kalthorne town and get us mixed up in a political mess we might not recover from. Stop Pièrre."

Charles nodded.

I sprinted to Madeline. The magic I gathered wasn't much but it was noticeable, held in my left hand like a stone. The rest I channeled through my feet and into the ground. I slipped, shoes slick with blood, and raised my left hand.

Waleran cut his spear up and redirected the magic as if it were nothing.

I had never studied the fighting arts, had never been interested in that branch of the noonday magic I so loved, but I knew an artist had to gather and channel it, and Waleran had no more hacks or apprentices left to channel for him. Even if he wore out, Pièrre would still heal him. No attacks I could think of would work.

So I stopped his horse's heart.

The horse collapsed, and Waleran fell with it, pinned beneath its side. I ripped my awareness from the horse and focused on Waleran. His leg was broken.

He tried to channel, desperate to be out from under his mount, and I severed the nerves in his arms. A whip of healing arts curled around his leg and healed the shattered bone, the magic too powerful and well done for me to break while the physician was still working, and I reopened an old, deep wound in Waleran's shoulder. Pièrre healed the severed nerves.

One of the soldiers Madeline had healed buried his sword through Waleran's neck.

I collapsed to my knees a few paces from Waleran. The soldiers with us moved in unison, turning their attention to Pièrre and the remaining hack. I waited for the last beats of Waleran's heart, but they never stopped. In the last dregs of magic I had left in him, I felt the structures of his throat repair themselves. There was too much damage, though. That was impossible.

The only way to heal such a wound was too replace the—

One of the soldiers screamed. Madeline scrambled away from the soldier she had been healing, her hands red and her face horrified. The flesh of the soldier's throat broke down until he couldn't scream or breathe, and all that was left was a wound identical to Waleran's. Waleran's heartbeat steadied, and he took a deep, chuckling breath. Madeline's gaze rose to something behind me.

A sliver of metal like the one that had killed Sébastien ripped through her shoulder. She let out a small gasp and looked down. The world stopped, singled in on the red stain spreading across her chest, and her knees slammed into the dirt. The power she had been gathering faded, seeping from her to the earth. Louis turned too slowly.

Another bolt caught him in the chest, knocked him from his feet, and landed him in the dirt next to Madeline.

I crawled to my feet to help them, and a hand curled around my ankle.

"That was my favorite horse." Each word Waleran said ground against the other, struggling to escape, and he flipped me over onto my back. "What an utter waste."

The spear in his other hand channeled magic in a circle around us, keeping the soldiers at bay. Too tired to gather magic without making the movement, I lifted my left hand. He pinned it to the ground with a sliver of metal.

Everything hurt, and I tried to push past it, to heal, but I couldn't while the metal still stuck there. A thin film of flesh, more like a

Stareater's wing than skin, sealed the wound. My fingers twitched and ached. I could feel the magic in my hand. There was too much. The ethereal pieces of me I took for granted were shifting, changing. Power corrupted.

Waleran yanked off his helm and stared at the odd white flesh of my wound. "You weren't meant to handle such power, and already your body is wearing down. Did you really think half-trained hacks with no grace in their veins could beat us?"

So many dead against so few.

"We had to try."

Waleran laughed and drew his sword. "Who's going to save you now, hack?"

TWENTY-EIGHT

Annette

W e should leave soon." Brigitte paced from door to window, keeping watch from the little room where we'd found Coline. It was mostly bare. The leftovers from the soldiers who had guarded Coline were useless, and we'd already divided up the two weapons that had been there. "We need to give them less time to scry or divine us. This will work better if all their attention is on the riot outside and not us."

"They killed their royal diviner," I said. "What are they going to do? Press their ears to the floor and pray?"

We'd watched the guards trickle from the building group by group. Every now and then, a growl would come crashing over the grounds like the warning cry of a hungry creature. His Majesty and his court could kill Laurel and make all the deals they wanted, but that didn't matter to most people. Those deals wouldn't come to fruition for months or years if we went to war with Kalthorne. Only

His Majesty would trust that a whole country would obey the rules of three people.

We had for decades, but now most of the chevaliers and artists were at the border and the soldiers in Serre were common. For once, His Majesty didn't hold all of the power.

"We're supposed to attack Kalthorne today," said Coline. "All eyes will be on Segance. It'll be him, Chevalier du Ruse, the royal guards, and whoever he had in court today to prepare for Kalthorne and deal with Laurel."

Chevalier du Ruse—the noble who had executed Estrel and Laurence.

I took a deep breath, exhaustion giving way to fury. "Let's go."

"Are you sure?" Isabelle's whisper was so soft, I almost missed it. Her fingers brushed my shoulder.

I nodded.

"Here." She carded her fingers through my hair, a fistful of brittle strands falling out completely, and braided it back from my face. "You're worn out."

"Aren't we all?"

"Not quite yet," Yvonne said.

"We're falling apart," I said with a laugh. "How's that for a portent?"

I grabbed the short sword from Coline's hand. There was too much power in the afternoon air, the desire to use it all overwhelming. I angled the blade in the sunlight until I could see a clear reflection of my face, the sunken eyes and cracked lips unfamiliar, and summoned up all my memories of Emilie. I had scryed her before, but now I summoned up the sound her voice and crook of her smile. She'd been so certain all those months ago in Bosquet. I needed her confidence now.

A chevalier, golden armor shining on top of a golden horse, broke through a line of Deme soldiers. Emilie threw up an arm. Power oozed like curdled blood in her veins.

"We're not attacking Kalthorne," I whispered. "The rest of the army's fighting the chevaliers."

And dying.

Coline muttered to herself, hands pressed together before her mouth. "This isn't just Serre." She inhaled and took back the sword. "There will be his personal guards, but if the army is revolting there, it might be elsewhere. Now's our chance."

"Great," I said. "One question—if we kill him, why are we immediately putting another noble on the throne?"

Brigitte pursed her lips, a grin twitching at the corners, and glanced at Coline.

"Annette?" Coline's hands clenched and unclenched at her sides. "Do you not trust me?"

"It's not about you." I ignored the pinch of regret in my stomach and sniffed. "Trust doesn't make you a good ruler."

"Aaliz said the same thing," Brigitte said.

"There will be a hole in power, and other nobles will attempt to fill that hole," Coline said quickly. "The revolts in Kalthorne failed, and the whole reason Laurel happened was to avoid a similar failure here. I have the resources to provide that security until it's no longer needed. Our neighbors value monarchies. They will try to conquer Demeine and take the throne if they think they have a claim to it. I prevent that claim." She looked at Brigitte who shrugged. "Also, I'm fairly certain if I don't follow through on my word, I'll be killed."

"That seems fair," Yvonne said. She held one of her vials up, magic bright. "I can maybe remove five guards from the equation, but I will have to be close to them. And this is for you."

She handed a yellow vial to Brigitte. Brigitte held it with her forefinger and thumb, as if it might burst at any moment.

"Anesthetic." Yvonne nodded to Brigitte's sickles. "Extremely fast acting, so cut them somewhere needful and it will numb the area within thirty seconds. Only lasts five minutes, though."

Brigitte tucked the vial into her chest pocket.

"All right." Coline laid one hand on Brigitte's shoulder and kissed her cheek. "Are we ready?"

I nodded and glanced back at Isabelle, a shadow over my shoulder. "Follow my lead."

She squeezed my shoulder.

We crept through the empty halls of the palace. The eerie silence in the walls and distant rumble of shouts stalked us. Brigitte whispered that Aaliz and some of the others had spent two days making sure the people who worked here knew enough to hide out but not enough to betray Laurel if they were so inclined, and Coline ran her hands along the walls like a child returned to an old home. She led us through the gilded wings, past portraits painted with gold flakes and the illusionary arts. Isabelle traced the lines of a portrait the size of a door that detailed the crowning of the first Henry du Rand.

"Guards," Coline whispered. "Four in front of the doors. Annette, can you scry to see if he's in there?"

She stumbled through the words, the beginnings of *father* on her tongue.

I leaned my forehead against the wall and looked into the crescent of Alaine's necklace—*Henry du Rand, weathered face weary, hands braced against a table covered in maps, Executioner René du Ruse at his side.*

"He's in there."

"One of the guards is coming this way," Coline whispered. She slunk back around the corner with us.

I slipped in front of her. "When he's distracting the others, take them out."

Yvonne made a sound behind me, and then the guard was on us, his eyes widening. A flush rose on his white skin. I closed the gap between us.

The magic in me surged, diving into his body like rain in a river, and I followed the path before me to the memories deep in the dark of his mind. Festering skin burned to the muscle and left to rot. Wriggling, writhing masses slipping through skin, burrowing into the recesses of the burn. White heads poking through red burns. Ever-hungry mouths gnawing at a leg and never leaving. The prickle of awareness that his body was not his own. Not anymore.

The illusion I created of his old injury was complete. The sight, the sound, the smell, the sensation. All of it real to him.

"No, no."

I stumbled back, skin burning under my nails, and blinked away the itch of his memories. The guard stared down at his arms and clawed at the sleeves. His nails tore through the thin ends.

"No, no, no. Not again." Blood beaded up along the scratches. Old scars, well healed and decades old, reddened under his nails. "Get them out. Get them out!"

He raced back to his fellows, arms held out before him, and screamed for them to help him.

Brigitte and Coline dashed forward. Metal clanged against metal. Bodies thumped to the floor.

I leaned against the wall and shut my eyes. Blood welled up across the skin of my forearms, matching the lines he had scratched through his clothes. Yvonne wrapped one arm around my shoulders.

"What did you do?" she asked.

"An illusion," I said. "Or a vivid memory. They work the same.

Illusion arts change how we observe the world on an ethereal level. I dredged up his old memories."

Yvonne let out a small sigh. "That's body alchemistry."

I had always been told the midnight arts couldn't change the world, only observe, but maybe a change in perspective *could* change the world.

I peeked around the corner—Brigitte and Coline still stood, but none of the guards did. We joined up outside the door, and Coline pushed a thin knife into Isabelle's hands "just in case."

"They certainly know we're here and will be prepared," said Brigitte. "That was not a quiet entrance."

There was no quiet now.

"Death isn't quiet," I said, the thump of Estrel's head hitting the scaffolding floor still heavy in my mind. An echo. A heartbeat. She died in me over and over and over again. "We shouldn't be either."

"Let us go loudly, then." Brigitte searched the guards' pockets till she found a key, and she paused with her hands on the doors.

Coline nodded, and Brigitte pushed open the doors. There were only a dozen people in the room at most, each one in the golds and silvers of Demeine. A long table of polished wood encircled the opposite end of the room in a half-circle, and they were spread out across it, their hands skimming over maps and scrying mirrors. René du Ruse—the executioner who didn't deserve the honor of a name—rose to his feet. At his side sat Henry XII, by the grace of Lord Sun and his Mistress Moon, King of Demeine. His gaze fell on Coline.

"Nicole," he said, voice bored, as if we had not escaped prison and pushed past guards bearing weapons. "I am much too busy for whatever foolish endeavor you are undertaking." He looked back down at the glass tablet before him, signed it, and made a cutting motion through the air with his right hand. "You may leave, alive, or you may die. I have reached my limits with you."

The other nobles in the room fled through a door at the opposite end. Coline turned her back on her father and gathered magic, sharp and writhing, in her hands and laid them on the door. The mechanism stuttered and clicked, and she glanced at me. Over her shoulder, her father glowered at being ignored.

"Fighting arts trick," she said softly. Her jaw tensed. "Laurence taught me."

They were cousins. I hadn't even thought about it, but how much hurt had Coline bottled up so she could do this?

She braced herself and turned. "Do you really think killing me will end this?"

"No, I think killing every damned rebel in this country will end this, but I can't do that at this very moment, so that leaves me with you." Henry let a loud breath and looked up, eyes steel gray in the sunlight. "And killing you, assuming you were to take command after me, will certainly be a blow to their morale."

Of course—he thought of his daughter as replaceable but his people as not even worth it.

"Deal with them," Henry said to the executioner and the six royal guards who had flanked them as the nobles left. "I would rather not have to kill my own daughter."

Coline took the sword from my hands. "I trust you. Tell me what to do."

I sunk to the ground. My fingers found Alaine's necklace, magic burning through them. Brigitte raised her sickle and approached the guards, and they hesitated. Isabelle sat beside me, channeling magic through her body and into mine, bearing some of the burden of my divining, and Yvonne's fingers brushed my shoulder. She upended a vial of silver filings in a crescent around us and struck flint against steel over it. Flames, moon-white and hot, flared to life between the guards and us. I grabbed her skirt and pulled her back to me.

"Magnesium," Yvonne muttered, pulling out a waterskin. "It'll buy us time."

And safety.

"You are brilliant." I leaned against her calf and forced the magic from Isabelle and me into Alaine's necklace. It quivered, silver rippling. *The royal guard nearest Brigitte struck out, short sword tearing through the air toward her right.* "Brigitte! Block right."

Metal struck metal. Boots scuffed across the floor. The thunk of a body against the floor.

I winced. Another image—*a guard thrusting his sword through Coline's right arm as she blocked another blade*—shimmered in the silver. I whipped my head up.

Coline raised her arm to stop a blow.

"Coline!"

Brigitte moved faster than I thought possible, sliding between Coline and the guard aiming for her arm. She hooked a sickle around his neck. She tugged. He died. Coline lived.

And blood stained the silver necklace red.

Only two guards were down, and my divinations were already wavering. Isabelle's hands were flushed, red-pricked pink, and blood oozed out from beneath my nails. We needed more. More power. More time.

We were not soldiers or noonday artists. We had never been trained to fight or to use our magic to protect us. Henry and his court had created a world where no one but them were trained to wield power. I channeled more magic, not caring where I gathered it from, and the power seared my skin, smoke curling free from the little cuts and scabs opening along my arms. An ache itched in my throat, a rotting wound where I had worn away from too much channeling. My neck creaked, more snapped twig than popping joint. Isabelle coughed, blood on her lips.

Another soldier swung, his actions clear in my divinations, and I shouted for Coline to duck. I heard her exhale. Grunt.

A body hit the floor.

I shouted instructions and the fight carried on, the sounds of the swords clashing beyond our dimming ring of fire. Not all of my divining was right, and each wrong future opened a new wound in Coline and Brigitte. I tried to channel more power with more precision, and it tore through my fingers and into the necklace. The image wavered, and a shadow covered my hands. Yvonne tossed water onto her ring of fire. White sparks skittered and melted across the stone floor. The table caught fire.

"Curious," the executioner said, the golden coat denoting his title of chevalier smoldering. In one hand he held a sword and in the other gathered magic, and the flickers of the noonday arts in him glowed like distant stars. His gaze settled on Yvonne. "You could have been very useful if you had not chosen this."

"Left!" I said and pulled Yvonne back with me until we hit the wall. Brigitte slid left and took out a guard too cautious after my shout. "Coline, lunge."

She did, and the final guard stumbled out of the way, feet tangling in his fallen comrade's coat. He hit the ground, and Brigitte hit him hard enough to keep him down. Yvonne tossed the waterskin into the flames between us and the executioner. The fire roared. He twisted his hand.

Power drenched our corner like rain. The fire died. Isabelle gasped.

I tried to breathe and nothing happened. The air was different, gone, and no matter how deeply I inhaled. Yvonne's hands went to her stomach, her chest, her mouth. She shook her head.

"The problem with alchemistry is that it relies too much on other people not understanding it," the executioner said, stepping over the remnants of our paltry defense. "And it's useless when there is no hydrogen or oxygen to burn."

He reached for Yvonne and opened his mouth. Yvonne spat a small white pastille into his mouth. The little ball shone with stored magic, and gagged, jerking away. The magic he'd channeled broke. I sucked in a deep breath, blood in my mouth. Yvonne coughed and kicked him away. He spat it out.

"What—" The words died in his throat. He croaked and narrowed his eyes at Yvonne.

I lurched, arms catching him about the knees. We fell, and I scrambled to grab his arm, his face, any part of him that would let my magic in. My fingers curled around his wrist.

The midnight arts flowed between us, a river of illusions and scrying, and dragged the man who had killed Estrel into the deep, dark past. He twisted and fought, like Alaine beneath the ice. I made him think he was choking. Made him gag. Made him scratch at the skin of his throat. Tear through the flesh and muscle and ash-white sinew of his body like his sword had torn through Estrel's.

Alaine died drowning, and so did he.

I didn't need their magic or power to change the world.

"No!" Isabelle slammed into me, knocking me from my seat on the executioner's knees. I hit the floor hard. Coline screamed.

Isabelle, Henry's sword buried in her right shoulder, whimpered. He hummed and wrenched the blade free. A stomach-rolling snap sounded as it tore from her, and she fell forward, still. I scrambled to catch her, and a thick hand took me by my throat. I grabbed Isabelle's dress, desperate to stay with her. There was supposed to be an after.

"This is unfortunate," Henry said, yanking me to my feet.

Winter had come and gone, and there was nothing left in me.

"You are truly more trouble than you are worth," he said to Coline, not even looking at me. He lifted me higher and higher until I hung from the gallows of his grasp. "Surrender to face justice, or I will kill her now."

TWENTY-NINE

Emilie

N o one would save me. No one could save me.

There was freedom in knowing the closeness of death.

I channeled more magic than I ever would have dared through his hand holding me, raking it across the muscles of his hands as I would if I were debriding a wound, and he pushed me away, the leftover magic creaking in my aching bones. A soldier tried to attack Waleran. The chevalier waved his hand, power leaping between them. Smoke curled from the soldier's nose and mouth. He gagged and fell.

As did the five soldiers around him.

Beneath the bright noon sun of a blue Demeine autumn day, Waleran was at full power. The soldiers couldn't touch him, and he needed only to channel a small gathering of the noonday arts to down five at once. I tried to reopen his old wound, and Pièrre's magic ripped me away from it. Charles looked from Pièrre to Waleran and then down at his own hand, his face inscrutable. I knew that look.

Charles had an idea.

I picked up a soldier's knife. Waleran's back was half to me, his face turned to stare at the soldiers. I sprinted to him and buried the knife in his shoulder. Waleran roared and flung his arm back, catching me in the face. I went flying and fell. He stalked after me.

Charles crept up behind him.

"You can't kill me," Waleran said. "What part of that statement doesn't make sense to you?"

I gathered magic so he wouldn't feel what Charles was doing, and Waleran laughed.

"I wasn't trying to kill you." I laughed and pushed myself up to my feet. "I was distracting you."

Waleran pulled the knife from his shoulder. The skin of his newly repaired throat reddened and swelled. He coughed, blood dripping from his nose, and threw the knife away. His breath caught in his chest, and he stumbled, fingers scratching at the scarlet rash seeping across the skin of his neck. The wound oozed, and behind him, Charles released the last of the healing arts he had been channeling. I laughed again and doubled over. Waleran fell.

Charles hadn't undone his healing.

Charles had *healed* him—altering Waleran's body alchemistry until his natural defenses recognized the new pieces as someone else's and attacked them. Charles had turned Waleran's body against him.

Waleran, again, for the final time, bled out in the grass.

A soldier whooped, and I fell back into the dirt. Madeline, healed, crawled until she was sitting next to me. I wanted to laugh or cry, but there was nothing left in me to fuel the movements. All I could do was stare at the sky.

Pièrre and his one remaining hack didn't surrender. The soldiers that were still standing surrounded them, keeping a good ways back after Pièrre stopped the heart of one. Still, he channeled through his hack. He wasn't worn down at all.

Charles sunk into the grass, legs crossed like a tailor, and nodded. "Let's heal the soldiers. We can deal with him after."

"Or during, if he tries anything," Madeline muttered, twirling the sliver of metal that impaled her between her fingers. "He knows he's lost. There's no telling what he'll do."

We walked through the field and healed the injured. Louis worked on a particularly complicated injury from Waleran's spear, his years of experience more useful than the other three of us combined. Charles finished healing a downed soldier and rose to his feet, knees shaking with effort. I hooked an arm through his, and we leaned against each other. He was a marvel of nuance.

The healing he had channeled was so well controlled and powerful that it held together the torn edges of a lung without wearing away at the rest of the soldier's body.

"He's good," I said, knocking the soldier out with alchemistry. I was certain that I would either be awake for days or sleep for weeks when this was over. "Next."

"Madeline, you've dealt with a liver laceration before, yes?" Charles cleared his throat and spat out blood. "There's a soldier to your left."

Madeline nodded and finished the soldier she was with before heading to the liver laceration.

"Head wound." I touched the cheek of a different soldier and checked his spine. He was unconscious, but he would live. "I would heal this, but I might miscount the number of bones and forget to fuse some."

Charles chuckled. "Do you need help?"

"No, rest a moment." I repaired the fracture skull, replenished the soldier's blood, and made sure he was set before turning my attention to Charles. A fever burned beneath his skin. He was exhausted down to his very bones where he had altered his own alchemistry too much to induce blood production in others. "Did you know that the majority of deaths for hacks are due to blood loss despite them rarely suffering a single injury?"

His head lolled forward. "Sounds like someone smart told you that."

"They're all right," I said. "A bit too close to death for my tastes."

"Really?" he asked. "I think I'm bitter enough right now to suit them fine."

My magic slipped beneath his skin and into the cracks of his bones, urging his body to work faster at repairing itself and funneling power from my body to his. "Charles…"

The words stuck to my tongue like bone.

I didn't love. That was it, wasn't it? What mother hated so much—I didn't love her, I didn't love our traditions, our history, or her love for me. I rejected all of it, cast it aside as easily as leaves shrugged off water. If I loved my mother, her hatred of me would have hurt me more.

But this wasn't about me. Charles couldn't die, not when he had so many things left to do—his assistantship, his family, and all those lives he could save. The world was better with him in it, and he deserved a long, happy life. It would be an honor just to live it with him, lover or friend.

"Please," I said finally. "Whatever happens with Physician du Guay and the rest of Demeine, survive."

The world shifted. Magic gathered behind me, too powerful for a single body to hold, and I stood.

"Get your filthy hands off me!"

We both whipped around. Pièrre flailed against the outstretched hands of one of our soldiers, who was weaponless and exhausted. There was nowhere for Pièrre to run now. Even his hacks, the one left awake and the ones asleep, were safely tied up. But still Pièrre channeled through them as if their mere existence as hacks were consent to use their bodies. Blood dripped from the ears of one.

Six of the soldiers trying to capture Pièrre fell, old wounds reopened at once. The three hacks on the ground groaned. The heartbeat of one flickered out.

Charles rose and sneered. "They were unconscious."

"I'm not surprised," said Madeline. "They're nothing more than extra scalpels or bandages to him."

"Fuck this," I said. "They used everyone else. Let dear Physician Pièrre du Guay bear the burden of his arts for once."

I moved before they could stop me. The soldiers around Pièrre writhed, and I leapt over them, body ready for one last stand. Pièrre turned at the last moment, his eyes wide, his hands raised, and I felt the crack of his arts before I saw it. I had broken my arm when I was twelve, and Pièrre rebroke it, the twin bones grinding together with each move. Old cuts and accidents reopened, slowing me down as I healed the worst of them. My arm snapped back into place. He paled.

"Break me all you want," I said, body so worn down already that snow spotted my vision. "You're done breaking down others to build yourself up."

I tackled him: no magic for him to counter, no wound he could heal. Let him try to kill me. He still had his back to the dirt, and my corpse would make a poor shield.

The soldiers grabbed his arms and legs, and we sat him in the middle of the field next to the bodies of the hacks and soldiers who had once trusted him to save them. He had used them and hurt them, and even now, their slow deaths didn't seem to bother him at all. He refused to heal them even when one of the soldiers threatened to kill him.

"You didn't ask their permission," I said, nodding to the hacks dying behind him. "I'm not asking yours." I turned to the others. "If we all channel and share the burden of wearing down, it might not kill us, and we might be able to channel enough power to save them, but we would have to use him as a hack."

"If we just channel through him," Charles said, "he won't do what we need him to."

"Then I'll do it." I leaned over Pièrre's form and grinned. "All those people who you hate and tried to use and kill? You're going to sacrifice yourself for them."

A sickle of a smile spread across Madeline's face. "Excellent."

"A hack must be willing," Louis said. "He isn't. If you direct the magic, you'll wear down as quickly as him."

"Then we save everyone quickly." I shifted next to Pièrre. "I can do this. Let me do this."

Let me save the people my legacy would have had me use and toss aside like Pièrre had.

We sat in a circle around Pièrre. Louis talked Madeline and Charles through the process, and I could see the magic slip through their bodies. They channeled it through Pièrre, the power reddening the skin it touched on him, and I pulled all that power into me. The world withered, and I bloomed. I could see everyone. Everything.

Lightning in a beautiful, bloody bottle.

The soldier nearest me had a broken ankle and torn ligaments, and Louis led me through how to heal it completely. I moved from person to person, Madeline setting a broken arm through me and

Charles scouring the acid and damage from a ruptured stomach in a soldier's chest. We forced bodies to regrow bone and blood and flesh until no one else lingered at the edge of death and life, and when the solders' bodies couldn't stand it, I used Waleran's corpse. The grafts were living things of alchemistry to make sure the new bodies accepted them, taking far more out of me than alchemistry normally did. We changed Waleran's donated parts at an ethereal level till his blood was not his blood and the new bodies wouldn't reject it. My own skin burned feverish with the power.

The soldiers Waleran had injured were harder to heal. Pièrre had worn down their bodies, their missing bones and muscles bleak holes. It was better I did this; I had no qualms about using the healing arts for such violence. The others were better than me, and Demeine would need them no matter what came next. I was doing something a physician should never do.

I used a few pieces of Pièrre to heal the hacks he had abused, and he fell forward, unconscious. It was what he had done to Gabriel.

The bones in Pièrre degraded, not enough to kill him but enough that he might never be the same, and the ones in the hacks rebuilt. Clean white edges reconnected. Muscles spread across the bone. We were only pieces. Everything was only pieces.

This regime had to be broken down and the pieces used to rebuild a new, better Demeine.

"I love you," I whispered to Madeline and Charles. "Goodbye."

Madeline sighed. "You are so dramatic."

Lightning ripped through me. I screamed, the shock yanking me out of the magic. My chest burned, smoke curled around the edges of my nose, and I couldn't smell anything but ash. I was on my back staring up at Madeline and Louis. Charles cradled my head in his lap.

"I can't believe that worked," Madeline said.

"I can't believe you did it right on your first try." Louis stared at her with an open mouth and something akin to fear in his eyes. "It took me three to get it right the first time."

"What?" I asked, and the words bubbled in my throat. I twisted and heaved into the grass.

"You were dead." Charles pulled back my hair and helped me sit up. "Your heart stopped, and Madeline restarted it."

I lifted my head. The ache rolled from my temples to the back of my head, a concussion in the making. The field around us looked razed, as if someone had come while I was out and set fire to everything, and the trees in the distance had shed their leaves. I ran my fingers through the black grass and groaned. Everything hurt.

Louis whistled. "We've got company."

With the grass dead, we didn't have to stand to see the faces on the other side of the river. Silver wolves and gold foxes, the steel beak of a hawk—Kalthorne's artists in their odd masks had come to see the commotion. One in the mask of a wolf whose hood was braided fur approached. The sword at their side was shaped like a talon.

The soldiers, all alive, all well, all shockingly energetic, closed in around us. Charles settled me on the ground and stood. Kalthorne was still a monarchy, and it might not take kindly to its neighbor upsetting that order. The wolf stopped a few paces from us.

"Sit, artist, before you fall," the wolf said. "Am I correct in assuming Demeine meant to attack us today? The divining arts have been unclear for weeks."

Charles sat back down next to me. One of his hands gripped my calf, the bite of each finger warm and sharp against my skin. I settled my hand between his shoulder blades.

"You would be correct." Charles bowed his head to the wolf.

"I am Hanne," the wolf said and removed her helm, the mask

slipping away with it. I knew there must have been magic in her armor, but I could sense nothing. "Who are you?"

"He's the duc des Monts Lance," I said, and by the way he flushed, I knew he had forgotten that advancement. "And the vicomte des Îles Étoilées."

"Why did you stop them?" Hanne's lips twitched, and she ran a hand over her closely cropped black hair. "We could not have held back them and your army."

"His Majesty Henry XII of Demeine lied about why he wanted to go to war with Kalthorne." Charles glanced at the soldiers around us. "The army didn't want to fight."

Hanne's eyes crinkled as if she were laughing, but her face didn't change. "We will talk more later, Charles. We will hope for peace but prepare for war, as your last kings have taught us. Rest. Let us wish your court agrees with you."

Hanne touched her chest and bowed, and she slipped the helm back over her face. Charles bowed as much as he could while sitting down.

"We did it," Madeline said, her disbelief painfully clear. "Maybe?"

"Good enough for now." Charles leaned into me. "A war stopped and only twelve dead."

"Only twelve?" I had thought for sure more were mortally wounded.

"Emilie," Charles whispered, "some of the soldiers you healed I'm fairly sure were dead, and there's nothing left of Waleran. Also, you ran out of pieces and got a little bit creative."

Louis held up his once-injured hand. Red lines like veins snaked through the leather, and when he pulled the glove away from his skin, they clung to him, leeches feeding the leather of their bodies.

I shuddered. He nodded.

"We shouldn't tell anyone that part," said Madeline. "Let's not give anyone bad ideas."

Charles wrapped his arms around me and pulled me into a tight hug, tucking his face into the curve of my neck. His nose brushed the shell of my ear. Tears pooled in the gap between us.

"You were dead." Charles's voice cracked. "You were very dead."

The pitter-patter of his heart was loud against my cheek, and I turned my head till my lips brushed his jaw as I spoke. "I'm sorry."

I tried to gather magic and channel it to heal the small cut on his jaw. It was little more than a paper cut and should have been easy. Nothing came to me.

Nothing lived in me. A sick pain rolled through me.

"We did it." Charles pulled away and helped me up, so we could walk back to camp. "We're alive and we did it."

I leaned against him. He smelled of rot and sweat, the earthy mixture of downed, wet trees and dead deer. He'd rolled up the sleeves of his shirt, and welts like freckles spotted his hands and forearms. When he moved, they wept a red that might have once been blood. I wiped his arms with my shirt. We were alive.

We were not all right.

"Yes," I said, and I couldn't bring myself to mention the yawning emptiness inside of me where my magic had once been. "We did."

There would be time for that later. All power required sacrifice.

We had lived; there was no sacrifice too great for that.

M agic gathered behind me. Henry laughed.

"Child, if you even attempt to finish channeling that, you'll only hurt yourself." His laughter rumbled down his arm and into my head, a sick, shaking sound that drowned out Coline's response. "You were not made to hold so much power. None of you were."

He dropped me. Air crushed into my lungs. Coline charged her father, and Brigitte attacked with her. I scrambled away from him and back to Isabelle, the memory of her hands channeling with me still warm against my arms. She groaned, fingers twitched, and I pressed my hands into the sieve of Isabelle's body. Yvonne crept to me and wadded her scarf up against the wound. None of it helped.

Wasn't this the plan all along? We couldn't fight back if we didn't know how. If we didn't have weapons. We couldn't do anything when we died early and our artists died at twenty-nine.

We couldn't heal ourselves when we did. We couldn't heal ourselves, not like they could. It was a culling.

"Yvonne," I whispered, voice rough as Estrel's. "I don't know how to fix this."

But no matter how much I channeled or wore down, my necklace showed me nothing—no past, no present, no futures. The silver cracked. Crumbled.

There was no way to win this fight.

"Quicksilver. Do you have any quicksilver?"

Yvonne stared at me, brown eyes wide, and she passed me a vial from her pocket. I dumped all of it into my cupped hand. The silver shivered, melting into a puddle. No bowl to help contain the visions. No time to focus right.

Coline attacked her father as Brigitte distracted him, but he had fought wars before we'd even been born. He dodged easily. Magic gathered in him, and he channeled it into his sword. The steel flattened into a shield. Both of their strikes clanged off of it.

Brigitte swung her other sickle up, and he leaned back. His foot hooked around her ankle and yanked her off her feet. Brigitte fell.

He brought the shield down on her neck. She rolled at the last moment, hair ripped away by the shield's base. Coline hesitated, eyes wide.

"Are we done now?" Henry asked, teeth clenched. He shook the shield, and it folded in on itself until it was a blade again. "This has gone on long enough."

A pink stain flushed his skin. As if this fight were getting to him. As if he weren't used to channeling so much magic by himself these days.

As if without his hacks, he wasn't half as good.

I pulled Isabelle into my lap. If we were dying, we were dying together. My left arm wrapped around her chest, the quicksilver slithering between the cracks in my fingers and clinging to the back of my hand. I tucked my chin into her shoulder, and Yvonne leaned her forehead against mine. Her hands still trembled in Isabelle's injury.

Magic seeped from me to it. Red streaked the edges, the blistered skin of my hands peeling away. I had been divining for so long today that channeling the magic was easy, the current of magic steady, but it ate at me, the weakened pieces of me giving way as I dredged the power from my bones. I had to find the right one. We couldn't afford the wrong future.

"What are you doing?" Yvonne asked, her hands lifting from Isabelle's shoulder.

I kissed her, only once, too quick to be nice. "What I do best."

All the magic I had ever gathered paled in comparison to what I channeled into the silver staining my hands. Silver swam in my sight, the world smeared by the power in my veins, and a single, certain future danced across the quicksilver.

"Coline! Left," I said.

She hesitated, her father's attack rattling up her arm. She stumbled back. He raised his sword and attacked again. I yanked at the future and held it tight in my hands.

"Retreat."

She did. Henry attacked, harder, faster, unyielding and giving up no ground, but when he reached to channel magic, he was close enough to grab. Coline and Brigitte tried to stop him, and he threw them off. They slammed into the wall, collapsing to the ground in a tangle of bruised limbs and blades. I hadn't wanted a future where we beat him. They were too few and far between, and there was too much red in them. I wanted a future where he got close enough for us to channel through him. My fingers closed around his ankle.

"Oh," I whispered, all the power he had wanted to use against us channeling through my skin. It was so easy to redirect. He was used to using hacks, to channeling magic through others, and I pushed all of it into Isabelle.

So I scryed the past as Estrel had taught me. I scryed what Isabelle's body had been before the hit. Henry tried to pull away, but I held tight. Isabelle jerked.

Her veins slithered across the opening. Yvonne ripped herself away, the red stain on her hands and clothes streaming back into Isabelle's body. The wound repaired itself from the inside out—bones snapping into place, muscles threading together, her skin as perfect as it had been an hour ago—and her eyes flew open. The only blood between us was mine, and it was a feverish pink. Isabelle breathed.

And Henry XII, King of Demeine broke free. Coline crawled to her feet behind him.

"How?" He growled and stumbled back, blood beading across the skin where I had channeled through him. "Do you really think the midnight arts, a mere reflection of my power, can overpower me?"

"No," I said. "But she can."

Coline grabbed his collar and forced him to his knees, so they faced each other.

"I don't want to be like you. I don't want your power. I don't want to wear down my country and use its people to keep myself alive." Coline slid the point of her sword from his arm to his neck. Blood welled over the point. "You're not powerful. You're a parasite."

All of the futures where he lived tasted like funeral pyres, but the ones without him were breaths of fresh air.

Henry plunged his hand into her side, the rings on his fingers transforming into a knife that glittered with the noonday arts. Coline bit through her lip but didn't scream and held her sword to his throat to keep him still. Her hands didn't shake.

"They will devour you," Henry said, voice low and shaking. He was too weak to stand, too worn out by what I'd done to him. "They would sooner eat themselves and shit on our legacy than let you rule them as they need to be ruled."

"Fuck our legacy," she said. "Demeine is worth more than our legacy. Our people are worth sacrifice."

It took more than one slice to sever a head. It took more than one slice to sever a head. Estrel had taught me that, as she had most things. Brigitte helped Coline finish the job.

I coughed up blood and silver. My arms shook, slivers of metal slipping from my skin like splinters. Flickers of the quicksilver darted beneath the cuts on my hands, sunk into the wrinkles of my palms, and solidified, silver scabs across my knuckles. The rapid beat of my heart fluttered in my head, and I tried to stand. A trembling hand curled around my wrist.

"Annette?" Isabelle's faint voice shot through me.

The wound across her shoulder and chest was still open and red, but the veins were sealed. The muscle had regrown. I could no longer see the sickly white of her bones. Her grip on me was loose.

I tried to say her name but only a rasp escaped. I pushed her back onto the floor, my hand shaking against her shoulder. She blinked up at me.

"You're bleeding." She lifted a hand and slowly touched the hollow of her throat.

I touched the same spot on me. The skin gave way, bowing beneath my nails like the thin wing of a Stareater. Her bleary eyes widened, and I knew I was right. Something was wrong with me.

Yvonne groaned. "Don't move. Don't touch it anymore. You need a physician."

She had a bloody nose from some hit or another, and I tried to sop it up with my sleeve. She let me. It didn't help much.

"My ears are ringing," I muttered.

She laughed. "I think that's just the door."

Someone was pounding on the doors, the hinges rattling like bells, but whatever Coline had done to the locks held.

We were alive. We were mostly intact. I ran my trembling hand down Yvonne's arm, savoring the feel of her warm skin. She leaned against my shoulder, touch for the sake of it instead of support, and the bitter scent of fire still clung to her clothes. Coline and Brigitte checked the royal guards they had downed at the start of the fight, and the two who had lived didn't put up a fight. They knelt before Coline and muttered in soft, steady voices. One stared at her father's head the whole time.

The other kept glancing at Isabelle and me.

I touched my face, and Isabelle pulled my hand away. Her shoulder creaked like a house settling.

"You look worse than whatever you're thinking." Yvonne turned my hands over and over, inspecting them like she usually did her alchemistry work. "I have never seen anything like this."

Well, at least I was interesting now.

"You glowed like a star come to earth," Coline said, crouching before me. "Can you scry what's happening with Kalthorne?"

"Absolutely not." Isabelle's arm tightened around my waist. "She's completely worn out."

I glanced at Yvonne who shrugged and whispered, "Your choice."

"Can one of us do it, then?" Coline ran her hand along her sword and cleaned the blade. "I need to know what happened with Kalthorne. If we attacked, if we're at war, there might be no going back."

Isabelle sniffed. "I'm no good at scrying."

"You two deserve a moment of rest anyway." Coline sat down, hard, and focused on the reflective surface of the sword. Nothing happened. She gathered no magic and did no channeling, but her eyes flitted about as if she were dreaming, and she smiled. "The army refused, and the Segance group isn't doing anything?" She paused, head tilting. "There was a fight, but it wasn't with Kalthorne."

Emilie des Marais, what have you done?

"Well." Coline, suddenly jittery, leapt to her feet. "We need to keep moving. This is good, but the other artists and my father's friends will try to take my place soon enough. I need to make sure the royal guards aren't going to do anything untoward and get Serre under control."

No. Coline had scryed?

But I hadn't seen it. I should've seen her channeling. I should've felt the tug of power flowing through her. I had always felt magic.

I rubbed my eyes and stared harder at her sword. No smears of power shone in it.

"Annette?" Yvonne touched my hand. "What's wrong?"

Coline and Brigitte helped Isabelle up, and while the three of them spoke, I turned to Yvonne.

"I can't see magic," I mouthed. The others couldn't know.

Had my use run its course?

"You're worn out. We'll try later." Her brows drew together in a familiar, confused wrinkle. "You need to rest."

Some hacks, after channeling for too long, lost the ability to use magic all together.

I opened my mouth, and she shook her head.

"It will be all right," she said, taking my hand in hers. "Think you can stand?"

She helped me up, and Isabelle stood on my other side. I hooked one arm through hers.

"Thank you," she whispered. "I'm sorry."

There were no words I could think to say, so I pulled her close and didn't let go.

Coline leaned in and kissed my forehead, then Isabelle's. "If either of you ever nearly die again, I will be unimaginably cross with you." She glanced at Yvonne. "You too."

"Now." Coline shifted her sword to one hand and picked up her father's head with the other. The skin beneath the blood splatter on her face was pale, old-milk white. She did not look at his face. "You two."

She rounded on the guards, and the one who'd been staring at Isabelle and me earlier flinched.

"You were members of the royal guards and protected my father. He was a very bad person and king to the majority of Demeine. That wasn't within your control. What you do now is," she said. "Will you protect me?"

The other guard licked his lips. "Traditionally, the old guard is killed with the king."

"Traditionally, the king doesn't replace his worn-out body with parts from his people," said Coline. "Anyone who broke the law, knew of that transgression, or abused their power will be tried, but I have no desire to kill for the sake of killing. However, if you refuse, that will leave us in a complicated position."

"I would be honored, Madame Royale Nicole," the staring one said.

Coline raised an eyebrow, blood dripping down her face.

The other one glanced at his companion and shook his head. "We would be honored, Your Majesty."

Coline swept to the doors and shouted, "Who knocks?"

The pounding stopped.

"We answer to His Majesty," a voice called out.

"Here is your king." Coline must have undone what she did, for she pushed the doors open and tossed her father's head into the hallway crowded by what must have been the rest of the royal guards. The two who had survived our fight flanked Coline and didn't so much as blink while glaring down their fellows. The dozen of them, red coats stitched with blue and orange, parted as his head rolled to a stop between them. One at the front stepped forward, but an older guard held him back. Coline's full named passed his lips.

"He instigated the war with Kalthorne, refused peace when it was offered, and was willing to sacrifice our soldiers to keep the war ongoing, all to distract the Deme people from the problems brought to light by Laurel. My father is dead, but his conspirators are not, and they may try to massacre Serre or kill me," she said. I hadn't noticed, but she had replaced her stolen sword with her father's, and that too she tossed to the ground at the guards' feet. "Demeine deserves better. The people of Serre shouldn't live in fear simply because their court is changing hands, so will you protect your people today? With Laurel? With me?"

The older guard nodded, the gold sun pin on his chest catching the light, and bowed his head. "Of course, Your Majesty."

Coline, thoroughly, rightfully, distracted spoke with Brigitte and the guards. I yawned, eyes fluttering shut. Yvonne leaned back and picked up my hand, and I lifted it to the light. Nothing called to me. There was no hum. No thrill of power awoke in my veins. There was only silver and light, a mirror streaked red beneath my skin.

"Are you worried?" Yvonne asked, eyeing the odd slices of silver writhing where open wounds should have been.

I leaned into her and shook my head, Isabelle's arm still about my waist and Coline's voice in my ears. "How could I be worried when I'm with all of you?"

EPILOGUE

Emilie

One Month Later

No one outside of us who had been there truly knew what had happened, but people gossiped and whispered about godly retribution, Thornish magic, and medical experiments gone wrong. We mostly let the rumors stand and kept what we had won in Segance between us, Her Majesty Nicole—who demanded I call her Coline—and the Thornish delegation of soldiers, politicians, and one ecstatic artist thrilled at the prospect of speaking to us. Considering we weren't at war, and Coline was much more concerned about Demeine than her father had been, no one seemed to mind.

Coline made it remarkably clear that her nobles needed to have more on their minds than previously.

My mother almost liked her.

Almost.

"At least she's doing things properly," she said on the eve of Coline's coronation.

I stared at her, unsure if I were unconscious and dreaming in the Segance infirmary somewhere. "She killed her father and took his crown."

"Only slightly less traditional than waiting for him to die." She tapped my teacup with her finger. "Drink."

Our relationship, in the strained month after the death of His Majesty Henry XII and peace with Kalthorne and reorganization of the noble houses—which was, to my mother's chagrin, still ongoing—had simplified. She mothered me.

Aggressively.

"You died," she had said to me days after the fight in Segance. She had traveled there to discover what had become of me, and Madeline had found her first. The words were an accusation.

I had nodded. "So they keep telling me."

She had not left my side since, and no amount of begging saved me from her endless teas and tonics.

I sipped the tea and let her talk. It was far easier than arguing, and, as much as I hated it, I was too tired. My ability to channel magic had never returned. It was as if someone had reached into my soul and plucked out a part of me, separating us forever. As if I were eternally walking down a familiar set of stairs and missing the same step every time.

"Have you decided what you'll be wearing tomorrow?" my mother asked softly. She fiddled with the vials of honey and medicines from Yvonne Lortet.

Her alchemistry almost made me wish I had gone to finishing school, but it was a very small almost. Without magic, I couldn't even see the power stored in her creations. It was an unbelievable ache.

"When you divined my future before sending me off to school and saw me in clothes you didn't approve of and no physician's coat, I think Mistress Moon was very truthful," I said. "I have a suit. I look very good in it."

Madeline, Annette, and Charles had not hesitated in buying new clothes for the occasion, and Madeline and Annette had taken a particular interest in torturing me with trips to a tailor's and dressmaker's and several other places where I had been poked and prodded while half-asleep and recovering. Annette, at least, I trusted to pick out something appropriate. Madeline was liable to pick out something solely to vex me.

"Good." My mother packed up her alchemistry curio and kissed my forehead. "You looked quite happy in that future."

I didn't know what to say to that. Our affection was a fragile thing, a careful titration, but I was still afraid to twist the lever and let my emotions flow free. It was a slow, steady drip, and for now, we were both all right with that.

The evening after Coline was crowned queen and her new council—one noble, one not—was selected, the stars fell. The coronation had started at dusk and the celebration would last till dawn, a new day for Demeine. As the last tendrils of red had seeped from the sky and faded to deep-ocean purple, falling stars had streaked through the dark, gold and burning. Annette, eyes silver in the light, stared up at the sky with the same tight-lipped smile she wore every time I saw her. Even without magic, she could read portents.

"What does it mean?" I asked, sliding through the crowd to her.

"Not a clue." She glanced at me. "Estrel had a pamphlet on

natural occurrences being misread as omens, but I left it in Bosquet. Seemed silly to bring it here after everything."

"Most things seem silly these days." I kicked my feet through the strips of dyed paper and pamphlets on Coline that littered the ground—all handwritten, some portraits, mostly frivolous. "What we did…"

"We did what we had to," Annette said quickly. "Do you regret it?"

Sometimes, if I looked just right, I could see the threads of quicksilver that still infected her. It made my head ache catching the flickers in the corner of my sight. Neither of us had left that day unchanged.

"No," I whispered. "I regret so many people died before Henry XII and his ilk were stopped."

Annette nodded. A gaggle of children raced by, splitting us and kicking up a fog of paper. One of the crinkled pamphlets caught in the lace of Annette's skirts, and she grabbed my arm for balance as she picked it from her dress. Her fingers closed around my arm, real and familiar. We had neglected each other during our swap.

We neglected each other no more, writing constantly to each other from my place in Delest and hers in Serre. She'd taken to accounting like I had taken to surgery, and within the first two weeks of working had found the "errors" of the noble houses. She had an eye for patterns, picking them out before the rest of us could even finish reading the ledgers. It turned out that quite a few noble families had taken to slightly adjusting their numbers in their favors. Coline had been thrilled.

There was so little accessible, tangible evidence of wrongdoing that we were clinging to everything we had to make sure the posthumous charges were believed.

"You were willing to die for people," Annette said softly.

I stiffened. "I always would have, as a physician should be."

"No, you wouldn't have." She shook her head, and the wrinkle between her brows deepened. "You wouldn't have. You'd have said it, but you wouldn't have."

"Please don't say that." I ducked, so only she could hear me. "I don't like hearing it."

It was true, of course. I had wanted to be a physician always, but being the physician had been the important part of that dream. The patients had been faceless and in need, and I had been their savior. Good deeds for the sake of good feelings.

"You might not like hearing it," she said, "but it's true."

"I know," I said. "I'm working on it."

Annette smiled, laughing. "Course you are." She squeezed my wrist. "What part of 'you were willing to sacrifice yourself' did you not understand as a compliment? I mean, it was ridiculous. There was no need and—"

"All right."

"—it wouldn't have worked—"

"I got it."

"—and you deserve better. Like I do."

A piece of celebratory scrap paper drifted down and landed on her nose. I left it there. "You live to mock me, don't you?"

"Absolutely." She hugged me and held up the pamphlet. "Look."

Portents and Propaganda by Estrel Charron.

"Well," I said, "that is my cue to leave. If tea leaves are beyond me, I can't imagine I'll be much better at deciphering how that got here."

"It's been odd." Annette tucked the pamphlet into her pocket.

For the first time all day, I laughed. "Unbelievably."

I had returned to university not as a hack but as a surgeon-in-training. Medicine without magic was a wholly different beast, and the new studies had distracted me from my loss. Charles was wondrously busy between school, his new project with Yvonne, and learning how to run Monts Lance for when the time came. We had gotten into several marvelous fights about the ethereal nature of bodies, though, and set to testing the more intriguing of the concepts. It was invigorating.

I had turned my quarters in Serre into a small laboratory to study. I went there now, needing the quiet. I was all right without magic—mostly, though Madeline said it made me very grumpy—and Charles, as so often happened, had been struck by the same inspiration as me. I opened the door as quietly as I could and peeked inside. He was writing on the glass board, one hand running through his hair and the other smeared with ink. His coat was thrown over one of the chairs.

"We are horribly predictable." I stepped inside and shut the door behind me.

Charles glanced over his shoulder, dropping the ink brush. "I love it. I was hoping you'd show up. I can't get this equation right."

"No math, please. I dream in mathematics now." I held up my hands in defeat and sat on one of the tall stools near him. "It's my least favorite class and the one with the most reading."

"You adore those classes." Charles stepped forward, slowly, and smiled. His legs nudged open my own till he was standing between my thighs and our lips were even. His fingers gripped my knees. "You're a very bad liar."

"I know," I muttered, nose brushing his. "It made this week very hard."

"May I kiss you?" asked Charles. "First, that is, assuming your news isn't life-shattering?"

"Please."

His lips pressed against mine. His hands slid up my thighs, my stomach, my chest, till he clutched the collar of my shirt in his hands, and I hooked my feet behind his back to pull him closer. He shuddered and pulled away. Only a hairsbreadth. Only far enough for us to breathe.

"I have a present for you." I kissed him, quickly, and uncurled his fingers from my collar; they started tugging the bottom of my shirt from my trousers. "Remember how you had an idea to test out infection rates but not how to actually do it?"

Charles laughed. His hands stilled, and he laid his forehead against my shoulder. "Really? Now?"

"Really." I ran my fingers through his hair, the little smolder of contentedness cooling at the base of my spine. "I know you Charles du Ravine as well as I know myself. You've been bored since dusk. Parties are not our thing."

He laughed again, the sounds rumbling in his chest and seeping into mine, hot and heavy. "We don't have to work. We can—"

Hurried footsteps raced down the hall outside. Charles untangled himself from me, and I straightened his suit and he straightened mine. His hair was a mess, delightfully so, and my fingers caught in the strands at the nape of his neck. He chuckled, leaned back against the table. It was our work space.

Surely no one would mind.

The door flew open. Madeline darted inside, locking it behind her. Back to the door and chest heaving, she held up her hand to her lips. Soft voices outside—the dreadfully attentive group of new physician assistants she had helped pick out and decided to tutor—called her name, and Charles opened his mouth to shout. I wrapped both hands around his lower jaw.

"Play nicely," I muttered.

He glared. His tongue flicked against my palm.

"Is that a promise?" I unwound my hands from his mouth. "Or a threat?"

"Promise," he whispered and cleared his throat. "Madeline, what are you doing?"

"I made the mistake of mentioning I needed to check on something within earshot." The right side of her lip pulled up in a sneer. "I wanted a break. Everyone keeps asking about what happened, and I do not want to talk about it."

"Join us," I said, waving my hand to Charles's glass board, "as we fail at equations."

Her eyes narrowed. "What even was that?"

Charles and I turned back to the board. The ink he had used had dripped until the equation was unreadable.

"If I can't even make ink correctly, I doubt I can do math right." Charles pulled away from me, head tilting as he tried to read what was left. "Oh well."

Madeline sighed. "Thank the Lord. I need something new to do."

"Yes." I leapt from the table and picked up a brush. "Let's see what we can do next."

EPILOGUE

Coline fiddled with the hem of her dress. The dress was violet, dark as night and sewn with gold threads. Coline hadn't wanted gilt at the expense of the people she'd have to swear to serve after what her father had done, but looking good was sometimes more important than being good. The dress was Vivienne's refitted, the seamstresses well-paid and spreading the rumors we wanted them to spread, and Coline looked, for all I could tell, good enough to be queen. She looked better than her father at any rate.

"You look divine." The mirrored collar of her dress was cold in my hands. She'd dozens of people to do this for her, but still I fixed it. "Today will be fine. Tomorrow too."

I couldn't divine anymore, use any of the arts, but hope was a portent all its own.

The door behind us opened. Isabelle's soft gasp made me grin.

"You look divine," Isabelle muttered, circling Coline with the eyes of someone who actually knew what she was looking at. "We should probably stop saying that, shouldn't we?"

"Not in private." Coline smiled and shrugged as much as she could in such a heavy dress. "I do love hearing it."

"We know." I stepped away and let Isabelle get her look in. "Was me saying it not enough?"

"You'd say I was pretty no matter what," Coline said. "I appreciate the adoration, but it's not helpful." Her smile tightened. "Do you think Brigitte will like it?"

If any of us would tell Coline she looked divine no matter what she was or wasn't wearing, it was Brigitte.

"She didn't leave your side as you recovered from your injuries." I leaned forward, kissed Coline's cheek, and moved to the door. "Remember?"

Coline hadn't had many injuries after, no one had, but most had slept for days or paced for days or switched between the two as if their body couldn't quite decide whether it was exhausted or exhilarated. Emilie and I had slept for two weeks.

Coline said it had been the longest two weeks of her life. She'd been struggling to become a queen while her friends hung between life and death.

Most of the surviving nobles were behind her—or too scared to say anything for now—and nearly everyone who had been there spread the same story.

"I'm going to find Yvonne," I said, curtsying. "I'll find you tonight, Your Majesty."

Yvonne and I were *romancing* each other.

Coline had cackled when she'd heard, and Isabelle had clapped. Infuriating.

"I'm glad I was only in charge of the drinks." Yvonne picked at what was left over from the morning's breakfast. Coline had been determined to feed anyone who came to see her crowned, and the kitchens had only just stopped cooking so that all the chefs and servers could take their places in the plaza before Serre church. There were only a handful of things left. "This you'll like, though."

"So long as it's not mushrooms."

Yvonne picked up a raspberry tart no bigger than a fingernail and fed it to me.

"Delicious," I said, voice cracking.

It did that sometimes now. The flesh of my throat had worn away, and I swore, sometimes, I felt moth wings where skin should've been. Emilie's wounds were even odder.

And Lord help anyone who looked at that battlefield in Segance. Nothing but corrupted things grew there now—trees with bark like nails, willows with leaves like hair, and earthworms segmented like long, long fingers. The university was having a great time studying it.

Yvonne chuckled and set it down, brushing the crumbs from the table. "My mother is right. You are too polite."

Her mother had said it as a joke when I'd been too tongue-tied to answer her if I wanted water or wine during dinner when meeting them for real last week. Yvonne's whole family—parents, siblings, a few extra cousins, and a stuffy uncle—had all raced to find her once they knew she had been at the fight in Serre. They'd been nice.

They'd called me part of the family.

My name was in all the gossipers' mouths, and Maman had written about that. Papa had showed up in Serre with Macé and Jean at his heels, but I'd still been asleep—unconscious, Emilie would've corrected—and they couldn't stay long. Isabelle had sent them away with promises to write as soon as I woke up.

I had woken up. I wasn't ready to write.

"Your mother may say whatever she likes about me." I nodded toward the door. "Are you ready to take our places?"

We'd been given chairs in the crowd—spots for retainers not quite noble enough to stand next to Coline. Isabelle was to sit on my other side. Coline had offered us spots nearer to her, but I'd enough of people watching me. I wasn't that Annette Boucher anymore.

I'd made my choice.

I was here.

"I've been thinking about alchemistry," Yvonne said slowly. "Demeine hasn't advanced with it in quite some time."

I leaned against the table. "Demeine didn't have you to advance it till now."

"Flattery will get you everything." She hopped up to sit on the table next to me, thigh pressed to my side, and looped our arms together. Her fingers threaded through mine. Softly. Tightly. "I'll be leaving for work in a week, and I wanted to know if you would like to come with me."

Oh.

I'd been looking for a home—a place, a building, a collection of walls that made me feel safe—and never found it, and I was a fool.

"Yes." I kissed her, quickly, carefully so as not to disturb the cosmetics she'd spent all morning on, and pressed my lips to the back of her hand. New magic. New people. New dreams I wanted to chase. "I would love to go with you."

She sighed and smiled, cheek against my shoulder. We understood each other. "Good."

That evening, long after the parties were supposed to be over, Yvonne and I made our way to the room Emilie was using as a study. Inside, Madeline and Charles were crowded around a board, and Emilie turned a thin letter over and over in her hands.

"We got this," she said.

Charles glanced over his shoulder. "It's addressed to all of us from Laurence and Estrel."

I still tried to scry sometimes. I didn't need my magic back, but I wanted to see Estrel again, even if only by scrying the past. It never worked.

Emilie showed the letter to me. Even Sébastien des Courmers was included and the sight of his name made Emilie wince. Charles's shoulders tensed.

"That's Laurence's handwriting," Charles said, and he picked up the letter with a trembling hand. *There were quite a few futures that did not come to pass, but time is a curious thing and many happenings occur across every future, repeating as if they are immutable events across all of time. We tried to prepare for some of these, and so, if there comes a time when you are in need of help or simply find that you are not enough for whatever it is you are facing, open the enclosed boxes. Though we are uncertain as to who in particular will need them across all possible futures, more likely than not, Emilie and Annette must be the ones to open them. It's a rather lovely bit of artistry we concocted. We'll explain it in greater detail the next time we see all of you. Love eternally, Laurence and Estrel.*

From the crate, Charles pulled out a large box I didn't recognize that he clutched to his chest. Emilie pulled it from him with gentle hands. I peeked into the crate.

It was Estrel's old lockbox, the one she kept beneath her desk and filled with all sorts of small, important things. I picked it up and set it on the table. I had one too. It still lived in the back of my wardrobe.

"Do you think they mean that something bad is going to happen to us?" Coline asked. "Or has it passed?"

"I would very much like to think that the coup was it," Madeline muttered.

"We should save them," I said. The box was impossibly heavy. It was only as long as my forearm and narrow as a quiver, but it weighed as much as a small child, and I ended up cradling it to me. "Whatever they meant, it doesn't matter. We don't need whatever it is now."

I glanced at Emilie.

She nodded. "We survived the worst already, and I would rather have the comfort of knowing these are here even if nothing as terrible awaits us."

"Agreed," I said. "We are enough."

Acknowledgments

There is a strangely deep sense of loss akin to grief when you come to the end of reading a book you love. Like me, Emilie and Annette experienced loss, and I often felt as though writing their journeys was writing mine—each fear, each triumph, and each push to do better tomorrow. Books were my constant companions before I found the people I call family, and the journeys I took on those pages shaped who I am today. I hope that Emilie and Annette are good traveling partners for readers on whatever journey they're undertaking. We lose people in life, but we find them, too, whether in books or the real world.

I am immeasurably lucky to have found mine. None of this would have been possible without my husband, Brent. I cannot put into words how comforting it is to know someone who understands my creative process and motivations so well. Thank you so much for supporting my dreams even when they're just a handful of characters with placeholder names and half of a concept.

Kerbie Addis is the best friend and writing partner a person could ask for, and I cannot thank her enough for all of the three-in-the-morning worldbuilding talks and rough draft readings. The thoughtful nuance and heart-lifting hilarity of Rosiee Thor's advice kept me going even when writing seemed impossible.

My agent, Rachel Brooks, has made my career possible. I can't imagine having gone on this publishing journey without you. Thank you, too, to the wonderful people at BookEnds Literary Agency.

As it always seems, I am in awe at how talented Annie Berger is as an editor, and I am so glad Emilie and Annette were in such capable hands. Nicole Hower and Billelis created a more beautiful cover for *Belle Révolte* than I could ever have imagined, and I'm so thankful for them. The Sourcebooks team is more home than publishing house. Thank you so much to Cassie Gutman, Sarah Kasman, Beth Oleniczak, and the talented editors, designers, and copy editors who made *Belle Révolte* into what it is today. Working with all of you is amazing.

Thank you, thank you, thank you to Ray Stoeve, Julie, and the brilliant readers who helped make sure *Belle Révolte* was a journey everyone could take.

And thank you to the countless readers, reviewers, booksellers, librarians, and bloggers around the world who make publishing possible, writing worth it, and reading a celebration of community and hope. I could never do this without you all.